The Cluny Problem

A Chief Inspector Pointer Mystery

By A. E. Fielding

Originally published in 1929

The Cluny Problem

© 2014 Resurrected Press
www.ResurrectedPress.com

Published by Intrepid Ink, LLC

Intrepid Ink, LLC provides full publishing services to authors of fiction and non-fiction books, eBooks and websites. From editing to formatting, to publishing, to marketing, Intrepid Ink gets your creative works into the hands of the people who want to read them.
Find out more at www.IntrepidInk.com.

ISBN 13: 978-1-937022-77-8

Printed in the United States of America

Other Resurrected Press Books in *The Chief Inspector Pointer* <u>*Mystery*</u> Series

RESURRECTED PRESS CLASSIC MYSTERY CATALOGUE

Journeys into Mystery
Travel and Mystery in a More Elegant Time

The Edwardian Detectives
Literary Sleuths of the Edwardian Era

Gems of Mystery
Lost Jewels from a More Elegant Age

Anne Austin
One Drop of Blood
The Black Pigeon
Murder at Bridge

E. C. Bentley
Trent's Last Case: The Woman in Black

Ernest Bramah
Max Carrados Resurrected:
The Detective Stories of Max Carrados

Agatha Christie
The Secret Adversary
The Mysterious Affair at Styles

Octavus Roy Cohen
Midnight

Freeman Wills Croft
The Ponson Case
The Pit Prop Syndicate

J. S. Fletcher
The Herapath Property
The Rayner-Slade Amalgamation
The Chestermarke Instinct
The Paradise Mystery
Dead Men's Money
The Middle of Things
Ravensdene Court
Scarhaven Keep
The Orange-Yellow Diamond
The Middle Temple Murder
The Tallyrand Maxim
The Borough Treasurer
In the Mayor's Parlour
The Saftey Pin

R. Austin Freeman
The Mystery of 31 New Inn from the Dr. Thorndyke Series
John Thorndyke's Cases from the Dr. Thorndyke Series
The Red Thumb Mark from The Dr. Thorndyke Series
The Eye of Osiris from The Dr. Thorndyke Series
A Silent Witness from the Dr. John Thorndyke Series
The Cat's Eye from the Dr. John Thorndyke Series
Helen Vardon's Confession: A Dr. John Thorndyke Story
As a Thief in the Night: A Dr. John Thorndyke Story
Mr. Pottermack's Oversight: A Dr. John Thorndyke Story
Dr. Thorndyke Intervenes: A Dr. John Thorndyke Story
The Singing Bone: The Adventures of Dr. Thorndyke
The Stoneware Monkey: A Dr. John Thorndyke Story
The Great Portrait Mystery, and Other Stories: A Collection of Dr. John Thorndyke and Other Stories
The Penrose Mystery: A Dr. John Thorndyke Story

The Uttermost Farthing: A Savant's Vendetta

Arthur Griffiths
The Passenger From Calais
The Rome Express

Fergus Hume
The Mystery of a Hansom Cab
The Green Mummy
The Silent House
The Secret Passage

Edgar Jepson
The Loudwater Mystery

A. E. W. Mason
At the Villa Rose

A. A. Milne
The Red House Mystery

Baroness Emma Orczy
The Old Man in the Corner

Edgar Allan Poe
The Detective Stories of Edgar Allan Poe

Arthur J. Rees
The Hampstead Mystery
The Shrieking Pit
The Hand In The Dark
The Moon Rock
The Mystery of the Downs

Mary Roberts Rinehart
Sight Unseen and The Confession

Dorothy L. Sayers

Whose Body?

Sir William Magnay
The Hunt Ball Mystery

Mabel and Paul Thorne
The Sheridan Road Mystery

Louis Tracy
The Strange Case of Mortimer Fenley
The Albert Gate Mystery
The Bartlett Mystery
The Postmaster's Daughter
The House of Peril
The Sandling Case: What Would You Have Done?

Charles Edmonds Walk
The Paternoster Ruby

John R. Watson
The Mystery of the Downs
The Hampstead Mystery

Edgar Wallace
The Daffodil Mystery
The Crimson Circle

Carolyn Wells
Vicky Van
The Man Who Fell Through the Earth
In the Onyx Lobby
Raspberry Jam
The Clue
The Room with the Tassels
The Vanishing of Betty Varian
The Mystery Girl
The White Alley
The Curved Blades

Anybody but Anne
The Bride of a Moment
Faulkner's Folly
The Diamond Pin
The Gold Bag
The Mystery of the Sycamore
The Come Back

Raoul Whitfield
Death in a Bowl

And much more!
Visit ResurrectedPress.com
for our complete catalogue

FOREWORD

The period between the First and Second World Wars has rightly been called the "Golden Age of British Mysteries." It was during this period that Agatha Christie, Dorothy L. Sayers, and Margery Allingham first turned their pens to crime. On the male side, the era saw such writers as Anthony Berkeley, John Dickson Carr, and Freeman Wills Crofts join the ranks of writers of detective fiction. The genre was immensely popular at the time on both sides of the Atlantic, and by the end of the 1930's one out of every four novels published in Britain was a mystery.

While Agatha Christie and a few of her peers have remained popular and in print to this day, the same cannot be said of all the authors of this period. With so many mysteries published in the period, it is inevitable that many of them would become obscure or worse, forgotten, often with no justification than changing public tastes. The case of Archibald Fielding is one such, an author, who though popular enough to have a career spanning two decades and more than two dozen mysteries has become such a cipher that his, or as seems more likely, her real identity has become as much a mystery as the books themselves.

While the identity of the author may forever remain an unsolved puzzle, there are some facts that may be inferred from the texts. It is likely that the author had an upbringing and education typical of the British upper middle class in the period before the Great War with all that implies; a familiarity with the classics, the arts, and music, a working knowledge of French, an appreciation of the finer things in life. The author has also traveled abroad, primarily in the south of France, but probably to Belgium, Spain, and Italy as well, as portions of several of the books are set in those locales.

The books attributed to Archibald Fielding, A. E. Fielding, or Archibald E. Fielding, are quintessential Golden Age British mysteries. They include all the attributes, the country houses, the tangled webs of relationships, the somewhat feckless cast of characters who seem to have nothing better to do with themselves than to murder or be murdered. Their focus is on a middle class and upper class struggling to find themselves in the new realities of the post war era while still trying to live the lifestyle of the Edwardian era. Things are never as they seem, red herrings are distributed liberally through the pages as are the clues that will ultimately lead to the solution of "the puzzle," for the British mysteries of this period are centered on the puzzle element which both the reader and the detective must solve before the last page.

A majority of the Fielding mysteries involve the character of Chief Inspector Pointer. Unlike the eccentric Belgian Hercule Poirot, the flamboyant Lord Peter Wimsey, or the somewhat mysterious Albert Campion, Pointer is merely a competent, sometimes clever, occasionally intuitive policeman. And unlike, as with Inspector French in the stories of Freeman Wills Croft, the emphasis is on the mystery itself, not the process of detection.

Pointer is nearly as much of a mystery as the author. Very little of his personal life is revealed in the books. He is described as being vaguely of Scottish ancestry. He is well read and educated, though his duties at Scotland Yard prevent him from enjoying those pursuits. His success as a detective depends on his willingness to "suspect everyone" and to not being tied to any one theory. He is fluent in French and familiar with that country. He is, at least in the first book, unmarried, sharing lodgings with a bookbinder named O'Connor, in much the manner of Holmes and Watson, though O'Connor disappears in the subsequent volumes.

While the early books fall plainly in the "humdrum" school with Pointer appearing almost immediately and much of story revolving on the business of tracking down various clues, the later novels are much more concerned with the lives of the characters surrounding the mystery. Pointer is much less center stage, often arriving instead at mid-book to clean up the pieces and insure that the guilty do not escape justice. It is, perhaps, this lack of focus on the detective, which has caused the works of Fielding to fade away while the likes of Poirot seem to attract the interest of each new generation.

One intriguing feature of the Pointer mysteries is that they all involve an unexpected twist at the end, wherein the mystery finally solved is not the mystery invoked at the beginning of the book. I leave it to the reader to judge whether Fielding is "playing by the rules" in this, but it does keep the books interesting up to the last chapter.

The Cluny Problem is the fifth mystery in the series involving Chief Inspector Pointer. Taking place almost entirely in the ancient French town of Cluny it provides some of the best evidence that Fielding was familiar with not only the French countryside and language, but with the French, themselves.

The English have always been suspicious of foreigners, in particular the French, and as much as they might admire the cuisine and the climate they can't help wondering why they can't act more, well, English. Of no French institution are the English more suspicious than the French justice system, which, after all is base on the Code Napoleon rather than English common law, and Fielding plays on this suspicion with her depictions of the local police commisaire, his assistant, and the *juge d'instruction*. All are shown as honest, earnest men, but quite capable of jumping to the wrong conclusion. Fortunately they have Pointer to keep them on the right track, though only, of course, as an observer.

Fielding doesn't restrict her comic portrayals only to the French, though. There is Mackay, the private detective with his almost indecipherable Scottish English and his fluent but weirdly accented French. There is also the young American woman, Vivian Young, who always seems to be in the middle of things and faces every adversity as befitting the daughter of a Texas Ranger.

Though it has a number of light hearted moments, *The Cluny Problem* is at heart a tragedy. Two Englishmen, having apparently held a duel in a locked room, have managed to kill each other. On the surface, the duel was over the wife of one of the dead men. But, as with all of Fielding's mysteries, there is much more hiding below the surface than a simple love triangle.

Despite their obscurity, the mysteries of Archibald Fielding, whoever he or she might have been, are well written, well crafted examples of the form, worthy of the interest of the fans of the genre. It is with pleasure, then, that Resurrected Press presents this new edition of *The Cluny Problem* and others in the series to its readers.

About the Author

The identity of the author is as much a mystery as the plots of the novels. Two dozen novels were published from 1924 to 1944 as by Archibald Fielding, A. E. Fielding, or Archibald E. Fielding, yet the only clue as to the real author is a comment by the American publishers, H.C. Kinsey Co. that A. E. Fielding was in reality a "middle-aged English woman by the name of Dorothy Feilding whose peacetime address is Sheffield Terrace, Kensington, London, and who enjoys gardening." Research on the part of John Herrington has uncovered a person by that name living at 2 Sheffield Terrace from 1932-1936. She appears to have moved to Islington in 1937 after which she disappears. To complicate things, some have attributed the authorship to Lady Dorothy Mary Evelyn Moore nee Feilding (1889-1935), however, a grandson of Lady Dorothy denied any family knowledge of such authorship. The archivist at Collins, the British publisher, reports that any records of A. Fielding were presumably lost during WWII. Birthdates have been given variously as 1884, 1889, and 1900. Unless new information comes to light, it would appear that the real authorship must remain a mystery.

Greg Fowlkes
Editor-In-Chief
Resurrected Press
www.ResurrectedPress.com

CHAPTER ONE

"ANTHONY!" Vivian Young made a laughing surprised clutch at a tall figure stalking ahead of her down the station platform.

The man turned sharply. At the sight of his fiancé he smiled pleasantly, though a sharp observer would have said that there was something in his eyes that suggested a man about to make the best of a position not entirely to his liking.

"My dear girl!" he ejaculated warmly, "what brings you to Macon? Did you get into the wrong train, or out of the right one, or what?"

"I'm on my way to Cluny. Buried, neglected Cluny. The town where the lace is made, and, less interesting to me, I guess, the town where there are some ruin that must be seen in order to be forgotten. I mean the ruins of that wonderful abbey about which the Frenchman raved at dinner last night. You started him off by asking him if he knew the place. But you didn't speak of coming on here yourself."

"Nor you!" Sir Anthony Cross spoke easily, yet the very swiftness of his reply suggested a hidden irritation.

"Ah, but I'm only marking time at Enghien with a sister! You're supposed to be rushing back to London to summon board meetings, and dismiss the president, I mean the prime minister, and generally make very important things hum. Is this the way you usually go back to England?"

"You can reach it via Macon," he said as lightly as she. Vivian was smiling up into his face. She was a very pretty young woman, in spite of the fact that she looked clever.

"Sure. Just as you could round by Constantinople," she agreed sweetly.

Again Anthony Cross smiled at her. Yet again there was that faint hint in his face of a man not entirely pleased with things.

"As with you," he began easily, "one might think that French professor has fired me up to look at his town. I'm keen on architecture, you know, and I ought to feel quite ashamed of myself that I've never been to the place. But the idea of your going there! Somehow one doesn't connect you with ruins."

"Why not? We all come to them some day," she spoke with the gaiety of under twenty-five. "Besides, as an American, I dote on anything we don't have over at home. If you're off for the same place, why, we shall have the whole long day to ourselves. You look charmed at the notion, Anthony, yet somehow I don't believe you really like it."

She never called him Tony. One could not easily imagine any one calling the man to whom she was speaking, to whom she was engaged, by a nickname. For, though young looking, there was so little of youth's softness in his face, that one suspected him of being much older than he showed. He had, in fact, crossed the forty line. Hard was the mouth, stubborn the jaw, obstinate the nose, and his fine eyes could at times cleave like a flash of lightning. He looked what he was, a man of high position, social and mental. But for an indefinable air of being a man of affairs, one would have guessed him a barrister.

"If so," he said rather slowly, "it's because I shan't be able to see much of you, or of the remains of the great abbey either." He looked at her meditatively before he went on:

"I suppose you're going back to Enhgien to-morrow?"

It was at that little resort so near Paris that he and Vivian had just got engaged. There in the hotel where her brother-in-law and his wife had been staying, Anthony

Cross and Vivian had renewed an acquaintanceship made earlier on shipboard.

She nodded. "You too, I suppose?"

"No. I may be delayed some days. There's history to be read in the stones of Cluny, I fancy—since it was made there once upon a time." He spoke as one turning some other thought over in his mind. Now he looked quickly down at her, as though he had decided on his course of action.

"You know the real reason why I'm back in Europe just now," he said in a low voice.

She nodded. She knew from him that there was a constant leakage from the parcels of diamonds sent to Amsterdam by the Diamond Combine in South Africa, of which Anthony Cross was one of the directors. That great firm's detectives had been trying to locate the leakage for months. They had decided that the master mind was not in Amsterdam, nor in Holland, but probably in France. Possibly in Paris. She knew, too, that Cross had left Capetown to make further, and personal, inquiries in the matter.

"Then, in confidence, I believe that in Cluny I may possibly pick up a certain piece of information which I very much want to get. Or rather, that something that I may learn from a man whom I expect to meet there may settle definitely a point that ought to be settled."

His jaw shut very tightly as he said this last. "And that's the reason, dear, why I may not have been as delighted at the thought of your coming to Cluny just now as I should otherwise be. In reality, but again in strict confidence, mine is entirely and simply a business visit. At which hotel have you engaged rooms?"

She told him.

"I think, on the whole, it would be better if we do not meet. I should in any case, of course, go to another hotel, but I'll let you take this coming train out there alone, and go on later. Sorry, Vivian, it's a rotten way to spend what might have been a most delightful time together, but there's no help for it."

She did not in the least see the reason, or the need, for so much mystery. But men have their own funny ways of doing business, she decided.

"If I run across you in the street, I'll ask you the way to the abbey in French," she promised gaily.

He smiled at that, genuinely this time.

"At any rate, our engagement has nothing to do with what takes me to Cluny. And I want it kept free of it. It's too beautiful a thing to drag into anything sordid."

He looked into her eyes with passion. It was a look that showed him to be possessed of a side not to be guessed even from a careful scrutiny of his very handsome but rather cold face. "And that being so, it means, as I said, that we'd better not meet at all. Cluny's a tiny place. Only some four thousand souls, and I may have to be there for some time."

The explanation explained nothing to Vivian. But if men were odd when it came to business, they were still odder when it came to sentiment. And, therefore, when both were mixed, they were oddest of all.

"Or perhaps I'll put off going there for a couple of days," he said ruminatingly. "Yes, I rather think I will—" He stood a moment in silence.

"You yourself are in no danger?" she asked suddenly. After all, detecting diamond stealers was dangerous work.

"Not in the least! Here's your train."

He helped her in. The engine pulled out. He looked very grave, very little the lover as he stood there, hat in hand, and yet she felt certain that he was deeply stirred, and trying to conceal the fact.

By what? He was very hard to stir, very hard even to know. And on that came the reflection that he would have had to own a singularly easy character for her to have plumbed it already.

It was only two months since their first meeting. Only a fortnight since their second. True, they had seen a great deal of each other during the passage out from Capetown. Terrific storms had kept the other passengers in their bunks. Officers and the doctor were too busy to have a moment to spare. Anthony had saved her from a rough-and-tumble with a wave when she first came out on deck, tight-reefed in oilskins borrowed from a stewardess. Neither had the faintest idea of who the other was. She had taken him at sight for a much younger man, and had treated him, as Vivian did treat young men, very cavalierly. He had responded in kind. They had quarrelled. But they were literally flung together half a dozen times a day. And, in spite of themselves, they grew first to tolerate, then to like, each other. When he told her his name, perhaps half-unconsciously expecting that it would impress her, she treated him as carelessly as ever. And Sir Anthony was considered one of the really great catches of the matrimonial market. It was genuine carelessness too, he saw. Not assumed to lead him on. Whether he were led on, or off, mattered very little to Vivian. When he grasped that fact, he was attracted still more strongly. Her prettiness, of course, had a great deal to do with it, but it was not everything. Then came the night of the all-but wreck in the hurricane. The ship was carrying a full load of steerage passengers. There were many gallant souls on board, but among them all, Anthony Cross stood out by his coolness and his organizing power. He held the frightened steerage quiet, not at the point of his automatic—though he had one in his pocket—but by his own calm personality, and Vivian worked among the women and babies as cheerful, as undismayed, as he. Save for the suffering it caused, she seemed to positively enjoy the danger, and Cross suddenly felt that his life would be incomplete without her. There was something wild and free in the girl that roused the hunter in him. If they lived, he told himself, he would capture her.

He followed her to France, to Enghien-les-bains, and found her in a moment of great depression. An unusual place for Vivian Young to be. She was a journalist by profession and by real preference.

She loved to watch the world with those pretty eyes of hers that were so unexpectedly shrewd, and she loved to shape what she had seen into words. To create an image of her thoughts, see it grow, and watch it stand itself, upright and whole. But she was not making enough to do more than support herself, and at Enghien she learnt from a sister, who prided herself on speaking the truth, that in the past, she had been dependent on her brother-in-law, not, as she had imagined, living on the money left by their parents. Her brother-in-law was an American doctor practising in Paris, and none too well off. Vivian felt that she must pay him back as soon and as fast as she could.

That evening Anthony Cross proposed. Vivian did not consciously take him as a means of paying what she felt to be a debt of honor. She was much more impressed by him than she let him guess. By him, himself, not by his position, or his name. There was something great in the man as she knew. And she divined also, with that sure instinct of hers, that under his calm, even cold exterior there was flame.

There was flame in her too. That night he all but won her. She believed that he had. But ever since then, she had felt more and more certain that he had not, which meant that he never would. For one thing, he was too old for her. For another—but what was the use. She had promised to marry him. Still, an engagement is but a trial run of the car, as it were. It's very purpose is to find out how one likes it.

At the first station beyond Macon, a young woman, also an American by the look of her, hurried towards the train where she sat. The new-comer was making for another compartment, but Vivian, at sight of her, flung the door open.

"Edith! Edith! Come in here!" she called.

The new-comer swung herself in and the two kissed

affectionately.

"My dearest Vi! Why, what brings you to this part of Europe . . . and just when we're off for Switzerland. ... I do call that real mean of things. We only started this morning. Adolphe left some papers behind him at Clermain that he must have. Adolphe's my husband, you know."

She threw in the explanation as though referring to the cat.

"We have a villa there all among the vineyards. But how just too frightfully maddening that you should be so close to us now. The house is shut up, or I should insist on carrying you off. Where are you making for?"

"Cluny." It was the first word that Vivian had been able to slip in. That had always been the way with Edith Metcalf as she had been in the convent at Paris, where they both had been sent to learn French. Edith de Montdore as she was now. Vivian remembered hearing that she had married a French wine-grower and that the couple lived near Dijon.

"Cluny? Don't tell me, Vivian Young, that you know the vamp?"

"Calm yourself, my dear girl, I've never heard of her. I'm on the way to Cluny for the purpose of self-education. Early Christian churches—wonderful abbey—marvellous abbot's palace and so on. . . . But this sounds much more in my line. Who is the woman? Does she vamp at Cluny? Or where you live?"

"At Cluny. I bet I should move if she came to Clermain," laughed Edith. "She's staying with her husband at a house there owned by a man we know. A Frenchman. But an awfully nice fellow."

"Staying with her husband? Where's the vamping then?"

"Oh, she's a subconscious one, child. She looks as meek as Moses, and as quiet as Lazarus before he was raised from the dead. But all the men rave about her. Oh, Adolphe too! One of the reasons I decided on going away

for a bit. I loathe Switzerland in a motor. So many roads
you can't go over. But anything's better than the vamp.
She's lips like a darkey's, and hair like one too, though
it's red, and she's no complexion whatever. Yet Adolphe
says she's a Rossetti, and a wonderful type. Don't let your
Anthony have a look at her. The best of wishes to you
both on your engagement, by the way. I did write them,
but allow me to embrace you, as they say here."

Edith Montdore did so, without a pause in her
chatter.

"Say, you have done well for yourself! And what a
splendiferous ring!"

Vivian was carrying her left-hand glove, a fancy of the
moment. On her third finger was a great clouded
sapphire, a Cross heirloom. Though not otherwise
particularly superstitious, Vivian had a dislike to that
fault in that particular gem. She said as much.

"Well, I guess I agree with you. Though the setting's
perfectly lovely. I told Mrs. Brownlow—that's the vamp's
name, by the way—about clouded sapphires meaning a
death in one's circle—or rather, only I told her that it
meant a loss, for she has some wonderful stones, but two
are a bit dark. And within the month after I told her, she
lost sapphires and all. I believe the thief got about five
thousand dollars worth of jewels off her altogether. I still
reckon in dollars, you see, the exchange bobs about too
much. My, she was mad! She was taking them to Paris to
have them re-set. That sort of makes it doubly annoying.
They were only insured for about half their value, it
seems. That was her husband's doing."

"What's he like?" Vivian asked. She was quite willing
to be chattered to.

"I always thought him a brainless, boneless, sort of
creature, until I met a woman the other day who knew
them years ago out in China—he's something to do with
silk. And this woman told me a story that makes me
wonder if he's such a weasel as he looks. It seems that out
there all the men fell for Mrs. Brownlow, same as they do

here. And one young fellow in particular went wild over her. So wild that Mr. Brownlow turned him out of the house one evening. And next morning the boy was found drowned in the river!"

"But what has that to do with the husband—I mean, I don't see " Vivian wrinkled her smooth forehead.

"Oh, but the young man had a brother who wrote to the British Consul that Mr. Brownlow must have shoved him in, Mr. Brownlow was all but prosecuted—so this woman said. Only there wasn't enough evidence. She herself firmly believed that he had done it. So did most of the people out there. That's why the Brownlows left finally. Thrilling, isn't it! I tell you that story made all the difference as to how I look at Mr. Brownlow now!" Apparently it had greatly increased her respect for the man. And Vivian burst out laughing.

"But surely they're not staying at Cluny year out, year in?" she asked.

"Pretty nearly," Edith Montdore said gloomily. "That's why we're off now. We weren't going for another month. But that woman gets on my nerves. Clermain is only some six miles from Cluny, and we're always meeting, and she makes me look, and feel, like a picture on a cigarette box. Frankly I'm in flight. You see, this Monsieur Pichegru—that's the name of the man they're staying with—runs his house, Villa Porte Bonheur, as a sort of paying-guest house. I believe he lost his money for a time—something went wrong with his vineyards—so he started this, and keeps it up because he likes it. He belongs to an awfully good family and knows every one for miles around. He's a duck, but the only thing is, he won't take maids or valets with people. He says that he hasn't the rooms to spare for them, and that they upset his own servants."

"I should be lost without a maid!" Vivian said in mock distress.

"You'll have to have one as Lady Cross!"

Vivian nodded. The prospect did not allure her in the

least. There was a short pause, then Edith Montdore babbled on:

"Monsieur Pichegru is unmarried, and at his age that means he isn't going to marry. By the way, he's giving a costume dance, masked too, this Saturday. Every one is going. I was, of course, only my frock turned out to be a ghastly failure. Lovely in itself but, my! I looked so homely in it when it came home, that I promptly devolped a heat rash. Suppressed. It seems you can have a suppressed rash. So I have it. The doctor has told my husband that it would only get better with change of air. It has—already." She chuckled gleefully. "Still, when Adolphe left those papers behind him, I insisted on being the one to fetch them. Oh, I'm only joking, but really that woman is the sort you read of." She meant "that you see on the films." Edith Montdore never opened a book—not even a novel. "You know, the kind that set all the men raving with one look."

The ticket collector came in. Mrs. Montdore had no ticket. She was sure that she had dropped it in the corridor. There was not room for more than two of them to hunt. Vivian sat on in the compartment. She was thinking. Vaguely at first, now with certitude came the idea that she had heard the name of Brownlow before. And recently. Quite recently. At the dinner last night when she had first heard of the existence of Cluny. Quickly, with that speed of thought which can flash a whole series of sights and sounds on the screen of memory at once, she seemed to be hearing Anthony Cross ask the French professor of archaelogy, who was one of the guests at her sister's table, "Is Cluny worth a visit, do you think?"

That had led to an account of the little town, and of what can still be seen there. A glowing account. Vivian, in swift retrospect, remembered now wondering a little that Cross, though quite an antiquarian himself, had not asked one question except about the state of the roads, the lie of the houses. And afterwards she had heard him step up to the other again, and say, even more quietly than usual, "You know Cluny well?"

"Very well. My brother is the *directeur* of its school of arts and crafts. I have just come away from the town."

"Indeed? Did you by any chance meet an Englishman there of the name of Brownlow?"

Yes, Vivian was certain that that had been the name murmured so softly by Anthony last night.

The Frenchman had not, and the talk was at once changed.

Funny the way one rarely hears a new name without hearing it a second time very soon afterwards! Vivian thought. But the entrance of her friend and the ticket, properly found and clipped, brought her back to the present.

"Say, Vi, I wish you could have a look at the vamp," Edith said, reseating herself and taking up the conversation where she had left off, as though it were a piece of knitting. "You're such a wonderful judge of character from one look at a face. Or you used to be. I sure would like to know where that woman belongs—with us hens, or out among the hawks. I know what! Go to Villa Porte Bonheur for a few days. Monsieur Pichegru won't take ordinary passing tourists, but he'll take any friend of ours."

"His house may be full," Vivian objected.

"It never is. He only has enough people nowadays to keep him from feeling lonely."

"But I'm intending to stay in Cluny for merely the one night," Vivian pointed out.

"But, why?" her friend asked. "Cluny really is charming. Why not stay for the dance on Saturday? This is Thursday."

"And go in my dressing-grown as 'A lady surprised by a fire'?" Vivian asked. "I'm a traveler, my child, not a bride with all her trousseau to choose from."

"Wear my new dress!" Edith pleaded. "I'll send it on to you. And we're very much the same figure. Besides it's the sort of frock that would fit any one. And though it doesn't suit me, it's a dream of cream and gold. Just your colors. 'Lady into Fox" is what it's supposed to represent. Adolphe designed it himself from some funny book or other. You would look a duck in it!"

"You mean a fox, surely!"

"Now, don't keep on joking!" Edith Montdore was really in earnest. "I want you to promise me to have a good look at the vamp, and give me your opinion. It'll be unbiased, you see. And mine can't be. And yet I really do want to hear what you think of her. Oh, Vi, why not? Monsieur Pichegru charges no more than the hotels do. You told me that Sir Anthony is going back to England, and that, until you joined him in September, you were just going to keep on staying at Enghien. That's a fortnight off. Why not put in two or three days down here instead? I'll get the frock when I go for the papers—it's still in its box—and send it off to you, to wait at the railway station until you have it fetched. And I'll telephone Monsieur Pichegru as soon as I get home— we're one station short of Cluny—you will, won't you?"

Once more Vivian laughed. How like Edith all his rush was! But she promised to think over the idea. It would depend on whether she liked the look of Cluny or not. When she saw, lying among the green Cevennes hills, a little gray town with spires and towers rising against the trees in a charming picture, she fell in love with the quiet nook. There were vineyards, and meadows, and a splashing stream rushing down the valley.

Clear of the station, she asked her way to the Villa Porte Bonheur. The name had stuck. Was it not tempting fate to give a house a name like that?

The villa, painted ivory, was one of the prettiest in the place. And the garden was a vision of pink roses and blue delphiniums. It was the garden that did it. At first. But the real reason that made her press the front door bell was a face, of which she caught a glimpse as she walked the winding drive towards the house. It was a woman's face, bending over an embroidery-stand under a tree. For a second Vivian stared, then she turned off down a little side path. That face! She knew quite well where she had seen a photograph of it. It was a very unusual face. Adolphe Montdore was right. It was the true Rossetti type. Inert to everything except the call of the senses, though for that very reason beauty-loving. And the photograph of it that she had seen, had been in the fingers of Anthony Cross only some three days ago. She had come on him suddenly standing staring at it. Lost to the world. At her touch he would have pocketed it, but she had caught his hand.

"Not on your life, young man! It's a picture of your mother, isn't it?" He had laughed, yet in the half-unwilling fashion of one who is annoyed by a sense of humor obtruding on what is not really funny in the least.

"No. She's a problem—a problem that belongs to the past." He now spoke very gravely. "Please don't ask me to tell you about her."

"Because I won't," his eye had said.

Vivian had changed the subject, biting back a retort that the problem out of the past had a most modern frock on. And now here was the original of that portrait—and of that dress.

This must be the vamp of Edith Montdore's outpourings. There could not be two women with faces like that in Cluny—in Villa Porte Bonheur. Something stirred in Vivian. It was anger. Anthony Cross had told her frankly the evening when he asked her to marry him, or apparently frankly, that there had been one woman in his life, in his heart, who had owned it completely for many years. Even though she had been married, and had sent him away from her, his passion had gone so deep that it had been beyond his power to uproot for many a year. But that now it was a thing of the past. Had been of the past for some time.

But this woman, sitting looking down at her embroidery with a slow, faint, oddly waiting look, a look that somehow stirred the imagination, was not of the past. She was of the present. And suddenly Vivian made up her mind to stay at Porte Bonheur if there were room for her. To stay and see whether Anthony Cross's visit were in any way connected with that face instead of missing diamonds. True, he had only asked the Frenchman about the husband—for Vivian was certain that here, close to her, sat Mrs. Brownlow—and Anthony had spoken to herself just now, as though only duty were taking him to the little town. But, Vivian remembered suddenly a lightly flung quip of his on board ship. "Oh, yes, it is always necessary to tell the truth. But it isn't always necessary to tell the truth."

It would indeed be an odd conjunction if it were mere chance that his inquiries into the stolen diamonds and the woman of his past—"the problem"—problem, very likely, because she had preferred her husband to him. Vivian thought cynically and irately—both met here in tiny Cluny. Vivian was not fond of coincidences in a novel and she did not believe in them in real life. And, then, that insistence that he should be left entirely to himself, like any other unattached man. . . .

It was with a very determined step that Vivian swung round, walked up to the front door, and rang the bell. She sent in a card of Edith Montdore's, on which that young woman had scribbled an introduction.

Monsieur Pichegru came down at once into the cold gray drawing-room—one of those typically French drawing-rooms that look chilly even on the hottest day. He was a pleasant-faced, elderly man with the alert, vigorous look of so many of his race. Edith had duly telephoned, and he pressed Vivian to stay at the villa for at least one night, and as many more as she could manage. The terms were very moderate for the comfort provided. He explained, as he showed her around, that he had injured his shoulder a little while ago while shooting rabbits, thanks to a young gun-bearer's brilliant idea of resting the gun that he was reloading on the wet clay ground, with the result that the barrel was blocked and the gun exploded. Monsieur Pichegru rightly thought himself very lucky to have got off with only a bruised shoulder and neck tendons. He usually, at this time of the year, had his house full of people who wanted a day at the birds, but now, with one exception, the villa only held some quiet people who, like herself, were interested in the ruins to be found in Cluny.

Vivian finally chose a charming bedroom looking over the old abbey gardens. At dinner she met the rest of the guests. They appeared to be very usual.

Mrs. Brownlow showed on closer acquaintance to be a very soft-spoken graceful Frenchwoman of approximately thirty-five. Unlike Edith Montdore, Vivian thought her very beautiful, and very finished. Though it was a type that repelled as well as attracted her. But Mrs. Brownlow seemed very gentle and kind. As for the husband, he appeared to be a silent, quiet, obliging little man. Remembering the tale passed on her, she smiled. It would have to be a very Eastern imagination indeed, she thought, that could picture him drowning his wife's admirer. Vivian thought that he was distinctly proud of her. And they seemed devoted to each other. So much for gossip, she reflected.

There were three young men in the house. Two friends called respectively, Smith and Lascelles. They seemed to Vivian rather superior beings, at least in their own estimation. Smith was in a crack cavalry regiment and was rather fussy over the fact that just now his host could not accompany him shooting, and that two friends of Monsieur Pichegru's, big bankers from Lyons, to whom he had been promised introductions, had not yet come to their country houses near by. Lascelles, Vivian learned, was a master in a smart preparatory school. He had the Cambridge manner to excess, and his account of the geological finds that dot what he called the Burgundian Passage, which once linked the Channel and the Mediterranean, was quite beyond her.

The two young men seemed only mildly interested in Mrs. Brownlow. Unlike the third young fellow, the possessor of ears like jug handles and great red hands and the name of Tibbitts, who was clearly her abject slave.

After dinner, Vivian sent down to the station for the box left for her by train. It was there. And with its arrival, she felt that she had definitely committed herself to at least a stay of over the week-end.

As to what Anthony would think of it—she did not greatly care. She would, of course, strictly keep to her promise if they met. But would they meet? That was the interesting point. If he really were coming because of those thefts. . . .

She felt a growing uncertainty as to what Anthony would do, and even as to what she herself might do, in the next few days. It struck her that possibly Edith Montdore might not obtain as unbiased an opinion of Mrs. Brownlow as she expected.

Had Vivian loved the man, the position would have been intolerable. But as it was, she confessed with some malice that not for a long time had she looked forward to anything more than she did to his arrival in Cluny.

Altogether, her stay in Villa Porte Bonheur promised to be most interesting. But she decided that it would be as well to start an article or two for her old paper. Very probably the next week would see her once more with nothing in front of her but her own earnings. And a very pleasant prospect too, she thought it. Even the "desolate freedom of the wild ass," has its points. At least it is freedom, and if you are a wild ass, that alone, not the warmed stable, nor the fenced field, calls to you.

CHAPTER TWO

IT was the afternoon after Vivian Young's arrival. The garden of Villa Porte Bonheur lay drowsing in the August heart which was robbing even the flowers of perfume and color. The very hills seemed to fling the light back into the valley, as though it were molten metal too hot to hold. Closed were the windows, empty the summer-house, deserted the tennis courts.

A man pushed open the iron gate, shut it, and looked about him. When he was near the house itself, he studied it attentively. He seemed to be registering the position of all the doors and windows, even of the chimneys, with his cool, light eyes. Then he walked up to the door and knocked. Could he see Mr. Smith?

He spoke in very fair French, but with an accent that bewildered the butler, who answered with a sleepy:

"*Monsieur desire?*"

"To see Mr. Smith," the visitor repeated clearly. He handed in a card. "Take that to the gentleman, and say that I've come to make some further inquiries about the money that Mr. Davidson lost in the express up to Paris a fortnight ago."

"Ah!" The butler became all interest. He showed the caller into a room.

"I'm right, am I not?" asked the young man in a friendly way. "A couple of Monsieur Pichegru's guests lost their belongings two weeks ago in the train de luxe between Macon and Paris, did they not? A Mrs. Brownlow lost some valuable jewels. And a Mr. Davidson lost a thousand pounds in money? While Mr. Smith and Mr. Tibbitts, who went by the same train, lost nothing?"

"Correct, monsieur. The losses nowadays in sleepers

are enough to make one thankful that one travels third class! Monsieur is connected with the inquiry?"

There was a certain alertness about the visitor's face and carriage and a shabbiness about his clothes that made the butler take him for a newspaper man.

"Yes, I am a reporter. Mr. Davidson is connected with my paper. He has entrusted me with the task of clearing up how the money was taken." He seated himself in an arm-chair, which seemed chosen instantly and at random, but which was the most comfortable one in the room.

The butler went in search of Mr. Smith. That young man was taking a siesta, and looked at the pasteboard with great disfavor.

"Mr. Mackay. *Aberdeen Mail*." The last was written in one corner, with the words, "Called for an interview about Mr. Davidson's loss in the Paris train."

"Tell him I know nothing whatever about the affair." Mr. Smith's French was exceedingly good. "Any inquiries he has to make should be put to the police. They have all the information and are handling the case. In other words, Honore, as far as I am concerned—throw him out! I don't intend to be bothered with reporters."

Mr. Smith relapsed sleepily on to his pillows again.

Tea was at five—a true summer tea, with iced drinks and sugary cakes and salad sandwiches.

Mrs. Brownlow superintended with the grace that seemed native to her. As the only woman—up till now—in the villa, she naturally played hostess for Monsieur Pichegru. Every one appeared to like the Brownlows, Vivian thought. And, indeed, they seemed to belong to the pleasant, unassuming type of people whom one so often meets, never saying anything worth remembering, and yet who are themselves remembered when brilliant wits are forgotten.

After tea came tennis. Some French neighbors drifted in, but Vivian and Mr. Tibbitts very wisely withdrew and played by themselves.

"Game!" she called finally, with the snap of victory in her voice; "and set!"

Tibbitts seemed to take his beating philosophically. He was a tall, weedy youth who yet conveyed a suggestion of hidden strength in the set of his sloping, narrow shoulders and the hang of his long arms. He had a weak face, and dressed in the very height of French fashion. Even here in Cluny, Tibbitts alone seemed to have no old clothes, no hats or shoes that only long affection saved from being discarded. His very flannels shrieked of their first month's wear. Vivian had met his type before, she thought; the sons of the newly-rich, with all the blemishes, but none of the brains and pluck, that had given father his rise in the world.

"I'm afraid I'm no good at games," Tibbitts said now in his Cockney voice.

"Sure," Vivian agreed heartily; "I am bad, but thou art worse, brother. I guess Mademoiselle Lenglen would wonder what the game was, if she watched us. But there are still two balls missing. And new ones too."

"It's about time to change, isn't it?" the young man asked doubtfully. "I thought I heard the bell, I mean the gong, go some time ago. Whereabouts do you think the balls are?"

"One, your's, was apparently off on a non-stop flight to my home town in Texas. Try over there, while I hunt here in these bushes."

She stepped back swiftly. As she did so, she felt beneath her heel, not yielding earth, but the very firm toe of a very stout shoe. Instead of a scream, she made a swift and amazingly sure lunge. She caught at a man's tightly-buttoned coat, felt her hand struck off with a jerk, and then the branches around her swished and eddied. She had seen nothing. Standing listening, she heard the swishing pass to the other side, then silence. No one was visible as she ran out on to the grass and looked about her.

For fully two minutes Vivian stood staring, then she

walked slowly back to the house. The average woman would have run, but this one walked almost reluctantly away, as though guided by prudence, as though impulse would have sent her after that unexplained figure.

From an open window came a contralto voice singing:

"Let us get all the blue overhead,
Let us soar like birds in their flight,
For it's while we are here that the roses are red,
It's after we're gone they are white."

Vivian had heard the song before, but not the voice. It was evidently Mrs. Brownlow. There was something caressing and passionate in it. The voice of a siren. It went well with Mrs. Brownlow's face, while her manner—quiet but indifferent—her way of speaking—cool though kind—went with neither. So thought Vivian as she ran on to her own room. She was in time for dinner. Most girls would have been late, especially if, like herself, they had no maid with them. But Vivian could hustle. One toss, and her tennis frock lay on the floor. Another toss, a plunge, a splash or two, a rub down, some more tosses, and she stood ready to go downstairs, her curly hair still damp around the nape of her white neck.

They all went in to dinner in a cheery, unconventional group. The two women first, the men following. Miss Young's seat faced the window, and she looked out of it a good deal, and very attentively.

"How have you been getting on with your history of Cluny, Mr. Murgatroyd?" Mrs. Brownlow asked of the only elderly member of the party. Mr. Murgatroyd sighed a little. He was a stout, short man with a ludicrous resemblance to Pickwick.

"I'm afraid I haven't done well to-day," he said apologetically; "the sunshine was too much for me. And the country-side too inviting."

"You have to be bored to work, don't you find it so?" Vivian asked.

"You mean you've got to work to be bored," Tibbitts corrected with a guffaw of startling loudness. Tibbitts was at his worst seen indoors. He was the kind of young man who gets hats and coats handed to him in the evening and is asked to call the car, with subsequent abject apologies for the mistake. His voice, too, fitted the nameless look about him of being a rank outsider.

"Ever tried it?" Smith asked with a supercilious yet measuring stare.

For some reason or other Tibbitts seemed startled.

"N-no. I mean to say—I was speaking airily." And very red in the face, he turned to Mrs. Brownlow.

Meanwhile Mr. Murgatroyd was talking to Vivian. She had made some remark about architecture, and then continued to watch the gardens. Was that a shadow, or a man, far away facing her? When she had finally decided that it was the shadow of a thick branch, Mr. Murgatroyd appeared to be finishing a short lecture.

The professor was evidently nothing if not thorough. He did his best to ensure that Miss Young should be able to recognize the Cluny offshoot of Burgundian architecture whenever she should meet it in later life. Advanced Romanesque it was, but he warned her that, in his humble opinion, she would be making a great mistake to call it pre-Gothic, though if she chose to refer to it as Early Pointed—with the careful stipulation that she was referring to Early Pointed on the continent—she would be quite safe, he thought.

"It was inevitable that the Cluny Benedictines would evolve their own perculiar architecture," he murmured finally, "since their thoughts were peculiar. Their own. Original."

"You think thoughts can influence buildings?" their host asked with a hearty laugh. His English was slow and labored. "The architect's thoughts—yes—and the brickmason's—oh, yes! But otherwise?"

"Buildings"—Mr. Murgatroyd looked across at him— "are made of brick or stone or wood. Are they not? Of thought manifestations, that is to say. And can, therefore, be influenced by thought."

"Then, let's have a week of high thinking," Smith said urgently; "and raise this ceiling for Monsieur Pichegru; he finds it far too low."

Murgatroyd chuckled. But he maintained his position.

"Every thought creates," he repeated, "in us and around us. And it creates in its own image. It draws to itself other thoughts of like kind, therefore other manifestations of like kind."

"I know what you mean," broke in Tibbitts with the air of an exhausted swimmer at last touching bottom with his toes. "I know what you mean, Mr. Murgatroyd. Misfortunes never come singly. And so on. . . ."

Murgatroyd nodded a little curtly. Tibbitts was not a favorite with him.

"Whatever causes one misfortune would be bound to cause another would be a better way of stating it," he murmured. "Take a criminal—I think that at the back of all our prison systems is the unacknowledged certainty that an evil mind should not be allowed at large to attract other evil minds. We hang a murderer because he must, not he may, cause other murders. The mind of a murderer will murder, in other words."

"It really comes to this," Monsieur Pichegru cut in, in his careful English, and in the tone of a man who dislikes the mysterious, "that talents for good or evil will draw to themselves their own opportunities. I think we can all agree on that?"

Monsieur Pichegru had all the Frenchman's love of a discussion at the dinner table. Not at lunch. The midday meal was for the passing of light items of news or gossip, but with the evening, the French spirit seems to expand and rejoice in exercise.

"What do *I* draw to myself, professor?" Vivian asked gaily, catching Murgatroyd's eye as he entirely agreed with their host's condensed version of his idea.

"Opportunities for using your very remarkable

quickness of observation, I should say," was his reply. It surprised her. Here was some one else who was quick too. "1 should think you would make a very successful newspaper correspondent, because by that law of which we're talking, events of interest would be bound to come your way, rather than the way of some duller person."

Vivian smiled a little as at a quaint phantasy, but on that came the startling reflection that here was the problem from Anthony Cross's past sitting beside Smith. Here, to the town, if not to the villa where she was staying, Anthony Cross was coming, perhaps on some errand of his own, perhaps really brought here by the hunt for the diamond stealers of which he had spoken.

Here, where just before dinner she had herself had the incident of the boot in the bushes on which she had stepped. And, why—yes, she herself—why was she here? Not as an ordinary tourist. . . .

"Law?" Tibbitts bit off a chunk of peach and talked through it. "You called it that before. I never heard of any such law. Where is it?"

"It's the law by which, unless we ourselves deliberately bury them, our gifts will surely get the chance to be used to their best advantage. It's a law we do not yet understand. But then, what do we understand?" The professor sighed.

"Nothing of what's been talked about just now," Tibbitts said bluntly.

Every one laughed. He flushed a little and thrust out his weak chin.

"I say, Miss Young, I've mended your bracelet for you."

He spoke loudly, in the tone of one who intended to show the rest that there were some things he could do better perhaps than they.

"Oh, thank you!" Vivian's bracelet, one of the heavy kind fashionable just now, had come undone during tennis, and had refused to stay fastened. Tibbitts had volunteered to put it right He now took it out of his pocket and held it out to her on the palm of his large, red hand—the hand of a laboring man in spite of its obvious acquaintance with soap and water.

It fastened perfectly. Thanking him, she snapped it shut.

"Talents, and opportunities to use them," Smith murmured lazily, with that undertone of careless contempt in which he always spoke to Tibbitts. "I didn't know you were a handy man, Tibbitts. There should be plenty of work for you if your tastes lie in that direction."

"I used to do metal work when I was a boy." Tibbitts looked uncomfortable. "Arts-and-crafts classes, you know. No end fond of it I was. That's where I got these weals on my palms."

"Just the lad for the garden roller," Smith said firmly. "Monsieur Pichegru, get him to have a heart-to-heart talk with it this evening."

Smith disliked Tibbitts, that much Vivian knew already. Mrs. Brownlow protested that Tibbitts and she were going to feed some carp in the Abbotts' Pond. She said it gently enough, yet Vivian was certain that she was not pleased with something. Was it possible that she did not care for her fag to slave for other people? If so, here was the first glimpse of one of the vamp's characteristics that Vivian had seen.

"No, no," Monsieur Pichegru said promptly; "I use Mr. Tibbitts for something better. Adrien, the chauffeur, thinks him a marvel. He thinks—"

"Who was that chap, a red-haired chap, who called here this afternoon," Brownlow asked the table in general, apparently not noticing that his host was speaking. "We met just outside the gate?"

"A reporter. He wanted to see me about Davidson's lost money," Smith answered in his drawl that struck Vivian as so affected.

"About my lost jewels, I hope, too," Mrs. Brownlow said urgently.

"He only wrote on his card that he came about

Davidson's loss," Smith explained. "I didn't see him—why should I? I told him to go to the police. They have all the facts. I loathe reporters."

"But why shouldn't he tell about my jewels too in his paper?" Mrs. Brownlow asked pathetically. She spoke perfect English, but with a very pretty French regularity of accent. "The same thief took both."

"The insurance company in London is investigating, you may be sure," her husband reminded her. "They won't thank us to insert articles in newspapers."

"But the things were only insured for half their value," she said accusingly. "All your fault too. And, of course, no company could be as keen on getting them back as I am. Do see if he won't write up a description of my jewels too. Who did you say the man was, Mr. Smith?"

"Name of Mackay. Scot evidently. Works on some Aberdeen paper."

"Then you may be quite sure he won't work for nothing," Browiiow pointed out to his wife.

Vivian was listening intently. This talk of theft. . . . And it was on account of thefts that Anthony had said he was coming to Cluny. . . . Was it, after all, really business that was bringing him? She had forgotten Edith Montdore's words about "the vamp's" lost sapphires.

Monsieur Pichegru explained, in answer to her inquiry, that a couple of weeks ago Mrs. Brownlow, another guest called Davidson who had now left, Mr. Smith, and Mr. Tibbitts, had all four gone up to Paris, taking the night Pullman at Macon. Mrs. Brownlow to join her husband in the capital, and at the same time have some jewelery re-set. Davidson to put some money into a tourist agency. Smith to have a couple of merry days with some friend, and Tibbitts to escort Mrs. Brownlow apparently; at least, so Monsieur Pichegru said with a twinkle in his bright, dark eyes.

In the morning, on their arrival at Paris, Mrs. Brownlow was minus her jewelery and Davidson had lost his wallet containing a thousand pounds in bonds—

international bearer bonds unfortunately. Neither Smith nor Tibbitts had lost anything. Except Mr. Smith, all the travelers had been chloroformed—by sprays inserted in holes pierced in the doors, the police thought. They had been the only occupants of the carriage, which had been put on at Macon. The porter seemed to have been drugged. There was nothing about the affair to distinguish it from other similar railway thefts, so Smith claimed when Monsieur Pichegru had finished.

"They tried to bore a hole through the panel of my door, but it was a new one. And teak!" he explained.

"These thefts on the French lines are getting as numerous as their accidents," Lascelles murmured under his breath to Mrs. Brownlow. He had only arrived yesterday morning, and was leaving at the end of the week.

After dinner some French neighbors dropped in again, this time for bridge. Smith, a remarkably good player, and his friend Lascelles excused themselves after a rubber, and sat out in the gardens close to a bed of rhododendrons.

In the thick undergrowth behind them there was from time to time a slight, noiseless ripple—a ripple that seemed to be steadily nearing the two figures. It had begun on the outer edge of the little thicket—then it showed towards the middle— then past the middle—now it was close to the edge nearest the backs of the two talkers.

It was on that movement in the bushes that Miss Young's gaze was fixed as she sat by her bedroom window watching the grounds through a very good glass, waiting for the first sign of the return of the man on whose boot she had stepped in the bushes. He was sure to come again she thought. She had looked for him all through dinner and ever since. Now she was certain that her glass was on him, though she saw nothing of any figure.

"I guess a Red Indian couldn't move better," she murmured, putting on a dark cloak, and slipping into her crepe tennis shoes. She made for a clump of bushes behind the two chatting men by a little detour, lingering until at last they got up and passed into the house again. Then she sprang forward into the thicket. The figure should be about here. . . .

It was her own shoulder that a hand grasped.

"Don't be frightened! Don't holler! It's quite all right!" The figure in the darkness was that of a man, the voice just now was low and very urgent.

Most young women would have needed some further reassurance, but Vivian Young did not try to pull herself away. She put her free hand instead into her pocket. Instantly a hand, that felt like steel, gripped it too, not hard, but very firmly.

"It's a torch, not a gun," she said quietly.

"Worse yet," came the swift whisper.

"You're an American, aren't you?" she asked. "I'm from God's country too."

"Has He only one?" came the tart question. "I'm frae Aberdeen, and—but whaur can we talk wi'oot being overheard?"

"Come with me." Vivian had made up her mind as to her course. "There's a summer-house not far off. . . ."

"Mind these laurel bushes!" he cautioned her. "They rustle unco' loudly."

She took his hand and led him swiftly, considering all things, to a dark outline not far off. There she paused, felt for a moment, opened the door, pulled her companion in, shut the door, and only then switched on the light.

They were in a pleasant, pine-walled, pine-ceilinged room, with a rug or two on the floor. Osier chairs in Mandarin blue with cretonne cushions on them, an osier settee and a small table by the fireplace gave the summer-house a homely look.

Seen in the bright electric light, her companion showed as a short, stocky figure with thick hair of a handsome auburn; a shrewd, freckled face lit by a pair of alert, cool gray eyes.

"Who are you?" she asked, though she guessed.

"Suppose I were to tell ye that I'm just the new under-gairdener wi' a taste for listenin' in?" he asked in his marked Scottish accent.

"I should know you for a liar," she replied promptly. "I'm from Texas. We use our wits out there. You're no gardener."

"And wherefore no?"

"Your hands—your fingers—and you called those rhododendrons 'laurels' just now."

He scratched his jutting chin and showed a very fine set of teeth. "Nane sae bad," he conceded fairly. His eyes swept her and studied her. "You yourself are?"

"A visitor to Porte Bonheur." She sat down. So did he. There was a pause.

"I'll e'en tak' a chance," the man said finally, after he had watched her intently for another moment; "I'll e'en trust ye. I'm a repairter on a paper in Aberdeen."

"Where's that?" she asked.

His reply was a look of boundless pity.

"It's the maist important toon in Grreat Britain," he explained modestly. "Well, I'm a repairter there, and yon affair of the robbery in the train of an Aberdonian, a Mr. Davidson, interested me. I've an idea aboot that theft. At least I had," he said, with rather a sheepish grin. "I've been sent by ma editor to speir oot hoo it a' happened. It's ma ain idea," he went on. "If I fail ma paper winna back me. You tak' ma meaning? If I'm caught oot, I'm just— well, whatever I maun hae to be. A trespasser or maybe even a burglar. But the pay promised if I succeed is grrand. And the credit too. I'd be a made man in ma profession. I'd like fine to succeed," he added in a tone whose sincerity there was no mistaking.

"I've got an idea that might be of use to you," she said brightly, and scribbled something on a magazine lying on the table. Tearing off the page, she handed the scrap to the man.

"That may help you in your search," she repeated

pleasantly.

He looked at what she had given him, and a dull red surged up in his lean face till his cheeks glowed like his hair. Then he turned and gave her rather a helpless look.

"You can read shorthand of course," she went on, "since you're a reporter."

For a second he stood biting his thin lips, looking at the little white tag. Then he raised his head and laughed a trifle grimly.

"You're a wonder! But you're richt. I'm nae repairter. But I thocht it wad be easier to gain access to the hoose, and your help too, maybe, if ye thocht I was a man belonging to a recognized newspaper. I wanted ye to have confidence in me," he wound up.

"I have confidence in myself," Vivian said placidly; "quite enough to risk associating with you, Mr. Mackay, or even helping you."

"She kens ma name! She kens everything!" he said in half-assumed, half-real admiration. "Well, I am a private detective, Miss Young. Here are my credentials."

He passed a thick note-case over to her. She studied its contents quickly—but quite carefully.

"You're one of the heads of the firm?" she asked, handing it back.

"I *am* the firm. A' there is to it." He spoke the last sentence soberly enough. His glance swept his thread-bare clothes, his shabby shoes, his ancient felt hat, with a meaning look. "It's make or break with me, Miss Young, this job."

Had he tried for a month he could have found no surer way to interest Vivian Young. "Make or break"—that was real life, she thought, with the feeling of a man who comes back after a long absence to familiar landmarks.

"As good as that?" she breathed eagerly. "My, there's nothing like just air behind one for helping to put pep into things. And putting pep into things is all there is to life," she finished with a laugh.

"As guid as that," Mackay repeated her words too, as

though he liked them. " 'Make or break' is guid, eh?" He seemed to consider the thought. "Well, I ca'd masel' a repairter as less alarming than a private detective," he explained after a pause. "I thocht I would hae a better chance for a crack wi' Mr. Smith."

"He seems to disapprove of reporters," she told him. "I must keep it dark that I'm one if I want to fascinate him."

"You're a reporter?"

"On the *Texas Whirlwind*," she said proudly.

"I *did* land a kelt when I talked of being a newspaper man to you!" he said with fervor.

Miss Young did not know what fish he meant, but she grasped the meaning.

"Sure did!" she assented blithely. She did not add that it was because of her descriptions of the scene, her work of rescue during a terrific fire, that her paper had sent her on a year's tour around the world. Nine months of the year were already gone. It was her great chance, she knew. And to think that so far it had only brought her the post of Anthony Cross's future wife. The thought flashed across her now with quite ludicrous dissappointment.

"Mrs. Brownlow, the woman who lost her jewels at the same time as Mr. Davidson did his money, wants you to work for her too, Mr. Mackay. Her husband rather turned the notion down, but I guess she gets her own way with him."

Mackay shook his head.

"By the terms o' ma contract wi' Davidson, I'm pledged not to undertake ony ither worrk till his job is dune. Or given up. And mind you, it's going to be a deefficult job," Mackay confided suddenly; "for every reason. Lack o' money. And on ma parrt lack o' training too. I'm but a beginner, ye ken. I bought the business wi' ma last poond-note and I've no succeeded as I hoped. So I come cheap. Which was why Mr. Davidson took me on. The prices o' a French detective made his hair fall oot. Forrby that he canna speak the language, and hasna any confidence in men that kiss each ither."

"It's a great chance for you!" she said warmly.

"It's one that I'll niver get again if I slip up on't." His face looked suddenly very young and troubled. She saw the over-sharp modeling of jaw and high cheekbone. Mackay could do with more food than he had been having lately, she thought.

"As far as determination is concerned I'll no slip. But it's ma brains, I doot, ma reasoning powers. And what you want in detecting, Miss Young, is logic."

"I'm only here over the week-end, but I'll help you find out anything I can," she said impulsively.

"What? Join forces wi' an unmasked gairdener and reporter?" he asked with a swift smile.

"I guess I can call most people's bluff," she said, smiling too. The pleasant smile facing her came off promptly.

"But if it isna bluff in yon hoose? And it may not be, Miss Young. Detecting isna a game for a leddy. Though I winna say but that there micht be bits of information and—well, juist bits like, where an insider could help a lot."

She rose.

"Well, I must go now. But I'll keep my ears and eyes open, and if I can think of anything brilliant I'll let you know. And if anything humble enough to entrust me with comes along you'll be so kind and condescending as to mention it, I hope."

He thanked her warmly.

"Ye're a plucky lassie," he murmured gratefully. "I kennt that weel the moment I felt your hand on ma coat. Not a tremble. Not a fumble, and not a soond. But is this suramerhoose safe for a crack?"

"It's stoutly built," she assured him. "I noticed this morning that you can't hear voices outside. Unless, of course, you were to put your ear against the cracks. But why not come to the villa? Call on me, if you like."

"I canna come ben," he said firmly. "Mr. Smith doesna like repairters, ye said yoursel'. And I've sent in ma name

as a repairter. But there's an old gentleman staying in
yon villa; I saw him fishing this evening. He and I passed
a word together. Maist interresting talk on the ruins we
had."

"Professor Murgatroyd, yes?"

"I'll watch for him, and mok' friends wi' him. He may
know summat that'll help. I feel a bit like a wee laddie oot
in his big brither's breeks," he confided whimsically.

"Your great chance will be the fancy-dress ball. Oh,
say, Mr. Mackay, it's masked! Until supper at one. Why
don't you come and go over to the bedrooms carefully, if
you suspect any one in the house. Do you suspect any one
in the house?" she asked. She meant, did he suspect
Smith or Tibbitts.

He could not, or would not, tell her.

"I'm not a guid detective," he said at once, "and never
shall be, but at least I dinna blab a' my thochts. But the
ball— that's a fine idea—I'll think that over—"

"Sakes alive, Mr. Mackay, you don't want to think
things over! You want to grab at them! Jump and land
them!"

"Na, na!" he expostulated in a deeply shocked tone,
"one should aye act according to the light o' reason, Miss
Young. After long and careful deliberation."

She gave him a derisive glance.

"You're young enough to learn better, fortunately. My
father was a Texas Ranger. One of the best. And his
motto was 'Leap before you look.'"

"Tut, tut!" Mackay clucked, shaking his head in open
horror.

"It's a good one," she said promptly. "None better."

"In Texas, verra likely," he said politely; "but in oor
parrt o' the globe, Miss Young, the licht o' reason is what
we maun go by."

"Shucks!" was Miss Young's reception of that bit of
wisdom, after which she arranged the hour of their next
meeting and said good-night.

CHAPTER THREE

NEXT morning, Vivian, Mrs. Brownlow, and Mrs. Brownlow's Faithful slave, Tibbitts, went out with Mr. Murgatroyd to an old fortress close beside the villa, from whose ancient battlements they had a good view.

It was a glorious day. Vivian shook off all fancies and riddles, and enjoyed it to the full. The meadows were one blaze of buttercups, the hawthorns white with blossom.

Behind them lay the wooded slopes of Fouettin and Saint Mayeul. A lane of lime trees, centuries old, still in full flower, led to the little town on their right. The smell of its blossoms, surely one of the sweetest smells in the world, rose all about them. Girls with big baskets on their arms were cutting off the thick clusters for the famous *tilleul tisane*. To one side the Grosne, crystal clear, glittered past meadows where maize was tossing its great golden plumes. There was a hint of ripening grapes in the air from the vineyards all around.

There is magic in Cluny by night or by day. A spell woven by man, and the mind of man. A spell from out the great days when:

> *"En tout pays ou le vent vente*
> *L'Abbe de Cluny a rente."*

The days when this little town was an asylum for kings, when its abbey led the world of Christian thought, and led it well; when Cardinals of Guise, and Richelieu, and Mazarin, and princes of the blood royal were content to be its "abbot of abbots"; when four Popes came from its grand old walls; when its library, and its learning, and its high standards; were only equalled by its power and its wealth.

Vivian leaned over the coping and studied the scene. For a while the historian let them idle, then he set to work. He had promised them a glimpse of the Cluny that he knew. A very different place from the sleepy *ville* that they saw.

Of the great Basilica, that monumental work of the eleventh century, the noblest church in Christendom of its time, he could only speak of as of a lost treasure, save for two towers of the narthex still left standing.

But he built it up again for them. In its green setting, with its triple roofs, its soaring steeples, its innumerable buttresses.

Then he showed them where the abbey ran, a world in itself, with its gardens, and its immense cloisters, its buildings, towers and ramparts.

Vivian was not greatly interested in architecture, but she liked hearing any man talk on what he knew well. Also, she had sent home a delicious little vignette of "The Professor at the Dinner-table," and she wanted another. Even if he had read them, Mr. Murgatroyd would only have been flattered, for she drew him with a very friendly pen.

Mrs. Brownlow seemed interested. But there was so little else doing at Cluny that Vivian suspected her of gracefully making the best of a dull day. Tibbitts shifted heavily from one big foot to the other and breathed hard. When he could, he leaned over the battlements and betted with Vivian on the various depths. He had a quite unexpectedly accurate eye, she found.

"And now"—Mr. Murgatroyd beamed at them like a father promising his youngsters a treat—"now we will go and have another look at the beautiful double-arched entrance gate of the old abbey. We won't go on to the museum. I don't doubt you, too, know that by heart."

"Bet your life!" Tibbitts agreed, adding in an aside, "I don't think!"

They walked to the school of arts and crafts, now housed in the old abbey, or part of it. Mrs. Brownlow said that she knew the gate well with its charming view. Why, Vivian asked herself, was she always so interested in Mrs. Brownlow? It was not only because of that odd incident of her picture in Anthony Cross's hands. It was something in the woman herself. Some charm that emanated from her, as perfume from a damask rose. Whether she were a vamp or no, Vivian could well imagine her to be a spell-binder.

Murgatroyd leading, they passed into the building. It was then that Vivian missed Tibbitts.

She believed that they would find him at some café outside, in front of an aperitif, but, to her surprise, looking over her shoulder, she saw him standing still on the handsome broad staircase, the original staircase, and bending down to examine the wrought iron banister.

"Gosh! I never saw finer work!" he muttered. "Old iron this," he went on touching it as Vivian had never thought that his thick fingers could touch anything. "Very old. Yuss," he bent down and studied it intently. Then he straightened up and grinned sheepishly at her before shooting a swift, rather nervous glance at Mrs. Brownlow's slender back.

"Don't often find things in museums and old places that interest me," he murmured apologetically; "first time I ever remember to've cared a damn for any of the rot they show you."

They walked on, Tibbitts sinking again into the dull young man with the efforts at heavy pleasantry that they knew at the villa.

It was when they were in the cloisters that he seemed to come to life again. He suddenly left them, turned at right angles and was lost to view. His action had something so definite, so purposeful in it, that the others followed.

"I told you the boy was only joking when he said that he had never been here before," Mrs. Brownlow murmured.

They found Tibbitts on his knees by a funny little

excrescence in the wall.

"Here is the spot!" he called exultantly. "They've built this doorway half over it, but here was the 'earth where that iron was puddled, bet your life, and drawn and hammered, and worked up, that we saw just now on that staircase."

Margatroyd gave an exclamation.

"You think you've located the blasting furnace of Brother Placidus?" His voice shook with excitement. "We've been hunting for that for years. I was certain that it was under some part of this later addition."

"Where else could it be?" Tibbitts asked contemptuously; "seeing the way the valley faces, it would 'ave to be 'ere, wouldn't it?"

His voice was the voice of a laboring man.

"Then you think this blackened wall—" Murgatroyd's tone was quite humble.

"I don't think! I know! You can see for yourself that part of the old sandstone 'earth is still 'ere. It would be lined with charcoal dust, you know. The pile of ore would go there. The 'earth would be filled up this-a-way with charcoal, and blanketed down with a muck of wet dust and small ore. Then you'd start the blast going, and keep adding more blanketing until you got a good heat, then you'd let the blast rip, and bit by bit the whole'ld turn to bloom."

"What's 'bloom'?" Mr. Murgatroyd was always interested in anything even distantly connected with his work. "What's 'bloom,' Mr. Tibbitts?"

Mrs. Brownlow watched the scene with a faint line between her rather thick, very long and low brows.

"Why, your puddled iron o' course. The stuff wot ye draws out and hammers and rolls. The stuff wot some bloke worked into those banisters we saw in the house back there, and that r'iling to the balcony just over our heads." He pointed up with one of his big red hands. "And I'll tell you one thing, the bloke wot designed them knew iron, knew wot it will do, and wot it won't. Beaten it with his bare fists in his time he must 'ave."

"Well done!" Murgatroyd was enchanted. "Well done! They are indeed both by the same master hand. Both by Brother Placidus. But that you should have detected as much at a mere glance—you are indeed a master craftsman, not merely the dilettante which in your modesty you claimed! Metal work was a genuine hobby with you evidently."

"Metal work, yuss." Tibbitts seemed to give a little start, and again he shot a rather timid glance at Mrs. Brownlow, who only turned and began to admire the flowers.

On the way out, Murgatroyd motioned them to follow him to a little room. He pointed to a painting in a corner representing a monk with a rugged, but intellectual head.

"That's Brother Placidus. Looks like a pilgrim with that staff in his hand, doesn't he? Well, he was one. We all are."

"Staff? That's a rabble, that is!" Tibbitts was staring intently into the dull, dim picture.

"And what, pray, is a rabble?" asked Mrs. Brownlow. Her voice was bored and indifferent.

"Why, what you rabbles with, silly!" was the unexpected reply. There followed a second of appalled silence. Then Mrs. Brownlow gave a forced laugh. There was nothing forced about Vivian's. She had to laugh or burst. The absolute stupefaction on Mrs. Brownlow's features was too marked and too sudden for her self-control. Even Mr. Murgatroyd was betrayed into one reluctant cackle.

"Really, Mr. Tibbitts," Mrs. Brownlow spoke with an effort at gaiety, "you are rather overwhelming as a tutor!"

Tibbitts turned scarlet.

"Sorry, Mrs. Brownlow, I spoke too quick," he mumbled; "I was thinking of that bloke there."

"You haven't told us yet what you rabble, and why you rabble," Vivian reminded him, with another burst of hilarity.

"A rabble is the long bar wot you rouses the boiling with," he said suddenly, and walked off whistling between his teeth. And with that, as far as Tibbitts was concerned, the interest of the morning seemed to be over. But on their saunter back to the villa, a saunter in which Mrs. Brownlow very quietly, but very firmly chose Mr. Murgatroyd as her companion, Tibbitts said suddenly to Vivian:—

"Brother Placidus, eh? That's the same as Placid I suppose?" Vivian said she supposed so too.

"Placidus"—Tibbitts swung his ornate cane to and fro—" 'e worked like 'is name. Placid. Nothing hurried about his work. No need to." Again there was a silence, and then he said half to himself:—

"Must be wonderful to do work like that back there. Work you 'ave a right to be proud of. Work you'd never need to brag about. It speaks for itself, it does. I used to think when I was a nipper that I'd do something like that bloke's wrought iron work some day. You couldn't do nothink finer if you was to try all your life! Yuss, I used to think in those days that once you was grown-up—why, you could do as you liked. Work to please yourself— "

He stopped again. Something in his brown eyes reminded Vivian of a homeless mongrel staring in through a window.

"I believe," she said encouragingly, "that wealth is just as much of a handicap as is poverty."

Tibbitts nodded, but he said nothing more. Mr. Murgatroyd stopped them a second later to point out a Merovingian wooden house. Suddenly Mrs. Brownlow gave a startled little exclamation.

"Ah!" beamed Murgatroyd; "you've noticed that added arch? It is indeed a dissonance. That must have been done when—"

But Mrs. Brownlow had turned and was hurrying down into the rue de la Poste without one glance at the anachronism which Murgatroyd fondly thought had surprised and shocked an informed eye.

Miss Young, as they walked on up the road that climbed to the villa, saw her hasten on towards a tall figure that was sauntering along with a leisurely

"All that I see,
Belongs to me!"

air as she called it. It was Anthony Cross. Vivian saw him stop at a word from Mrs. Brownlow and take off his hat. Mrs. Brownlow drew him to one side, and together he and she, after a few minutes animated conversation, walked back towards the center of the town.

Mr. Murgatroyd, since this was a matter unconnected with sticks and stones or past ages, had noticed nothing. He burbled on. Tibbitts melted away into a cafe. Vivian Young threw the historian a word now and then, but she was thinking hard.

Anthony and the problem from his past! Apparently he had just arrived. He was carrying a small bag. She had noticed that at Macon there was no word or sign of his valet. She would do nothing to deliberately put herself in his path, she had decided. That should be left to Fate. Besides, always at the back of her mind was the knowledge that Anthony really was engaged in a most important search, one which, though he had denied its presence here at Cluny, was not unconnected with danger.

She wondered whether he would learn that she was staying at the Villa Porte Bonheur. She wondered, whether, and if so, when and how they two would meet.

At dinner that night, Mrs. Brownlow spoke of Cross.

"I met an old friend of ours unexpectedly this morning, Tom," she murmured. "It's Anthony Cross. Fancy meeting him again and of all places here! I asked him to drop in for a chat after dinner."

"Anthony Cross?" Tom Brownlow repeated rather vacantly. "Oh, yes, of course! Coming in this evening, is he? Good!"

Surely this was overdoing it, Vivian thought. Surely a couple who had spent the whole afternoon together would have talked over a friend's arrival. Why then this public announcement and this apparent difficulty on the husband's part to "place" the friend?

"What brings Cross to Cluny?" Brownlow went on.

"The abbey remains. I suggested his asking you for a room, Monsieur Pichegru. Perhaps he will. If he stays on at all for any length of time. Apparently he has only made up his mind definitely to one night, and took a room at the hotel near the station. If you hadn't happened to be taking us on that historical tour of the town, Mr. Murgatroyd, he might have come and gone without either of us knowing of it. He was so surprised to see me walking towards him." This last to her husband, who nodded carelessly.

"Are you talking of the Sir Anthony Cross?" Smith asked with interest "One of the directors of the South African Diamond Combine?"

The Brownlows said that that was the man.

"He's on his way back to London on some matter connected with the syndicate, so he told me," the wife added.

Vivian saw Smith flash a quick, inquiring glance at his friend, Mr. Lascelles, who returned it blandly. Catching Vivian's gaze on them, both men dropped their eyes with a haste that looked positvely guilty, and began to crumble their bread.

"Perhaps we can persuade him to let me put him up, though but for one night," suggested Monsieur Pichegru, and again a message of the eyes passed between Smith and his friend. "Any friend of yours, Brownlow, can always count on a room here. And a rest in this quiet spot might do such a busy man as Sir Anthony good."

"I am sorry to seem discourteous," Mr. Murgatroyd said in his clear voice; "but if Sir Anthony Cross were to become an inmate of Villa Porte Bonheur, I should be constrained to go to one of the hotels. Under ordinary circumstances that would be no matter, but half-way through my book it would entail, I confess, a certain amount of adjusting of impediments. . . ."

"You know Anthony Cross?" Brownlow asked curiously.

"I have never met him," explained the professor; "but some years ago my brother was very anxious to establish a leper colony not far from one of the mines owned by his company. He had just been appointed a director, I remember, and it was owing to his active and passive resistance that all efforts fell through. I feel that the abandoning of a project of bringing help to a class of human beings who certainly needed it sorely was due entirely and solely to him. And feeling that, I very strongly object to meeting him. His standpoint was—" Mr. Murgatroyd pulled himself up, but his eyes flashed. He looked very different from the placid scholar of the morning.

He shook his head at himself. "The French are right; to be angry and to make bad blood is one and the same thing. Sir Anthony must have brought down on himself enough ill will without my adding to it."

"It does not seem to have harmed him, so far," Mrs. Brownlow put in, with, for once, a touch of sarcasm in her voice.

"So far," Murgatroyd repeated. "Remember the words of the wise Solon: 'Account a prosperous man happy only when he ends his life as he began it.' Sir Anthony is still a comparatively young man, as age goes nowadays."

It seemed to Vivian that the rest of the dinner was unusually quiet.

Smith, his friend and Mr. Murgatroyd all seemed lost in thought. Only the Brownlows, Monsieur Pichegru and she kept up a desultory chat, with clumsy contributions from Tibbitts.

After dinner, Vivian took a walk by herself through the gardens. For the present she had decided to act exactly as though Anthony Cross were not in the town.

She finally strolled back to the summer-house to which she had taken Mackay. It was the hour at which they had agreed to meet.

As she shut the door, some one rose in the dusk inside. It was the detective.

"Sure, it's verra kind of ye, Miss Young," he said, with evident pleasure. "Naething to report, I tak' it? I hope to find some clue when I tak' a luik at the hoose to-morrow nicht. The nicht o' the dance. For I shall come to it. I've met a mon who'a a director of a great diamond combine for which I did a bit o' warrk a couple of years back. He's doon to tak' a luik. at the ruins, and is putting up at the same hotel as I am.

"I've had a crack wi' him. I tellt him what brings me here—in strict confidence, o' course, and I spoke aboot the ball tomorrow. Balls are a bit oot o' ma line. But he thinks, like you, that I must na miss seeing the inside o' a' the rooms when the parties are engaged below. It seems he kens the leddy who lost her jewels—yon Mrs. Brownlow—and through her he'll meet Monsieur Pichegru, and will ask him for twa invitations for Saturday nicht. Ane for himself, though he doesna expect to be here to use it, and ane for a friend. That's me! Certes, I shall use mine."

"You mean Sir Anthony Cross? Mrs. Brownlow spoke at dinner of having met him in the town. If you've worked for Sir Anthony, perhaps he can put you in the way of some really good job." Vivian was thinking of the diamond thefts.

"A doot that," Mackay said with his self-deprecatory smile. "I'm no the class o' detective that Sir Anthony Cross wad employ. What I did for his combine was nobbut looking up some clerk's Edinburgh guarantor. And that class o' warrk is a' I'm guid for, I fear me. Ye see, detecting differs. I've always worked on business questions. Tracing checks, asking aboot characters, and the like. But private warrk—like Mr. Davidson's—it pays the best, o' coorse, but it's the sort I'm no cut oot for, and that's a fact. However, I shall just use ma een to-morrow nicht, and if I find naething after all, I'll awa' to Paris, and try to work at the bogle frae that end. For when a's said and dune, 'tis by the light o' reason alane problems are solved."

"Father solved his with his gun—alone," Vivian said dryly, and Mackay laughed. A laugh that suddenly spoke of youth and a sense of humor, however repressed.

"What are you coming to the dance as?" she asked next. "We ought to be able to recognize each other."

"I thocht o' a ghaist," he said tentatively. "I canna spend ony money on it. And for a ghaist a' I'd need wad be but a sheet and a pillow case—over and abune ma ither claes," he added hastily. It was Vivian's turn to laugh. Suddenly an impish idea struck her. She would have dearly like to suggest that Mackay should go as "The Ghost of a Young Man Drowned in Shanghai," but she bit back the speech. After all, though the tale linking his death with Mr. Brownlow might be false enough, the young man had probably really died. And besides that, Vivian was no spreader of idle gossip.

"White's rather a poor color for snooping," she said instead.

"True." He thought a moment. "Forbye giving some servant lass the fright of her life. Hoo aboot a collector then? That micht do. Juist ma Sunday blacks—ma frock-coats gey shiny at the seams, and I'll rip it a bit here and a bit there—and ma top-hat has seen better days—and wi' ma sma black bag in ma hand, I'd do fine, and widna be seen a mile off. Aye. It'll be as a collector I'll come. A debt-collector, ye ken. And you, Miss Young?"

"I'm 'Lady-into-Fox.' Chiefly a woman, but turning back into the fox that I once was. With a fox's head on my hair. But about what brings you to Cluny—I came here simply bursting with something that happened this afternoon, and yet which seems too monstrous."

She stopped as though she really meant the adjective.

He looked hard at her. His bright, alert, gray eyes

were trying to read what she had to tell him before she spoke. His resolute, freckled, rather plain face was alight with interest. Was he to hear something that would help him?

"If only you were hunting for Mrs. Brownlow's jewels instead of, or as well as, Mr. Davidson's money, it might help you tremendously," she said slowly; "though, as I say, I can't believe—no, I can't!" She stopped again.

"I cann't warrk but for Davidson the noo, but I'm as keen on knowing what happened to Mrs. Brownlow's jewels as she can be," he said eagerly. "The twa thefts were the warrk o' the ane thief. There's na doot aboot that. It's not entirely the money I'm working for, Miss Young," he added, as she still did not speak, "though I canna deny that a bit o' siller wad be useful. But it's the thocht o' mebbe beating a criminal at his ain game. I'd like fine to do that!"

She nodded. "Well, this afternoon, while I was practicing some serves, I happened to look towards the house just as a gust of wind blew back the curtains in one of the first floor rooms. You'd call it ground floor. And there stood Mr. Tibbitts by the window with a string of black pearls in his hands. He nearly dropped them, and looked ready to drop himself when the curtain billowed around him and he saw me on the grass.

"He sounded me when he came out as to whether I had noticed some beads he'd bought in the village as a present for his sister at home. Now, of course, that's quite possibly all the scene meant. But—it's funny! It sure is! He looked appalled when that curtain blew out like a sail and left the window free. Yet I can't think that Mr. Tibbitts is a thief! He is supposed to be a rich young man! But it was a string of black pearls that Mrs. Brownlow lost along with some sapphires, and those in Tibbitts's hand were just the length of hers—long enough to go around the neck—a choker string. And I never saw a lovelier sheen. They looked like black grapes. And Tibbitts was on the car the night they were stolen from

Mrs. Brownlow— altogether—" she shook her head with
its bright waves of light-brown hair—hair that matched
her eyes in color.

"Which window was it?" Mackay asked at once.

"A long window in a room they call the cedar room.
It's a sort of extra room. Hardly ever used."

"Not the room where the safe is?" Mackay asked. She
shook her head.

"That's in Monsieur Pichegru's study. I know, because
he wanted to lock away any jewelery or money of mine I
might have with me. But about Mr. Tibbitts—" she looked
inquiringly at Mackay, who only stood thoughtful and
silent.

"Sakes alive, why don't you say something?" she said
laughing.

"I'm thinking," he replied gravely.

"But I want to know what you think about what I've
just told you—about Tibbitts—"

"It takes time to think," Mackay said judicially; "to
think wi' any degree of usefulness, that is. But I'll admit
that it's queer," he conceded with one of those boyish
smiles that lit up his lean face.

"So are many little things about the house," she said
in answer to that. "To-night at dinner, for instance, when
Sir Anthony's name came up. Mr. Smith and a friend of
his, a Mr. Lascelles—the two you were watching when we
met"—Vivian's eyes twinkled like brown diamonds at the
recollection—"he's leaving to-morrow morning, by the
way—looked so oddly at each other. A long, meaning look,
especially when Monsieur Pichegru said he would put Sir
Anthony up."

"Is he going to?" Mackay wanted to know.

"Mrs. Brownlow thought Sir Anthony wouldn't be
staying long enough to make it worth his while changing
over from the hotel. Besides dear old Mr. Murgatroyd got
quite mad at the mere notion. I thought Mr. Smith, and
Mr. Lascelles, too, both looked very disappointed.
Certainly they were very silent for the rest of the meal.

Say, Mr. Mackay, it all sounds so silly, gossiping like this. But I like talking to you. Partly because I sure am glad to have some one to speak to who reminds me of home. You look like the kind of men I'm used to. Though, heaven knows, they'd beat you when it comes to grabbing on to things! But also you never know what bit of idle chatter might not help a detective."

"Not this detective! Not me!" Mackay said gloomily. "I'm plum oot o' ma depth. But I'll dae ma best!" he finished sturdily.

She laughed. "My grandmother used to say:

> *"Do your best*
> *And leave the rest,*
> *Angels can't do better."*

"But the trouble is it isna angels I'm up against," was his only comment on grandmamma's philosophy. "I've been trying to think things oot. But even if I had ma suspicions, hoo can I prove them?"

There was a short silence, then she told him of the morning at the abbey.

"Mr. Tibbitts was too funny. He grew just like a workman. Dropping his aitches and speaking like what we call a Bowery tough. And the way he turned on Mrs. Brownlow, when she was fed up with his talk about a rabble and asked him what it was. Asked him in the tone that says you don't care a cuss what it is—you know the tone." Vivian laughed again. "It sure was funny!"

"Do you think she likes Tibbitts?" Mackay wondered.

"She treats him very nicely. In a sort of elder-sister way that's quite charming. But, then, she is charming in everything she does."

"And her husband—Mr. Brownlow?"

"He speaks to him always in a very civil tone. More I can't say. Mrs. Brownlow told me that they met Tibbitts at Monte Carlo simply flinging his money away right and left. He was a mill hand. She thinks—she doesn't know—

and his father emigrated and made a fortune suddenly and then died. She explained to me that they wanted Tibbitts to stay a while at the villa with them and learn to pick up a few things—"

"Such as Mr. Davidson's thousand pounds, and her jewelery?" asked Mackay grimly, and they both rocked in unseemly mirth.

"How mean we are to talk like this! Say, she fascinates me, Mr. Mackay. She's a wonderful woman."

"She's a face that doesna attract me," he said rather shortly.

"But she's so graceful!"

"Aye. She has a nice walk," he agreed. "I've heerd that Isadora Duncan walked that gait."

"I should like to know her better," Vivian went on, half to herself. "I'm sure she'd be interesting to know. Yet I can't think why I'm not sure."

She rose to go. But she had one question to put.

"Mr. Mackay why did you ask me where Monsieur Pichegru's safe is?"

"I've known of a missing paper once being a' the time in the man's own safe," he said darkly. "That's why, Miss Young."

Vivian thought this over on the way back to the house. And the more she thought it over, the less she understood exactly what the private detective meant. Did he know himself? But her thoughts now were really on Anthony Cross. Had he arrived? Would he and she meet? To-night?

She heard her name called, and found Mr. Smith behind her on the path.

"I thought I heard voices in the summer-house. Have you left poor Tibbitts locked in?" he asked languidly.

"Oh, no," she spoke as casually as he. "I was talking to an acquaintance of mine who didn't know where Monsieur Pichegrus boundary runs. A man who's putting up at the Hotel de Bourgogne. By the way, he's an acquaintance of this Sir Anthony Cross's too."

"Why don't you bring him up to the house," Smith suggested in what sounded a sociable tone; "do you know if he's any good at squash racquets?"

"Let's ask him," she suggested.

They found the house, as she knew they would, empty. It had a window that looked on to the opposite side of the path, and she had talked to Smith as they walked towards it. Unless he wished to be found then, Mackay would be out over the sill and through the bushes, like a young salmon over a rapid; of that she was quite sure.

Smith murmured some vague word of regret about the squash racquets and strolled back, while Vivian took a turn through the orchard, enjoying the beauty around her.

Coming back to the villa once more, she saw ahead of her, in a corner of the thickly-wooded drive that made a little bay here, two people standing talking. One was Anthony Cross. He was speaking very earnestly to an over-dressed, over-painted woman. Or rather the woman was talking earnestly to Anthony Cross. She was a remarkably handsome woman too. Vivian thought that she must have been a singularly lovely girl. Standing still in the shadow of some trees she looked at them. By Anthony's expression she saw that he was trying to escape. But the woman would not let him go. There was something absolutely desperate in the very bend of her neck as she seemed to be pouring out a string of entreaties. Twice he tried to leave her, but she only stepped after him and continued to talk. Finally Anthony's face flushed at something said, and with a little twitch of his shoulders very familiar to Vivian—it had reminded her the first time she saw it of a Roman senator adjusting his toga—he almost pulled his arm from her hand and turned away. An exclamation from the woman stopped him. Even to Vivian's far-off ears it had had a tragic sound. He looked ashamed of himself, she thought, and turning, he stood patiently for another moment or two. But by the set of his jaw, when he replied, Vivian could guess that he was not giving way. Indeed it looked to her as though he were delivering some sort of an ultimatum, or even warning the woman not to continue her argument, her pleading, her—whatever it was. And when he had done speaking, he turned away in a manner that brooked no further stopping. Resolutely he walked towards the house, out of sight.

The woman stood where he had left her, in the middle now of the path. She stared after him. Her face was towards Vivian. It was pale, and there was a sort of desperate hatred in it, a sort of unable to believe that all was lost expression on it that kept Vivian rooted to the spot. She shivered. What could make a woman look like that at a man? Tragic and almost frightening in their wild fixity, there was a passion of hatred in her magnificent eyes that had to be seen to be believed.

"I wouldn't like any one to look after me like that!" thought Vivian. She wondered what it meant. She was far too experienced, knew too much of the world, to think the worst, as a nicely brought up young woman of the mid-Victorian period would have done. But still—it was an odd look. . . . It did not admit of many interpretations. . . . Vivian went on. The woman, hearing the steps on the gravel, turned, gave her one glance and then walked away swiftly towards the gate. Vivian was half-minded to catch her up and chance some excuse. After all, she was Anthony Cross's fiancé. Or was she? No, to be honest, she didn't care a rap how many old flames, or new ones either, Anthony had. She was quite sure that she never had cared, and never would care. And on that thought, she slowed up, turned and walked away. At the first possible moment she intended to take her freedom back.

That wild night on the ship, something big about the man had imposed itself on her and blinded her to many smaller facts—their different upbringing—their different walks in life. A girl, of course, can marry a man of quite another world, but she must want to become a member of

that world. Vivian didn't. She was a born fighter. She
loved a struggle. And there would be no fighting, no
struggling, as Lady Cross. Anthony was not a self-made
man. He had shown her some photographs of his family
place that had much impressed her. It must be a dream of
a house, of a park. But even at that moment of semi-awe,
Vivian had known in her heart of hearts that it was no
home for her. You couldn't add anything to Quarry Court.
You could only keep it up. And keeping up what others
had had the fun of making did not appeal to Miss Young.

Arrived at the villa, she went to her room. By the
reflection on some ilex bushes below her window, she
could see that the lights were on in the cedar room—the
room where she had seen Tibbitts standing with the
beads—or could it possibly be the pearls—in his hand.

Leaning out, she could even catch a voice, Anthony's
voice, speaking quietly as ever. In fact, speaking a good
deal more quietly than usual, she thought. Then came a
laugh. Mrs. Brownlow's throaty gurgle. And another! Her
husband's this time. Anthony did not seem to join in, and
he had a very hearty guffaw when he was amused. Next
she heard his low tones making what seemed quite a long
speech. Evidently the Brownlows had carried their friend
off from the drawing-room to this quieter spot. There was
only one other room in the wing. A sudden wonder struck
her as to whether the Brownlows already knew of
Anthony Cross's engagement to her. It would hardly be
possible for him to be talking so long without telling old
friends of the most important step that can befall man or
woman. If so, would he learn of her arrival here? Here in
the villa? Would he think it a coincidence if he did? He
might. But she knew the quickness of his perception, of
his reasoning. He was not a man whom you could easily
hoodwink. He had an uncanny—at least she thought it
uncanny—way of putting just the one question that you
did not want him to put, the one and only query whose
answer would inevitably give him the kernel of the
matter. She decided that if Anthony heard of her arrival,

it would be no use pretending that it was not linked with the sight of that photograph, with her overhearing his question about a man called Brownlow.

And on that came the thought to go downstairs now, it was only a little past nine, and leave it to him to meet her as a stranger, or present her as his fiancé. Which would he do? What a delightful, awkward position for him. Vivian was a bit of a minx. The idea appealed to her immensely. She was down the stairs within the minute. She was almost at the door of the cedar room when came the reflection—was it fair to Anthony, supposing the very unlikely case that he did not know of her presence in the house at all; would it be fair to him to spring a meeting on him in circumstances of which he had had no idea when he had asked her to meet him as a stranger? That halted her. Then came the thought that, apart from fairness or not to Anthony, she was sure that he could be very stubborn. In which case the jest might be a rather awkward one in the end. Suppose he let himself be introduced to her as to a stranger, and suppose her vague feeling of thin ice, of undertows, was all wrong, and these people at the villa were all that they seemed, how could she ever explain away the facts when they learned them? And since the Brownlows were "all right" and friends of Anthony's, they were sure to learn of them, unless—

Could she save his pride if not his heart? Could she perhaps prevent him telling others of that engagement which she firmly intended to break. She decided to step into a room near the one from where the voices came—it was fitted up rather in an hotel fashion with several little writing-tables—and wait there for his departure, which could not now be long delayed. She would slip out through one of the long windows when he should pass the door and meet him outside the villa gate. She would be frank with him, she would tell him that she had acted on impulse when she had accepted him. That his personal magnetism had swept her judgment off its usually firm set. As to more sordid motives, Vivian refused to acknowledge them, even to herself. They were not really part of her. In that she was right. She was no parasite.

Vivian settled herself in an arm-chair. She did not switch up the light which was back by the door.

It was some minutes before a sound roused her from her thoughts. It was the faint fall of footsteps outside, or rather beside, the room. They died away. Then they came again. Again they died away. Some one was lightly, all but noiselessely, walking up and down a carpeted side-passage which ran between the room where she sat waiting and the room where Sir Anthony sat talking, presumably alone with the Brownlows.

Vivian waited until the steps passed once more, then she noiselessly opened her door and looked out. To her surprise the passage, too, showed no light. Whoever was there was in the darkness. And must have switched off the row of lights that had been shining like pink pearls a minute ago.

She hesitated. For after all, she, too, was waiting in the dark. That other person out there might be equally justified in hoping for a word with Anthony Cross. And for an equally good reason perfer, too, not to be seen waiting.

On that, however, came a sudden realization that Anthony Cross claimed to be in Cluny on a mission both secret and important. A mission connected with a theft that ran into many figures. He had laughed at the idea of danger, but the danger might be here just the same.

She knew now that she was not in the least in love with him, but she would always be his friend. Was that figure, doing so soft a sentry-go outside the cedar room, a friend?

She was just on the point of slipping out and switching up the lights, when the door of the cedar room itself opened and shut swiftly, as some one—a man—stepped out. She heard a "Sorry! I had no idea there was any one here!" in Brownlow's voice. He had evidently collided with some unseen person.

She heard an answering, "I can't find the switches. I want the room where Monsieur Pichegru told me that I should find plenty of writing paper."

It was Mr. Lascelles! Quiet Mr. Lascelles, then, who had been taking that promenade up and down the dark passage. Vivian was surprised. The next instant she jumped to her feet. For Brownlow, still speaking very pleasantly, said:

"Oh, that's the other side of us. This way—"

They were coming in here, and she, Vivian, would be found sitting in the dark and apparently waiting—for whom? For what? It was an impossibly ridiculous situation since she could give no explanation. There was no time to switch up the light, as the men had already turned the corner and would see the streak under the door and hear the click.

Intensely vexed at the whole affair, she stepped behind the long curtains over the windows. The glass doors themselves had patent fasteners, which were too noisy to dare to open—for the moment—or she would have slipped out now, at once, into the garden. She was delighted when she heard Lascelles say rather nervously:

"Oh, thanks! Thanks so much. I only—eh—wanted some paper to take to my room with me. This will do nicely. Thanks."

"Sure there's nothing else?" Brownlow asked. And was it Vivian's fancy or was there something mocking in the question so solicitously put. "Nothing, thanks," was the reply, and a minute later she heard the two men pass on together down the passage to the main hall.

She waited where she was. One of them might come back, and the villa's carpets were frightfully thick. A moment later she heard some one actually in the room. Some one who now closed the door. Vivian had noticed that her curtains by no means covered the whole of the window recess. She had not dared to touch them for fear of a fold continuing to quiver. Now peeping out, she saw that it was Mr. Brownlow who was back again in the room. But a Brownlow quite incredibly changed. Hands in his pockets, his shoulders hunched, his heard thrust forward, he stood staring at a table beside him with unseeing eyes. And as he stared, his face grew more and more malignant.

The forehead, never lofty, seemed to flatten as she watched. The little eyes to move closer together. His jaw thrust forward till the yellow lower teeth jutted out a good eighth of an inch beyond the upper ones. It gave him a horrible resemblance to a wolf. Vivian had seen many seamy sides of life in her newspaper work, but she had never looked into a more criminal face than this man's was—now—seen like this, off his guard.

The story her friend Edith Montdore had told her in the train came back to her. For the first time she thought that the gossip linking the husband with the lover's disappearance might well be true. She could easily imagine this man in front of her, this hitherto unseen, unguessed-at man, jumping on another in. the dark, holding his head down under water until the heaving and the struggles should cease. . . . She kept very, very still. Vivian was frightened.

For a full minute she had the benefit of Brownlow's horrid and ferocious look, then, with a sudden gesture as though he had made up his mind, he opened the door again, stood a second, apparently listening, switched off the light, and passed noiselessly out of sight.

She was after him in a flash. That was no face to let roam a house where a man on a dangerous mission might be sitting all unsuspecting.

She flattened herself against the wall, even though he switched out each light as he came to it, so that the corridor leading to the cedar room was quite dark, as dark as the one which Mr. Lascelles had been patrolling. Had he gone back to his post? she wondered. Apparently this idea struck Brownlow, too, for at the corner he turned and gave the side-passage a long scrutiny. From the sound of his steps, she thought that he even tried a door at the farther end which led into the garden. Then he came back, and again he switched off each light. All was in darkness now, except that some leaded panes at the other end shed a sort of blurred luminosity all along the corridor.

By it Vivian saw Brownlow tiptoe to the door of the cedar room, and bending down, press his ear to the keyhole.

In the stillness she heard Anthony's voice talking, apparently pleasantly, and a moment later came another peal of laugher from Mrs. Brownlow. Vivian had never heard her laugh much before. Then came a sentence or two in her voice, but said with great animation.

Evidently it was not sober business that was going on behind that door. The man outside it stayed as he was for several minutes, then he straightened up, and, as Vivian backed into the room where she had been, he passed her walking swiftly on into the main part of the house. She followed cautiously until she saw him enter the billiard-room with some word that she did not catch, in a pleasant, ordinary voice.

She moved away, took up a book, and sat down in a corner of the lounge close to the room where she now heard the click of balls.

She had plenty to think of. First of all, she considered Mr. Lascelles's silent pacing of that dark passage. Mr. Lascelles—was he here by some arrangement with Anthony? Was he the man whom Anthony expected to meet? That might be possible. And that long, quiet interchange of glances between himself and Smith at dinner, when Anthony's name had first come up, could her idea explain that too? It must, if it were the right one. She saw the look again. Not stealthy exactly, yet not open. But then came the thought that Anthony's mission, or quest, was he here by some arrangement with Anthony? Was he the of it, of course. That might include Mr. Lascelles. But it obviously did not include Smith. For Mr. Smith had not been acting, she felt sure, when he had inquired whether Mrs. Brownlow's chance-met friend were the Anthony Cross. But Mr. Lascelles might have had something he wanted to ask of Anthony—some favor. That might explain his acts to-night, and that look between the two friends. . . .

Her thoughts passed on to Brownlow. The man was madly jealous. Of that she felt certain. Most dangerously jealous, too. That sent her mind racing back to the photograph of Mrs. Brownlow, to the "problem" in Anthony Cross's past, to the vamp of Mrs. Montdore. The last term she thought, but the fears of a wife with a slightly uncertain husband. But the photograph, Anthony, and that awful look on the husband's face. . . .

She made up her mind to see Anthony as early as possible to-morrow morning and warn him of what she had seen. It was too late to-night for the talk that she had hoped to have with him outside. And in the villa, he would be accompanied to the door for certain by some member of the household.

She told herself that she ought to leave Porte Bonheur if there was any idea of resurrecting Anthony's past. But she found herself very reluctant to cut herself off from any chance of knowing what happened after she left. The clicking of balls beside her stopped.

"By Jove," came in Brownlow's voice; "my wife and Anthony Cross seem to have a lot to say to each other." How jocosely he said it, and now, as he stepped out of the room, how pleasantly he smiled at her as he passed her chair.

After a moment Smith came out too, and, also after a moment, went on down the same way.

Vivian closed her book and decided that it was her turn to get some note-paper from the writing-room.

Neither man was to be seen. But she heard Brownlow's voice. Evidently he had joined his wife. She looked at her watch. The talk in the cedar room was certainly a long one. Yet, as a rule, Anthony was a man of few words. She went to her room. It was not till nearly one o'clock that the light ceased to shine on the bushes in front of the cedar room, and only then did Vivian, fearing she did not know what, leave her window, and go to bed.

CHAPTER FOUR

NEXT morning, Vivian was out early. She intended to stay out until she met Anthony, even though it was the day of the dance, and the frock made for Edith Montdore needed a few adjustments. Pins would have to do, if necessary. The point was to see Anthony and warn him not to trust to any specious appearance of friendliness on Mr. Brownlow's part, but to realize that the man was a menace, or could be. Vivian had seen that evil face of his in her dreams. She had been glad when it was time to get up.

She was used to a hotter, fiercer land, but this temperate country-side seemed to her very lovely this morning. The Grosne is a true angler's stream; to-day it was clear as the air above it, the speckled trout casting dark shadows on the pebbly bottom as they lazily fanned themselves with a moving fin, or opened and shut their mouths in that foolish, contented way that causes a fisherman to see red. The swallows and martins glanced like blue arrow-heads above them. The water plants were alive with the shimmer of dragon-flies' wings. She watched a little water vole sitting up and munching a spray of marsh-wort in two tiny hands. Near her a cuckoo was calling the one "true" interval of bird song—that mysterious, alluring call. A dipper caught her eye, and paused on a shallow stone to curtsey politely before he started off to take one of his strolls along the bottom.

From a turn in the road, she saw two men fishing. One was Anthony. One was Mackay. Just now, they were apparently comparing their tins of bait. Anthony went off to another swim of the river. She came on him again by the Pont de la Levee. Mackay was out of sight around a bend.

"Anthony!"

He turned, glanced all around them, and shook his head, not very indignantly, at her. They were quite alone.

"Woman, indiscretion is thy name!"

"Oh, don't joke! I've something to say to you. First of all, I'm staying at the Villa Porte Bonheur."

He looked at her impassively. She felt that he was angry, very angry, but he made no remark.

"I met a friend in the train who knows Monsieur Pichegru," she hurried on. "She recommended me to try his villa. And besides—but never mind about that. The point is this. Last night, while you were talking so long to Mrs. Brownlow, I came downstairs in order to meet you in the garden on your way out. Well, I heard some one walking up and down in a dark passage quite close beside the room where you were."

She described what happened. She described also the fiendish expression on the face of Brownlow when standing in the room which he thought was empty.

"Now, don't misunderstand me," she finished. "My only concern is that you should know that the man is dangerous. Wildly jealous. He looked capable of anything last night. And I heard a very dreadful story, if true, about him in the train from my friend. A story she had heard from one who knew them out in Shanghai."

She told it. Anthony Cross listened to it, too, without a change of his face. Certainly he did not look at all grateful.

"Do you really think, my dear girl," he asked coldly when she was silent again, "that I am so little capable of managing my own affairs"—there was the faintest emphasis on the possessive pronoun—"as to need to be guarded and shepherded, however charmingly?"

She knew by his tone that he was, if possible, even angrier than at first.

"I expressly asked you to keep clear of me during my stay down here," Anthony went on. "Did you by any chance overhear me ask Monsieur Bonvy if he knew a man called Brownlow in Cluny?" He spoke in a very level voice.

"I did," she replied promptly. "And also, when I saw Mrs. Brownlow, I recognized the woman whose portrait I had seen you looking at, and remembered what you had told me about the one woman you had loved. Any other questions?" Vivian too was angry. To think that she had given up a much-needed nap this morning in order to be up and out and warn this ungrateful brute.

"And so you deliberately went to Porte Bonheur? In order to keep watch on me?" he asked with deadly politeness of tone.

She nodded.

"Did you speak to the Brownlows of me at all?" she asked as quietly as he. "Did you mention, I mean, that you were engaged?"

"Certainly not," he said almost sharply.

She drew off his ring, and held it out.

"Then I can give you this back now. Thank you for the loan of it, Anthony." Her face was gentle again. "But it was only a loan. I guess we both knew that in our hearts. It really belongs to—some one whom you haven't met yet."

"Just as you like." He spoke as carelessly as though she were returning an umbrella that he had lent her.

Vivian was relieved and amused and pained all in one.

At that moment Mackay appeared around a bend. Both she and Cross seemed to welcome the sight of a third person.

"Good-morning!" she called out first. Then as he drew nearer, she went on, "You and Sir Anthony are fishing together, I suppose?"

Anthony nodded.

"More or less. We're putting up at the same hotel. How did the fishing go?" he asked, turning to the other man.

"Caught anything?"

Mackay had not.

"Like me. And to think that scientists would have us believe that fishes can't hear. I believe that they have all our five senses, and another five of their own as well." Raising his hat to Vivian, Anthony moved off.

"For ma ain part," Mackay said sadly; "I've come to the conclusion that to catch roach you maun think like a roach. I micht do better if the river wasna a strange one."

"I guess you mean if you knew French better, so as to catch up with the thoughts of the French roach," Vivian said laughing. She felt strangely happy. The thing that she had funked—oh, yes, indeed she had—was over. She was free. What a glorious morning it was. How the shadows of yesterday seemed to have passed away. Back at the house she felt the same lightness of heart. It was as if some fairy had changed her eyes. Everything now resumed the usual aspect that things wore in the usual lives of usual people. Such as she was. Such as, she felt sure to-day, were those of the people around her.

True, Mr. Brownlow had looked like a fiend last night. She did not weaken on that. But he might have had "a toothache in his temper." Evidently he had got over it to-day. For he was in high spirits.

In the afternoon she wrote a little on her article. But there was too much noise for her thoughts to come easily. And, though she had a good style, it was not yet good enough to do without the support of some thinking.

The house was invaded by a chattering mob of gardeners, and cooks, and furniture movers, and florists' assistants. She found herself at a loose end. Mrs. Brownlow was invisible. Her husband seemed to be spending his time trying to see if his sitting-room chimney smoked. At least, so he explained to Vivian, when, alarmed at a thick puff of smoke rolling down their mutual corridor, she had run along to find its cause.

He was beating a flaming paper to pieces on the hearth.

"It's all right, Miss Young, I'm trying the chimney with a newspaper. We haven't had a fire in it since we've been here. But my wife wants one for to-night. One feels chilly after a dance, don't you think?" Vivian agreed. Ever helpful, she would have flown to his assistance, but something in the small eyes fixed on her—something about the whole mild, smiling face made her alter her mind. She left him to get the better of the smoke by himself.

"My!" she said to herself, "his tooth must be aching again. He looked as though he would have bitten me if I had come one step nearer. And that wasn't a newspaper he was burning either."

It was at lunch that she heard that Anthony was coming to the dance.

"He has telephoned to Lyons to send him a pierrot dress, if there's still one to be had," Mrs. Brownlow said, "though I don't suppose he'll do more than look in at us frivolous folk."

Vivian felt like saying that on shipboard there had been few better dancers than Anthony. But she kept silence, though there was, for the first time, a rather aggravating air of proprietorship about Mrs. Brownlow's way of speaking of Anthony. It irritated her, and suggested an incipient toothache of her own.

"Will you let him have a room for the night, monsieur?" The soft voice went on, "You offered it so kindly last night, and as he's leaving early in the morning, I think it would be more convenient if he could change here, than if he had to walk back to the inn?"

Monsieur Pichegru at once made for the telephone to ask Anthony Cross to send his things over to the villa, and stay there for whatever time he intended to remain in Cluny. In a few minutes he came back.

"He'll send his things over later on. I'll tell Honore to put them in the red room. And as he spoke of letters which must get off to-morrow, and which he may have to finish tonight, I've put the cedar room at his disposal, since none of the empty bedrooms has a sitting-room attached to it. We must be sure and leave a couple of chairs for him. And a writing-table can be moved in from the next room. He won't mind the fact that everything else is cleared out for the dancers."

"What with writing and dancing all night, and traveling all day, the strenuous lives rich men lead make me thankful, Tom, that you aren't a millionarie," Mrs. Brownlow said lightly.

"He has asked for two cards for a couple of hotel acquaintances," Monsieur Pichegru went on, going to a side table and rummaging in a drawer.

"Men?" Mrs. Brownlow asked; "and good dancers?"

"One's a lady. A Mrs. Eastby. I will call on her this afternoon. The other card I'll hand to Sir Anthony when he gets here." And the conversation drifted away from Anthony Cross.

Mrs. Eastby—could that be the name of the woman in the garden, Vivian wondered. But if so, had Anthony asked for an invitation for her? But then, why the whole scene?

That afternoon, Monsieur Pichegru was wanted urgently on the telephone. Monsieur was trying on his fancy dress—the good man was going as Saint Urban, patron saint of vineyards—and rustled in his robes and miter to the instrument. After which he flung his sacerdotal garments wildly off, called for his car to be sent around at once, got into his ordinary clothes, and tore his hair all in a few brief seconds.

His bonded warehouse in Dijon had caught fire. His Chablis, his Mussigny, his Pommard, his Chambertin, his Beaune and his Mercury, not to speak of—as he did promptly and wildly—his Saint Georges and his Montrachet, were in danger. And French laws as to salvage are very trying to proprietors. He was insured, naturally, he called over his shoulder, in answer to sympathetic inquiries from his guests. It was not a money loss but a loss to the world of wines and good cheer that was threatened.

He begged his house party to continue just as though he were present to-night. He might indeed be able to return and join in the dancing, but that was very problematical. In the meantime he delegated the Brownlows as his representatives. But Brownlow refused the honor. "I'm no good as the convivial host," he maintained, laughing.

"The British shyness!" scoffed Monsieur Pichegru; "then you, Monsieur Smith, must represent me. I will take no excuses from you! Oh, that reminds me: the card for the lady friend of Sir Anthony Cross, and the recipe for my iced claret-cup which has no equal from the Channel to the Mediterranean—like the little stories dear to your friend who has just left us."

Smith and he walked off, the one receiving, the other giving directions. When at last night fell, the weather was perfect. Mrs. Brownlow was greatly relieved, for she had suggested that the many windows of the music-room, which was being turned into a ball-room, should be taken out and plants and sham plaster pillars be arranged so as to hide the wall-spaces between. The effect was good. Room and garden seemed to merge into one blossoming whole. The lawn had been brought up to the edge of the parquet flooring and level with it.

All the invitable part of the neighborhood was at the dance. Some of the dresses were gorgeous affairs from Paris or Lyons ateliers. Many were simple, and others were humorous.

Mrs. Brownlow wore an ordinary, but very lovely, evening dress of soft silver brocade and lace, over which, from shoulder to hem, front and back, ran a bright blue half moon. On her head was a diadem of wired crystal beads that spelled the word "ONCE."

"Once in a blue moon" was her obvious meaning, and her mask was another blue half moon. It was but decorative. She made no attempt to disguise her identity.

Her husband was "a bottle of Macon"—a shiny roll of

black cardboard, duly labeled, and wearing a cork hat.

Vivian looked quite charming in her creamy frock with its gold lace cap and fox's mask a-top of that. Across her face stretched tawny velvet with a deep gold fringe. Edith Montdore had not intended to be easily recognized.

The guests were only announced by character. Mackay came early. With Dundreary whiskers made from horse hair, clad all in shabby black, with his shabby little bag, he was a good figure. Taken for "the gas-meter man," he was much applauded.

"Have you seen Sir Anthony?" she asked as he stepped to her side. He replied Scots fashion by another question.

"Why should I have?"

"Oh, no reason. Only he's late."

"Perhaps he isna coming at a'. He's too sensible a mon to care for this sort o' thing."

"You talk like your own grandfather half the time!" Vivian scoffed.

"Wouldn't you give the whole of it for juist quiet under the stars?" he asked suddenly. "I wud. There's an awfu' lot of wishy-washy talked aboot dances. A nicht spent in the open, the sicht o' the sun coming up in the morning, or sinking in the west; yon's worth while. But this—it's juist mak'-believe!" He spoke contemptuously. "I canna thole mak'-believe," he added, quite unnecessarily.

"But it's not make-believe." She spoke with certainty; she had only half-heard what he had said. "I've a feeling, 'a pricking in my thumbs,' that something's stirring to-night in the Villa Porte Bonheur, Mr. Mackay. It may not concern either of us, neither you nor I may ever learn what it is, but I tell you I feel it. Mr. Murgatroyd said people like me attracted things to their neighborhood. That if they were going to happen, they'd happen near them. I wonder if he was right. And I wonder, too, if so, what's going to happen here."

"Well, it's no great happening, but for ane thing I'm awa' to search the upper rooms. I've been over yon

Tibbitts's. I found naething. If he still has a string of black pearls, then a' I can say is that he wears them."

There were several pierrots, most of whom wore a round, pale, cardboard pierrot-face as a mask. Anthony Cross was one of these, but he was easily recognizable by his great height. He made no attempt to find Vivian. On the contrary, he avoided her, choosing Mrs. Brownlow's vicinity with marked preference. Brownlow did not seem to mind; at least he immediately stopped for a genial word with him.

Vivian had not yet seen the woman to whom Anthony had spoken last night in the garden. But after a little while "an Egyptian lady" was ushered in, with a white yashmak up to her khol-darkened eyes. Her dress, to Vivian's scrutiny, was made up chiefly of shawls and yards of black tulle from the local shop—a traveling dress evidently. A question of Smith, who was "Le Grand Chef" in white cap and apron, told her that her guess was right.

"But don't say that I gave her away. She happened to speak of rigging up something Eastern. I called on her this afternoon, you know; her husband's a colonel in a camel corps. Did you ever see such eyes?. . ." He broke off to watch the latest arrival. Evidently Smith was struck with Mrs. Eastby's looks. And no wonder, Vivian thought.

"She's here having a look at the ruins," Smith went on. "Met Sir Anthony, who's an old friend of her husband's, it seems, coming down in the train. Funny world! He's over from South Africa, she from God knows what oasis back of beyond, and they meet in a branch line running from Macon to dead-alive little Cluny." He tucked his cardboard pate more firmly under his arm, and waving a farewell with his soup ladle hurried away to claim his partner. Smith was positively human tonight, Vivian thought.

She watched the veiled figure move towards the tallest pierrot, who was not dancing at the moment. Vivian drifted in that direction too.

"How is my dress, pierrot? Not so bad, considering

that it consists of a couple of shawls and window curtains?" The "Egyptian" spoke coquettishly.

"It seems all right to me," Anthony's voice answered indifferently. "Well, I hope you'll enjoy yourself, but frankly, I—well, I was surprised that you cared to come." There was something like suspicion in his tone. And in his eyes, too, as they looked out of his cardboard face.

"Oh, I like being with people who are having a happy time," she said, with a little catch of her breath.

Anthony nodded agreement as he moved away to talk again to Mrs. Brownlow, who had now left her post by the door. Sugar slide was the dance of the moment. Mrs. Brownlow said that she would show him the steps and took him to a quiet corner of the lounge, so shut off by palms that it made a little room to itself. Vivian could not follow there. Nor did she want to. There was only too little mystery about their mutual infatuation, she thought. They were not even pretending an interest in steps. Heads close together, they were sitting and talking. A moment later and they got up and passed into the larger room. Anthony looked as though he were immensely pleased with something, Vivian thought. He had a triumphant air. And at that look a pang stabbed her. Not for his lost affection—not entirely. But for himself. That he should be content to solve the problem in this way. It was not a problem any more, Vivian thought; the solution was only too simple, too easy to guess.

She was dancing with Mr. Brownlow. They were doing a sort of in-and-out around some rose bushes when, turning to look at him, she caught a glimpse, just a flash of the face that she had seen—herself hidden—in the writing-room last night. The expression passed in a second. He had been staring over her shoulder. When next she faced that way, she saw that Anthony and Mrs. Brownlow were again together—again talking. Mrs. Brownlow seemed to be yielding to some suggestion of his, but yielding unwillingly.

Finally they turned and went indoors, at an almost

peremptory gesture of his.

Brownlow laughed. A very forced laugh, Vivian thought it.

"Dear me! I shall have to call out Sir Anthony before breakfast to-morrow morning, if this goes on. 'Pistols for two, and coffee for one.'"

"He's leaving very early," Vivian said lightly. Though she did not feel like taking the situation lightly.

"He'd better!" Brownlow said under his breath in a tone of such fury that she drew away. She of all people did not intend to be dragged into any quarrel between Mr. Brownlow and Anthony and Alys Brownlow. Let the husband look after his wife better. Certainly to-night for the first time she had met the vamp. Mrs. Brownlow was consciously trying to attract, and, of course, succeeding. The very turn of her head over her shoulder as she passed into the house in front of Anthony was alluring, mysterious, provocative.

Brownlow made some excuse and practically left Vivian *plante la*, as she called it. But some one else came towards her with the unmistakable step of one who at last sees that for which he has been hunting.

It was a man's figure, wearing a long robe, the hood drawn over the head, with slits in it for eyes.

"Just in time!" he murmured; "not yet a fox, lady, are you? Do let me have one dance before you change completely."

Vivian studied him. It was Mr. Lascelles, she felt sure. But Mr. Lascelles had left that morning, so she had been told.

"What is a member of the Ku-Klux-Klan doing here?" she asked.

He gave a protesting shudder. "I am a Florentine!" he expostulated. "A Brother of the Misericordia," he gave his hood a tug. "If you are struck down with plague this night, I would bear you to a hospital. On the other hand, should you intend to murder any person or persons with whom you are annoyed, here I stand, ready to help give them Christian sepulchre."

"I had no idea you were useful," she murmured.

He bowed.

"I felt sure that you did not guess my worth," he murmured. "But where is it, Jane?"

"Where is what?" she parried. Jane! Then he did not know her. Jane. . . . Vivian looked about her as she danced off with him. The only woman of her height and build was the Egyptian lady. She was old enough to be Vivian's mother, the girl thought, a little piqued, but, of course, under such a mask as hers, and with lappets of gold lace fastened under her chin as well. She had thought when first she saw him that Mr. Lascelles looked as though he could dance well. Now she found that he could indeed. He had a jockey's sense of balance. She enjoyed herself in silence for some minutes. When they were resting, he asked her again urgently: "Well, Jane, how about it? I've come for it."

"For what?" she piped in the treble squeak that she had adopted to-night.

"The portrait you promised me," he replied on the instant. But she noticed that her next partner was already at her elbow. Would his reply have been different had they been alone?

Mr. Lascelles had looked a most cautious man to her. How he watched her to-night! He, who had barely glanced at her yesterday. Always, wherever she went, she saw that figure in the long robe. He seemed to dance with no one else. To have eyes for no one else.

She had no dances to spare. But twice he passed her with a murmur of, "I've come on purpose, Jane." She only laughed.

Shortly after his second inquiry, Vivian noticed that Anthony was in the ball-room, looking keenly towards the main door, as though he were expecting some one. She saw him standing there again a few minutes later, as she swung past, and again looking as though he were waiting for some one, or for something. He had avoided her with great care all the evening. As she had him. But now she felt a sudden impulse to go up to him. He was leaving next morning. She did not want them to part like this. But just then Smith claimed her for the dance.

"Does one good to get back to this sort of thing," he said, as he improvised some new steps with the skill of an expert.

"Mr. Lascelles, too, evidently couldn't stay away," she said after a moment.

"Lascelles?" he started. "Have you seen Lascelles here? To-night?" His tone sounded genuinely amazed.

She pointed out the tall *frater*. Smith eyed him keenly, then he shook his head.

"That's not Lascelles! That's—I forget who, some friend of some one's, but it's not Lascelles."

Vivian did not believe him. Was he honestly deceived, she wondered, or merely trying to mislead her.

"You'll see at supper-time that it isn't Lascelles," he said positively. "But what's that? The gong? Then it's close on midnight, and time for Pichegru's iced claret-cup.

"Bring forth, he said, the mazers four
My noble fathers loved of yore."

The doors of the ball-room opened, and in came a file of four chefs in white, each with his attendant scullion. The chefs carried silver trays from which artificial icicles hung, piled with what looked like snow, in which was embedded the local and enlarged equivalent of a mazer bowl. The scullions carried smaller trays wreathed with flowers on which rested small silver boxes.

Smith struck the foremost bowl twelve times as the clock in the lounge chimed midnight.

"The drink of obligatory!" He called in French, "I, *le grand chef,* present to you, in Monsieur Pichegru's most regretted absence, his especial *Coupe de Bourgogne a la mode de Cluny,* invented by him in honor of this occasion."

A bottle of local wine was emptied into the well-filled bowls. Then Smith took the silver boxes up one by one.

"Herbs of immortality and health, plucked in the meadows, according to the secret rites handed down in the Pichegru family," he explained.

The contents, woodruff, and raspberry leaves, and lemon and cucumber slices, and various flavoring herbs, were tipped into the drink. Smith gave four stirs with his huge spoon that set the ice clinking, then the claret-cup was ladled out.

No one needed a second command, the drink was exceedingly good, very mild, and ice-cold.

Vivian saw Brownlow pledge Anthony with mock formality. Both men seemed on the best of terms with each other. She thought that Mrs. Brownlow, standing a little behind them, eyed them very closely. The /rater was nowhere to be seen. Nor the Egyptian lady. Bar these two, all the dancers that interested Vivian were present.

When she had finished her own glass, Anthony had disappeared. After the next dance she decided to look him up. She remembered their host's words about the letters that Sir Anthony might have to write. Hurrying down the passage towards the cedar room, she saw, to her surprise, that the Egyptian lady was ahead of her, walking very softly and yet with purpose in her swift glide. She stopped in front of a mirror to powder afresh. The yashmak dropped. She was the woman of the garden, and the expression that stared into the mirror was not unlike the one which her face had worn yesterday. It was the look of an utterly desperate woman. She did not see Vivian, the latter was sure of that. Her lips were moving swiftly, hurriedly, as though she were saying something over and over to herself. It occurred to Vivian that as she herself was going to see Anthony Cross for what might well be the very last time, it could do no harm if she were to freshen herself up too. After all, though she did not own magnficent eyes, nor was a Rossetti type, there was no real need for her to look her worst.

She spent some little time in her room. Finally, she slipped down again and into the same passage. The villa was built, roughly speaking, like a Z, the main body running north and south, the two projections east and west. At the end of one was the ball-room, at the end of the other this cedar room. Before she reached its door, she passed the room where she had waited in the darkness last night. It opened now, and out bounded Mr. Murgatroyd, looking like a man beside himself with indignation or burning wrath. Now the professor had spoken of possibly watching the revelry for a while from the first floor landing. But this was not the first floor landing. And the way in which he had burst from the room suggested a very different man from the gentle lecturer who was deep in the life of the Benedictines. He had shown some of this violence last night, however, at the mere mention. of Anthony's name, as she now recollected.

At sight of her now, he jumped back into the room as suddenly as he had leaped forth, and closed the door. She felt sure that, had she tried it, she would find that he was holding it shut. It almost seemed to her that she could hear his quick, excited breathing from the other side. She was quite sure that she caught a "Not now! Some one's passing!" in a tone of extreme warning.

Vivian stood quite still. What was astir all around her? She walked on into the cedar room. Anthony was alone in it. His pierrot overalls, his pierrot cardboard face were off. He was in gray tweeds, standing with bent head staring at the floor. He swung around as she entered with the expression of a man who says "Here you are at last!" Yet the underlying look on his face, the look that Vivian felt sure had been there before she touched the door handle, was of a cold fury. Both looks, the underlying one and the sudden flash that crossed the other as two beams of light might cross each other, left his features when he saw that it was Vivian. Yet she felt that the anger was still there, if anger it should be called, for she had a feeling that it was deeper, larger than mere anger.

He took a step towards her.

"Not now, Vivian," he said quietly. "I haven't a moment to spare now—not even for you."

And taking her gently, but firmly, by the shoulders, he. turned her round with a very masterful touch. As always with him, or nearly always, he impressed his will on hers. He dominated. She murmured some word of apology, and like a timid schoolgirl left him.

What in the world made him look at once so fierce and so icy? And what had made Mr. Murgatroyd look as he did? She decided that as there was bitter trouble brewing between Anthony and Mr. Brownlow, Mr. Murgatroyd had been called in to arbitrate or to smooth matters over. Vivian thought that the look on his face must have been caused by indignation at the whole affair. That probably Mrs. Brownlow was in that room of which he had held the door shut, and that he had been trying in vain to reason with her. At any rate, Vivian was sure that husband and old friend were quarreling over the wife.

For once she accepted defeat. It was not a case in which she could interfere. She would leave in the morning. Or no, she must know how events shaped themselves. When Anthony left early next morning, would he leave alone? One thing she had decided on. She would not watch him, nor Mrs. Brownlow. She had tried to-night to say some parting word to the man with whom, for a couple of short weeks, she had been on terms of such intimacy. But he had no time for her. Yet Vivian had a feeling that he had not parted in anger. Rather there had been a quick tenderness, not very profound, of course, but still there, in his voice and his touch. Poor Anthony, she thought, caught loitering too near to danger, overtaken by the lava stream of what he thought was an extinct volcano and about to be swept away by it. As she stepped out of the door again into the passage, she caught sight of a now familiar figure at its end.

"Dash it all!" she thought fretfully; "there's that Laseel les again!"

She dived into the side passage. A couple of curtains were looped at its entrance. She unfastened them swiftly. The corridor was very poorly lit to-night. All available lamps had been carried off for the dancing wing. Lascelles, she imagined, thought that she had stepped back into the room out of which he saw her come, for he hurried forward.

"Jane," he said in a cautious voice, "are you there?"

And on that appeared from nowhere the woman whom Vivian felt sure answered to that name, "the Egyptian lady." Vivian had not seen her come, but then her range of vision was limited to the end of the passage beside her. She saw the hooded figure put his hand on the knob of the cedar room door, she saw the woman snatch the hand away with a low, but almost frantic:

"No, no, Reggie! Remember your promise!" The voice of the woman whom Vivian now called Jane was very determined. She stood on tiptoe and whispered something swiftly into her companion's ear. Then both turned away, and, obedient to the woman's urging, passed together down the corridor.

Vivian waited some minutes, then she cautiously slipped across and around to the ball-room by a different way.

"My, but masked dances can be queer, especially in this bouse!" she ruminated.

On the floor, she saw Mrs. Brownlow and her husband dancing together, and apparently in a most friendly fashion. That seemed to her to be queerer still.

At supper-time a telegram was read from Monsieur Pichegru. He sent excuses and good wishes to all his guests. He could not hope to be back in Cluny for another day at least, but all was going well. The fire had been got under, and everything had been salvaged.

Masks were now taken off. Mrs. Eastby dropped her yashmak as well. Vivian stared at her. She looked ten, nearly twenty, years younger than the distraught figure out on the gravel path pleading with Anthony last night, or than she had done just now, desperately powdering her face and mouthing some words over and over to herself.

No woman in the room could touch her, either for looks, or for a certain magnetic warmth that she seemed to spread about her. Mrs. Brownlow, more painted than Vivian had ever seen her, was but a shadow beside her. Though she tried to take the ascendancy that she usually had in any company at Cluny, the other woman out-shone her beyond all comparison.

Vivian looked around at the people, most of whom were strangers to her. At no table did she see the Brother of the Misericordia. She leaned across to Mrs. Eastby, who was having supper with an utterly fascinated Smith.

"Where's your friend, the Ku-Klux-Klan man as I called him?" Mrs. Eastby looked at her. For a second her eyes wavered, then:

"I don't know whom you mean," she said lightly enough. "What clan did you say?"

Smith explained.

"I saw you and he talking together, or rather I heard you, outside the cedar room," Vivian went on pleasantly. She saw no reason why she should not try to get at least a little daylight on some of the puzzles.

Mrs. Eastby's eyes did not falter, but some champagne was jerked from the glass around whose stem her fingers were curled.

"Did you give him what he came to fetch?" Vivian persisted lightly, but with a keen glance.

Mrs. Eastby did not seem to hear. She said something to Smith, at which the man laughed immensely. In another moment the woman's eyes rested on Vivian's. The glance was triumphant. Almost sarcastic, though a little too shining and radiant for that ugly word. Certainly there was nothing either guilty or nervous in it. Vivian told herself, and with real relief, that she was making mountains out of molehills. And on that she, too, turned her attention to her companion, a young French officer, eager for a flirtation with an American girl.

When the last dance was over, and the last laughing guest had driven, or walked off, Smith looked about him. Vivian and Mrs. Brownlow were the only ones to be seen of the house party.

"How about tea and another rasher of bacon apiece before we part?" the deputy host asked. Yes, Smith had certainly changed into quite a pleasant person, Vivian reflected. He evidently was one of those young men who need amusement.

Mrs. Brownlow shook her head. The early morning light was anything but flattering to her. She looked very fagged.

"I'm going to bed," she said sensibly. "How well it all went off!"

"Thanks to you!" Smith said warmly. "You were simply splendid!"

"I can't think where Tom is hiding," Mrs. Brownlow spoke with considerable irritation. "He must know I'm dead for sleep, and don't want to be waked up hours from now."

"I'll root him up and send him along," Smith promised. "Don't wait down for him."

He went off down the corridor calling "Brownlow! I say, Brownlow! Your wife wants you. Show's over. No need to hide now."

But Mrs. Brownlow ran down the stairs and past him. She swept along the halls, calling her husband's name as she hurried to each room and looked in.

Vivian would have followed, but Smith stopped her.

"This is where little girls get sent to bed," he pointed out. "It's clear what Mrs. Brownlow thinks has happened, and she doubtless knows her good man," he finished in a low whisper.

"You mean?"

"Well, she evidently suspects that 'dear Tom' has looked too long upon the wine when it was red, or the whisky when it wasn't. Beastly bore if it's so. Don't know what the people around will think of two Englishmen not knowing when to stop."

"Two?"

"Oh, yes, Tibbitts had to be assisted up to bed long ago. Funnily enough, Brownlow was the one who helped the butler guide that winsome boy's feet up the stairs. He never could have climbed them unaided. And still funnier is the fact that Brownlow professed to be positively furious at the whole business. I say, can't you stop her calling so loudly and banging on the doors?" he asked with a pained frown. "The noise she's making is positively shattering."

"Where's Sir Anthony?" she asked suddenly.

"He left long ago. Oh, well, if you insist " He stepped aside with a look of thinly-veiled disgust at her insistence.

Vivian hurried after the other woman. Something, some wave of emotion sent out by Mrs. Brownlow was reaching Vivian and acting on her oddly.

They were now close to the cedar room.

"It's locked!" Mrs. Brownlow said, wheeling.

Smith nodded as he peered into it.

"From the inside. Key's sticking in the lock. That's why—" he finished a trifle curtly.

Her only comment was to beat with a small clenched hand on the panel.

"Tom! Tom!" Her voice was hysterical.

"Now, Mrs. Brownlow," remonstrated Smith, "the last thing you want to do is to make a fuss—collect the servants—and so on "

"Don't be silly, Mr. Smith! Tom could drink the ocean dry and not feel it."

"Probably," was the laconic comment with a more than usually bored look at her distraught face. "Monsieur Pichegru doesn't bottle the ocean."

"Something's happened to him!" Her hand went to her throat. Her eyes grew terrible. She seemed to Vivian to be struggling not to scream aloud.

"Something's happened to him!" she said again in a sort of terrified whimper. "He isn't anywhere else! And the door's locked!" Her voice now came as though half strangled. "He must be in there!"

"Now, look here"—Smith spoke firmly, with a fair amount of kindness and a great deal of impatience in his tone—"this won't do. Positively. You and Miss Young go on up to bed, and let me grapple with the situation."

Mrs. Brownlow turned on him. Vivian had a wild notion that she was going to strike his rather supercilious face.

"Tom's ill. Or else—something has happened to him!" She was shaking violently. Vivian laid a hand on her arm. A comforting hand. But Mrs. Brownlow flung it off almost savagely.

CHAPTER FIVE

VIVIAN moved away from her and joined Smith, who, preceded by the butler, went around to the windows of the cedar room by the outside garden path. Fortunately the steel shutters had not been let down, though the thick draw-curtains prevented any view into the room.

"Got a knife, Honore?" Smith asked. The butler produced an instrument which seemed fitted for every emergency, from putting up a tent to shoeing horses. With a great deal of difficulty, he finally raised the catch on one window and got it open. Smith stuck his head in through the overlapping hangings.

"Let me see! No, Mr. Smith, let me see!" Mrs. Brownlow had come up behind them. Her voice brooked no denial. In a second, reaching over Smith's shoulder, she pulled wide the curtain. Then she went down as though poleaxed. Vivian caught her and helped Smith to lay her down on the grass, then she stepped after him into the room and stooped over a figure close to the window.

Mr. Brownlow was dead. Shot through the heart. From a marksman's point of view, it was a very good shot. He was in evening clothes—his cardboard bottle-dress stood in another part of the room. Facing where the men were staring, Vivian saw, in the opposite corner, a second figure. Also lying motionless. Here, with an exclamation of horror and pain, she touched an out flung hand from which the revolver lying beside it; had apparently dropped. The hand was icy. Anthony Cross, too, was dead, and must have been dead some hours. Well, Vivian thought grimly, he had sent his antagonist to his account. For she came from a part of the world that has until recently had to police itself, around which still lie wild districts where lead settles quarrels, if they are only bitter enough. She did not lose her head now. Neither did the butler nor Smith. It was the former who took command in his master's absence.

"A duel!" he muttered. "We must send for the police all the same. Though under the circumstances, they will only do the most necessary."

Mrs. Brownlow staggered in through the window.

"He isn't dead! He can't be dead!" she cried in French, and in a tone of anguished incredulity. Then she flung herself on her knees by her husband's side. "He's only fainted. I'll get my smelling-salts. They're in my handbag " She babbled on and hurried out and up the stairs, to rush down them a moment later, a little bag in her hand.

Vivian, for her part, went to the telephone as soon as the butler had finished calling up the police. She got the Hotel de Bourgogne and asked that Monsieur Mackay be summoned. It was urgent. She heard him answer almost at once.

"Mr. Mackay, please come back to the villa immediately. I can't say more over the telephone. But please come immediately; it's most urgent." And with that she hurried back to the cedar room. Here she found that Smith was almost forcibly lifting Mrs. Brownlow away from her husband's dead body.

"I'm most frightfully sorry," he was saying, and as though he meant it, "but you mustn't alter his position. Not until the police have seen him. He's quite dead. I swear to you that both men are dead. There's nothing we can do for them. Here! One of you women help her up to her room and stay with her. Don't step on that revolver!"

Vivian returned to the hall. There were plenty of women servants. She was not needed.

Was Mackay never coming? She wanted him. He might not be much use as a detective, she suspected, but she liked him as a man. She felt sure of him, and these last few minutes that had come to mean something.

She finally heard steps coming up to the front door,

which stood wide open, with the butler as a sort of distracted sentinel every now and then stepping through it to see if no one was in sight yet.

It was the private inquiry agent. He was followed by a police sergeant and two of his men. They tried to stop Mackay from entering ahead of them. He got past by a very dexterous sort of sideway duck.

He jumped over the mat and made for Vivian, while they, led by the butler, turned off towards the cedar room.

Mackay listened to Vivian with a look of absolute stupefaction on his face.

"A duel?" he muttered in an incredulous tone; "but that's clean impossible! Did you say a duel?" He spoke as though she had told him that the room in question contained a dinotherium.

"Sure thing," she replied confidently. "Each has his gun beside him. Apparently Mr. Brownlow beat Anthony Cross to the draw, but Sir Anthony got his man." There was a friend's pride in good work done in Miss Young's tone. "Got him dead. His was the better shot."

"Losh!" muttered Mackay feebly, and said nothing more for a moment. Then he asked, "Whaur's the wife?"

"In her room. She's half crazy. But only on her husband's account. Oh, I hope she's satisfied now with her work!" Vivian felt a sudden surge of anger race through her. "But I shouldn't say that! She's sorry enough now it's done."

"Do you think she had any idea there was trouble on?" he asked after another pause, during which, by his face, he seemed trying to get his bearings, and not succeeding over well.

"I think when her husband didn't turn up, she pretty well knew. Oh, yes, she guessed then what must have taken place. As who wouldn't? Still I don't want to talk as though she was the sinner and they just sheep led astray by her. They were all three equally to blame. If there's any blame due anywhere. After all, one must live one's own life. No one else is going to live it for you. And when a man's dead, it seems to square up accounts somehow."

The telephone bell whirred. The sergeant strode to it. Followed a series of those grunts which only a perfect sense of intonation preserve from sounding like the language of pigs. Finally he replaced the receiver and turned to Smith, who had drawn near.

"Our commissaire is attending an international Conference at Macon, presided over by the *chef de police* of the department. But, by good luck, a high officer from the *Surete de* Scotland is attending the conference too, and he is accompanying our commissaire down here. A great compliment to us, that! He will be a witness to the fact that it was a duel between two English gentlemen, and that none of us was to blame. That the deaths were not due to any negligence on the part of the police of France. *Enfin,* that our licenses are not to be endorsed— on this occasion."

"I tak' it the mon means Scotland Yarrd?" Mackay asked.

Smith nodded loftily as he turned away towards the stairs. He had assumed an air of ostentatiously dissociating himself from the villa and all that therein was.

A little later he and Murgatroyd came down the stairs together.

"Brownlow!" Vivian could hear the stress of utter incredulity on the name of the dead man, "did you say, Brownlow?"

Vivian could not hear Smith's reply. But finally she heard the other saying in shocked tones of profound horror: "Terrible! Terrible! And utterly incomprehensible. To me, at least. What could have caused those two men— " again she lost the rest. But a moment later the historian came into view, making for the cedar room itself.

He was not admitted. Even though, like Mr. Smith, he was known to be an acquaintance of the commissaire. This was Mr. Murgatroyd's first visit to Villa Porte Bonheur, but it was by no means his first stay in Cluny.

Year after year his rotund little form had been seen paddling backwards and forwards between the museum and his hotel.

Finding he got scant attention and even less information from the police, the professor made his way back to the lounge, where Smith was buried in a time-table.

"Poor Mrs. Brownlow!" he said once more; "I wish I could stay and offer her my poor attempts at consolation. But the affair is too terrible. . . ."

"Horrible!" said Smith. "Positively shattering!"

". . . And she has her own priest to help her. That being so, I am afraid I cannot put off my departure even because of this terrible event, as I shall explain to Monsieur Pichegru when he arrives, as, of course, he must, at once."

Now Murgatroyd last evening had not spoken as though he intended leaving the villa for another fortnight at least.

Vivian drew Mackay into the little lobby and murmured as much.

"I sure do think it funny of him to fly off like that!" she finished.

But Mackay thought it only natural.

"And natural that he should repeat Mr. Brownlow's name in a tone of such amazement when he heard that he was dead?"

Vivian continued. "He didn't exclaim over Anthony Cross's!"

Mackay made no reply to that.

"He evidently expected Brownlow might go for Anthony Cross, but he didn't seem prepared to hear that Anthony Cross had held his end up, and that sure seems strange. He couldn't have—Vivian stopped herself. She was about to say "known Anthony Cross well."

"Mr. Murgatroyd hasna anything to do wi' their deaths," Mackay began heavily.

"I know that!" Vivian agreed hastily. There was a

little pause.

"Why, say, that's just the sort of thing Mr. Murgatroyd spoke of," she murmured; "that if things had to happen, I should be in the midst of them—because I like being in the midst of things. Not that I like being in the midst of this thing!" She shivered a little.

Now that the sheer excitement of the terrible discovery was wearing off, her heart began to make itself felt. To have lost a friend, any friend in such a way! Let alone one who for two weeks had been very near and dear to her indeed. Perhaps not that last—no, in all honesty, not that last—but a friend certainly. It was emphatically all his fault. She had warned him. It was as though he had been bewitched. Had he been bewitched? He, with those standards of right and wrong which were otherwise so unbendable that they were one of the things in him which made her uncomfortable! Vivian always liked exceptions to be made—for herself, for those she loved— but Anthony never made any. Not even for himself. In those days. A fortnight ago. And now—dead on the field of dishonor. . . . The thought stung. She jumped up again. Could she be mistaken? A duel, yes, but for another, some other reason? Then she shook her sensible little head. No. All that lead up to it had been too clear. He had deliberately put himself into the path of temptation again. He had disregarded all warnings in his blind infatuation. He had provoked a jealous man past all bearing. . . . Neither Mr. nor Mrs. Brownlow were people who had, or who could have, any connection with his company. Their meeting—the whole fact that it was to the wife not to the husband that Anthony had devoted himself so utterly, all went to prove it. And what had it brought him? Death. A tarnished memory. And not even the love of the woman for which he had paid so dear. Mrs. Brownlow had not so much as glanced at Anthony Cross's dead body. Suddenly, that seemed to Vivian a very pathetic fact. For it was a fact. She had staggered to her husband, she had fallen on her knees by his side, Smith

had had almost to tear her from him, but she had not
even looked towards Anthony Cross's dark corner. It was
quite clear where her love really belonged. But Anthony
must have had good reason for thinking otherwise.

Vivian remembered Edith Montdore's belief that the
woman was a vamp. Certainly she had tried by every wile
known to a clever woman to lead him on, as Vivian
herself had noticed this last night. And it was all a
mistake, or play, or self-deception?

Now Cluny is but fourteen miles or so from Macon,
the capital of its department, Saone-et-Loire, and there,
as the sergeant told Smith later, a big international
conference was being held while the dance at Villa Porte
Bonheur was but beginning. It was the closing night of
the conference. Monsieur Cambier, the commissaire of
the Saone-et-Loire police, was its vice-president. He gave
the closing address, and wound up with the words:

". . . and above all, my dear colleagues, let us beware
of the clever, the tortuous, as opposed to the simple
explanation of any crime. It is so easy to be unexpected
and so tempting."

Monsieur Cambier sat down amid applause.

The president nodded his head approvingly, and
turning to a young man on his right, asked in tolerable
English, "You, I know, Chief Inspector, agree with me,
our *confrere*? The English character of itself answers that,
with its love of the plain, its well founded distrust of the
complex."

Chief Inspector Pointer of New Scotland Yard made
some noncommittal reply. He was pre-eminently a man
who could keep his opinions to himself. His pleasant, but
inscrutable, glance said as much. So did the quiet dignity
of his manner, an unconscious dignity that suggested
unusual force of character.

With the formal closing address, the circle of men
sitting around the table shifted more comfortably in their
chairs and started fresh cigars. No one was in a hurry.

Tales such as you could hear to-night would not come any one's way for another twelvemonth.

When it was over, Pointer walked back to his hotel. He wished most heartily, as he went to bed, that English mattress-makers would turn detectives and find out the secret of French beds. But he was a man who, by nature and training, could do with very little sleep, so that, in spite of springy ease, he was up early next morning. There is nothing in dull little Macon to take a man into the streets before the rest of the world is astir. Like most French towns, it has, to English eyes, a peculiar desolation and grubbiness, due in part to the lack of flowers, gardens and trees.

True, Macon has a past. It was a Roman camp. It had a cathedral. Lamertine was foolish enough to be born there. Macon also has a present—its innumerable factories. While the view of Mont Blanc from the bridge which links past and present, is, like its wine, of no great interest.

Pointer decided to stay where he was and listen to Sir Walter Scott instead. He turned to the *Journal,* a traveling companion old and tried, and was losing himself in a page, when the night porter, after the quickest and lightest of taps, slipped into his room. Pointer was wanted immediately at the police station. A car was waiting for him below. A message was being wirelessed for him from London, which the police thought that he would prefer to receive in person.

Pointer was soon listening in. It was New Scotland Yard that was speaking, and in its own often-changed code. Worked out it came to this:—

Two Englishmen had been found dead at Cluny, quite close to where the chief inspector was. The French police were still a little on edge over the remarks made about their handling of the recent case of a drowned English-woman in Paris. The Home Office wanted to pay them a marked and soothing compliment, and had asked Scotland Yard to let Chief Inspector Pointer proceed to

Cluny, to act as the British official observer for whom the French police had just asked. The assistant commissioner, who was speaking, added that since Pointer's leg had not yet recovered from the injury that it had received in his last case, he would on no account be allowed to go on active service again for another couple of weeks. Pointer grunted at that, but finally sent back the equivalent for "I hear and obey" which was expected of him.

The commissaire, Monsieur Cambier, came in as he was finishing.

Pointer explained the request that he had received, and his own acceptance.

"Like myself, the *chef de police* of our district will be overcome by the honor done us." Cambier bowed deeply. "It is indeed a most unlooked-for favor that an officer of your position should be willing to watch a simple little local case. But on the other hand, as the two gentlemen concerned appear to belong to your 'high life,' your mere presence will be a guarantee of the complete impartiality of the investigation, and will, therefore, be of immense comfort to the English nation." Monsieur Cambier made a superb gesture and proceeded to thank Pointer on behalf of himself, of his colleagues, of the *chef de police*, of the prefect of the department, and was apparently working his way along to the president of the republic when some one brought in hot milk and coffee, which was poured, in the dexterous French way, in two simultaneous streams into a couple of cups.

"Cluny," Pointer repeated; "any connection with the Hotel de Cluny?"

In Paris there runs a legend which recognizes three kinds of French. The French of the *Academie*, the French of the man in the street, and the French spoken by the English and Americans. But Pointer spoke the tongue well. His consonants popped, or came with the crisp patter of pebbles on metal. His sentences turned up their tails.

"You mean the museum? It used to be the Paris house of the abbotts who lived, *et ma foi,* ruled, in Cluny. The town is small. Lace and pottery-making are its chief claims to notice —bar its ruins, of course."

They stuffed their *croissants* and rolls into their pockets and hurried down to the car below.

In it was a bright-eyed, dark-haired young man who sat writing fast in a pocket-book. As they opened the door, the breeze caught a loose end of paper and whirled it into the air. Pointer did not seem to make any movement, but his fingers closed on it and he held it out to the young man who jumped up.

"Parbleu, I should like to meet you with a foil, monsieur!" Cambier introduced him.

"This is Rondeau, my aid. He thinks himself a detective, but he is young." In Cambier's tone was an affected discontent. In his eyes great friendliness. "He is a *revolutionaire.* In detective theories only, I can vouch for that. Also, he is a writer of detective stories. And detective stories, monsieur, should be forbidden by law. They are poison to the intelligence."

"I follow Poe and his Dupin," Rondeau said cheerfully. "I build with humble bricks an altar to intelligence, to the Goddess of Reason. Monsieur Cambier, my *chef* here, would make her a slave, chained to the heels of old boots, coming after blobs of candle grease—an old *chiffoniers,* a rag-picker."

"Detection is a science," Cambier said sternly.

"It is an art," Rondeau maintained; "all the groveling after clues in the world is not worth one pinch of fl—"

"Say the word *flair,* and you fly out of this door!" thundered Cambier; "the detective's flair is the criminal's mascot."

All three laughed.

"Detective stories discourage crime," Rondeau pointed out.

"Not yours, my friend. *Your* detectives are calculated to increase the number of murders a hundredfold. But what did you learn on the telephone while I was upstairs? Anything of importance?"

"The men who are killed are a Baron Cross and a Monsieur Brownlow." They looked inquiringly at Pointer, who tried to place a Lord Cross—and failed.

"I know the house where this lamentable thing has happened," Cambier explained to Pointer. "I know the owner of Villa Porte Bonheur. He is a Monsieur Pichegru—a gentleman of the utmost respectability, an owner of some small, but good, vineyards. A couple of years ago his entire crops of grapes failed, and he took into his house what you call 'paying guests.' It was a revolutionary idea! But it saved our good Pichegru. And since then he has continued to have some foreigners always with him. In case the crops failed again! His villa is well run. It is well staffed with local servants, who say that it, and the people staying in it are always, in every way, of the most correct." Cambier ran over the names of the inmates as known to him.

"I have met one of the dead men—Monsieur Brownlow—once or twice. He played a good game of tennis, and was a fair shot, besides seeming a most agreeable companion. Unfortunately his wife is young and beautiful—"

"Her age is given on her *permit de sejour* as thirty-two," cut in Rondeau. "But I agree that she is very interesting-looking, though I ask myself—"

"You agree! Interesting-looking!" scoffed Cambier; "ah, the presumption of youth! How old is Baron Cross; did you learn that?"

Rondeau said that he had. The baron was between forty and fifty apparently.

"Present at the fancy-dress dance which was given at the villa last night were——" Rondeau enumerated the names of the guests as telephoned to him.

"Here we are!" murmured Cambier, who was looking out of the window. "Here, at what was once the hub of the world. Here, in this deserted nook, where prelate and prince came to have their disputes settled, where sovereigns make a pilgrimage. The Abbot's Palace is now the *Hotel de ville*, with which you, monsieur, will doubtless become well acquainted before the formalities are over. I do not expect that it will be a long business "

"One never knows—" began Rondeau hopefully.

"But one learns!" retorted Cambier. "You, *monsieur Vin-specteur-en-chef*"—he turned to Pointer—"have naturally an absolutely free hand. In every way, in every respect. Any observations with which you honor us will be carefully treasured and at once embodied in the official reports. Ah, here is the villa gate!"

A moment more, and the three were out on the gravel. Another moment, and they were met by the police sergeant on guard, who described the finding of the "duellers," first by the inmates of the villa, then by the police.

"This way, *mon chef.*" He took them to the cedar room. All but one set of curtains were still drawn. The commissaire snapped on the electric light as well.

"They fought in the dark," murmured the sergeant, stand- ing bare-headed by Sir Anthony's body. "Here is a switch most convenient to turn out the light."

The police bent over the bodies in turn. The doctor was waiting for them to be handed over to him, but he showed how Baron Cross, as he called him, though mortally wounded in the side, had had time to fire and kill his adversary with one fatal shot. Death in Brownlow's case had been instantaneous. By each man's side lay the revolver which had presumably been used. Both jobs were what the doctor called neat. Bleeding had been chiefly internal.

"The facts seem clear enough. I regret deeply"— Cambier turned to Pointer—"that there is nothing here to show you what we can do. Husband—wife—husband's friend. The door locked on the inside. The key in the keyhole. Bah, it explains itself—so far. Not even a detective of Rondeau's could miss the truth. Not even in the first chapter. I do not suppose that you know either of the dead men's faces, monsieur?"

Pointer did not.

The sergeant reported the servants' gossip, which was to the effect that "milord Cross" had devoted himself entirely to Madam Brownlow last night. Evidently monsieur had either misunderstood, or understood— according to one's point of view.

The sergeant had been making inquiries over the wire. No one of the guests to whom he had telephoned— very guardedly —had any idea, as far as he could judge, that there had been anything in the way of an accident at the villa last night.

"Just so," nodded Cambier. "It was a duel to the death —in the dark—between these two, of which every one else was in ignorance probably. Except, perhaps, madam. We shall come to her by and by for that point to be cleared up. Though what could the poor woman do? Having done all the mischief, she would now have had to stand on one side and let the consequences work themselves out."

"Yes, but I ask myself—" began Rondeau. His chief cut him short.

"Do not embroider, do not twist, Rondeau! Do not, I beg, be subtle! Here we have two men and a beautiful woman. Some incident heats their anger to fury. Each fetches his revolver. They stand in corners opposite to each other the length of the room apart, turn out the light, and *voila!*—that is all."

"I have an idea that it is not so simple!" insisted Rondeau.

"An idea!" scoffed Cambier. "Have you a fact? Let us see what we can find?" He looked about him keenly. "Here is a tiny pin on the inkstand—"

"Such as is used to pin together bank-notes, eh, *mon chef*?" Rondeau asked excitedly, drawing in his breath, as he bent over the first find, as though the air were laden with some wonderful perfume, the perfume of a pin.

"And other things, my lad! You always forget the

other things, the every day other things." Cambier
continued to go over the room, inch by inch.

He examined the disguise worn by Brownlow—the
cardboard bottle of Macon. It showed no marks of a
tussle.

"It has many straps inside. None of them are strained.
He took it off quite calmly, without haste." Cambier
passed on

"There are no finger-prints on either pistol," Rondeau
murmured.

"*Tien*, and I thought the thinker despised clues! But
as we both know, more often than not, with people whose
hands are clean, and cool, no prints are left." Cambier got
up and dusted his knees. "I think we can leave this room
now. Locked up, of course. The photographs have been
taken and are being developed?"

The sergeant said that was so.

"And how about the room of milord?" Cambier next
asked.

He was told that it had yielded nothing significant.

"Then I think we will interview that poor lady,
Madam Brownlow. She has my most profound sympathy.
After all, it was God, and not herself, who gave her her
strange, troubling beauty and a charm that mounts to the
head like our own rich wine. Rondeau, you can finish your
report in the next room. Hand it to my secretary, who will
be here shortly. But, as railway freights have again risen,
and it will eventually have to be sent to Macon, may I
suggest a little more compression than last time? As for
Monsieur Pointaire and me, we will now go up to the
room of Madame."

CHAPTER SIX

A GENDARME approached the commissaire. After a few minutes' talk, Cambier turned again to Pointer.

"It appears that there is an English private detective already on the spot. He is investigating the loss by a gentleman who was staying at Villa Porte Bonheur of a considerable sum of money in the Paris *rapide* some days ago. He speaks a French which can be understood—with a little trouble—and he can understand whatever is said to him, which is all that really matters. Fortunately this private inquiry agent has met the dead milord, and can, therefore, positively identify him as Baron Anthony Cross."

Anthony Cross. Pointer at last placed the dead man. One of the directors of the big South African Diamond Combine. He decided mentally that Rondeau would certainly start asking himself questions when he heard of that fact. Even he, Pointer, wondered whether. . . .

"The sergeant rightly did not care to allow him the run of the room until we should *viser* his papers," went on Cambier. "Would you be so kind as to do that for us? Since we have the inestimable benefit of your presence." Cambier spoke to one of his men. A minute later and Mackay entered. One glance and he stepped up to Pointer.

"You'll be yon chief inspector frae Scotland Yard they are talking of outside as having arrived. Here are my credentials." He handed the same wad to Pointer that he had shown to Vivian Young. Pointer also went through the contents carefully.

"And here's a letter frae Mr. Davidson, who's my employer for the time being, referring to some question I asked him. And here's a line frae the dead mon, Sir

Anthony Cross, enclosing me an invitation for last nicht's dancing. I did some warrk for his firm not long ago. Looking up a doubtful reference in Edinburgh. I hadna met Sir Anthony till I chanced on him here." Pointer handed him back the papers, and introduced him to the commissaire, who shook hands.

"It seems a clear case of a duel," Cambier repeated thoughtfully. "Is there anything known to you that explains the ill-feeling between the two gentlemen?"

"I'm afraid I can't be of the smallest use to you, except by saying that one of the dead bodies is certainly that of Sir Anthony Cross," Mackay explained, in his fairly correct, but very weirdly-accented French.

"Pity. We were on our way to question Madam Brownlow," Cambier continued. "You, too, monsieur, are welcome to hear what she has to say."

Mrs. Brownlow was very pale, very haggard even, yet not the distraught figure that might have been expected. She was in a short, black dress of some shimmery silken stuff that outlined her really lovely figure in a way which would have caused a sensation before the war.

All the men thought that she was made up. But made up to hide, not to accentuate the marks of grief and shock.

The whole terrible affair had come as a complete thunderbolt on her, she said in the soft murmur of a well-bred Frenchwoman. She knew, she had always known, that her husband was jealous almost to the point of madness. That was really why she was thankful to stay on here in Cluny. She and Sir Anthony had flirted a little to-night. But it was only a flirtation, a game. Only a pose. Her husband must have known as much. True, he had once before objected to her acquaintanceship with Sir Anthony, and that was why he and she had not seen anything of each other for so long.

"Was your husband a violent-tempered man in private?" the commissaire asked.

Mrs. Brownlow wiped her brimming eyes. "It took a tremendous lot of feeling to break through the restraint habitual to him. He rarely lost his temper, but when he did, he lost it completely."

Coming to last night, she said that he had seemed vexed with her for having sat out a good many dances with Sir Anthony. But the dead man and she had naturally a good deal to talk about. Her husband had scolded her, and she had been very indignant with him. Then, later, he had apologized, and they had made it up. But evidently the feeling had remained behind—and this was the result!

"Madam," Cambier said gently, "come, now, be frank with us. It will go no further. You were planning to elope last night with Sir Cross, were you not? It was for that that he had come here?"

Mrs. Brownlow's head sank lower yet. She did not reply until the question—a guess—was repeated, still more gently.

"Yes," she whispered all but inaudibly. The Frenchman looked very sympathetic.

"I am so desolated, madam, to have to press the point, but we must, you know. You and Sir Cross intended then to go away together? And your husband learned of the plan?"

"I think he must have," she murmured brokenly.

"And when did you decide on it?"

"Last night. Before the supper. I did not notice the time. I—oh," she broke down apparently, but there were no ravages visible on her tinted cheeks when she raised her head again, though she was very pale and looked very unhappy. She looked very lovely too. Hers was a type of face that needs emotion to kindle it.

"And you knew nothing of this duel?" pressed Cambier.

"Absolutely nothing." She spoke very earnestly. "I am willing to swear that on the crucifix."

"I believe you, madam," the commissaire said gently. He questioned her as to when she had last seen each of the two men. Mrs. Brownlow could not be sure. She had no idea of the exact hour, but in Sir Anthony's case it had been before supper; and in her husband's case it had been some little time after supper. Perhaps half an hour, but perhaps less or more.

Pointer and Mackay listened attentively. Cambier now turned to them. "Is there anything you would like to ask madam, messieurs?"

Mackay fidgeted a moment on his seat, then he burst out:

"I canna get the affair properly into ma head," he said at last. "There's nae logic intilt. To kill a mon—it takes a lot o' feeling to gae that far. I canna hear that Mr. Brownlow showed any sign of jealousy before. The general opinion, on the contrary, is that he was anything but of a jealous temper."

He looked at Mrs. Brownlow questioningly.

"But you see he was," she said sadly. Speaking in English too.

"He never betrayed himself before," Mackay went on obstinately; "for a mon o' oor race to kill anither—na, na, ma'm, I canna think ye're richt! I feel siccer there was mair nor that behind these deaths—this fecht. Ye maun forgi'e me, Mrs. Brownlow, but ye see I ha'e met your guid man, though but at this dance. He didna strike me as in a tooring passion at ony time last nicht. Na, na! It wasn't jealousy! Judging accordin' to the licht o' reason, I canna think it that. I canna! There maun be some ither cause." Mackay spoke very firmly.

"But you see, Sir Anthony and I were going to run away together," she said, hanging her head with its top-heavy mass of thick, rather coarse, dusky red hair. "And somehow he must have learned of it—and Sir Anthony has a quick temper—so that, between them, they quite lost all sense of proportion."

Still Mackay shook his head. Still he looked absolutely unconvinced.

"Tisn't logical, ma'm. To suddenly fecht a duel—he's a law-abidin' mon a' his days. 'Tis too sudden. There maun be some ither cause."

"Oh, it isn't the first time!" she replied in French, her voice marking acute pain. "I—I ought to have been on my guard. I am so terribly to blame!" She buried her face in her slender, long, beautiful hands for a moment, and shuddered. The commissaire looked sympathetically at her.

"There was another time," she went on in a little, hushed voice barely audible, and still in her native language. "It was years ago. In China. A young man used to come to our house a good deal there. He was such a nice boy, and so homesick. And so frank and friendly. I was so dreadfully sorry for him. I never guessed, until the last evening, that—well, that he didn't look on me as a sort of temporary sister, as I thought. That last evening—" she paused. "Mr. Brownlow came in and found him saying good-bye to me. My husband wouldn't listen to any explanations. And next morning poor young Jackson, that was the boy's name, was found drowned in the river near our house. And some people said"—she bit her trembling lip; she was genuinely shaken by the old story—"some people said that Tom had drowned him." Her voice was a mere whisper of horror.

"Had he?" the commissaire asked bluntly.

"I was never sure." Alys Brownlow shivered. "I was never sure, but"—she lifted her head and looked at the three intently listening men—"I think that he did. I think there was a quarrel over me by the river, and Tom flung young Jackson into it without caring, at the moment, whether he could swim or not."

"Was the affair never cleared up?" Cambier asked.

Mrs. Brownlow shook her head.

"It never came to a trial. There was no evidence. But many people, as I say, thought that he had. You see, Mr. Mackay, many people guessed what you can't seem to believe, that Tom Brownlow was a very hot tempered and very jealous man in his heart."

There was a long silence.

"Thank you ma'm, for explaining," Mackay said finally. "You've pit the logic intilt that it lacked before. There's nae doot in ma mind the noo but that you were richt, and that Mr. Brownlow was a maist dangerous man."

Again there was a silence. Finally Cambier turned to the chief inspector.

"If there are no questions you would like to ask madam, I have no further queries to put for the moment."

On Pointer and Mackay both murmuring a negative, the commissaire rose, said a few words of respectful sympathy, and led the way downstairs. It was understood that Mrs. Brownlow would remain in the villa for the present, though they hoped not to have to disturb her again.

When the newly-made widow was alone, she rang and asked if Miss Young would speak to her for a moment.

Vivian came with great inward reluctance. She was angry and very disappointed in herself that this should be so. Mrs. Brownlow had taken nothing from her worth keeping, or that had ever been really her's. She knew that it was only wounded pride that made her wish never to see the woman again.

But after a little delay she came. She found the other stretched out on a chaise-longue. Vivian thought she had been lying with her face buried in the cushions. More, it looked to her swift glance as though a corner of the cushions had been bitten by sharp, small teeth.

"Oh, Vivian—may I call you that—please stop with me!" Mrs. Brownlow laid a hand on the girl's shoulder and drew her down closer. "I couldn't tell those men, they wouldn't understand it—but, oh. . . . Don't shrink from me"—Vivian had made her back stiff—"you can't blame me as much as I do! But oh, I'm punished! For you see"— she gulped down a sob— "you see, it was my husband I loved! Not the other man at all. Now it's too late—I know that. Now it's too late!" There was desolation in the tone. There was desolation in the large but narrow eyes, in the whole sunken face.

Vivian's kind heart melted.

"I'm very sorry for you, Mrs. Brownlow," she said, and meant it.

"Stay with me!" pleaded the other; "I can't leave here immediately. I don't feel able even to think. Tom decided everything for me for so many years. Tom—" Her eyes over flowed, her lips quivered, and snatching her hand away she burst into passionate sobbing.

Downstairs, Mr. Murgatroyd had asked if he could speak to the commissaire for a moment. He explained that he did not want to be detained at Cluny. That he very much wanted to catch the next Paris express at Macon.

Now, as has been said, Monsieur Cambier knew the professor. For the latter had special access and permits to what remained of the old abbey library, where he often worked for days at a time. Mr. Murgatroyd went on to explain that he had no faintest notion of anything that could throw any light on why Mr. Brownlow should have shot Sir Anthony Cross, nor why Sir Anthony should have wanted to shoot Mr. Brownlow. He had not met either of the men until he came here to Cluny this last time. And on that, and leaving his address, Mr. Murgatroyd was assured that since he said that he must leave at once for Paris, no objections would be raised, though he was asked to remain in France until he heard from the commissaire. That official did not add, what he did later to his superior, the *chef de police*, that seeing that all the guests who had attended the dance had dispersed, one more, and that one who had not been present, might be allowed to go on too.

As soon as Mr. Murgatroyd had left them, Monsieur Pichegru arrived from Dijon. He was in a state of mind that, had the matter not been so serious, would have been funny.

Added to his shocked horror as to what had happened

to the two dead men, was an intensely human curiosity as to why it had happened, and what Mrs. Brownlow would do. Also how it would affect the name of the villa itself, which, as he explained, he advertised as a quiet retreat, a perfect nerve cure The Brownlows had been the first people of the party now staying in the villa to answer the advertisement.

"I looked up their references, which were in every way satisfactory," Pichegru went into details. He now furnished the information that had been given him. Brownlow was a member of three good London clubs, and was engaged in silk importation. Apparently he was a man of considerable means. His wife had some unusually fine jewels, a part of which, as the commissaire knew, had been stolen lately. They were so fine that Pichegru would only allow them in the villa on the understanding that they should be locked up every night in his safe.

As to Sir Anthony Cross—he explained how slight was his knowledge of that gentleman.

"And now, monsieur, or rather messieurs, what ought I to do? I am really needed in Dijon, and badly. The warehouse is but a riddled sieve of a building. You know what happens if good wine is carelessly handled—on the other hand, I would not for the world appear wanting in respect—"

He was called to the telephone. A question had arisen which only he could solve, and only he on the spot. Monsieur Pichegru was distracted. Cambier finally advised him to go to Dijon, and from there keep in touch with the villa over the telephone. He could be summoned at any moment. He would be so summoned should his presence in Cluny be of the slightest help. Meantime his household staff would carry on, the butler in particular, as Monsieur Pichegru pointed out, enjoyed his entire confidence. So finally, half-relieved, half-apologetic, the owner of the villa jumped into his car and made off once more for Dijon and his hogsheads and his bottles.

Mr. Smith was asked to come into the room. He shook

hands with the commissaire. They had faced each other on the hard courts many a time. He ran over the finding of the two dead bodies, explaining that he had first thought that Brownlow must have fallen asleep, then that he had had a glass too much, when he failed to reply to the calls for him.

As to when he had last seen either man, Smith was very vague. Around one o'clock, he fancied, in each case. But Cambier's closer questioning made him say that time at a dance was not, as far as he was concerned. Simply was not. He had one curious little incident to relate, however.

"Sir Anthony came out of the cedar room as I was passing, shortly before midnight. Or shortly after it. He was without his pierrot mask and dress, and asked me if I would act as co-witness with Mr. Murgatroyd to his signature. It was a financial paper that was to be signed, he explained, and he said that he regretted that he could not let me see the contents. I followed him into the room, and found that he had folded the paper so that his signature, when he wrote it, was the only thing visible. Below it Cross had written the words 'Witnesses to my signature,' with a bracket within which we signed, Murgatroyd and I."

Smith added that, seeing the position of Sir Anthony, he had not given the matter a second thought. He had found, and he had left, Murgatroyd in the room with the baronet. Now he thought it highly probable that Sir Anthony had in reality been asking him to witness his will, but, for fear of arousing comment, had preferred not to state the truth. Though why he should have told a lie about the matter, would, Smith thought, need some one who knew him to understand.

Sir Anthony had proceeded to say good-bye to Smith as the latter left the room.

"You say 'seeing the position of the dead man,' monsieur," Cambier next asked, looking up from his notes. "What exactly did you mean by that? His social position?"

"His position as a director of the South African Diamond Combine."

The commissaire blinked. Rondeau gave an exclamation.

"Diamond Combine?" both asked together.

Smith explained that Sir Anthony had been a director, and a most energetic one, of that great cartel for many years. Smith left with them *Who's Who*. Pointer opened it at the dead man's name. He was put down as the only son of the Right Honorable Sir Henry Wykham Cross, seventh baronet of Riston. Educated at Winchester and New College. Called to the Bar by the Inner Temple. Went the South Eastern Circuit. Two years later went out to the Consular Court at Shanghai. Shortly afterwards followed his uncle, Mr. Herbert Cross, as a director of the South African Diamond Combine, and his father as eighth baronet.

Pointer translated line by line. Rondeau made copious notes.

"And he was apparently making his will last night—before that duel to the death—nothing more natural . . ." Cambier mused.

"Though I ask myself whether his many interests might not be for something in this mystery," Rondeau struck in.

"Do not use the word 'mystery' so lightly, my dear fellow," corrected Cambier. "As far as I can see, *l'apropos manque*. But I would like a word with the professor. He might know definitely whether that paper was a will or not. He was in the room, Monsieur Smith says, when the latter entered, and he left him still in the room."

Inquiry for Mr. Murgatroyd showed that the historian had already left in a car, for which he had telephoned very urgently to the one local garage.

"I have the name of his hotel in Paris," Cambier said placidly. "I will write and ask him the question I intended to put personally. The answers mean but little. The paper signed might have either been a will, as we think, or concerned some money affair which Sir Cross wished settled before he died. Madam Brownlow believed, as you know, that he has no relatives living. We will, of course, communicate at once with the London office of his firm. What is it, Chevron?"

It was Mr. Smith again. Mr. Smith wished to be allowed to go on to Vichy, where he expected to take a cure. He had been going later on, in any case, and now, very naturally, preferred to leave at once. The commissaire jotted down the name of the doctor—it was one known to him, for Vichy is fairly near to Cluny—and said that, provided Mr. Smith would hold himself in readiness to give any evidence which he, the commissaire, frankly did not think would be needed, there was no objection to his proceeding to the spa at once. And Smith, looking quite grateful, left the room hurriedly to make his arrangements.

The commissaire now turned his attention to the servants. Rondeau was told off to have a look at Sir Cross's bedroom. Pointer and Mackay followed him. Sir Anthony had sent on his suit-case to Paris from the hotel yesterday afternoon.

"There are only two bags of his here." The sergeant showed them to Rondeau. In the one were the dead man's night things, the other was empty except for two novels.

"There are no letters in either, nor on him," murmured Rondeau thoughtfully; "like that witnessed paper, he must have, himself, posted anything that he wrote, I suppose." He looked troubled. But after a moment he suggested rejoining the commissaire downstairs. The latter was finishing his questions. None of the servants had anything new to tell him apparently. One of the footmen had tried the door of the cedar room somewhere between half-past one and two o'clock, found it locked and passed on. He had been in search of a chair. Now he had a fancy that he had heard steps inside the room, or at least a sound as of some one stirring; but as he was very young and very much excited at the two deaths, Cambier placed a big question mark beside his impressions. All of the servants, now that the event had happened, were sure that they had noticed that Mr. Brownlow was very jealous of Sir Anthony, and that the latter was absolutely indifferent as to who noticed, or who did not notice, his flirtation with Mrs. Brownlow. Apart from her, the baron, as the servants called the baronet, had, as far as was known, spoken to no one else while in the ball-room, except that the butler had seen him once talking to an English lady staying at the Hotel de Bourgogne, a Madam Eastby, a friend of Sir Cross's, he believed. He had heard, he explained, that when his master was summoned to Dijon, Mr. Smith had called on her in his stead with an invitation extended to her at Sir Anthony's request, made over the telephone yesterday afternoon.

Proceedings were now halted long enough for some one to telephone to the hotel in question. Madam Eastby had left. She had returned to the hotel around two o'clock, changed, and had driven off in a car that seemed to be waiting for her. A sleepy night porter was not very exact. The lady had left no address. She had only come for a couple of days to study the historical remains of the place, so she had said on arriving. When had she come? By the same train as Sir Cross, though apparently they were only slightly acquainted. The hotel had only seen them exchange a few words once or twice in all.

"Probably train acquaintances," murmured Cambier when the telephone information was passed on to him.

"She is said to have been very handsome," Rondeau added. It was he who had telephoned.

"Just so. That's why train acquaintances," snapped his chief. "The points—the only points of interest to us— are that she apparently did not know Mr. Brownlow, and that Sir Cross's behavior towards her was not one to arouse any jealousy in any onlooker. This is a duel, remember. Kindly let that fact clip a little off your imagination's wings."

Rondeau subsided. His last effort had "explained" a man injured by a mule's kick into a violent attempt at highway robbery on the part of four armed apaches.

"We will see what the two others guests staying in the house can tell us." Cambier had the butler once more summoned. He learned from him that Monsieur Tibbitts, who had been helped up to bed by Brownlow and the servant last night, had gone out for a spin to cool his brain at some early hour in the morning.

"If a man—a foreigner not accustomed to wines—will prefer Burgundy to our light claret—" the butler shrugged his shoulders. He was a *Clunyois*, well known to Cambier and the police as a most respectable character.

Questioned as to the hour of Tibbitt's retirement from the hall, he gave it as around half-past twelve. Early this morning, one of the temporary footmen, who was a waiter at a nearby inn, had happened to see Mr. Tibbitts driving alone in a little sports car. The car belonged to Monsieur Brownlow, the butler added, though Monsieur Tibbitts often used it. As to his early drive, he had done this once or twice before after a bottle too many, and might be expected to return before lunch very much the better for his outing.

"Meantime, the young lady is available," he suggested.

Vivian was requested to speak to the commissaire for a moment. The questions put to her were purely formal. Neither of the Frenchmen asked her if she had met Sir Anthony Cross, nor yet Mr. Brownlow, before arriving at the villa, for, knowing from the butler's account of Sir Anthony's first visit that she had not met him then, and aware of the fact that she was an American on a tour of the world, it was taken for granted that the one was a total, and the other a comparative, stranger. She added nothing to Cambier's knowledge of what had happened, merely corroborating the butler's and Smith's accounts of how the bodies had first been found.

The doctor's preliminary report was handed in before Cambier had finished this dull but necessary part of the inquiry. A fuller one would follow later. This first one merely established the fact that, as had been thought, the bullet that caused each man's death fitted the weapon found beside the other man, and had been fired from the front in Mr. Brownlow's case, and sideways in Sir Anthony's case, but at a distance that precluded any singeing of cloth or powder marks.

In Mr. Brownlow's case death had been instantaneous, while in Sir Anthony's, the wounded man had, as they all knew, had time to kill the other before himself expiring.

"Just so," Cambier nodded in agreement with the medical finding. "Verdict, so far, is death in both cases as the result of a duel. Fought without seconds. Because of the intention of killing. The press can have the news now, Rondeau."

"Though I still ask myself—" his *aide* began.

"Ta-ta-ta!" snattered Cambier like a cross gander; "do not ask yourself anything! Tell yourself, on the contrary, that everything here goes to constater a duel. Nothing to suggest a crime."

And on that the conference broke up. The two Frenchmen began to collect their notes; the chief inspector drifted out into the corridor. He was only an observer, it was true, but he had observed one thing as he passed down it. The four pewter plaques on its walls that represented the four seasons were not in their correct order.

They ran Spring, Summer and Winter on the long wall, and on the end, opposite to the door of the cedar room, hung Autumn. It was this one that Pointer now looked at. The plaques hung by stout chains and plate-hooks from the picture rail. This plate had recently been shifted on its hooks, as two similar bright marks, the same distance apart, but a little to one side, showed. Nor did the name hang true now. Pointer turned his attention to Winter on the long wall. It, too, showed two bright marks on its edge, just a thought farther to the right than the hooks that now held it.

So both the third and the fourth in the series showed signs of a recent interchange. Why? He had another look at Winter. It was very much ornamented with lumpy work. A close inspection showed something that looked like a sun in the midst of a haystack, supposedly snow-covered, that bulged to one side. Pointer looked at the door of the cedar room. Had this plaque hung fourth in order, on the little end wall, it would have been exactly opposite the door. There was no one about. He jumped on a chair. The "sun" in the haystack was a small bullet, such a bullet as an automatic might have fired. It had not gone through the thick metal, but had embedded itself very deeply in it.

He turned around as the door of the cedar room opened. The two French officials were going to have a general inspection of the gardens. Pointer joined them.

"Nothing amiss," Cambier said finally; "as was to be expected. You agree with me, messieurs, do you not, that the gardens tell nothing?" He addressed Pointer and the private inquiry agent. Mackay nodded. Chief Inspector Pointer said nothing.

"It tells you something?" Rondeau said instantly, all alertness.

"You mean?" Cambier was no less interested.

"I think some one has searched the garden already," Pointer said finally.

"None of our men. The sergeant did not trouble, seeing that the deaths—so far—look like a duel. You think some one has searched here—this morning? May I permit myself to ask why you think that, monsieur?" Cambier asked.

Pointer showed them some leaves here and there which, he thought—and he was a country boy—had been either disturbed or turned over. The morning dew, thick and heavy, was what he went by.

"But there are no footprints—" Cambier was examining the ground very closely. "A dog, perhaps; some animal?"

Pointer thought not. He thought that the marks showed that some intelligent person had been looking for something and had had an idea of where to look.

"I think it was some one who had lost or dropped something on the way between the front door and the gate and retraced his steps looking for it."

"Losh!" muttered Mackay. "Mechty me!" he added after a pause.

"Ah-h!" breathed Rondeau, with that eager intake of his breath that suggested a dog trying for a scent. "Ah-h!"

"But what makes you think the same person searched as lost?" Mackay wanted to know. "Why wasna it some one searching for what some ither person had dropped?"

Pointer thought that the searcher was both too vague and too precise for that. He had, so he believed, turned over or prodded some leaves from every bush on the right-hand side —supposing he were walking away from the house that touched or bordered the winding main drive.

"You think the leaves and plants that have been disturbed are only in that direction," murmured Cambier. "We will see."

But he could not agree with the man from Scotland Yard. There were many signs to Pointer's eyes that the other missed, perhaps because he did not believe that they held any message bearing on the case.

"No footprints, messieur, no mark of a hand in the ground," he finally pointed out. Pointer quite agreed with him.

"What object would you think it was?" Rondeau wanted to know.

"Something small and flat," Pointer thought; "small enough and flat enough to be hidden under those primula leaves, for instance, back there. Something that he was carrying in his right-hand pocket, or in his right hand on leaving the house.

"A love-letter," breathed Rondeau with kindling eyes.

"A bank-note!" retorted Cambier with a laugh at him. "Do not embroider, Rondeau! Anything else you can tell us, monsieur? You think it was in his right hand?"

"Assuming that he lost it on his way from the house. And, as we have learned of nothing missing, it looks as though that were the case. Besides, he does not look for it at night. Or we should have heard of a lantern or electric torch being asked for."

"Ah, here is a mark!" Cambier bent down low; "fingers of a hand or glove have swirled those leaves over. *Voyons—voyons—*" he pulled at his lower lip. "Monsieur Smith walked down this drive, did he not?" He spoke to his sergeant.

"Waiting for messieurs to arrive," the man agreed. "He did. And as he walked, he slashed at the plants with his motoring gloves. He was carrying them in his right hand. He waited for you quite a while by the front gate."

"There is our mark explained." The commissaire turned to Pointer with a smile. "It is a habit of Monsieur Smith to cut at things idly with whatever he holds in his hand. I have noticed it on more than one occasion. But many thanks for pointing out what might have been of the greatest importance."

Cambier turned away, and with his *aide* made for the Hotel de ville. Mackay hunted on.

"I'm trying to recover Davidson's money, ye ken. I'd like to find what was flung awa'. Ye never can tell what may help in a search—that's logic. I dinna ken whether your guess was richt, or yon Frenchie's, but I'll luik a bit longer." He did. But finally he gave it up.

"Yon's a terrible thing to have happened," he said half to himself as he straightened up. "But what's the use!"

"The use of what?"

"Of arguing according to reason in this affair. Ah, here comes Miss Young. We maun stop, for she's seen us. And if she wants to speir oot hoo things stand, she wull."

Mackay's tone of resignation made Pointer smile. But

Miss Young was only told what the papers would soon know, and what she knew already: that a duel to the death had taken place at the villa last night, and that both the men who fought it were dead. Vivian nodded sadly.

"Well, I'm glad that there's to be no long drawn out investigation. And so will Mrs. Brownlow be."

CHAPTER SEVEN

MACKAY was very flattered by an invitation from the chief inspector to join him at a second breakfast of rolls and coffee—the badly-made coffee of your provincial French towns. They were both putting up at the hotel nearest to the station, and were discussing some of its discomforts, when Rondeau came hurrying in.

"Losh, he's been asking himself something again, by the look o' him!" Mackay muttered.

But it was the commissaire himself this time who requested that the two gentlemen would return at once to the villa. Monsieur Cambier had had a telephone message, Rondeau explained, as the three hurried up the winding, shady Promenade de Fouettin—on to which the villa gardens opened—a telephone message from some one in Enghien-les-Bains. Rondeau would not say more, but he was fairly bursting with excitement.

The commissaire, too, though a quiet man, and, like most of his race very sparing of gesture, seemed stirred, Mackay thought, as they all three stepped into the writing-room—the room earmarked for the police investigation.

He repeated that he had just had a telephone message from Enghien-les-Bains.

"A Madam Gatwick there wished to speak to the official in charge of the inquiry into the death of Sir Cross. I asked her how she had heard of the death. She told me that the valet of the dead man had just telephoned to the hotel in Cluny, asking to speak to his master, and had learned that he was dead. Incidentally, of course, the hotel asked the man-servant for his own address, and I have had him summoned here at once. But to return to this lady—she tells me that Sir Cross has been staying at Enghien-les-Bains with her and her husband and her sister. Was it true, as the valet had been told, that he was supposed to have met his death in a duel over some lady down here? She evidently intended to receive a reply. I said that we thought so. The voice of this Madam Gatwick then replied that that was absolutely impossible, and went on, in her truly distressing French, to say that her sister was Sir Cross's fiancé, and that that gentleman had certainly not fought a duel over her sister. Wait, *mon aim*"—he silenced Rondeau—"do not give vent to those suppositions that I can almost see thronging to your lips! Stranger things are yet to come. I inquired—tactfully, I trust—when the engagement had taken place. And *ma foi,* it is odd!" Cambier made a grimace. "Just now! A fortnight ago! I asked her where her sister was. I expected to learn that she was on her bed, dissolved in tears, or even under medical treatment, but I confess I did not expect the answer that I received."

He paused.

"The answer!" implored Rondeau breathlessly.

"The answer was that Mademoiselle Young—that is the lady's name—is here in Cluny. More, is here in the Villa Porte Bonheur itself."

"Mademoiselle Young!" gasped Rondeau, and actually seemed too surprised to ask himself anything at all. Mackay jumped in his seat.

"Now," insisted Cambier, "this piece of news is very interesting, and very dramatic. And perhaps it changes much. And perhaps it changes nothing. An engagement may be entered into for reasons of, shall we say, good sense? An affair of the heart might persist in spite of it. You young men are not the only romantics. Unfortunately. And now we will again question Miss Young. This so very reserved young lady."

"Reserved!" Rondeau threw up his head. "It is more than reserve that we have here, *mon chef.* I ask myself—"

"Softly! Softly!" cautioned the older man; "remember the facts! A young lady suspects her fiancé of an entanglement with an old flame, a married woman. She comes down on the quiet, though without changing her name, to investigate. She knows who the woman in the case is, for she goes at once to the house where that woman is staying. She keeps out of sight of Sir Cross, for the first evening at any rate. Until she is sure. Then— now Rondeau, you are fond of guessing, what then?" Rondeau refused to rise to the bait.

"Then, I think, she has an interview with Sir Cross next day," Cambier continued. "She would have done much better to have placed the affair in the hands of her brother, the head of her family. But apparently she did not even consult him. Young ladies nowadays are of an independence! But is the world any the better? The safer? It is not. On the contrary!"

"Why do you think she had a meeting with her fiancé?" Rondeau asked.

"Because she makes no move to interfere the night of the ball—last night. She lets things take their course. I think that means that she had had an interview with this baron, and herself breaks off the engagement in fact, which he had already broken in spirit. Not reflecting that in these days, since the devastations of the war, good husbands are easier lost than won. Carried away by his passion for Madam Brownlow, he accepts his freedom. Then comes this duel. He is killed. The young lady sees no reason to relate a very sad little episode—a very humiliating one for her. . . ." Cambier went over with characteristic French penetration to suggest the feelings that might have prompted Vivian to keep silence.

"*Enfin*," he wound up; "that is what I believe to have happened. And that is why I say this new development, which seems such a *boulversement* in reality, may alter nothing."

Even Rondeau was of this opinion after an interview—a long one this time—with Miss Young. She seemed perfectly candid throughout. But Pointer noticed, so did Mackay, that she waited always for Cambier's lead.

She acknowledged that she had been engaged to Sir Anthony, but said that she had broken off that engagement yesterday morning. She had come to Cluny really to see its interesting architectural remains. But on her arrival, recommended to the Villa Porte Bonheur by a friend, Madam Montdore, she had recognized Madam Brownlow as a lady whose photograph she had seen a few days before in Sir Anthony's hands. The rest ran very much as Cambier had outlined it. She did not speak of the reason for his visit to Cluny that Anthony had given her, because she did not believe it to be true since the evidence of the duel.

It was very painful to all of them, this showing up of the dead man, this forcing the girl to tell of what was after all a humiliation, though Vivian refused to consider it as such. But she asked for absolute silence about it. And the commissaire promised her, that the facts should not be made known by the police, if it were possible to keep them quiet.

When it was over, she turned to Mackay, who walked away with her into the gardens and up to the old fortress beside them.

Both were silent at first.

"I'm sorry!" he said in a low voice. That was all, but she felt strangely comforted.

"So'm I!" she said quietly. "I'll be frank with you. I didn't love him. But I respected him tremendously. Oh, tremendously!" she repeated. "But as far as myself, my own feelings went—I wouldn't say that in that room; it seemed unfair to Anthony somehow—but I wanted to break off the engagement anyway."

"You did?" Mackay was relieved to hear that. He had feared a broken-hearted girl.

"Say, do you think I would have let Mrs. Brownlow have a walkover if I had loved the man?" Vivian demanded indignantly. "Not on your life, Mr. Mackay! My

father was a Texas ranger. He never sat with his tail
between his legs while people went off with what
belonged to him. No more would I! I let Mrs. Brownlow
try her hardest because I didn't care. And mind you, she's
right in saying the tragedy is her fault. She did try. By
leading Anthony Cross on. Of course, though"—Vivian
corrected herself—"I must remember that he was very
hard to read. My, yes! Too hard. I like franker people. I
wouldn't say that to any one else, but it's the truth. I felt
more and more that I might live a hundred years beside
him and never know what he was feeling deep down—"

Suddenly she broke off in that way that means that
an opposite thought had just struck home.

"Yes?" he asked with interest.

"I saw him really moved just at the end," she spoke in
a gentler tone. "I mustn't forget that. He must have cared
tremendously for Mrs. Brownlow to have looked like that.
He was all out to win. Say, when he turned at my
entrance into the cedar room, I could fairly hear the
swish of steel in the air. I wouldn't have guessed he had it
in him. He was on the warpath, sure enough. Oh, he was
out for Brownlow's scalp. Perhaps it was only that I didn't
really stir him, just as he didn't me, that made me think
him so cold and calm and self-controlled. You see we met
under exceptional circumstances. . . ." She told Mackay of
the storm at sea, of that wild and yet wonderful night
when each had found in the other a courage, high and
serene, that neither waves nor wind could touch.

"If Anthony had kept on being the man of that all but
wrecked ship, and I reckon that if I'd kept on being the
girl of the same, we wouldn't have drifted away from each
other so quickly. But even on board I never saw him look
really roused. Not like last night! It took the woman he
loved to do that. Every one could see how things were
shaping all evening. Every one but himself and her, I
suppose. But I guess he didn't think there was any risk.
He and I once practiced at a floating target, and my! he
sure was a crack shot, and swift as lightning on the

draw."

"Aye," Mackay said dully, and fell into his reverie again.

"Talking clears the mind, you know," she said encouragingly.

"What a clear-minded worrld we ought to live in," he said with his swiftly appearing, and as swiftly disappearing, flash of even, strong teeth. "It dosena clear mine. It addles it. Now, thinking on the ither hand— meditating according to the light o' reason on the facts as known—"

"Oh, *do* can that!" she begged. Opening her heart just now was a relief to her. "Or at any rate let me give you something to meditate on.

"Why did Mr. Lascelles come back on the quiet last night? What did he want from me, when he thought I was 'Jane'? Apparently he and the woman Anthony Cross wouldn't talk to were in some plan together. And she surely looked as though it had gone off well at supper. Oh, yes, I know that Anthony's and Mr. Brownlow's was a duel fair and square, but apart from that, there sure were strange things on foot here in the villa last night."

"I doot but the explaining o' the strange things is far beyant ma powers. There's nae logic here. And wi'oot logic, I'm a helpless mon." Mackay looked very tired. And in the sharp morning light he looked shabbier than ever. Vivian, who had watched, not once but many times, the turn of the card that might have meant absolute poverty for herself, looked at him sympathetically. He was not likely to make much out of his present job.

"Did Mr. Murgatroyd explain what he was doing in that writing-room last night?" she asked next.

"He never mentioned it," Mackay said, still with his thoughts somewhere else. "He said he had nae suspicion that onything was wrang between Brownlow and Sir Anthony."

"My!" Vivian looked shocked. "Say, he can tell them when he wants to, can't he! Like the rest of us, I guess.

But I suppose he didn't like to talk over whatever it was Mrs. Brownlow had said to him. He sure was in a difficult place. For surely to goodness *he's* what he seems? But apart from him, there's all the rest of things I can't understand. There's—"

"Aye!" cut in Mackay in the tone of one who doesn't want to talk. "There's a' that. A' things for which I'm nae guid.

"Ye see," he went on after a pause, "in stories it's invariably the private detective that wipes the eye o' the police. He's ca'ed just in time to prevent a terrible miscarriage o' justice and in the last vairse the police officer is shaking his hand, and saying, wi'tears in his een: "Whaur should we be but for you, Mr. Knowell?' Aye, it's like that in buiks. But in real life?" He shook his head. "Tak' ma job—"

"I wish I could!" she said with spirit. "Say, *I*'d make things hum!"

"How?" he asked pertinently. She thought awhile, and then agreed that there might be a few difficulties about getting under way. . . .

"I searched the rooms overhead last night and found naething," he pointed out. "Naething at a'. But, of course, I canna search them as a policeman wud. Pulling this and tearing up that. I have nae richts at a'. I havena an army of helpers dotted o'er the land." He spoke bitterly. Vivian studied him. She was not particularly fond of people who failed. Nor over lenient in judging them. She herself had never failed. But somehow—she was sure sorry for Mackay, as she expressed it to herself. The young man's face, voice, carriage, spoke for him as a man who would do his best—who had done his best honestly.

"You're all right," she said encouragingly, "all you want is a bit more drive. More hustle and less logic." At the sight of his face she broke off in her exhortation to exclaim in horror, "You're not going to quit?"

He made no reply.

"But you can't leave now!" She was in open dismay.

"Say, Mr. Mackay, you simply can't leave now!"

He made no promise except that he must, of course, stay until the inquiry, short though it apparently would be, was over. Vivian lost patience with him for his willingness to accept defeat.

"*I* can leave, but I wouldn't. Not for anything! I must know just how things happened. Of course, I know how they happened—but I want it proved. Besides, I've promised Mrs. Brownlow to wait here until—well, I guess, until she can get away. Oh, I know it's a funny situation. But it's less painful for both of us not to rail at each other. Besides there's Mamie, my sister, Mrs. Gatwick. She's on the way down here already. Worse luck. Say, I do hate being cried over."

But Mrs. Gatwick did not look as though she had come for that damp purpose as she hugged and kissed her sister in the latter's bedroom a few hours later.

"My dear girl, you can't stay in this house! We'll go back by the afternoon train. What a horrible little place this is. I didn't see a single decent store as I came up the street. And dust! Now, you get to your packing, or are you through already?"

Vivian disentangled the arms around her.

"Mamie," she said resolutely, "I'm staying right here until Mrs. Brownlow is able to get away. She's waiting to take her husband's body home with her. And I think it looks better for us to be friends. There's no reason why we shouldn't be."

"Waiting for Mrs. Brownlow!" echoed her sister shrilly and indignantly. "Mrs. Brownlow!"

"She asked me to stay with her."

"She sure has a nerve!" was the sister's indignant comment. "I don't know what's come over you, Vivian. To be taken in by that sort of creature. Mrs. Brownlow, indeed!"

The married sister sniffed.

"Now, Mamie," Vivian said as patiently as she could. Which was not anything wonderful in that line. "I know how you feel, and why you feel like that, just on my account. But you needn't. I had broken off my engagement with Anthony yesterday morning. He was free. He wasn't running away from me," she finished a little proudly.

"Why did you give him up? Because of this woman?" Her sister continued hotly, "Vi, I'm surprised at you! Anthony Cross loved you, and you alone. I don't care what she says. He loved you!"

Vivian put up a hand to stay her. Mamie's cheeks were flaming. She could be a terribly red-hot partisan, as her sister knew.

"Don't, Mamie, dear! It's not fair to any of us to weigh which of the two women he loved the better. *I* know. And so does Mrs. Brownlow—and I don't mind. No, no!" in answer to her sister's opening mouth, "don't Mamie! I know how you mean it—just out of championship for me—but the sympathy's not necessary. Not for me, and— what you say isn't true."

"Vivian Young! Why, how you talk! Of course it's true!"

Vivian shook her head.

"Anthony told me himself about her," she said finally. "He told me that it was over and done with. I know he thought so." She shut her eyes to the doubts about that.

"Vivian," Mrs. Gatwick spoke more quietly now. The two were sitting on the couch at the end of the bed. "There's something wrong about all this. I don't believe it was a duel at all. I believe that woman is lying out of whole cloth when she says that she was going to run away with your Anthony. What have you got to go on but her word? I didn't tell you, but Anthony Cross talked to me the day before he asked you to marry him. He thought he was too old for you. And too—well, too conventional for your fancy. He spoke of his love for you. I wish I could repeat his words, and above all, his tone. He loved you, dear heart. Loved you really and truly. Nothing, no lies, no police theories, *nothing* would make me think that the man who spoke of you like that could, within a month, be trying to run off with another man's wife. Not a man of Anthony Cross's character. I was ever so pleased when you took him. That was why I told you about George helping you out as he did. It seemed brutal, but I thought you might not take him otherwise. And about this old love affair of his, he told me, as apparently he did you, that it was absolutely done with. I guess he would find it easier to talk to me about her than to you. He said he's seen her quite lately, and found that not a spark of his old feeling remained. That even if she were free, he wouldn't marry her. He added, it's true, that she still wasn't free, but he assured me that he hadn't the slightest trace of love for her left. And you think, after that, that he would run away with her?"

"No," Vivian said, feeling exhausted with this flood of argument which did not stir her; "no, Mamie, but I think he was talking like that to you because he wanted it to be like that. And perhaps he really thought it."

"I don't believe anything of what they say here. Anthony Cross wasn't the sort of man to have duels," Mrs. Gatwick said vehemently.

Oddly enough, the dead man's valet, who was speaking to the police just then, was saying very much this same thing as the last sentence of Mamie Gatwick.

He was a typically quiet-spoken, quiet-eyed man. Starling had been with Sir Anthony Cross only a little over a year but he felt quite certain of his employer's characters, though Sir Anthony was a man who never, under any circumstances, took him into his confidence in any way.

"Or any one else, as far as I know, sir," he added laconically to Chief Inspector Pointer.

As to the engagement to Miss Young, Starling had heard of that. He had ventured to congratulate Sir Anthony, who had replied that he considered himself a very lucky man. He, the valet, knew of nothing whatever that would explain a duel between his master and Mr.

Brownlow, a name he now heard for the first time.

"But is it the sort of thing that surprises you?" Mackay asked. "I mean, was your employer the kind of man to fight another man easily?"

"The very last man in the world, I should say," Starling replied decidedly. "If it hadn't happened, I should say it was the sort of thing that couldn't happen. I never knew Sir Anthony lose his temper. And, if I may presume to say so, that was the character I had from his late valet when I took the place."

The list of articles found on Sir Anthony and in the bags was handed to him. As far as he could tell, nothing was missing, but Sir Anthony had packed his smaller bag himself. Starling knew nothing of its contents, which must have included the revolver that he now identified as a revolver which his late master generally carried while traveling. The smaller bag was one exclusively used, as far as he knew, for important papers and such like. Papers which Sir Anthony had probably dealt with by now.

"About coming to Cluny, do you know if it had long been in Sir Anthony's mind?" Cambier next asked, through Pointer.

The valet thought it a sudden decision. "We were staying at Enghien-les-Bains with some friends of Sir Anthony's. Yes, Mr. and Mrs. Gatwick and Miss Young. Sir Anthony was going back to London to-morrow; Mrs. Gatwick and Miss Young were to join him in August at his place in Yorkshire. It was three days ago that my master told me suddenly that I was to pack a bag for him—that he was going away for several days and would not want me till his return to Paris to-morrow. He told me to put a dress suit in, and gave me my instructions as to reserving seats and a cabin for our journey back to England. That evening he dined with Mr. and Mrs. Gatwick, and afterwards he gave me some final directions. Sir Anthony spoke of looking over the monuments down here for two, at most, three days."

"Was he interested in such things?"

"Very much so."

"There was nothing out of the way, nothing that now strikes you as odd, about his coming down here?"

"Nothing whatever, sir."

"Did he often go without you?"

"Sometimes he would, sir. When it was a case of any business he would often be good enough to dispense with my services."

As to who was the person of Sir Anthony's family to summon to Cluny to take charge of the body, Starling said that he has already cabled the dreadful news to Mr. Maitland, a great friend of his master's. Mr. Maitland, therefore, might be expected to arrive, or at least, cable some instructions, any moment.

"Was your master a good shot?" Rondeau wanted to know.

"Very."

"Was he fond of dancing?"

"Uncommonly fond of it," was the answer, and with that he was dismissed.

"Yet Sir Cross did not dance last night," Rondeau remarked when they were alone. Like his chief, he considered that the use of the Christian name implied familiarity or affection.

"He was possibly carrying a loaded revolver on him," Cambier pointed out dryly. "Well, messieurs, I see no reason to change my verdict. A duel. Not a crime. The bodies of the two men will be free when the doctor's final report is made, and can then be coffined and taken away in due course." He stopped. The door was jerked open and Mrs. Gatwick bounded in. No other word describes her energy or her action.

"Say, chief, I want Mrs. Brownlow arrested for the murder of my sister's fiancé, Sir Anthony Cross," she began. "I told you about the engagement—"

"Very clearly indeed," murmured Cambier hurriedly.

"Well, I've just had an interview with that woman,"

Mrs. Gatwick went on, in her fluent but faulty French; "and there's not a word of truth in her story. I believe she shot poor Sir Anthony because he wouldn't run away with her, and then killed her husband to prevent his giving her in charge. And what are you going to do about it?"

Evidently order the French equivalent of Black Maria was the least that the lady expected. Mrs. Gatwick resembled one of those electric eels put into fish tanks on long journeys to insure that the fish caught will keep in good condition, for only by great agility and an uncommon turn of speed can they escape. Yet to look at, Mrs. Gatwick was a small and pretty blonde, with rather gentle, wistful, blue eyes.

The house was in a turmoil within five minutes. It took the whole of her hour's stay in Cluny to induce her to allow matters to continue as they were. But occasionally folly, or what seems like it, is justified of her children too. This was such a case, for half an hour after Mrs. Gatwick's very disgruntled return to Paris and her children—her husband was in bed with a chill—came a piece of news that made her accusation against Mrs. Brownlow no less wild, but at least less preposterous.

The fully-completed autopsy brought a staggering fact to light. There was no possibility of doubting the proofs adduced, and they altered everything.

As was known, both men had drunk of Monsieur Pichegru's claret-cup at the same time. In it had been woodruff, and the stages of the absorption of that herb into the system is as accurate as a clock.

Medical examination showed that Sir Anthony had been killed about an hour after the drink. Whereas Brownlow could not have received his bullet until nearer an hour and a half had gone by. In other words, there was an interval of around thirty minutes between the two deaths, and it was Anthony Cross, the injured man, who had died first. Probably a couple of minutes after the infliction of the wound in his side. What had been taken for a duel, now stood out as a crime, or two crimes, very cunningly camouflaged by the criminal or criminals.

"*Mon dieu!*" Cambier stood for a moment as though the doctor's final bulletin had been a spell depriving him of the power of moving. Then he came to life with a bound. Orders rattled swiftly.

He turned to Pointer.

"The case is from now on, of course, in the hands of the *juge d'instruction*, or I should at once question Madam Brownlow again, but he will be here immediately. Until his arrival I have enjoined absolute silence in the matter on all my men."

The *juge d'instruction* is an official whose powers and duties might be loosely compared to those of an American coroner. Or one of our own coroners; sitting, however, without a jury, and on an inquest which continues until, in his opinion, the case is sufficiently clear for him to have an arrest made, and decide whether the arrested person shall be sent up to stand his trial or is to be released. He has most formidable powers of loosing and binding.

"But what about Monsieur Smith off in Vichy?" asked Rondeau under his breath.

"He will be safe enough there. Nor is there any question of Monsieur Smith—as yet."

"And Monsieur Murgatroyd in Paris! And what about Monsieur Tibbitts, still at large," Rondeau went on.

"What about all the guests at large!" snapped Cambier; "we must take the case as it is, not as we would have it. We are not writing a novel, we! Besides, remember, whoever staged this little tableau in the cedar room here thinks that he—or she—has hoodwinked us. Let them continue to think so. As for Tibbitts, he will return. Whether innocent or guilty, he will soon return. Why should he not? But let me see the key of the cedar room again." He hurried to the room in question. "Yes, yes! Here are marks that might have been made by ring-nippers such as hotel thieves use, such as we detectives use, to turn a key—left in a keyhole—from the other side of the door." Cambier frowned down at the scratches in question. "But this means that a professional, a trained criminal, has been at work here. *Sapristi!*" He turned to Rondeau with a wry smile, "Well, for once I acknowledge that the simple explanation was too simple. *Eh bien*, we must build another. We know—what do we know? That Brownlow could have killed Sir Cross, and that a bullet from his automatic probably caused Sir Cross's death—though the make is very usual. And we know that a bullet from Sir Cross's automatic killed Brownlow later on, for his revolver is not usual, but that Sir Cross could not have fired the shot himself.

"I think these odd facts mean that both men were shot by some third party who had possessed himself, or herself, of their revolvers, and, after inveigling them one after the other into the cedar room, shot each with the other's revolver, knowing of the jealousy between them. Knowing perhaps of the contemplated elopement of Madam Brownlow. Anything else would mean a combination of chances so strange that they would verge on the improbable. To suppose, for instance, that Brownlow killed Sir Cross, and then, some half-hour later, was himself slain by another hand. . . ." Cambier shook his head. "That is highly fantastic. For that presupposes two murderers—two motives—"

For once Rondeau made no reply. He was thinking too hard over the absolute reversal by the final medical bulletin of all that had been taken for granted. Then he broke out:

"But I ask myself, what if Monsieur Tibbitts does not return? He went off very early. He should have been back by now "

"You forget, *mon cher*, that this is supposed to be a duel!" Cambier reminded him dryly; "there is no reason why all the world should not come and go, therefore. As for Tibbitts, he has probably had a breakdown, or, since he was in the state suggested by the butler, a smash-up somewhere is delaying him. In any case, since he is using that particular car, we need not worry, for—"

At that moment the sergeant came in. One of the police had found a small, round-barreled, slotted key in the garden. He had found it by chance as he stooped to retrieve a dropped cigar. It was lying in a cut of the turf, quite hidden from view, though apparently not buried in any way.

The commissaire had the finder and the object found brought in. He eyed the key closely.

"Not well finished. . . . Very good metal. . . . No number on it. ... Where exactly did you find it?"

The man took him to the exact spot. Rondeau followed like a terrier. The key had lain close to the gate, under some leaves, and on the right-hand side of the drive going away from the house. The cut in the turf into which it had fallen, or had been thrown, or hidden, was very close to the path, a bare inch from it, though completely out of sight.

"Ah, *mon chef*," Rondeau said as the two walked back together; "you always beg me not to embroider. Very well, this time I do nothing. I content myself with admiring the pattern presented by the facts."

"Just as well," Cambier thought. "For one of the guests may have dropped it—though it has all the look to me of a handmade key. There is something in the barrel—we will have it analyzed at once. But first I will ask Monsieur Pichegru and Madame Brownlow if either has ever seen it. Just to make sure—"

"I asked myself at the time if the officer from Scotland Yard was not right in thinking that something had been hunted for—on that side of the path," Rondeau muttered half aloud.

"And why should not an English official be right— sometimes?" Cambier spoke with conscious generosity as he reached for the telephone.

A little later Pichegru rushed up in his car, gasped at the latest news, stamped about the floor, and raved at the impossibility of being in two places at once. He seemed genuinely distraught at the conjunction of a murder at his villa and a fire at his warehouse.

As to the key, he disclaimed all knowledge of it. There was a safe in his study, but its key was quite different. He now handed over all his house keys to the police, insisting on their examining everything.

"Search anywhere you like," he begged; "but you will not find why those two mad Englishmen decided to shoot each other—ah, I forget, it is not a duel! But in any case, what can I do? I am not of the police. But I must—I must superintend the re-racking of my Chambertin!"

The commissaire was all sympathy. He told him to wait for the arrival of the *juge d'instruction,* a personal friend of Monsieur Pichegru's.

Meanwhile Madame Brownlow was shown the key. She said that she was sure that she had never seen it before, and that it could not, therefore, belong to her husband. All his keys were accounted for. As to whether it belonged to Sir Anthony Cross, she could not, of course, say.

But the valet was positive that he had never seen it before. Though that might not mean much. Vivian Young, though that meant even less, was equally sure that she had never seen it in Anthony Cross's possession.

The guests of last night were asked over the telephone whether any of them had lost a key. The same inquiry was passed around the shop assistants and other helpers. Though a great many could not be reached, all those to whom the question could be put replied in the negative.

The analysis of the dark matter found in the shaft proved to be dried blood, and dried in such a way that it must have lain in a little pool of it, and not been used since.

Now, the only pool of blood was in the clothing—over the heart—of Brownlow. The key contained nothing else, no fluff of any kind, and no dust, which rather suggested that it had been used immediately prior to the shooting. A hint of oil bore this out. The police analyst thought it was a key that had been fairly frequently used, that it was of amateur make, and that, as the commissaire suggested, it was possibly the key of a safe.

Pointer looked it over carefully too. Mackay stared at it hard.

"It's not unlike one Mr. Davidson had in that pocketbook he lost," he said finally. "I'm na sure o' course. He juist said twa keys, and described them. Now, wud it be possible to send this to Mr. Davidson?"

The commissaire explained that that would be quite impossible. If Mr. Mackay really thought the key tallied with that lost by his employer, a subpoena would be at once issued, and Mr. Davidson would have to appear in person. The key could not be allowed to leave the Hotel de ville, where it would be deposited within the hour.

Mackay scratched his chin.

"He wud be pleased!" he murmured to Pointer. "He's juist stairted in on a maist important job. If he was ca'd off doon here, whether it was his key or no, he'd shoot me for having brought him awa frae Paris juist the noo. I'll na risk it."

He looked at the key again. "The mair I study it, the less resemblance I find to Mr. Davidson's," he said finally; "and that's true enough. Not juist said to avoid being shot by Davidson."

"Probably it belonged to Sir Cross," Cambier said, taking it back and carefully locking it in his steel box. "We knew that it was not Monsieur Brownlow's. Or at least we have cause to think so. Ladies are as a rule only too eager to get hold of the keys of their husband's safes— their contents are not subject to death duties with us, you know. But as to who dropped it by that gate—why it was flung away. . . ." Cambier stood looking down at his locked box as though it were a crystal.

"I ask myself if it was not some one who thought himself suspected," Rondeau burst out. "I might wonder, for instance, if the some one who had taken it had not taken something more valuable, say the pocket-book which contained this key, and that he did not want the key, and flung it away as being only an additional danger if found on him. Flung it from a motor car, say—in other words I ask myself if Tibbitts was not the loser. The man who left so very very early and has not returned—"

"Tranquilize yourself," murmured Cambier; "even should he not intend to return—which would be absurd with that nice little duel set in the cedar room as I have told you before—still, should he not return, thanks to Detective Good-luck we should not have the slighest difficulty in tracing his car. I will ease your mind by telling you that that is being done now. At this minute."

Turning to Pointer the commissaire explained that a car of similar make, and with an all but similar number, had been wanted for a long time for vine-stealing on a large scale from the vineyards around. It was a French make, bought in Lyons.

"We said nothing about it to Monsieur Brownlow, but twice his has been stopped by over-zealous gendarmes because he was driving her."

"Yes, and I ask myself why he did not resent those stoppages and questionings," Rondeau said, in the tone of one who intends this time to finish his sentence, come what may.

"Now Rondeau, I beg you!" his chief threw in, but in vain.

"I have been talking with one of the agents who did the stopping, and I ask myself why a man should be polite when he had a right to be angry. Why Monsieur Brownlow was always polite to the police—almost deprecating. As though he wished, at all costs, to avoid any trouble with them. And that makes me proceed to—"

"To superintend the search in the gardens, my lad. From end to end," finished Cambier. "You are younger than I am, so that a couple of years spent in probing into the reasons for Monsieur Brownlow's ordinary civility means nothing to you, but at my age time is more valuable. *Allez, travailler!* Here comes the *juge*. Once he gets indoors, of course, all hopes of keeping it to ourselves that there is a crime to investigate will be gone," He gave his orders to the sergeant. From now on every one coming to and going from the villa, unless well-known tradesmen or the men investigating the case, were to be followed. All telephone messages were to be taken down. All letters banded to him, Cambier, to distribute.

CHAPTER EIGHT

MONSIEUR GRANDPOINT, the *juge* in question, was at the villa before Cambier had finished speaking. He was a severe-looking man, with a narrow forehead and bleak eyes. In manner he was distant but very patient, with a patience that was inexorable rather than gentle. He could be a formidable cross-examiner, unhurried and persistent. But he absolutely agreed with Monsieur Pichegru that the latter could be of no more help to the police in Cluny than in Dijon, and of infinitely greater use to himself in the latter place. Monsieur Pichegru's alibi had been tested. There was not a moment of last night when he had not been accounted for.

On being asked to tell them all he could about Tibbitts, before he left, he said at once that he knew very little about that young man. As a rule, he was exceedingly careful who his guests were. He felt that he owed this to his neighbors, he added, with a bow to the *juge* who bowed in return. But unfortunately in the case of Tibbitts—Pichegru explained that the young man was the Brownlows' protege, who had come upon him at Monte Carlo making ducks and drakes of his money and getting into a most undesirable set. When Brownlow, came to Cluny to recuperate, Tibbitts had accompanied the pair. He, Pichegru, had not cared for his presence in the house, but Mrs. Brownlow had been so sorry for the oaf that he had not liked to press the point. They were all three leaving shortly to return to England.

Mrs. Brownlow had told him that she had an idea that Tibbitts had been a clerk in a drapery shop when he came into a big fortune. Mr. Murgatroyd had happened to mention to him, only last night, that undoubtedly the young man had been a metal worker of some kind, that his knowledge of foundry work was first-hand and thorough. Pichegru had no further information apparently to give on the subject of the young man. Questioned as to Tibbitts's infatuation for Mrs. Brownlow, an infatuation which the *juge* had noticed when he had dined at the villa, Pichegru, with a faint smile, said that it was Tibbitts's one redeeming trait. Certainly Brownlow had not seemed to mind it. Not in the least. Monsieur Pichegru was quite certain on this point.

"About that journey to Paris a fortnight ago, in the *rapide,* when two of your guests lost, the one a large sum of money, the other some very valuable, and insufficiently insured jewels, monsieur," put in the commissaire; "Tibbitts was one of the party, was he not?"

Monsieur Pichegru agreed that Tibbitts had been there, as had Monsieur Smith.

Now Smith was still considered by the police as definitely out of the possible suspects—like Monsieur Pichegru himself. Not only was he a subaltern in a crack regiment, a cavalry regiment, but last night he had been in the public eye practically all the time.

True, it only takes one second to fire a shot that kills a man, and only two, therefore, to kill two men; but in Smith's case there really seemed no motive to raise any suspicion of his having played a part in the tragedy.

Monsieur Pichegru was asked a few more questions and then dismissed to his car with the official blessing, as it were. And the *juge* turned his attention to the real members of the circle. He proposed an interview with Mrs. Brownlow first of all.

The *juge* had dined at the villa only a fortnight ago and had talked to the Brownlows a good deal. More to Mrs. Brownlow than to her husband, but then, all men did that. And she was his compatriot by birth.

The four of them were shown into her sitting-room now. She was seated in front of a writing-table, apparently reading old letters. Very evidently she had been crying.

At the sight of the *juge* she rose to greet him with a gasp of surprise.

"Oh, how glad I am to see you!" she said prettily.

"Madam, prepare yourself for a shock," the *juge* said gently; "the doctors have just handed in their final report. And everything is changed. Monsieur Brownlow died about half an hour after Sir Anthony Cross. You understand? There was no duel. It could not have been Sir Anthony Cross who killed your husband. The revolvers lying beside each man were blinds. False evidence. Yet we still think that a bullet from the revolver of Monsieur Brownlow killed Sir Anthony Cross. And your husband could have fired it, madam. You comprehend?"

Mrs. Brownlow looked too stunned to understand anything. She covered her face with her hands for a long moment. They were trembling violently.

"I understand your emotion, madam," the *juge* said, with a touch of real feeling. "Would that I could respect it and leave you to your thoughts—your memories. But I must continue. It is quite possible that both men were shot down by a third person, for we have just been told that Sir Anthony Cross was the head of a large diamond syndicate. The South African Diamond Combine."

Mrs. Brownlow lowered her hands to her lap very slowly. Over her face came the look of a wanderer who, lost in the dark, at last catches sight of a light.

"So *that* was why!" she breathed. "Not on my account. Thank heaven! But because he was helping Sir Anthony Cross in some deal, my husband was shot down!"

"Helping Sir Cross in a deal?" repeated Cambier; "you said no word of that before, madam!"

"I never thought of it till now. I thought that it was I—that it was over me—" She drew a deep breath. "But, as a matter of fact, Mr. Brownlow was acting for the time-being as a sort of secret go-between for Sir Anthony, either for the purchase of, or the sale of, some big stone or stones. I think that was why he went to Paris a couple of weeks ago. The time when I lost my jewels in the *rapide* on joining him."

"But this is very interesting!" said the *juge*. Every one nodded. "But I thought there was ill will between your husband and Sir Anthony?"

"Not until this visit down here. But when I was told that a duel had been fought, it seemed that it must have been over me. For"—she looked at Cambier—"as I told the commissaire, Sir Anthony and I were thinking of going away together. It was madness on my part—a passing madness. But I feared that my husband must have learned of our intention. I never even gave a thought to the possibility of murder!"

"And this business between the two? Can you be more explicit, madam?"

"About a month, or six weeks ago, I happened to notice my husband reading a letter in Sir Anthony Cross's hand-writing. I saw him tear it up very carefully into tiny scraps. I asked him how he came to be hearing from our—old friend he had once been very jealous of him and me—and why he said nothing about the letter to me. He told me that Sir Anthony wanted him to undertake 'a rather delicate bit of business'"—she gave the last words in English—"that the terms were so tempting that he intended to accept, but that the business in question was a close secret between himself and Sir Anthony. That he would not have spoken of it even to me yet, but for my noticing the writing. He went into no details. And I may even be wrong in thinking that the visit to Paris was connected with the receipt of that letter. But I think it was. Or he would have taken me with him. When I ran across Sir Anthony down here in Cluny, I thought, of course, that he had come to see Tom. But neither man would acknowledge as much. At least, Tom refused to say one way or another, only he told me to be sure and refer to the meeting at the table so as to give him a chance of speaking of Sir Anthony before the others. When I did so, he himself spoke as though it were years since he had heard from Sir Anthony. Sir Anthony was coming in after dinner for a chat, so he had said, when I met him. My husband told me to have everything look like a mere chance meeting of old friends. He was most insistent on this point. So insistent" —she passed a hand across her eyes—"that now I realize that he believed there was danger in anything else. But whom did he dread? Who was there at the table with us who had to be misled?"

She stared at the men with fear-distended eyes.

"The man who took the revolvers and locked that cedar room door from the outside—but with the key on the inside," Cambier said gravely. "And, now can you tell us whether the murderer might have obtained possession of your husband's pistol fairly easily?"

"Very easily indeed. My husband kept his automatic in that little locked cabinet on the wall, there where you see the crossed foils. The key was always in the copper vase standing on the top of the cabinet."

"It does not seem to have called for a vast amount of scheming to obtain possession of the weapon," Cambier murmured dryly; "but who would know of the place where it was kept?"

She thought a moment.

"I think all the other guests must have seen him take it out or put it back. The shooting gallery is on this floor, you know—the picture gallery which Monsieur Pichegru uses for that purpose. And on dull afternoons my husband used to practice with our host, and with Mr. Tibbitts, too, a good deal."

"Ah, with Monsieur Tibbitts," nodded Cambier. "With no one else?"

"With Mr. Smith, of course. And yesterday with Miss Young."

"Ah," murmured the *juge*; "Mademoiselle Young—she can shoot then?"

"Very well indeed. She beat Monsieur Pichegru, and

he is as good as my husband was."

"And Monsieur Tibbitts, was he good?"

"I don't think so. But, really, I don't know."

There was a short pause. Cambier broke it. "So then, if Sir Cross was equally easygoing as to the place, probably his bag, where he kept his revolver last night, it, too, could have been obtained quite easily. . . ."

"However it was managed about the revolvers," Mrs. Brownlow spoke as though that part of it were of small importance; "at least their deaths have nothing to do with me! I shall not have to drag out my days under a feeling of guilt almost too heavy to be borne."

". . . And the revolvers were changed afterwards—changed to put us off the track," Cambier murmured slowly.

"By the man who shot my husband," she finished. "Unless, of course, they might have been changed by accident. Monsieur Smith, and Mademoiselle Young, and the butler, were all in the room before you came. So was I, of course. How easy to take up the weapons to look at and get them mixed in putting them down again. But of one thing I feel sure. My husband either disturbed the murderer of Sir Anthony, or, equally with Sir Anthony, was in the murderer's way. And because of that, both men were killed."

"And then the scene was set for a duel. . . ." Cambier nodded.

"How about your husband's papers?" asked the *juge*; "we must look through them, madam."

"Certainly. But he kept few notes. He prided himself on his memory. As to business papers, they would, I expect, be in his London safe. In the city. His partner is a Mr. Tenby," she gave the address; "but he would know nothing of any business between my husband and Sir Anthony. He was not at all in Mr. Brownlow's confidence, except as regards the actual business of the firm."

She sank back as though exhausted, and certainly looked it.

"Oh, my poor head!" she gasped. "Please send for Dr. Bourelly; I feel so faint. Perhaps Miss Young would come to me?"

"We will see to it that she is asked to come, though first I want to have a little talk with her. But, madam, for the moment, not a word to any one of what has been discovered by the doctors. Not a word. Not to any one!" the *juge* repeated impressively.

On that they left her. Half-way down the stairs the sergeant met them.

"We have news of Monsieur Tibbitts. He was last seen driving very fast away from Autun."

"From Autun? That means he's making for Paris!" ejaculated Rondeau. "And as a rule—"

"I permit myself to suggest that, before giving us that rule, you thoroughly investigate Monsieur Tibbitts's rooms at once," his chief threw in with ominous politeness. Rondeau leaped up the stairs again and whizzed round the corner like a skater.

"He is as good at finding truffles as any pig in the land," Cambier said tolerantly; "only he lacks experience when it comes to cooking them. But he will make a good detective in time. Oh, much, much time—when he ceases to ask himself so many questions." He rapidly explained to the *juge* as they passed downstairs how Tibbitts came to be making for Autun, or Paris, in Brownlow's fast car.

A moment later there came a theatrical whisper of "*Mon chef!*" down the stairs. Rondeau was beckoning excitedly.

"Shall we see what he has found?" Cambier asked Pointer.

Mackay attached himself to them, and the three joined the commissaire's *aide* in the large room that had been assigned to Tibbitts on his arrival with the Brownlows. It was rather a bare-looking place, but a couple of folding double doors, now locked, connected with the Brownlow's rooms.

Rondeau was holding out a pair of dancing pumps. On

the glass-smooth soles were smears of reddish brown.

Cambier took them from him and touched the stains with something from a bottle that he had put in his pocket early that morning. They were bloodstains. The commissaire whipped off his own footwear and looked at the soles closely.

"No there are no marks on mine."

Nor were there on the shoes of Chief Inspector Pointer or Mackay.

"These shoes of Monsieur Tibbitts—if they are really his —walked over that carpet downstairs in the cedar room when the bloodstains there were quite fresh."

Now, though he did not need to recall it to the minds of any of them, the only stains on the carpet were around Sir Anthony Cross. That unfortunate man had fallen sideways. Certain marks made it look as though he had raised himself on his elbow and shifted his position before he died, though they now knew that he had not, as had been at first thought, then fired the shot that killed Brownlow outright.

"So Monsieur Tibbitts was in this cedar room, apparently. And probably he could have possessed himself without any great difficulty of the revolvers of both Sir Cross and Mr. Brownlow. Also, he must have been aware of the jealousy between the two men, and might have known of madam's intention of leaving her husband with the other man. Monsieur Tibbitts is supposed to have been helped to bed in a state—well, verging on intoxication. That might be a clever ruse. A very clever one."

"Then it wasna Tibbitts's," Mackay said contemptuously.

"Ah, do not be too sure!" Cambier retorted meaningly; "these stupid young men can be very clever sometimes. Rememher that one of the men murdered was one of those who helped him up to bed—would be convinced, therefore, of his helplessness. That would lull any suspicions to rest—supposing even Brownlow had them.

And yet would leave the butler to report the occurrence to us. A very useful alibi is helpless drunkeness."

Cambier and Rondeau both searched the room from end to end but they found nothing more. Of any such pliers, or nippers, as would have been necessary to lock the cedar room door as it had been locked, they found no sign.

What they did find was a strange mixture of wear. Tibbitts's underclothes varied from silken splendor, bought, judging by its little tag, in Monte Carlo, to cotton, very much in need of mending, or the dustbin.

Cambier, leading the way, then locked the door, and rejoined the *juge* in the writing-room, where he sat reading over the notes.

Cambier showed him the shoes.

"He forgot these," he said laconically. "Some day there'll be a criminal with a really good memory. But, so far, there is not."

"And this young man was very infatuated with Madam Brownlow, as I myself noticed," the *juge* mused. "We will see about identifying the shoes."

This was done within ten minutes. They were undoubtedly Tibbitts's.

The commissaire turned to Mackay.

"You must have had your suspicions of this Tibbitts, monsieur, or you would not have been staying down here. You, who are on the hunt for the stolen money."

Hitherto the private investigator had been only tolerated as far as the police went, now he moved up into the position of an ally.

Mackay was answering with caution. A caution that impressed the commissaire. This man had brains. Only a man with brains, in the commissaire's opinion, held his tongue. Cambier finally drew out of Mackay the confession that he believed it possible that Tibbitts had stolen the sum of money lost by Mr. Davidson.

"Did Monsieur Davidson suspect his fellow guest and fellow traveler of having stolen his money?" the *juge* asked Mackay. The private inquiry agent nodded.

"Aye, he suspects him strongly, as is logical. But we have nae proof. Nor am I sure in ma ain mind that it was he who took money or jewels."

"Monsieur thinks?" queried the *juge*.

"I have a notion that it was Brownlow," Mackay said, after a moment's hesitation.

"Brownlow!" All the men stared at the private inquiry agent in surprise. "But the drugging—" Cambier protested.

"Oh, Tibbitts was an accomplice, no doubt. But I have na heard anything that proves that the money and the jewels werna stolen before the train started. Brownlow was at the station to see his wife off. He claimed—and would have got the insurance put on them. A low enough insurance, but five hundred is a useful bit o' siller. In ma opeenion," Mackay said finally, "the jewels were too peculiar to have been stolen by a clever thief. Broken up, they would not have been of any great value. None of the stones was of remarkable size as far as I can learn."

"But Brownlow is a wealthy man!" protested Cambier.

"Are you sure?" Mackay asked sceptically. "If he's in Chinese silks, then he's in troubled waters these years."

"That might explain why he was so willing to take on the offer of Sir Cross," mused Cambier.

"Supposing that it was ever made," Mackay said to Pointer.

"*Quoi?*" asked the *juge*, catching the tone.

Mackay repeated his remark in his Scottish-French.

The *juge* raised his very arched eyebrows.

"You think Madam Brownlow was lying?"

Mackay refused to commit himself to that, but she had not convinced him that she was telling the truth, he said. Not at any time throughout the interview.

"So far, I see no reason to doubt her statement," the *juge* said coldly. "She is a lady for whom all we who know her have the greatest respect. As for her husband—my only impression of him was of a well-traveled, well-educated man. A man of the world."

But coming back to Mackay's doubts of the lady's statement, the *juge* wanted to know what caused them.

"Sir Anthony wasna a seller or buyer of diamonds," Mackay went on; "and he wad hae mony a mon to his hand if he wanted some particular stane. It doesna stand to reason that he wad hae written to a mon he hadna had any dealings wi' for years juist to dae a thing like yon for him. Brownlow was in silk—not gems."

"Still, in the case of some particular stone or gem wanted, that would not matter," the *juge* said slowly. "The Brownlows had just come from Monte Carlo, where the most amazing jewels can be seen at times. I can imagine that Sir Anthony had noticed the Brownlows' name as present at some dinner or entertainment given by the person whose jewels he hoped to buy. Oh, at Monte Carlo dinners are given with no other reason at times! No, Monsieur Mackay, I think you are prejudiced in your suspicions of Brownlow. But pray, proceed. Do I understand that you doubt madam's account of the letter that she claims her husband received from *le feu baron?*"

"Perhaps I was over hasty in saying what I have," Mackay now confessed. "I go a bit carried awa', and that's the truth.

"For myself," Cambier said decidedly; "for myself, the criminal, so far, seems Tibbitts. We know that the key on the inside of the door has been turned with very up-to-date ring nippers. By an expert. Who would be more skilful in their use than the metal worker Tibbitts? I believe—I myself—that this young man tacked himself on to the Brownlows because of Monsieur Brownlow's intention of joining a big banking concern in Lyons, the Banque Agricole et Commerciale. He was considering, so we have been informed for some time, the opening of a branch in London, after he had become a partner. In spite of your suspicions, Monsieur Mackay, I can assure you that your dead compatriot was considered in banking circles in Lyons as a man of considerable, though tied-up means. Yes," Cambier repeated thoughtfully, "it looks to me as though this Tibbitts had thrown himself in the way of the future banker at Monte Carlo and played both at being a fool, and a rich fool. It is only an idea, but—"

"But it fits!" echoed Rondeau enthusiastically. "I asked myself more than once why a young man should bury himself here in Cluny. Even the fine eyes of madam would hardly compensate for the lack of other things to look at."

They were back at the villa, and the *juge* proposed to question Mrs. Brownlow once more, this time with a view to further information about Tibbitts. But Mrs. Brownlow was no help whatever. She had not the faintest idea, she said, who Tibbitts was, nor whence he came. All she knew was that at Monte Carlo he was so obviously a sheep waiting for the shearers that first her husband, and then she herself, had been interested in the young man.

"Why in him especially?" Mackay wanted to know. "If it was juist that the sprockle flung his sillar aboot daft like."

Mrs. Brownlow looked a trifle impatient.

"How can one say why one is sorry for one person and not for another?" she asked in the tone of one putting an unanswerable question. "Perhaps it was because he seemed to like us so much. My husband doesn't often care for young men of his type, but he asked me to do what I could to get him away from the set with whom he was mixing. I did. And the result was that Mr. Tibbitts followed us here, or perhaps that's too strong a word, but when he asked if he could come too, as he was at a loose end for a fortnight, neither Tom nor I minded. Personally, I was glad. The poor boy at least was grateful for what we had done and were trying to do for him."

There was a pause. The *juge* broke it.

"Well, he may come back to the house any moment. He may have had a breakdown, and this absence that looks so doubtful be explained, but it looks odd. Very odd."

Mrs. Brownlow gave a sort of strangled cry.

"You don't mean that you suspect Mr. Tibbitts of — she stopped, as though too appalled to finish the sentence. The idea seemed to stun her.

"There are several things about him that have an odd appearance," the *juge* said quietly. "And there is another point. I am sorry to grieve you, madam, but I must refer to something that you told us. Do you think that this Monsieur Tibbitts knew that you were about to run away with Sir Anthony Cross?"

Mrs. Brownlow's eyes widened. Evidently this was a new idea.

"You mean that he—that because—" she broke off, trembling a little.

"It might explain the murder of Sir Anthony. It might explain the murder of your husband," the *juge* said slowly. "Mind, I do not say that it does. Or that it will. All I say is 'it might.' But there is this, madam; we have here a young man of whom nothing seems to be known to his credit who could possibly have, or think he had, a motive to kill either or both of the men we have found dead. That connection between their deaths may not be the business bond which for the moment linked your husband and his old friend, but it may be in this young man's evil mind. Jealous of the friend—jealous of the husband."

She seemed thunderstruck.

"But what—you must have something to go on," she said finally.

He did not reply.

"It may have been no affair of the heart," Cambier now put in; "but a much baser motive. Going back to that time, a fortnight ago, when you lost your jewels on the *rapide*—" He questioned her very closely as to the movements of each member of the party. So did Mackay. The upshot was that Tibbitts was by no means cleared of the possibility of being the thief of both money and jewels lost on that occasion. Each of the four had had a compartment to themselves. The whole carriage had been empty but for them. Three of them next morning claimed to have been drugged. But Tibbitts had insisted on the doctor attending to him last of all. At the time, Mrs. Brownlow now said, she had put it down to unselfishness. Now it transpired that when Tibbitts's turn came he had been able to stagger up and go for a walk in the air, and that, therefore, he received no medical attention whatever.

Cambier raised his eyebrows. But he made no comment.

Further questioned, she agreed that Tibbitts had shown a remarkable knowledge of metal work while with herself, Miss Young, and Mr. Murgatroyd. Up till then she had thought that he had been a clerk in a little haberdashery shop somewhere in the Midlands.

She had not seen Tibbitts since just before, or after, supper last night. She forgot which. Her husband had told her, in answer to some casual inquiry on her part, that he had helped him to his room.

"You think," she asked, her hand held to her head, "that Tibbitts had got on the track of whatever it was that my husband was doing for Sir Anthony Cross? And that that was why he seemed so devoted to us? That he didn't care really for either my husband or me?"

The silence of the men told her that that was exactly what they did think. The *juge* began some questionings about the letters from Sir Anthony.

Pointer meanwhile moved quietly around the room towards the book-shelves. Taken unawares, and a violent death nearly always takes a man unawares, much can be learned of his character from what he reads. More than from the companions he keeps. For the latter may be chosen for reasons of diplomacy or business, and not from liking. There were several rows of light reading, probably sent up by Monsieur Pichegru for the use of Mrs. Brownlow as well as of her husband. Suddenly his glance stopped and went back to a preceding row. Yes, he was right. There was a French as well as an English translation here of Assomoff's *Along the Old Trade Routes of Kublai Khan*. The English book looked quite new, the French was very old and neglected, yet apparently its leaves had only just been cut, for the top edges showed like curly antennae. He took out the English translation, which was from a later edition, and had come from a shop in Paris. Brownlow's initials were inside the cover. Only three pages had been cut, he saw, and they were in the middle of the book. Pointer wondered what subject had so interested Brownlow—one of the dead men—that he had apparently had a dip into both books, his own and Pichegru's, for the French copy was not likely to be in the room, unless Brownlow himself had taken it upstairs.

Standing back of the lady, who was utterly engrossed in her talk with the police, Pointer turned the three pages. One he held level with his eyes. A mark had been put to a sentence, and then rubbed out, and very carefully smoothed down. It was this last that interested him most. The sentence in question merely spoke of a road that here joined another road, the first one leading to Krasny, with its nomad herdsmen, and of the writer seeing a camel-caravan bound for the town. That was all.

A little French brochure stood beside it. A French translation of Sven Hedin's comments on the Russian work. Here again a mark had been rubbed out. The marked passage concerned the course of the Uluh Kema river, which, the great explorer pointed out, ran in a different direction to that assigned it by Assomoff, with the remark that the town of Krasny would have to be moved some hundred miles farther towards the Gobi Desert to be able to stand on the bank of the river as the latter was sketched in *Along the Old Trade Routes*.

Pointer put English translation and French brochure back and picked up the next book. It was a French treatise on *The Territories of the Soviet Union*. It was of the current year. Here again, only part of the pages had been cut. This was the section dealing with the Turco-Mongolian races.

The writer was fond of flowery phrases and disliked precision. Pointer gleaned much unsought-for information of a vague kind, but finally he came on one familiar word. The name of a town. And again that town was Krasny. Mr. Brownlow seemed to have a genuine interest in the place.

He carefully looked at each of the other serious works. They had not been even handled, for every volume, as he lifted it, showed a little scollop of fine dust on the shelf where it stood. Evidently the feather whisk of the maid had only given the shelves a flick, and evidently Mr. Brownlow was a man of narrow tastes. But when he reached the last volume, a fat book on *Chess Openings*, he found a glossy surface below it. Yet the book was some thirty years old, and could hardly interest a man able to obtain up-to-date works on chess. Pointer's interest, therefore, was in what might lie behind it. From this dark nook he drew out a little Turkish-English grammar with a sheet of paper in it. The writing on the paper was the same as that on the letters in Mrs. Brownlow's lap at the moment. Brownlow had evidently been working out an exercise. Now Pointer's hobby was the learning of languages. He knew nothing that so rested the mind wearied with heavy thinking. At the very moment he was learning Persian, working just as Brownlow evidently had been doing. But Farsi is the same, beautiful, elegant, flexible for the traveler as for Hafiz. But no one ever learned Turkish because of its literature. It has none. Surely it was not for the purpose of reading the speeches of Mustapha Kemal Pasha in the original, that Brownlow was working out the Osmanlee equivalent for "The miller's daughter has the cat"? Besides, Turkish, such as this little grammar taught, was only for traveling purposes. It is not the Turkish spoken by the upper classes. It is really Tartar, the *lingua franca* far and wide in Asia.

So Brownlow was preparing himself to travel somewhere where this language would carry him. . . . To

Krasny? Turco-Mongolian Krasny? Pointer replaced the grammar and the fat book on chess and turned away. The others were preparing to leave Mrs. Brownlow alone again. He followed them down into the writing-room, used by the *juge* for the moment as the consulting room. Cambier asked the chief inspector if he would find out through Scotland Yard if anything were known about— which meant against—Tibbitts. Pichegru had left them a snap-shot cut from a group that Murgatroyd had taken. And they also had what it was reasonable to assume were the young man's finger-prints on many objects in his bedroom.

"As I say, in his case, Detective Good-luck will be our best assistant," Cambier said with an anticipatory smile. "Even now my *agent* is tracking that car, village by village, on its route. Luckily no remark was ever allowed to leak out as to its number. Therefore no comment could ever have reached Tibbitts to show him how much attention it roused in every policeman whom he passed."

A *portrait parle* was at once drawn up of the missing man. That is to say, a catalogue of his features classified with a truly French minuteness of detail. By these "portraits" of their's they claim that their detectives can pierce through any disguise to the anatomical features of the face sought for. In practice Pointer knew that the French, lose far more criminals than we do, just as he was aware of the vast number, comparatively speaking, of wrongly-condemned persons languishing in their terrible prisons. As to disguise, nothing can pierce a really excellently done one, seen hurriedly, or in a place that is out of keeping with the criminal's position in life.

Though there was a long list of "wanted" men in France, who, like Landru, did not even trouble to disguise themselves, did not give up one of their usual habits; merely changed their address, and ignored detection, *portrait parle* and all.

Meanwhile, Rondeau was told by telephone that the car of Brownlow's which interested the police had been located at several more places along the route nationale leading to Paris, but was not yet caught up with. Probably the end would come in Paris itself.

"His arrest is only a matter of hours," Cambier said with evident relish.

"Just so. And in the meantime, we will question the other lady in the house." The *juge* pushed away the pile of notebooks. "There are odd circumstances connected with Mademoiselle Young. I do not mind saying that I find her behavior throughout very strange. I will leave it at that, gentlemen. But we will now confront the silent fiancé of the dead baron and hear what she has to say about the changed situation— about the murder of two men, and not about any supposed duel between them."

Vivian was already downstairs in the lounge. The news of the arrival of the *juge* d'instruction at the house had spread among the servants. The upper housemaid had whispered to her that something fresh must have turned up—something most important.

"The *juge* is in the sitting-room of Madam Brownlow," finished the maid in a confidential whisper; "he is well advised to turn to her!" She pulled herself up on that and would not explain her meaning.

Apart from her words, Vivian felt something stirring around her. And when she went downstairs, the perturbed faces of the servants, whose look of decorous shock for the fatal duel was now replaced by a very personal disquietude. would have told her that something quite new was on hand.

CHAPTER NINE

VIVIAN stared at the stony look on all four faces turned to her. On Mackay's features such an expression meant a warning, she felt sure. A warning that something important was afoot, and that she should be careful. The eyes of the *juge* were like icicle points. She took an instant dislike to Monsieur Grandpoint. One of those dislikes that are always mutual.

"Mademoiselle," he began sternly, after the preliminary introduction; "why did you not tell us that Sir Anthony Cross, your fiancé, was down here to meet Mr. Brownlow on business?"

Vivian was more amazed by the question than she had been since the discovery of the two dead bodies. But she was a reporter. A very good one. Trained to keep her face under control. She did not show any signs of the surprise that she felt.

"Because I did not know it," she replied coolly. "Is it a fact?"

"You had no idea that Sir Anthony was down here in Cluny except to run away with Madam Brownlow?" he asked sarcastically.

Vivian caught her breath.

"I don't understand," she said after a second. "I guess there's something new happened that I haven't heard of."

Still she spoke in a calm tone that made the *juge* privately believe that she knew all this already.

"We have learned that there was no duel," he said very coldly. And proceeded to tell her what he had just told Mrs. Brownlow.

Vivian only opened her eyes a little at the end. She glanced once during the recital at Mackay who nodded imperceptably. As for Pointer, he only watched her with his pleasant gaze that gave sharp-witted Vivian the feeling that she was made of glass.

"No, there was no duel," the *juge* repeated again; "but there are two murders. Two crimes. Possibly connected with this visit of Sir Anthony to our quiet little town. Possibly not connected with that visit at all."

"Oh, yes, it was. too!" Vivian spoke, as she had to listen partly, through Pointer. A proper interpreter was on his way from Lyons, but for the moment the chief inspector filled the post.

"My! Yes, it was!" she repeated Anthony Cross's words to her of expecting to get some information down here in Cluny from a man whom he was going to meet. The *juge* listened attentively. Vivian, after a second's hesitation, went on to speak of the constant thefts from parcels of diamonds sent to and from Amsterdam which had brought Sir Anthony to France in the first place.

"And you said nothing of this 'mission' of Sir Anthony's up till now? Not when he was found shot?" the *juge* asked very quietly.

"I thought, like every one else, that it was a duel. I guess I thought that more than any one else," she said firmly. "And that being so, Sir Anthony had asked me to consider everything he told me about the losses to his company as absolutely confidential." She went on to say that she understood from him that inquiries were on foot which any talk or publicity might quite frustrate. She, personally, knew nothing about these inquiries, except the fact of their existence. Sir Anthony had only referred to them in general terms, as explaining what had brought him to Europe just now.

The *juge* thought a moment. Adjusting his gold-rimmed glasses, he sat for another moment reading through a page, of notes.

"You say Sir Anthony knew that you were coming down to Cluny, and yet he, who was also coming down here, did not accompany you?" There was something like disbelief in the cold eyes on her. "And you made no effort to see him here? To meet him?"

She explained that he had wished it so.

"You had not quarreled with him about his coming down here?" The *juge* spoke as though he doubted all that she had told him.

Vivian again repeated what she had said. "Sir Anthony was coming down to Cluny on business, so he told me," she finished. "And for that reason we did not come together. I doubted whether the reason that was bringing him down was really business when I recognized Mrs. Brownlow from a picture I had seen him looking at not long before. And because of that doubt of mine, I came here to the villa. But it was due to his own wish that we should not be seen together, that we met, as we did, outside the house."

"Mrs. Brownlow's portrait—" Cambier pulled at his moustache.

"And yet," the inexorable voice of the *juge* went on; "yet, mademoiselle, knowing what he had told you of what brought him to Cluny, you did not connect the two deaths with this errand of his, this so secret errand?"

"Certainly not. Because I was told it was a duel, and because I had seen for myself that Mr. Brownlow was jealous of him. I guess motives were a bit twisted up all around. Also, I sure didn't reflect that a man can be doing business with another and yet have a private grudge against him."

"M-m-m," hemmed the *juge*. Again there was a silence. Strictly speaking only the *juge*, when he was present, could question a witness. Some leaves in a notebook turned by him was all that broke the rather tense stillness of the room.

"Apparently, mademoiselle, you were the last person to see Sir Anthony Cross alive?" There was something ominous in his stare. The words came with harsh emphasis.

"I guess the man who shot him was the real last," she

said composedly. It was a composure that did not please Monsieur Grandpoint. He thought Vivian hard. And truth compels one to admit that not even her best friend could call her soft. Just now, however, all personal grief had been dynamited away by the startling news that Anthony Cross's death was a crime. And a most puzzling riddle.

Vivian's very eagerness to understand, to solve the riddle, took the whole fact of the death away, as far as she was concerned, from the heart—the warm realm of feeling—into the mind, that cool place where problems dwell.

"But, putting the moment of his murder on one side," the *juge* resumed; "you, I say, mademoiselle, are the last person of whom we have any record who spoke to the dead man. Now that is a very important point."

He said this last very meaningly. Pointer translated. Vivian's French was a little clouded by her anxiety not to understand it wrongly.

"Say, don't let him forget that they learned that point from me!" she said with her usual spirit.

"Oh, quite so!" agreed the *juge*; "told us, however, while his death seemed to be due to a duel. But to pass that by for the time being, kindly tell us, once more, exactly what Sir Anthony was doing when you saw him in the cedar room."

Vivian went into every detail that she could remember. The *juge* worried her. Her own very anxiety tripped her up sometimes. And every fresh detail, or trifle, that she mentioned, would be met by the harsh remark of, "You did not mention that before, I think." Vivian would reply that she had not remembered it till now, or not thought it worth noticing. It was a true French scene. Utterly hopeless from the point of view of helping an innocent person who really was trying to aid the law, though well calculated to confuse a guilty man or woman. Pointer had met it before. He knew the French theory that when a witness adds anything to their first testimony, this addition is to be considered as most suspect. As either unconscious self-deception, or conscious effort to "embroider" the plain facts, as Cambier put it.

The *juge* finally rose.

"Now, mademoiselle, kindly accompany us into the next room and show us how, and where, each of the bodies was lying. You were the first to reach both."

Vivian hesitated for a fraction of a second.

"It's not fair," Mackay began hotly in an undertone to Pointer; "they didn't ask that of the wife. Then why of the lassie?"

"You forget Mrs. Brownlow's a Frenchwoman by birth," Pointer said dryly.

Vivian quickly overcame her shrinking from the thought of again stepping into that room where but a few hours before she had seen so horrible a sight. Leading the way in now, she explained very carefully what she had seen.

The *juge* studied the photographs which he held.

"And you say that you passed over to Sir Anthony, stepping just beside Mr. Brownlow's out-flung right hand?"

Vivian nodded.

"It must have been a narrow passage way between that hand, and that table leg there."

"It was," she agreed; "but I don't take up yards of room."

"No. And the revolver, where was it?"

Vivian looked at him for a second, a long, intent look. Then she stared at the part of the floor of which they were talking.

"You have forgotten the revolver?" the *juge* asked icily. "You have describe very closely many trifles, but you have forgotten to mention stepping over it?"

"It wasn't there," Vivian said finally.

"That means to say?" he asked, raising his eyebrows.

"That it certainly wasn't there—then. Oh, I know it's on that photograph probably. Now I come to think of it, it was lying close beside that table leg when I came back into the room, but some one must have moved it out a little—" she stopped herself.

"You said that you lifted his, Mr. Brownlow's, right arm to see if he were really dead."

"Yes, I lifted the hand, which lifted the arm."

"And you did not see the revolver underneath the arm either?"

"No." She spoke rather curtly. "No, judge, I didn't."

"Yet Monsieur Smith and Madam Brownlow and the butler all saw it lying out right where you claim to have stepped."

She made no reply. "It got moved out," she said again after a pause. The *juge* pursed his lips and made a note. He pointed out to her, quite dispassionately, that the leg of the table in question was one of those thick, solid, ormolu-mounted affairs which, dividing at the base into three equally solid branches supporting the table top, quite negatived the idea of the revolver having slipped farther away from the body before it had been inadvertently moved in closer.

"You are quite sure that you yourself did not move the revolver?" he asked finally. "You are quite sure that you did not change them in some way? For changed, of course, they were—by some one."

Vivian began an indignant protest. He raised a white, thin hand.

"*Doucement, mademoiselle, plus doucement!*" he said, drawing himself up. "I am here to ascertain the truth. Not to please you by my sympathetic remarks."

"I guess I don't care what you're here for, I didn't touch those revolvers!" she said indignantly as before, and from that stand she refused to be browbeaten. Finally, she was dismissed with a curt request to hold herself in readiness to answer further questions if necessary.

Vivian made a tart reply, which Pointer, for the once, softened in translation. She went up to her bedroom as in a dream. Not a duel—murder! Anthony had been murdered! And so had Mr. Brownlow!

Then that revolver had been "planted" so as to have the two dead men look as though they had fallen in what, in France, is still considered fair, if not lawful combat—a duel. The bullet that had killed Anthony fitted the weapon that had been found lying beside Brownlow's outstretched right hand. Of that there was no question. But how had that weapon got there? Or rather, when? For Vivian was certain that there had been no revolver in sight when she had first bent in shocked surprise over Brownlow's body. She had done more than lift a hand or an arm. She was very strong. She had half-raised the body to be sure that life was really extinct. There had been no revolver lying hidden beneath the dead man. But if not there then, how had it materialized later close to his hand? By whom, and when, and above all, why?

She, and Mrs. Brownlow, Mr. Smith, and the butler. . . . They four were known to have been in the room between the time she moved the body, without seeing any weapon, and the time when the weapon lay there for all to see. Also, possibly a maid had stepped in to help Mrs. Brownlow up to her room. But Vivian dismissed the servants. It was not as though either man had been killed in his own house. Here could be no question of feudal loyalty, she told herself grimly. But was there a gang at work? And like a flash came the thought of Mr. Lascelles—of the "Egyptian Lady," Jane Eastby, and of her evident fright lest Lascelles should open that cedar room door. What would he have seen? What would any one have seen? A dead man? There had been that in the woman's tone which made the terrible question ask itself now in Vivian's groping mind.

For Mrs. Eastby had tried to hide the urgency of her fear. Vivian saw again the forced and frightened smile with which she had pulled his hand away from the knob. And such a woman as Vivian had seen staring after Anthony Cross that first evening, the evening before the dance, would be capable of almost anything. Mrs. Eastby could not have produced that revolver, but what about an accomplice of hers?

Mrs. Eastby, Lascelles, Smith. . . . Was that the way the wheel turned? But Smith had not left the room this morning early until after she herself had returned from telephoning. Had he the revolver already on him? She mentally ran her eye over his trim chef's dress of white linen. It had fitted beautifully. But an automatic takes up little room. And if not Smith, then there only remained Mrs. Brownlow. Was it possible that it was she? Vivian remembered the smelling salts and the velvet handbag that Mrs. Brownlow had clutched as she ran past the telephone in the lounge where Vivian was trying to get Mackay. That handbag. . . . Now, in retrospect, Vivian seemed to notice how stiff and rigid it hung. Had it been heavy? Revolver heavy?

She tapped her even little teeth. She realized now that few are the crimes, and very simple, that are capable of being solved en bloc.

She went downstairs and found Mackay looking at the pewter plates that had so interested the chief inspector.

"They're too fussy for my taste," Vivian said, drawing him away. "Say, Mr. Mackay, that judge has a grouch against me."

"Na, na!" he protested. "Only you were a bit short wi' him. And in a republic, as you should ken weel, Miss Young, you mustna be short wi' officials. It's only in a monarchy that ye daur be rude to a mon in office."

"Instead of freezing me, if he'd only concentrated on that revolver that *wasn't* there when we first broke into that room this morning, he might give the case a shove forward. He didn't even see the point. That Englishman did though. I caught his eye."

Mackay's own eyes were on her now, waiting.

"As far as I can see," she went on in a low voice; "Smith could have produced the gun if he had had it on him. But Mrs. Brownlow could have fetched it, or its mate." She told him of the bag, the "smelling salts." "Mr.

Brownlow may easily have had a brace of automatics."

Vivian knew of many men who had always carried a pair. Such as her own revered father, for instance. Men who, like him, had to go into wild places. Such places as China was nowadays. Yes, Mr. Brownlow, once of Shanghai, might well have owned a pair of automatics. Or his wife might have had the mate to the one which he usually carried.

"There's nae logic in the supposition that the wife had any hand whatever in the deaths," Mackay began, in the didactic fashion that made Vivian want to laugh and want to pinch him at the same time.

"I'm not saying that she had," she retorted swiftly; "all I claim is that she muddled up the trails. And mind you, Mr. Mackay, she must have known at once what make of bullet had killed Anthony Cross. The bullet hadn't been extricated by then. She knew it so all-fired surely that she did on the instant the one thing that made it look like a duel. If she knew so much, did she know more?"

Vivian could not help it, but the wild words of her sister flashed through her mind.

"Aye, that's the point," Mackay conceded; "did she know, or didn't she?"

"But if Mrs. Brownlow mixed things up so as to start that duel idea," she went on in a still lower voice; "then she cared more than that should be thought, than that the murderer of her husband should be discovered. For she confused the trail hoplessly, as she thought. That looks " she hesitated.

"Hoo does it luik?" he asked slowly.

"As though she were protecting the man who killed him." Vivian's face was horrified at her own words.

"Na, na!" Mackay was positive on the point. "She couldna hae known o' her husband's death or she wud hae put the automatic doon then. That's logic. Besides, her whole manner tells that. She just grasped at the first straw that came to hand to save his reputation. And her own."

"Na, na!" Vivian imitated him. "She sacrificed her reputation. And now that we know it was no duel I can't for the life of me help wondering whether—well, whether things were as she represented them between Anthony and herself. She may have made more of that than really existed—supposing she knew that her husband shot Anthony Cross. She may have wanted every one to think he sure had cause for the shooting. You do get into some awful muddles if you don't stick to the truth," Vivian continued, with what an unkind observer might have called a reminiscent air. "And if she helped stage that duel idea by putting a revolver by her husband's side, she sure has made a muddle. But one can't blame the poor soul for trying to make things look their best for her husband. Any woman would do that."

Mackay felt that Vivian certainly would. She left him on that and went to the telephone. There was no question now of her leaving the villa. The *juge* had intimated as much in no uncertain way.

Her telephone conversation over, she waylaid Chief Inspector Pointer when he came out of the conference room, as the room beside the cedar room was now called.

"Could I have a word with you, alone?" she begged.

He followed her into an empty room.

"Chief, will you find out for me who murdered those two men? Or at any rate who murdered Sir Anthony Cross. Though I guess they're linked. The man who got the one, got the other too."

But Pointer explained that he was only an observer in this case. That he had no standing other than that. Nor could have. The *juge* begged him to help him out with a piece of English at that moment, and Pointer left, with another word of regret to the girl.

"Too bad," Vivian said in considerable vexation to Mackay when she met him a little later and recounted her failure. "I wanted you and him to work together."

"But I'm pledged to Davidson—" began Mackay.

"I telephoned to him," Vivian said triumphantly; "the

butler here has his address, and I asked him if I couldn't get you to help me in this inquiry. He was most frightfully sorry to hear of Mr. Brownlow's death, and said that of course you could take it on. He seemed surprised that I asked him, and not you! But I didn't intend to speak to you about it before knowing that you could say yes—if you wanted to. And, of course, you do want to!"

Apparently Mackay did not.

"Davidson or no Davidson, I'm nae guid. I canna see ma hand before ma een," he said despondently. "There's nae light o' reason here to guide my deductions."

"But you can't refuse!" she protested. "My, I simply can't look on and see a man kick his chance down the stairs and out the front door! Sakes alive, man, don't you know a chance when you see one? When I caught sight of Mrs. Brownlow," she went on; "and recognized her from the photograph I'd seen in Anthony's hands, I jumped to the conclusion that he had been telling me an untruth. Even otherwise truthful men don't always think it necessary to tell the truth to women. But now I know that he was murdered, shot down from the side before he could draw his gun perhaps; why, remembering what he told me, I begin to have a different idea of things. And"—her face softened—"and now I understand his manner when I gave him back his ring, and when he told me last that he had no time for me. He seemed so casual because he had no idea that it was the last time. He sure thought there would be many meetings later on when we could thrash things out. He was all hot on some trail. Mrs. Brownlow says her husband was helping him in some deal. Whether she's right or wrong— I can't make up my mind about her—here's your chance, Mr. Mackay, your great chance!"

"Too great for me," he insisted quietly.

She stamped her foot.

"I *won't* let you talk like that of yourself! I know you can catch murderers if you only give your mind to it. And they must be caught. I was engaged to Anthony Cross. I

liked him immensely. I'm going to find out who killed him
and who killed Mr. Brownlow. You and I are going to
work this together, Mr. Mackay."

She looked very capable as she spoke, with her chin in
the air. But Mackay did not seem impressed.

"It's nae worrk for a wumman. Forbye a young one."

"I'm a good reporter," she said hotly; "and a good
reporter is a good sleuth."

"That sounds gey fine," was his only rejoinder; "but
there's nae private investigator to touch the police."

"Say, Mr. Mackay, your grandfather must have been a
wonder," she said dreamily.

"Eh?" he asked.

"You must be his image. I guess you forget at times
that you're not ninety-nine—yet. Well, good-bye; though
it's one more disappointment. For you sure have brains,
though you don't know how to use them. And I had
another piece of news to discuss with you." She flung this
over her shoulder as she moved towards the stairs.

It was not in human nature not to prick up its ears.
Vivian was generous.

"It's this. Mrs. Brownlow hasn't an idea who Mr.
Murgatroyd was talking to down here in the waiting-
room last night. So she says, and I believe her—there.
Then who was it? Why was Mr. Murgatroyd there at all
at that hour? And looking as mad as mad could be."

"Mad?" queried Mackay, but with a grin.

"Angry. Vexed. That sort of mad. And why did he skip
off before any one could question him? Of course, while
we all thought it was a duel, and while I believed he had
been having a heart-to-heart talk with Mrs. Brownlow, it
was different. But now! I think he knows something! Only
that, of course. I guess even I don't connect a well-known
lecturer and a crime. Though I don't know. . . . He might
have been just acting a part. I'm beginning to think he
was too good to be a real, and that mortal man couldn't be
honestly as keen on history and stones as he was. But I'll
tell the world he really knew a lot. My, he really did!"

"Sure did!" Mackay agreed; "but whaur do I come in?"

"In finding out more about Mrs. Eastby," she said promptly. "I saw her trying to detain Anthony, you know, and him trying to shake her off. It was the face of an absolutely desperate woman, Mr. Mackay."

"He sent her an invitation to the dance!" Mackay said disbelievingly; "and argueing by that . . ." he shook his head.

"Then there's Mr. Murgatroyd's odd behavior that night. I think now that he was talking to her—to the 'Egyptian Lady.'"

"There's nae wumman nor yet a professor in last nicht's terrible events," Mackay said firmly. "It wad be against a' reason."

"That's to find out," Vivian countered smartly.

"Aye, find oot," scoffed Mackay. "Ye'd better apply to Monsieur Rondeau, that bright-eyed French laddie o' the police. He writes detective mysteries, and like you he's amazing good at asking questions."

"But—like me—no good at solving them?" Vivian was piqued.

"Well"—he temporized before the sparkle in her eyes—"hoo wud ye find oot aboot Mrs. Eastby, for instance."

"Why, I—I'd " she thought hard.

"She hasna left an address. The police cud trace her, but I canna," Mackay went on. "Whaur I score wad be in reasoning, in mature deliberation—but there's no chance for that in this case."

He paused to let that said fact sink in.

"Haven't you any idea yourself about the link between those two murders," she asked finally?

"Aye. But it's nobbut an idea. Ye canna arrest a mon even in France, I'm thinkin', on an opinion. There's ower mony o' Sherlock Holmes's case wudna haud water in court."

"But you have an idea!" She was all agog. "Oh, my! Mr. Mackay won't you give me an inkling of it—of who—"

"A' I can say at present is that I dinna think a wumman did either. Let alone baith," was his cautious reply.

She chuckled impatiently.

"You sure are the lightning calculator of your year! But I'll drop one more pearl before I go. Find out whether the link between Mrs. Eastby and Mr. Lascelles isn't Mr. Smith. Or what about Mr. Tibbitts? It seems to me every one's forgotten him. He hasn't come back yet, you know."

Mackay did not tell her that the police were quite cognisant of that young man's existence—and of his whereabouts.

"You're always talking of reasoning, of deliberation—" she began swiftly.

"It soonds like a gey varied conversationalist," he murmured.

"But why not meditate on Mr. Tibbitts? Here's a man who's prepared an alibi beforehand, as it were, and yet one that would take him away from the ball-room for the rest of the night. Say, Mr. Mackay, I think you ought to concentrate on Tibbitts as a murderer as well as a thief."

"Na, na!" he said firmly. "He hasna the kind o' mind that a murderer maun have." And with that Mackay left her.

Vivian was not so sure. Tibbitts might well represent the link between the deaths of the two men, she thought. She was certain that the deaths were closely connected. She did not for a moment believe that in the same quiet old town, in the same villa, on the same night, two murders, separate and distinct, could have been planned and carried out. On the whole now, thinking over the various people who could have had a hand in the tragedy, Vivian's darting suspicions joined up with those of the commissaire, and hovered rather persistently around the head of Mathew Tibbitts.

CHAPTER TEN

THE *juge* wanted the chief inspector to go over a letter that had just arrived, sent by air mail from Geneva. It was from Mrs. Eastby, who apparently lived at Winchelsea when in England. Mrs. Eastby claimed the French equivalent of three hundred pounds from the effects of the late Sir Anthony Cross. She wrote that the sum in question had been handed by her to Sir Anthony on the night he met his death. The receipt, which was made out for her, had gone on with her luggage to Como, but it had been witnessed by a professor staying at Villa Porte Bonheur and by another guest, Mr. Smith. The money had been handed in notes of a thousand francs to Sir Anthony in order that it might be at once invested by him in a particular company and under special circumstances, and was almost too late to be so used. She could not give the number of the notes, as the numbers of French notes are never taken, but all but six of them were thousand franc notes, and as she had pulled out the bank pin to count out one of the packages to Sir Anthony, in the cedar room, she had torn the top note across, and had mended it with a strip off the flap of an envelope from the rack on the writing-table. The lady wrote that the matter was extremely urgent. She hoped that as she had the receipt signed by two men, who were doubtless still present at the villa, there would be no delay made in finding the sum and Returning it to her— without the necessity for legal intervention.

There was a hint in the last line that such intervention would quickly follow any effort to withhold the money.

"So it wasn't a will Monsieur Smith signed, as he thought. It was evidently this receipt of which the letter speaks." The *juge* looked at the sum in francs and pursed his lips. "Here is an interesting piece of news! There is no trace of any such sum. None whatever. Sir Anthony has only some loose notes, amounting to a thousand francs in all, on him."

"That pin found on the ink-stand!" Rondeau almost whispered.

Cambier nodded. "That pin!" he agreed. "But there is another interesting piece of news. Rondeau has found out that a Mademoiselle Fumier—she is the daughter of a doctor who lives in a little village near us"—he explained to the chief inspector and Mackay—"overhead a conversation while sitting out with a partner not far from the open window of the cedar room. She understands English and speaks it well. I have just questioned her. She could not hear much of what was said, but the conversation was of the nature of a quarrel. It took place before supper, and between Sir Cross, whom she could see now and then coming towards the window—he was apparently walking up and down the room—and some other man. Englishman probably, as the conversation, the quarrel rather, was in English. As to this other man, she could only hear a low-pitched man's voice speaking very quietly in between Sir Cross's indignant outbreaks. She thinks this other man was urging some course on Sir Cross which the latter was indignantly refusing to take. But that, of course, is only her interpretation of the affair.

"Once, when Sir Cross stood looking out into the garden for a moment, she heard him say as he turned away, in a very threatening tone, 'It's a case for a criminal prosecution.' That was the only sentence— complete sentence, which she heard. But in the beginning she had caught a very significant word. That was the word 'thief!' Spoken in a tone of positive fury. Later she heard the word 'money' many times. So many times that she was sure the disagreement concerned that common source of friction. She, of course, was under the idea that the talk concerned some third party. Some political

discussion even. We can make a better guess. 'Thief —
'money' —it was Tibbitts's, we may be sure — that quiet
voice speaking so softly. The honest man is not concerned
with the open window, with the possibility of a listener.
But a dishonest man, a thief — ah, he is not forgetful of
eavesdroppers. Never!"

Cambier went on to explain that Mademoiselle
Fumier had not spoken sooner because, though she had
heard of the duel almost at once, her father had objected
to her concerning herself in what seemed a
straightforward, but unpleasant affair — until the report
reached him that it was no question of a duel any longer,
but of murder. Nor did she think, at first —that which
she had overheard was of any importance.

All the Frenchmen evidently knew the young girl, and
equally evidently were tremendously impressed by what
she had to say.

"The money she heard spoken of was very likely this
money of which this letter speaks," the *juge* murmured.
Cambier nodded.

"But in that case one asks oneself why Tibbitts was
concerned with it—" Rondeau ventured. And this time
Cambier allowed his query to stand, even nodded
agreement to it.

Meantime, the car that Tibbitts was believed to be
driving had just been traced to an hotel in Paris in the
Latin quarter. The *Surete* was taking the matter up. And
evidently both expeditiously and well, for within half an
hour came the telephoned news that Tibbitts had been
arrested in a room of the small hotel in question. On him
had been found several wads of thousand franc notes, one
of which had a top note that had been torn across and
mended, apparently with a strip from a gray linen
envelope, on which the beginning of a "V" was legible, an
envelope from Villa Porte Bonheur.

Oddly enough, as soon as she heard of the arrest,
which was early next morning, Vivian began to have
doubts of Tibbitts's guilt. She knew nothing of the letter

of Mrs. Eastby, nor of the torn bank-note found on the young man.

"He fits all right—bits of the puzzle—but I can't think it was that poor simp!" she confided to Mackay, whom she met walking towards the villa after a hasty breakfast.

"Brownlow murdered Sir Anthony, Miss Young," he said suddenly. "I'm as certain o' that as though I had seen him do it. And it was because I was sae sure that I wadna tak' on the job when you asked me yesterday. His wife has suffered eno' by the husband's death. I wadna be the one to add to her grief."

"But, surely to goodness, you thought it a duel at first like all of us!" she protested, amazed and a little indignant. He shook his head gravely.

"Never. Not once. But it isna ma case. I'm engaged to get back Mr. Davidson's money—if I can. As for the twa deaths—" he hesitated. "Miss Young," he said suddenly and very earnestly; "I havena been able to say a worrd o' ma inner-maist thochts for fear o' being laughed at. For a man should reason—and reason according to the rules of logic. But I ha'e the gift. The hielan' gift. Some ca' it 'second sicht.' Ma faither was the seventh son o' a seventh son and baith he and his faither were borrn on a Sunday. I can aye see bluid on the hand o' a murderer. Believe me or no. When I first lookit at Brownlow, I said to myself 'There goes a murderer!' For, though he had gloves on, to me his palms were red and gory."

Mackay's voice suddenly rang out. There was that in his tone and eyes that spelled conviction, however fantastic his words might be.

"Gosh!" Miss Young breathed in amazement. She had never thought of connecting this steady-eyed, red-haired young man with anything occult.

"You mean to say that you can see further into these murders than the police?" she asked finally.

"Aye and no. The gift comes and gaes. And, as I say, I'm working on ma ain case. But of this I feel certain, Tibbitts is nae murderer."

There was a pause.

"Hoo's Mrs. Brownlow takin' a' this talk aboot Tibbitts the noo?" he asked next.

"Haven't you heard? She's so ill that they've installed a nurse. The doctor talks of inflammation of the brain. Poor thing! And yet—I wish I could quite place her in all this. . . "

"So do I!" Mackay agreed fervently. "I canna read Mrs. Brownlow. Neither by the light o' reason, nor by any gift I possess!"

He hurried off at that, and Vivian took a turn through the orchard, thinking over what he had just said and what she knew of the affair.

She was not a believer in things occult, but it was possible that Mackay had a sensitiveness to the thoughts around him that often goes by that name. At any rate, he evidently thought that he was endowed with some special powers. They had not seemed to lead far, but one never knew. . . . This was a most perplexing problem. The morning paper, *Le Petit Clunyois*, had been full of it. The paper mentioned that Maitre Lenormand, the great Paris avocat, had been briefed to assist Tibbitts, and would arrive in the evening. This was very unusual. Lenormand's fees were on a scale that usually precluded his being called in so early in a case. Evidently Tibbitts, or some one behind Tibbitts, had money to spend on his behalf.

The villa became the center of a whirpool of activities. Reports in inconceivable number were drawn up by the doctors, by the detectives, by the police, and by reporters for their papers. Every one who had been present at the dance and could be reached was interviewed. The stationery shops of Cluny did a roaring trade, and were cleared out of sealing wax.

For an hour before he questioned Tibbitts the magistrate busied himself in reading over the reports tabulated for him by his chief clerk. Then he sat and thought over the whole very carefully. Now and again he paced the well-worn strip of carpet in the bare room of the Hotel de ville, whose beautiful proportions and noble ceiling had once been part of the palace. But its present use was suggested in the ink-stained green baize cover over the long table in the center, in the dusty chairs with their once leather seats, and in the files that ranged the walls.

Chief Inspector Pointer and Mackay were both present at the interview.

As it progressed, a formidable total was built up against Tibbitts.

The servants one and all claimed to have noticed that he was madly in love with madam, though she, apparently, treated him like an indulgent elder sister. There was only one witness, the woman who acted as Mrs. Brownlow's maid when wanted, who did not agree with this at all. She maintained that Madam Brownlow on many occasions did her best to turn Tibbitts's head. But the woman disliked the newly-made widow, and by her own dislike spoiled the credibility of her evidence. Miss Young was called, and did her best for both the accused and Mrs. Brownlow. She considered Tibbitts's attachment rather of the knightly adoration type than of the passionate apache kind necessary for such a double crime. But here again, her evident wish to help harmed her testimony. Then came the facts of the journey to Paris, when the thousand pounds in money and the jewelry worth more than another thousand had disappeared. The Pullman attendants and the doctor who had been summoned to attend Davidson and Mrs. Brownlow and Smith—of whose unconsciousness there was no question—remembered many little trifles, which, put together, seemed definitely to prove that Tibbitts could not have been drugged as he said.

Tibbitts himself made a very poor impression on every one. Pale, hunted-looking, he faced the *juge*, his guard behind him. Unshaven, and apparently unwashed, his whole appearance spoke of guilt and shrinking dread. He put up such a lathe-and-plaster defence that, had the occasion been less terrible, it would have been ludicrous. He himself seemed made of putty. And was in some state of secret terror which, like a frightened driver, made him swerve into the very things he wanted to avoid.

Within half an hour the *juge* wrung from him the acknowledgment that his tale of the drugging was false. But he protested that it had only been told with some silly idea of not seeming luckier than his companions. A confused jumble of an explanation that did not explain, least of all to the magistrate with his chill eyes.

Suddenly the *juge* produced the key found in the garden near the gate.

"And now about this—" he said in dramatic accents.

One thing was evident about it. It froze Tibbitts. His face went livid, and yet there came a gleam into his green-gray, watery eyes that made them flash like a cat's at night. He looked as though he could have made a leap for the little piece of metal lying on the *juge's* table. Then he stammered out that he had never seen it before. And this with such abject terror that his denials only strengthened the idea that he connected that key very definitely and very terribly with one at least of the dead men.

The *juge*, after he had adjourned for lunch, gave the commissaire instructions for the reconstruction of the double murder, which he intended to carry out at midnight. Tibbitts was to be confronted with the room as it had looked the night before last, the night of the dance. At the writing-table would sit a figure very like that of Sir Anthony Cross. Into the room, later on, would come another agent made up as like Brownlow as possible. The *juge* hoped to get the truth before dawn.

Which meant, so the commissaire thought, a confession from Tibbitts. The magistrate neither agreed nor disagreed with this. He only looked very thoughtful, and pursing his thin lips, plunged into the reports again. Cambier was expecting every minute further information from Lyons as to Brownlow's plans there. Plans that now looked as though they might link up with Sir Anthony Cross, for Brownlow, it seemed, had spoken of a very wealthy backer who might be coming in with him. No name had been mentioned, but it might be ferreted out, and the name might be Anthony Cross.

Mackay was very silent at lunch—a lunch which he hardly tasted.

"It's awful!" he said at last, giving up the pretence of a meal, "seeing a man ye believe innocent being caught up and hurried into God knows what. I'm as certain that Tibbitts didna kill either of yon dead men as though I were the recording angel and knew it a'. D'you think they'll send him to the block?"

Pointer thought that they would. His bloodstained shoes, not in the least explained by his assertion that his nose had bled, an assertion proved to be false by a dozen trifles as soon as put forward; his knowledge of where the revolver was kept; his probable jealousy of the husband as well as of the lover, unless the crime could be proved to be connected—as Cambier hoped so to prove it—with money concerns alone—all tended to fasten the guilt on Tibbitts. "If you think him innocent," Pointer finished; "how do you account for his evident feeling of guilt? He doesn't consider himself innocent."

"I can only explain it logically by wonderin' if some joke wasna played on him. Some ghastly hoax. Convinced as I am that Brownlow murdered the ither, I think he then got hold of thus puir fule and made him think that Mrs. Brownlow had done it. To save her, I think, Tibbitts is taking the blame."

Pointer did not agree. He, too, had been told of Mackay's gift, but he felt sure that Tibbitts really believed himself guilty.

"Weel, then," Mackay said suddenly; "Brownlow may have told him that he was drunk at the time, and that he killed Sir Anthony while drunk. That's a possibility that's quite in accordance with good reasoning. You could make

Tibbitts think black was bright silver if you only worked hard enough. He's but a puir working lad, who by some chance has been pitchforked into, for him, great society. He eats wi' his knife when he isna thinking."

"A poor working lad . . ." Pointer shook his head. "I've just passed on a report sent over by air from the Yard. Tibbitts's finger-prints have been identified as those of an extremely able safe-breaker, who started as a thief, proved himself quite a wonder as a lad at breaking into shops and tills, was sent to Borstal, ran away, and went in for regular safe-cracking. He never was caught. Oddly enough, for he's not clever. It's thought that his accomplices themselves protected him. He's such a wonder at his work. I take it, his arts and crafts classes were rather of the nature of self-help and self-tuition. Though doubtless night classes all right."

Mackay asked more details.

"There's na doot he took the siller and possibly the jewels on the *rapide,*" he said when he had heard them. "That's ma only reason for mixing in the affair. I promised Davidson I wad get his money back. And I mean to get it—somehow."

Pointer agreed that Tibbitts had probably had something to do with the missing valuables.

"He was very fond of working in the garage here, we have just been told, and of doing little repairs to the car, which he practically alone used. The repairs may have included key-making. Some of that dust in the garage is powdered cuttle-fish, or I'm mistaken. Than which there's nothing better for taking impressions. He recognized that key. I shouldn't be surprised if he had made it."

There was a long silence.

"Yet," Mackay said at last, "there was anither man, a third man, in yon death room. It wasna Tibbitts." He shook his head. "Tibbitts a thief, aye. A safe-breaker possibly. But nae murderer."

The chief inspector rose.

"Well, Cambier and the *juge* think we shall know to-night. The commissaire is convinced of Tibbitts's guilt."

"But the *juge* isn't?" Mackay asked.

"I think he doubts it," Pointer gave Mackay a faint smile; "but I think it's only because he rather believes that Miss Young is mixed up in the affair in some way."

"Yon great lawyer is coming by the evening train; he may see some way oot," Mackay murmured.

"Unless the way is out of the room where Tibbitts is safely locked-up, I don't see how he can be of any help. But his coming shows that Tibbitts has some friends concerned for him. He looked a very astonished man when he heard of Lenormand's expected arrival and partisanship."

"I thocht that put on," Mackay said, rising in his turn. "Weel, I'm more than ever glad that ma pairt is juist the money—the siller. This life and death business sickens me. I felt like a lad watching a rabbit chased by stoats this morning. And to-night will be waur. For that puir fule hasna the wit to help himself."

But there was no reconstruction of the crime that night. At seven Maitre Lenormand arrived from Paris. He dined in his room at the inn and about eight-thirty, after a careful reading of copies of all the reports, sallied out to interview his client. The client was not there. Tibbitts had escaped. An escape that is still talked of in Cluny. A quick investigation by a furious Cambier brought out the truth.

This was not the maitre's second visit, but his first. Yet at half-past seven some one wearing his big black hat and black cloak, both well-known garments of his, on which even the morning paper had commented, had arrived at the wing of the Hotel de ville where Tibbitts was housed on the first floor, with no exit except through a guardroom, or at least a room always occupied by at least two busy policemen writing their reports.

The great *avocat* arrived, handed in his card, and was at once shown into Tibbitts's room. He mentioned that he would have to go back to the hotel almost at once for an important paper which he had forgotten. He had a largish bag with him. In about five minutes he passed out again, at least the police thought it was he. This time he made no remark, but was in a great hurry, as was natural. Nearly half an hour later the men in the outer room went off duty. While they were still talking to the men who were to take their place, handing over the reports and discussing the items of the day, the man they took to be Lenormand, still in hat and cloak, came out again from Tibbitts's room.

"This time I am really off for the night," he remarked pleasantly.

"We did not see you come back," the agent nearest him said quickly.

"No! I will report myself at the table each time after this," the so-called Lenormand said very civilly, offering the man a couple of cigars and wishing them all good-night.

That was all. But it was enough to make Cambier nearly break a bloodvessel when confronted with the maitre's denial of any such previous visit, and the abundant proofs that he had not left the hotel since his arrival at seven until now, half-past eight.

"It was some accomplice of Tibbitts's," Rondeau murmured; "some apache friend. French, apparently —"

"Certainly," rectified Cambier. "His accent was that of a Frenchman. And besides—the neatness of the whole plan—its admirable simplicity—"

"It must have been some one who knew that our police are changed at just that hour," Rondeau thought; "that looks like a local man. It sounds bizarre, but have you reflected, *mon chef*, that Monsieur Pichegru is just the height and build of Maitre Lenormand? It sounds bizarre, as I say, yet I ask myself whether—" he left the sentence unfinished.

"Monsieur Pichegru?" almost yelled Cambier; "what an idea! And the motive? And how did he escape recognition?"

Rondeau was silent for once.

"My lad, whoever released Tibbitts was himself the murderer," Cambier said firmly. "Do you not agree with me?" he asked the chief inspector and Mackay.

Pointer said that he did. Mackay said that he would have to think it over before deciding.

"Whoever it was," Rondeau said aloud, "was evidently provided with a double set of the great Paris avocats well-known cloak and broad-brimmed black hat. One he wore, one he carried in his bag."

Cambier nodded. Rondeau went on:

"He put those in the bag on Tibbitts, who walked out swiftly, without saying a word—ostensibly to fetch the paper that had been forgotten—down on to the street, around a corner, and into a car waiting for him. The other waits nearly half an hour in the empty room—he has a nerve that one—and then, still impersonating Lenormand, comes out at a moment when he knows that there is always a good deal of bustle and confusion, when no one can be certain whether he came back before or not. . . . Besides, who would suspect the great Lenormand of conniving at the prisoner's escape? And as you say, *mon chef*, who would run such a risk unless it were vital that Tibbitts should not be questioned further. Tibbitts must have known the secret. Tibbitts must have been about to betray something absolutely vital. I even ask myself if Tibbitts—"

"It is unendurable!" Cambier fairly shook with bottled fury. "As to what the *juge* will say, the devil only knows!"

But the *juge*, though scandalized that such an escape could have happened in a case that Scotland Yard was watching, was not greatly perturbed. He did not think that Tibbitts was guilty of the murder, he now said. Though he had hoped by reconstructing the crime, as they believed it to have happened to wring from him some important, perhaps vital, clue to the baffling problem.

As for Monsieur Pichegru, though that gentleman was unable to furnish an alibi during the hour Tibbitts escaped, Monsieur Grandpoint agreed with the commissaire that the idea of his. being either criminal or accomplice was ludicrous.

"His son is in the income-tax department," Monsieur Grandpoint .said severely to Rondeau, who murmured that he had only asked himself the question.

"A far more likely guess would be Monsieur Smith," Cambier said suddenly, who had been thinking hard. "He, too, was of the same height and figure and would not be too well known to the policemen. Quick! the telephone!"

Over it Cambier learned that Monsieur Smith, who was staying in one of the best hotels of Vichy, had been out all afternoon and evening in a car—yes, driving it himself—he had not yet returned. He had spoken of running up to Mont Dore.

Cambier wished to be told the instant that he returned. He next spoke to the Vichy police, asking them to see when Monsieur Smith got back, whether the car tires suggested Mont Dore dust or Cluny's softer loam. Then he had a talk with Maitre Lenormand.

The great *avocat* was only a little less curious than was the commissaire at the trick that had been played. But he wished silence on the affair. He was leaving at once. Returning to Paris, he said, in a tone that suggested a man flying back to civilization. The police agreed with him that no word should leak out as to Tibbitts's escape. Only those actually concerned in the inquiry were to be aware of the fact that that young man was not locked up *au secret*.

Then came the report of Smith's arrival back in Vichy, after a lapse of time that might have meant an excursion to Mont Dore or to Cluny. The tires refused to say which. Smith himself said that he had just run around the country generally, not stopping anywhere, merely trying the car with an idea to buying her. The police, who searched the little tonneau, found a piece of a torn envelope with a Swiss stamp; the postmark was Geneva, though the date was very blurred.

"Geneva!" repeated Rondeau; "where Madame Eastby wrote from—where she is staying! *Sapristi*, but I ask myself—"

He was bundled from the room.

The *juge* next morning left Tibbitts on one side and concentrated on a fact that interested him greatly, which he had discovered late yesterday afternoon. That was, that there was one of the guests at the dance who had only been seen masked. Who must, therefore, have left before the one o'clock unmasking and supper. It was the footman who had first given the *juge* the clue in some answer of his, but the butler, too, when his attention was called to some of the facts, bore out his fellow servant's idea. Both men now recollected that the tall figure, wearing a long robe with a hood pulled over its head, had only been seen by them near Miss Young. The "Lady with the Fox" as they called her. They could not recollect having seen the man in question talking to any one else, though this was only a vague impression. But both were certain that they had not seen the man after unmasking time. The butler could not recollect what name had been on the card handed in by the guest in question. He had happened to arrive at the same time as a group of local people, one of whom, "Good King Rene," had mislaid his crown, and in the confusion until the royal regalia was complete once more, the stranger had passed on. The servant only remembered one point about his appearance —that his hands were unusually dark for a European.

"African combine—dark hands!" Rondeau ran his hands delightedly through his curly hair.

Now the *juge*, a fervent Roman Catholic, was the author of a book on *Roman Catholics and the Ku-Klux-Klan*. As the garb of the unidentified guest was described to him in detail his face grew longer and longer.

"What have we here?" he muttered, all but crossing himself. "What have we here? And remember, *messieurs*, this man so dressed, this guest who was not seen after the unmasking, kept entirely to the company of the fiancé of one of the dead men. And remember also that we have only her word that it was she who broke the engagement off. Everything suggests that it was Sir Anthony, rather than she. Everything! And now, recollect that this same stranger was apparently no stranger to her. We have the evidence of one of the waiters, now back in Macon, who heard him ask her to 'give him what he had come to get.' Personally, gentlemen, I find here in this mysterious figure, and this mysterious fiancé, a conjunction more suggestive than in the thief of the *rapide*—Tibbitts and some accomplice. I will question Mademoiselle Young yet once more."

Vivian sensed the increased antagonism of the *juge* at once. In his manner, in his eyes, in his voice. Her own dislike answered to his.

Questioned, she replied that she recalled the figure perfectly. It was Mr. Lascelles, she felt sure. She explained Mr. Lascelles, as far as she knew him. She had not seen the figure after supper either, that was to say, after the unmasking. There was something in her tone that made the magistrate sure that she was holding something back or not telling the truth. Personally, he thought the latter.

"What is your religion, mademoiselle?" he asked unexpectedly.

"I am a Christian," she answered blandly, for Pointer did not need to translate the simpler sentences to her.

The magistrate frowned. This was levity. Or downright mockery.

"Are you a Roman Catholic?" he asked shortly.

"No."

"And Sir Anthony Cross?"

To his disappointment the *juge* learned that he was not one either. Vivian assured the magistrate, after many further questions, that she knew nothing whatever of the *frater* of the Ku-Klux-man beyond meeting him at Villa Porte Bonheur as Mr. Smith's friend. The *juge* did not believe her. He sensed that she was not telling all that she knew. For Vivian at first kept back the strange episode out side the door of the cedar room between the *frater* and the "Egyptian Lady." She hoped that Mackay might yet make some good use of that. She wanted that lame duck of a self-distrustful young man to swim. So finally the *juge* dismissed her with some acerbity.

"A very determined young lady!" was his comment; "and yet, according to her own story, we are to believe that she stood aside and let things take their course?" He shook his head slowly and firmly. "That, I do not believe."

"That is what I ask myself," Rondeau burst out excitedly; "did she do that or did she not? I learned, though at the moment I thought it of no importance, that she practiced pistol shooting on the very morning of the dance together with Monsieur Smith in the shooting gallery. Now that is an odd way for a young lady to spend her time, just before her lover came down to see an old flame again."

"Mademoiselle is an American," Cambier put in dispassionately. "I understand that in that country pistol shooting is part of every lady's daily round."

The other Frenchmen nodded. Yes, they, too, were aware of that, but still, in this case. . . .

"She brought her pistol down with her, and it is an automatic," Rondeau pointed out. "And I ask myself if she did not bring it intending to use it on Sir Cross."

"Rondeau, do not embroider!" begged his chief. "Her automatic was not the one that killed either of the two men. And a national amusement does not mean a crime."

"But, *la bas*, I understand that every one shoots at least one person in their lives. So I ask myself—" Rondeau murmured, but Cambier asked him to jot down instead some inquiries about Lascelles which were to be made by telephone and wireless.

"It is very curious," the commissaire went on, "that all the men who were at the villa just before or during the time of the murder have disappeared. Mr. Murgatroyd is unfindable. He is expected back home in September, and you"—he turned to Pointer—"your people cable you that all researches into his past are of a most ironclad respectability. That he is, as we here always took him to be, a savant, a writer on many works of the past. As to respectability, that, too, seems to clothe Monsieur Smith."

There was a short pause.

"Have you inquired of Monsieur Smith the address of his friend, Lascelles?" asked the *juge* of Rondeau.

The latter had, but Smith had said that he hadn't the faintest idea where Lascelles was hanging out, bar the fact that both had arranged to meet at Zermatt in a week's time and try the Matterhorn by a different traverse. Yes, he had heard from Lascelles since leaving Cluny. But the letter was only posted en route, from Geneva, he thought, but he couldn't be sure.

This was all that could be got from Smith, and it was very unsatisfactory.

"We have no reason, however, to think that either Smith or Lascelles knew the dead men before coming to Villa Porte Bonheur," the *juge* pointed out. "Madame Brownlow, before she became so ill, poor lady, told us explicitly that she and her husband knew none of the guests staying there. Except, of course, Tibbitts—and except, as came later, Sir Anthony Cross. He, we know, came to Porte Bonheur villa because of Brownlow, whom we now know was not merely an old acquaintance, but a temporary partner of his."

"Whom we have been told was. I dinna believe that last part," Mackay remarked as always.

In the afternoon Mrs. Eastby arrived. Nothing could make her anything but a very handsome woman. But her wonderful eyes looked as though they had spent some hours staring into black depths. The lines around her passionate, rather disappointed-looking mouth had grown a great deal deeper than when Vivian and she had watched each other at the supper table the night of the dance. She explained to the *juge* that she and her husband, Colonel Eastby, were old acquaintances of Sir

Anthony. Her husband was in a nursing home, or the whole affair would have been carried out by him—doubtless very much more cleverly. This pleased the *juge*. It was the correct attitude for the other sex. She went on quickly, but clearly, to explain that the friendship between the three of them, though of long standing, had never been a very close one. On coming down to Cluny to see a town of which all the world had heard, she had met Sir Anthony in the train—to their mutual surprise. He had happened to speak of a new business venture which he was about to sponsor. He had not gone into details, but he had let it be seen that it would make the fortunes of those who got in on the ground floor.

"Now," Mrs. Eastby went on with winning frankness; "I'm under fearfully heavy expenses just now, with my husband ill, and I asked Sir Anthony at once to invest in it some savings which I had been able to make out of our very tight fit of an income." He had put her off, but not definitely. She had hardened herself and waylaid him for an invitation to the dance at the Villa Porte Bonheur—a dance of which the hotel was talking, and where she hoped to find him in a more genial mood. Her hopes had been justified. He had taken the sum which to her was so big, to him so tiny, and had promised to invest it at once for her as she wished.

"But I must—I *must*—have my money back, since it's not been invested as I hoped. I simply must have it!" She was extraordinary pale, and in her eyes was a look as though she were fighting down stark terror.

Terror of what? wondered the two Englishmen.

Vivian had talked over Mrs. Eastby with both the Chief Inspector and the private inquiry agent as soon as it was known that that lady was coming to Cluny.

Mackay had advised silence.

"That puir wumman had naething to dae wi' the deaths," he said for the tenth time. "Why drag her affairs oot for general inspection? It was some wee matter o' her ain, sic as we a' have."

"Is that according to the light o' reason, or second sight?" Vivian asked with her disarming laugh.

"It's all very well for Mr. Mackay to say that Mrs. Eastby had nothing to do with the two murders," she went on. "I don't think she had actually, but the Ku-Klux-man? Those words I overhead were sure funny! Do you mean to say, Mr. Mackay, that you won't even make any use of them?"

"I'm on ma ain job," he replied doggedly, undeterred by her half-incredulous, half-pleading face.

Chief Inspector Pointer had now spoken, and very gravely.

"You ought to tell everything you know, Miss Young. Possibily Mackay's right, and Mrs. Eastby has nothing to do with this double crime. But that's not for any civilian to decide. The responsibility is too tremendous. The very thing you keep back

might help the criminal to escape. Even a detective, who has a theory of the case, can't possibly tell what's important and what isn't until near the end, let alone you. By you I mean any outsider."

"Have you a theory of the crime?" she asked quickly. Vivian liked the chief inspector, or rather she would have liked him had she seen more of him. But he held himself very aloof as he moved to and fro in his pleasant, unobtrusive way. She was quite sure that nothing escaped those fine eyes of his, but neither did anything escape his firm mouth.

"I'm too busy asking myself questions—like Rondeau—to have a theory as yet," he said with a smile.

So Vivian now finally told the *juge* of the scene outside the cedar room between Mrs. Eastby and Mr. Lascelles, or rather, between the "Egyptian Lady" and the hooded friar. It was after Mrs. Eastby had had her first talk with the officials that Vivian made her statement. It was received very noncommittally. Then came a surprise. Mrs. Eastby denied the whole incident—denied ever having met a man called Lascelles, or ever having spoken to the hooded figure at the dance, except, perhaps, some light, passing word.

If Miss Young were telling the truth—she shot a baleful glance—then some one made up in a similar dress had impersonated her, Mrs. Eastby.

Vivian was aghast, but Mrs. Eastby was not to be shaken. Nor was Vivian.

The *juge* eyed the American girl with all but open suspicion. Mrs. Eastby turned on her in a burst of almost hysterical fury:

"I didn't shoot either of those poor men," she cried wildly when Vivian had left, a very ruffled Vivian, a Vivian by no means at her best. "I wish to God Sir Anthony Cross were here alive and well. But that girl? The girl who could tell such a wicked untruth is capable of anything!" And she began to cry shakily.

Pointer, watching her, thought that her grief was even deeper than she wished to show. The others thought the same.

"She loved him," Cambier said firmly, after she had left them; "yes, poor woman, she is, I think, agonized by the fear that by handing him over the money, she may have been an indirect cause of his murder. For three large piles of banknotes . . ." the *juge* shrugged.

"But that money was not to be invested!" Rondeau said almost violently. "I have learned that Mrs. Eastby was seen talking to Sir Cross at the station in Enghien by a porter. Therefore she followed him down here. Oh, there is more behind that sum of money than an investment! I have a feeling that there is more!"

So had the *juge*, and he was a very experienced psychologist.

CHAPTER ELEVEN

RONDEAU spent the afternoon in a frenzy of activity. His chief, the commissaire, was busy too. Between them they learned that two other people had seen Mrs. Eastby and the tall, hooded figure talking very earnestly together. In each case, unfortunately, the observer did not speak or understand English. But each thought that Mrs. Eastby was soothing her tall companion, or adjuring him to do something that he did not want to do.

Rondeau found out that a youngish man with very dark hands had driven Mrs. Eastby away from the hotel. Questioned, she refused to give the man's name who had driven her or any information as to the car. She tried to pass off the finality of her refusal as the merest decency to an absent friend, but the explanation was patently false.

But, whoever the man in the robe or the driver might have been, it did not seem possible that he was Lascelles. For Rondeau finally located that young man. And Lascelles referred the police in Geneva for the night of the dance, to an hotel there which had known him for years, with whose resident proprietor he had often gone climbing. Inquiries proved that unless the whole hotel staff, as well as the Swiss who owned it, were all in league together, Mr. Lascelles had most certainly spent the fateful night there. Investigations at the frontier showed that his passport had duly passed through in the later evening. So, in spite of Vivian's fancy, whoever the man in the long robe was, it could not have been Smith's friend, the young science master.

Vivian was at first incredulous, then utterly dumbfounded. As for the *juge*, he plainly showed that this shaking of part of her testimony gave him the gravest doubts as to the rest.

"But I thought—say, I was dead sure—" she stammered to Mackay in the garden.

"Aye. One thinks!" he retorted; "and one's dead sure. But half the time one's wrong!" And on that he fell silent.

"Are you coming down to the village, I mean the toon?" he asked, as she made for the gate.

"I am. Before that judge has me arrested I want to return something I've stolen." She waved an umbrella at him. As to her words about arrest, Vivian had no idea how possible, in the magistrate's opinion, that step seemed.

Mackay had already noticed the umbrella hanging on her arm, and noticed, too, that it was of a size and make unusual in her belongings.

"Whose is it?" he asked.

"Don't know. A couple of strangers came to the museum yesterday, in which I am being driven to take an interest, very much against the grain I do assure you. Like Mr. Murgatroyd these two, however, obviously came to worship. I left before they did, and the man in charge of umbrellas gave me this instead of my own. As Mr. Murgatroyd said, it's always to me, or near me, that things happen!"

"What makes you think this belongs to those men you saw?" he asked grumpily.

"I happened to notice the men walking up to the museum. One of them had this very umbrella swinging on his arm. As it's no use to me, I intend to return it."

"If you've identified it as well as you did Mr. Lascelles's voice," he began with unkind frankness.

"That alibi of his may be phony after all," she said at once, but only half-heartedly.

He shook his head. "Better give me the brolly," he suggested. "I'm going that way, the way of the only hotel in the place where strangers are likely to put up besides my own, and they're not staying where I am."

But Vivian did not let go.

"Tell me what he looked like and I'll find him out," he persisted.

"Why shouldn't I have some interest in life?" she countered. "As to what he looked like in the museum—an undertaker taking a friend to see his mother's grave. That's what he looked like." And with that brief sketch of the umbrella's owner, Vivian turned down the avenue of limes. He kept beside her.

"You've quick eyes if you can be as sure as that of the owner," he repeated after a moment.

"Sure. When all this terrible affair is over, I'm going into partnership with you, Mr. Mackay. We'd get on fine. You could do the reasoning, and I the mistakes."

Mackay looked at her. His careworn young face lighted. For a second she thought that he was going to speak and say something pleasant, but the usual cloud of taciturnity swept down on him again.

"It's a ruined concern, Miss Young," he said wearily; "yet, if I pull off this thing, I might take you at your word," he finished, giving her a keen, searching look, "but I doot it's beyond me."

"The dice are sure loaded in this game," she said gently. "It would take some one like that chief inspector to play them."

"You think he's so good?" Mackay asked without any look of pleasure; with something that sounded like jealous disparagement in his voice.

She nodded with certainty. "I know that make of man. And I know your make."

"And the difference?" Mackay asked shortly.

"You're a man of action," she said kindly. "And that's the trouble. Detecting doesn't take action. But here's the hotel. I'll go in and ask if any one answering to the man I saw with this is staying here."

But Mackay insisted on doing it for her, while she sampled some ices and cakes at the town's best confectioner's.

Vivian was never more sure that America was God's country than when she was in a French cake shop. But Mackay found her doing her best to initiate the young woman in charge into the mysteries of a Texas sundae. The best local equivalent seemed to consist of jam and cream and strawberry ice. Mackay shuddered at the sight, but Miss Young thought it quite fair for a first effort.

"Did you find the man? *Is* he an undertaker on his way to his mother's grave?" she asked Mackay on his return.

"He's a Swedish art critic, who only speaks Swedish, so our interview was short. But he recognized his umbrella."

"And what about mine?" Vivian asked. "Consider me as crushed as you like, still I want my umbrella."

"The chap, whose gamp was given you, has sent yours to the villa."

"But how did he know where I was staying?" she persisted in surprise.

"The mon in charge told him your name and address. A' the lot of us at the villa are marrked men and women, ye ken."

"But the man in charge of the umbrellas doesn't know me! I went to him at once about it before I came away. He sure didn't know me from Adam—or let's say, Eve. He told me as an excuse that he was new to the town. Say, that's queer!"

"Some other official supplied the information then," Mackay said carelessly.

Vivian returned to the villa, where she found her umbrella. It had been left by the chasseur of the hotel where the strangers were staying. She was sufficiently intrigued to walk on to the museum which shared with the Hotel de ville the honor of being housed in what had been the Abbotts' Palace. The same man was in charge of umbrellas.

"I received my umbrella safely," she said at once; "did

you give the man who took mine my name?"

"But I do not know your name, madam," he said in open amusement.

"Didn't he come and ask you for it?"

He had not. The man assured her that he had not had any questions asked about either her umbrella or the one given her by mistake, except from herself. She decided to ask the same question of the man at the door. But he was talking volubly in low tones to a couple of gendarmes. Just behind their heads was an open window, so high up that any one standing there could probably not be seen but could hear. Vivian had passed that room coming out. It was empty now. She stepped back into it and, as she hoped, her head was barely level with the sill. She listened intently. She felt quite sure that it was of "the Problem" that they were talking. It was. And, as far as she was concerned, it certainly was news. For it was of Tibbitts's escape they were speaking. And the men, being among themselves, doubted whether he ever would be taken. The man was a foreigner, they pointed out, and would probably make for home; and once outside of France—well, all Frenchmen knew how slender was the chance of any one finding a criminal when they couldn't.

Vivian, slipping out in time to meet the man returning to his post, found that he, too, had had no questions put to him about any umbrella. She walked home very much mystified. But foremost was the escape of Tibbitts. How it was accomplished she had no idea. Evidently it was not supposed to be known, for there had been no hint of it in any newspaper.

Meanwhile, through information at once furnished him by the London office of the South African Diamond Combine, the commissaire had been in telephonic communication with the chief detective employed by them to trace the perpetrator of the constant thefts. The man was a Dutchman called Oor, with a number of men under him working in various capitals. Oor was personally certain that Sir Anthony's murder could not be connected with the inquiries proceeding. They were not yet far enough advanced to need any such panic measure, nor were the men he was after "killers."

He also maintained that neither the head of the small gang nor any member of it could have been near Cluny, or south of Paris since over a fortnight ago. They were all under observation, and knew it. As to Brownlow, the man killed at the same tune as Sir Anthony, being in any way or sense a helper in locating the diamond thieves, Oor negatived that quite definitely. Apart from the fact that Sir Anthony was notoriously a man who only believed in professional help, this especial tracking was not one where the cleverest amateur could assist. It could only be solved by a close inside knowledge of the postal routine of two continents and the seas between. Had the late Brownlow been a retired officer of the merchant service or some postal official, there might have been a possibility of Sir Anthony having asked his help; but a silk merchant!

As to a suggestion that Sir Anthony had come to Cluny to meet some other person still who might throw light on the losses, the speaker had been in secret telephonic communication with Sir Anthony on his leaving Enghien, and the baronet had not mentioned the matter. Yet Oor was absolutely certain that he would have done so in that case. Sir Anthony was a very loyal man, who took no step without talking it over with the men engaged on the task. Nor could he have stumbled by chance on any proof at Cluny which might have brought about his murder or the murder of any helper.

Oor again repeated that the case was not far enough advanced for anything of that sort to be possible.

The *juge* murmured that he had felt sure all along that Mademoiselle Young's suggestion as to Sir Anthony having come down on any inquiry connected with the diamond thefts was but a blind, a false trail.

"She is deep, that young lady!" he said gravely. "Very deep!" As to whether Brownlow was helping Sir Anthony as a go-between for some purchase of a stone or stones,

Oor could not say. All he did know was that such a purchase would have nothing to do with the firm, but be a purely private matter.

Meanwhile, Pointer, by wireless via Lyons, had been getting all the information possible about Mrs. Eastby. As far as was known, neither she nor her husband had ever been in any trouble, and until he exchanged into a camel corps, he had generally been stationed in some home garrison where all possible facts were available.

They had one son. This son had entered the counting house of the Johannesburg branch of the Diamond Combine two years ago. He bore, as far as was known, a satisfactory character in every way. He had been nominated by Sir Anthony Cross, and inquiries showed that it was Sir Anthony again who had told him to take the four weeks holiday which was due him this autumn, now, in July. Young Reginald Eastby was over in London it was thought, though his only address there was a small club much used by army men from Egypt. There Pointer could get no present address, only a vague idea that young Mr. Eastby was in France.

It was the existence of the son which was the important point. Why had Mrs. Eastby said nothing about him? A son, moreover, who was old enough— twenty-six—to be in the employment of Sir Anthony's company, though not, it appeared, in any capacity that brought him into personal touch with that director.

A confidential inquiry had been "beamed" to the firm as to whether Sir Anthony had in any way seemed to especially favor young Eastby. The reply was that, considering that the young man was his nominee, Sir Anthony had always seemed ultra-critical of his work. Eastby had just been recommended for a very important rise, a vacant post in London, to which the other directors thought him especially fitted, but Sir Anthony had opposed the recommendation, saying that he did not think the young man up to the new position's difficulties.

An idea of the *juge*'s was swept away by these later

facts.

"Otherwise, of course, one might think . . ." he said vaguely, shaking his head; "yes, indeed, one might think. . . . Fortunately Sir Anthony Cross's legal adviser and personal friend is, I understand, on his way here. He will represent the family. And from him we may gain a great deal of help."

The *juge* was referring to Mr. Maitland, who was on his way to Cluny to take Sir Anthony's remains back to the family vault. He was, it seemed, one of the executors of the baronet's will, a friend of many years, and up till now the solicitor in whose hands the Diamond Combine, at Sir Anthony's instigation, had placed all its legal business, just as he had transacted everything of that kind for the dead man for many a year. He had just retired a few days ago—to enter parliament, it was thought—but seeing the urgency of the situation, he had volunteered to continue working as heretofore for a few weeks more, giving the office in London the benefit of his advice and intimate knowledge of Sir Anthony's plans.

Meanwhile, Cambier had been furnished with approximate measurements and a photograph of Reginald Eastby from England. They showed that it was not impossible for this young man to have been the Florentine Brother of Mercy at the dance, and that, later on, he might have driven his mother away from the hotel. If it were he, why had he come to Cluriy for so short a time? Why gone, without apparently making himself known to his host?

Mrs. Eastby was asked where her son was. There was such stark terror in her face at the question, which was suddenly shot at her after several quite casual ones, that all the men in the room were sorry for her. She stammered something unintelligible with pale lips.

"Madam," the *juge* said not unkindly, "you had better give us his address at once. We shall have to have it. We have evidence showing that he was here the night of the dance."

"But I don't know where he is!" Mrs. Eastby cried in something near to a shriek. "Somewhere in Bulgaria—fishing —and then he was going on to Cyprus."

"It sounds an expensive holiday . . ." murmured the *juge* who, like most of his nation, did not travel. "I understood that your means were straightened."

Mrs. Eastby replied that Reginald traveled third class and was doing it extremely cheaply. Most of it on foot. How could she reach him? She replied that she had no means of doing that. That when his month was up he would come back to London.

"Perhaps!" muttered the *juge* with dreadful clearness. "Madam, I am sorry to wound a mother's feelings, but we have to-day—now—learned that Sir Anthony requested your son to take his holiday at once, and at the same time that a chartered accountant was instructed to go through the young man's accounts. There was no reason given. But it speaks for itself."

"Because he was appointed to, or as good as appointed to, a very much better position in London," Mrs. Eastby cried, twisting her fingers until the small knuckles—the knuckles of a woman of feeling and impulse, but not of much logical capacity—seemed to crack.

"Sir Anthony had at the last moment scratched through that appointment, Mrs. Eastby. That was a proceeding, madam, that might well arouse passionate fury in the breast of a young man, who perhaps thought he had a right to extra favoritism on the part of Sir Anthony Cross.

"You were overheard telling him not to go into the room where Sir Anthony was." The *juge* now inclined to believe that Vivian had told the truth. "He asked Miss Young, taking her for you, for what he had come to fetch. . . ."

Mrs. Eastby had pulled herself together by this time. Again she maintained that her son was nowhere near Cluny on the occasion of the recent dance—that he and Sir Anthony were on as good terms as any young man in the firm's employment. As to Sir Anthony having started him with rather a better paid post than most beginners had to take, that was due, of course, to the dead director's friendship with her husband and herself. Her husband had asked him to do his best for their boy, who had just left Oxford with a scraped-through pass. Sir Anthony, she thought, was rather afraid that, having done as much, Reginald possibly, and certainly the other members of the staff, might think that he intended to make a favorite of the boy. For that reason he had gone out of his way to show that, though he had put the young man in his position out of kindness to the parents, his kindness ended there. There was no question of any intimacy at any time between the two.

She was very good indeed now, very matter-of-fact, very clear, very detailed. Yet there was that in her eyes that told of her back against some wall.

"She is shielding her son," the *juge* said when she had been released from the rack. That was the impression that the Scotland Yard man and Mackay both had. "Yes, she is shielding her son. The poor woman! Of course he came here. Came to meet 'Jane.' His mother's name is not 'Jane.' Nor do I think he would call her that. I think 'Jane' is some one else— perhaps some one who did not come. It is perplexing—very, very! Now, the latest information which we have just received is that Mrs. Eastby is in some financial difficulty. That she had asked, less than a month ago, for a loan of a hundred pounds from her bank and was refused, as she had insufficient security to offer. Her husband's pension ceasing at his death."

Pointer had just ascertained these facts from the bank manager in question.

"Yet we find her handing three times that amount to Sir Anthony Cross. Still, there are ways. . . . There are gambling tables, there is a lucky deal on the stock exchange. There are the *petites economies* so dear to ladies. The savings in the stocking, never referred to, but always produced when it is a question of a remarkable chance. Yes, yes, we understand all that . . ." murmured the *juge*. "It is the son, in that extraordinary garb. Even without believing that fantastic tale of the young American girl's, it is the son that is of interest to us," he went on ruminatingly.

A policeman interrupted. Saluting, he brought information that on the Paris express from Macon had arrived not Mr. Maitland, the expected representative of the family and Sir Anthony's personal friend, but a very important person none the less, the head clerk of the London office of the combine, a man who spoke French as well as he did English or Tal. Mr. Heimbrot, the clerk in question, brought with him a letter that had reached the office after the death of the writer, Sir Anthony. It was dated the day of his death, and had been collected by the midnight collection in Cluny. Evidently it was one that had been posted by himself late in the evening. In it, he not only withdrew all his objections to young Eastby's obtaining the London appointment, but strongly urged that he should at once start in his new sphere on his return from his holiday. Heimbrot believed that Sir Anthony had intended to do this all along, and had had the young man take his leave now instead of later with this in view.

Mr. Heimbrot went on to say that he had written to congratulate young Eastby on the good news, for this letter quite settled the appointment. Where had he written? To Mr. Eastby's club in town. It would be forwarded. Mr. Eastby was in France at the moment. Sir Anthony had referred in a previous letter to having met Mrs. Eastby in Enghien-les-Bains, and Eastby was traveling with his mother.

Mr. Heimbrot, a middle-aged man with shrewd but kindly lines on his face, looked uneasy at something in the eyes of the Frenchmen fixed so eagerly on him. He paused in his narrative.

"Mrs. Eastby and her son in Enghien? Oh, yes. The

name of the hotel? I want to get into touch with Mr. Eastby," murmured the *juge* with an air of content that relieved Mr. Heimbrot. But the head clerk did not know at what hotel the mother and her son had stayed. The dead baronet's reference had suggested a chance meeting.

The *juge* next asked for all possible details concerning Reginald Eastby. Heimbrot told everything that he knew concerning the young man. No fresh material was added to the known facts, though he supplied the secretaries of the officials with plenty of dates. Young Eastby had done very well in the office where he worked, and had shown executive and financial ability quite above the average. For which reason he had been proposed for the unexpected vacancy in London, which meant a big rise in position, salary and prospects.

Yes, the head clerk had understood from Sir Anthony that he did not intend to recommend Reginald Eastby to the post, but evidently, on reflection, he had recognized his undoubted fitness for it.

"And can you tell me why he had a chartered accountant go through the young man's books while he himself was away on a holiday, a holiday which the murdered man had practically ordered him to take?" asked Cambier. The secretary pursed up his lips.

"Suspicious, I should say. It looks like that. But evidently unfounded, or Mr. Eastby wouldn't have got the rise. I think some one must have been telling tales, false ones, that set Sir Anthony against young Eastby. There was no reason for them. You see, I'm from the Jo'burg office myself, a couple of years ago, and I keep in touch with my old friends out there. Reginald Eastby is as steady as a rock. Hard working and clever. Lives quietly with his mother."

"What about Colonel Eastby?" asked the *juge*.

Heimbrot opened his eyes.

"Colonel Eastby's in an asylum. Has been there for donkey's years. Got kicked on the head by a camel just after he joined the camel corps. And no hope of recovery, they say."

"In a lunatic asylum?" queried Rondeau, half-rising from his seat. "A maniac. Homicidal?"

The secretary nodded pityingly. "So they say—a certified lunatic."

"And where is this asylum?" breathed Rondeau.

"At Passy. Close to the American hospital there. There's a man there said to be a marvel. But he hasn't been able to help the poor colonel, I understand. He's been going from mental home to mental home for years and years. No good."

"How long ago was his injury?"

"I understand that it happened when young Eastby was a little chap. He's twenty-six now. About twenty years ago, I suppose."

"And now," the *juge* leaned forward and dropped his voice; "now, about Mrs. Eastby and Sir Anthony Cross?"

Mr. Heimbrot only looked at him.

"The—the friendship between them was of long standing, *hein*?"

Mr. Heimbrot could not seem to say. He had apparently became quite vague as to details. He could not say that he had ever heard any talk connecting Mrs. Eastby's name with that of the dead man. But he did know that Mrs. Eastby had come to Johannesburg years ago, just after the accident to her husband, with her little boy. She lived there very simply. Heimbrot added that every one was uncommonly sorry for the lovely girl—she was little more than that at the time. For herself and for the ghastly fate that had overtaken her marriage. The Eastbys were not badly off, but their modest resources were strained to penury by the expensive charges for the colonel, and had so remained ever since.

"I saw the letter some four years ago in which she thanked Sir Anthony for having got her son a post," Heimbrot went on. "She had marked it 'Personal,' but it got into the wrong pile. Most touching letter I ever read," he said after a little pause. "And a credit—both to the woman who wrote it and the man who got it," he finished warmly in English.

"Well done!" breathed Mackay to the chief inspector sitting beside him.

The *juge* asked a few more questions. As, for instance, how Sir Anthony and Mrs. Eastby had come to meet at Enghien. Mr. Heimbrot had no idea. He did not know either where Mrs. Eastby was at the moment.

Did he think that possibly she and her son were traveling with Sir Anthony? Mr. Heimbrot did not. He added that there was a belief in the office that, personally, Sir Anthony rather disliked young Reginald Eastby. Pressed, he confessed that he, too, thought that the baronet was inclined to be over severe on that young man's work.

The next question concerned the leakage of diamonds from the parcels sent to Amsterdam. Mr. Heimbrot was very reticent, but he agreed that Sir Anthony's presence in France was due to some investigations now going on. That was all for the time-being, and Mr. Heimbrot, with many thanks, was allowed to stroll around the little town at his leisure.

There was a moment's silence after he left.

"So it was Madam Eastby—not the husband, who was in a lunatic asylum—who asked for that post for her son," the *juge* murmured. "And she and her son were together at Enghien. And she followed Sir Anthony Cross down here. And the son? I think we may take it that he followed with her. And Sir Anthony had refused to give the son this rise." He took off his pince-nez and rubbed them clear. "Does a man of Sir Anthony Cross's apparent strength of character give an underling a post because of such persistance? Is it not rather calculated to make him stand still firmer to his refusal? You, monsieur," the *juge* turned to Mackay, "have met him; do you think he was the kind to yield to pressure?"

Mackay did not. "But he was the kind, to yield to common sense," he said. "Evidently the more he thought it over, the more certain he grew that this young Eastby was the man for the job. As Mr. Heimbrot says—and as seems logical."

"Then why did the mother say nothing about the son's presence here?"

"Pride," Mackay said at once. "She didna want us to think he had to beg for it. Aye, and verra likely she didna want the son to know what was up. Ma idea is that Mrs. Eastby had him—her son—on hand, if need should arise, if Sir Anthony should want an interview with him, but that she didna want Sir Anthony to know that Eastby was there unless he asked for him. Thae worrds Miss Young overheard, they might fit in wi' that theory."

The *juge* pondered this, eyes on the notes taken.

"You forget that we have here a double crime of singular ferocity," he pointed out; "a double crime. And a cunning one. Locked door on the inside, revolvers beside each man. The detective in charge of the inquiry into the disappearance of the diamonds is certain that there is no one in Cluny connected with that."

"I do not say that I agree with him," Cambier cut in as the *juge* turned to him. "But on the other hand, he is certain that Monsieur Brownlow, whatever Madam Brownlow's idea was, cannot have been taking any part in the search for the missing thieves."

"Yes, but I ask myself—" put in Rondeau.

Unheeding him, as usual, the commissaire went on: "I think Mr. Oor's reason for that belief is sound. I confess it appeals to me more than his certainty that no criminal connected with the thefts from the combine could have come to Cluny. Tibbitts for one—and in some way, Smith too? Though of him I do not feel really suspicious. But now this little perplexity about the son of Mrs. Eastby. . . ."

"What I ask myself," Rondeau announced; "is where is the colonel? The mad colonel? Have we not here—"

"A forged document," the *juge* finished, speaking very solemnly. "That, messieurs, is the great, great question

on which much hangs." He paused. You could have heard
a piece of paper fall in the attentive silence. "Is this letter
a forgery?" He held up the one Heimbrot had brought
him. "Was it a final desperate effort on a mother's part to
get her son into a good position, or on his own part, with
her connivance? Was Sir Anthony already dead when this
letter was concocted, or was he killed to prevent the
inevitable discovery that it was a forgery? And the death
of Mr. Brownlow, was that, as has been already surmised
might prove to be the case, an effort to cover up the first
crime? Did he intrude on the murder— or the forgery?
Was he silenced by the only means that spells perpetual
silence? Since, I take it, in the next world we shall not
need tongues. Our experts will decide the question of
forgery at once. I think it looks very dark indeed,
messieurs. Not so much against that poor wife and
mother, whose fate has certainly been in life's shadows,
but against the son. Evidently ambitious. Else why the
quiet life, the attention to duty, of which that kindly
disposed head clerk has just told us.

"What do you think, Cambier, you are an expert on
such a point?" He handed the note over and went on:
"Personally, I think the note looks unlike Sir Anthony's
usual writing, of which Mr. Mackay provided us with an
example. If it be a forgery, then we come back to the
theory of the impassioned pleading of the mother,
resulting in one more absolute refusal to place the son in
a position for which she thinks him so well suited, for
which he has strained every nerve to fit himself. That
dislike of the son—it looks as though at some time the
mother had put the son first and Sir Anthony second," the
juge said slowly.

Cambier looked up long enough to nod.

"That's what I think." That was what Pointer thought
too.

"One can imagine . . . one can imagine"—certainly one
could almost see the *juge* at it—"a young wife, very
beautiful, kept to her duty by the little son. And a man

rich—of the nobility—also young, accustomed, perhaps, to being all-victorious, who found that, because of that son, the mother stood firm where the woman and the wife would have weakened. Well, Cambier, what of that letter?"

"It is hard to say." Cambier had all the reluctance of your expert to commit himself.

"The difficulty will be to find the son—the masked young man who was no more seen after the hour for unmasking."

"If nothing leaks out, he must return when his leave is up," Cambier thought. "Then of course—"

Rondeau came in with fresh information. He had just been called to the telephone. His researches had borne fruit. Mrs. Eastby and her son had stayed at one of the small hotels in Enghien while Sir Anthony was there, arriving the same day that he came, and leaving the day that he left. Apparently Reginald Eastby had never been seen with the magnate, but spent most of his time on the Enghien golf course. But on four occasions he had been seen in the local teashops with a young, fair American girl.

"Young, fair American? *Sapristi!*" muttered Cambier.

"Does it fit Mademoiselle Young, that description, or does it not?" purred the *juge*.

Rondeau went on with his gleanings. Reginald Eastby seemed to have spent a very quiet time at Enghien. Neither he nor his mother went near the gaming tables, which was surprising, for one only goes to Enghien-les-Bains to gamble.

"I ask myself," Rondeau said, laying down a copy of the report, "whether it was Tibbitts whom Mademoiselle Fumier heard in the cedar room. Suppose it was young Eastby with whom that quarrel took place."

"Ah," the *juge* nodded, "ah! That would fit well. Mademoiselle Fumier heard the word 'thief,' and many times the word 'money.' " He paused and repeated, "Thief—a chartered accountant to go over a clerk's books—a mother who insists on paying to the director three hundred pounds which she can ill afford to spare. Oh, *messieurs*, here, I think, lies one end of this tangle. We will see that poor Madam Eastby once again."

CHAPTER TWELVE

MRS. EASTBY came in looking as though some inner fire were scorching her up.

Rondeau had found a piece of evidence which the *juge* now used with very good effect. Rondeau's find was a waiter, at present in Lyons, who had been sent by a local *pattissier* to help at the villa the night of the dance—the night of the double murder, as it was called in the local press. He had been told to fetch a small table from a window in the passage that ran between the cedar room and the writing-room. He found that the table had already been taken, but while looking about for it he, too, had seen that strange interlude which Vivian had watched and overheard between the veiled Egyptian woman and the tall hooded figure.

He had seen Vivian too, and his confirmation of her presence and of the pantomime—he understood no word that was said—now bore out the girl's story. Even the *juge* accepted it. Mrs. Eastby was told that a second witness had been found who definitely identified her son, a witness who had seen him at Enghien-les-Bains, where he had been staying with her.

Mrs. Eastby's rouged thin cheeks went blue-white. So did her lips. Her eyes had in them the unforgettable look of a hunted deer when the dogs close up. There was only profound pity in the faces of those watching her, but they were all the hounds of the law. Pledged to run down the guilty without pity. Mrs. Eastby pulled herself together splendidly after one second's hesitation.

She explained, with an appearance of great frankness which only the look in her eyes made unconvincing, that she had so hoped to keep her son out of this terrible affair. This was what had happened. She wanted Sir

Anthony to invest the three hundred pounds for her as
she had already explained, but her boy had a dislike of
Sir Anthony and a great objection to making any use of
him. But she wanted her son to come with her; after all,
should it come to a difficulty in talking over money
matters, a woman liked to lean on a man, even on her
son. She gave a bright smile at this, a smile that she kept
flying in face of the deepest gravity around her. So, in
order to have Reginald with her in case of some hitch,
and yet not have him know what she wanted of Sir
Anthony, she told him that a girl with whom he was very
much in love, an American girl whose first name was
Jane, would be at the dance in fancy dress, and masked,
of course. He had come for that reason. Miss Young was
the only English-speaking young woman present, and
though considerably taller than her son's "girl," the
difference between them was attributed by him to the
costume and mask and the effort to be disguised.

She, Mrs. Eastby, by the way, had a bet on that no
one would recognize him. A very big bet. It did not apply
to "Jane," as otherwise he refused to come with her, but
to every one else. That was why she did not want him to
enter the room where Sir Anthony was, who would, of
course, have known him from his voice, if from nothing
else.

With whom was this bet?

She declined absolutely to say. Unfortunately her son
had an understanding with "Miss Jane" about a
photograph of hers that she was to give him if—well, as
an answer to a letter which he had written her. Mrs.
Eastby did not know what letter nor what answer, but, of
course, one could guess. Again her heart-breaking smile
flashed around. Her son, as she said, had at first
mistaken Miss Young for this other girl, but he chanced
to overhear her speaking to Mr. Smith in her natural
voice, and on that he had very indignantly refused to
stay, either to supper or later. She had remained behind,
delighted that Sir Anthony had taken over the money for

her, and after supper and a change at the hotel, her son, who had been driving about to cool off, had come for her as had been arranged and driven on with her to Macon, where they caught the Geneva express.

By this time, for the *juge* did not let her story go unquestioned, the report of the specialists was put in his hands. Three of the five experts considered that the letter brought by Mr. Heimbrot, the head clerk, was written by Sir Anthony Cross, though under the stress of considerable haste and emotion. Two were sure that it was a forgery.

He read it through, handed it around, and then turned to the woman, who passed her tongue over her lips.

"Now, madam, I am sorry, but there is one more point. One of the dancers heard a man quarreling, or at least having a very hot disagreement with Sir Anthony Cross just before he must have been murdered. This man was your son." He spoke with great certainty.

Mrs. Eastby stared at him in apparently genuine bewilderment. "A quarrel?" she asked more quietly than she had yet spoken.

"A disagreement of the strongest kind, let us say then." The *juge* pursed his lips, as though he had no need to quibble about trifles. "The word—forgive me for hurting a mother's feelings—but the word was 'thief,' and there was a constant reference to 'money'—to the three hundred pounds you brought back. There is a suggestion," the *juge* went on," that the man speaking to Sir Anthony Cross was Tibbitts. But he denies that flatly. I am inclined to think it was your son."

"Oh, no!" Mrs. Eastby said eagerly. "Oh, no! He was dancing with Miss Young at the very moment. I heard that talk. I and"—she swallowed hard and tried to turn her *et*—she was speaking French—into a cough.

"You and Mr. Murgatroyd," finished the *juge*.

His shot went home. Mrs. Eastby again paled, a sickly pallor. Her hand went to her heart.

"I too as it happens, heard part of a long talk between Sir Anthony and a man," she went on steadily enough. "It was before I had my talk with him."

"Sir Anthony and Tibbitts, I presume," the *juge* said wearily.

She shook her head. "Oh, no. I had talked to Monsieur Tibbitts that evening. This was a gentleman speaking. The voice was cultured. The intonations quiet."

The *juge* was rather surprised, though he did not show it, that she had not snatched at the idea of the speaker being Tibbitts.

"Did you hear what was said?" the *juge* asked noncommittally.

"Unfortunately, no! I was too engrossed with—my hopes that Sir Anthony would invest the money for me to pay much attention. I only listened to hear when the voices would stop and I could speak to him again."

"You heard enough to tell you what they were talking about, doubtless?" the *juge* asked.

"I only heard the word 'tufa' said very clearly once."

"Tufa?" the *juge* looked puzzled. "What meaning has that word in English, madam?"

"The same as in French. It's a kind of volcanic rock, I fancy." There was a pause. The *juge* was inclined to believe Mrs. Eastby. The word overheard was not of the kind which one could see any reason for her inventing.

"How was it used?" he asked next. "I mean, was it in a sentence or by itself? Said as though in explanation or in a question?"

"Said in great anger," she replied at once. "Sir Anthony said it. It seemed to be in reply to a long sentence on the other man's part which I didn't hear—as I say I wasn't listening to what was said—but this word came like a sort of whip-crack; 'Not tufa!' as though that ended things. There was a long silence after that, and the rest was carried on in a lower voice, and again I paid no heed."

Mrs. Eastby was allowed to leave them for a brief

respite, and Mr. Heimbrot was asked to come in again, after the *juge* had studied an English-French dictionary very carefully and consulted an encyclopaedia.

Mr. Heimbrot was at once asked if he had ever heard of tufa in connection with Sir Anthony's interests or in connection with the combine's properties.

Mr. Heimbrot thought a while.

"If you mean 'volcanic tuff,' which used to be called 'tufa,' there might be a connection—if Sir Anthony were talking to some one who was not familiar with diamond earth. I don't know of any diamonds that have been found in volcanic tufa, but we're always on the lookout for that possibility. The Great Matan stone was found in a layer of it in Borneo. For years it was held to be a diamond, though now it is considered a rock crystal, but it's very close to being a pure diamond. Just a little more of this, or that, and it would have been one of the finest stones in the world. Three hundred and sixty-seven carats, mind you. The Great Moghul was only two hundred and seventy-nine. Yes, I shouldn't wonder at all if the talk was on diamondiferous earths, which always are volcanic in origin, of course. Volcanic breccia generally."

"Do you think Sir Anthony was about to start any new enterprise? Form any new company?" the *juge* went on after a pause, "One into which he might let a friend on the ground floor now, but which would be closed to further capital on such advantageous terms very soon?"

Heimbrot was all eagerness. The *juge* repeated most of what Mrs. Eastby claimed had passed between herself and Sir Anthony Cross about the investigating of the three hundred pounds which she asserted that she had handed him. Heimbrot was like a ratter who hears a rustle in the hayrick. Nothing could quiet him down. He pelted the *juge* with questions. It was only when he was really convinced that no one in the room could tell him more that he returned to the role of the questioned, not the eagerly questioning.

Evidently getting in on the ground floor with Sir

Anthony Cross was a privilege not to be lightly turned down.

Then followed an adjournment for refreshments. Mackay caught sight of Mrs. Eastby's face at the window of one of the rooms. Again he thought of the deer and the closing in of the hounds. Instantly he wheeled and went back, opened the door of the room, and went up to her. His usual shyness gone. He took her hand hi his. It was as hot as though she were in a fever.

"Don't give way," he said abruptly enough, but in a voice that turned her to him. "Things look black, but your son is all right, Mrs. Eastby. We know he didn't hurt a hair of either man's head, and we'll prove it yet. Trust me." There was a ring of certainty in his voice. Her other hand closed around his lean brown one with its big knuckles.

"He's innocent, oh, he is indeed!" she said in a gasp; "but —but—" She looked at him in a haggard terror.

"I know he's innocent," Mackay said again. "I have the gift of second sight, Mrs. Eastby. It hasn't let me down so far. I saw your son the night of the dance. He's no murderer!"

Her eyes lost a little, but only a very little of their terror. "If you can bring the others around to your way of thinking, Mr. Mackay, I'll bless you—wherever I am. The mere suspicion of a crime would ruin his career. He would never get over it. Never! And he's worked so hard to get on, and has had such an uphill fight. And he's so proud " She turned away, her face working convulsively.

A gendarme entered. Would monsieur step back into the conference room? Monsieur Maitland, the representative of the family of Sir Cross, the dead baron, had arrived at last.

Mackay gave Mrs. Eastby's arm a warm, encouraging touch, and hurried off. But he stopped before the Winter plaque on the wall and looked at it very long, instead of going at once into the room where the *juge* was receiving the newcomer.

Mr. Maitland proved to be a tall, thin, very reserved-looking man of around forty, with a sensitive mouth and rather unusually dreamy eyes for his profession.

He soon supplied the police with a large amount of fresh facts concerning Sir Anthony Cross's life and activities.

"Have you any idea what piece of financial activity Sir Anthony was contemplating which would be to the advantage of his friends to invest in, should he permit it?" the *juge* asked finally.

"You mean the Mongolian Exploration Trust?" he asked doubtfully. "I doubt if that would exactly be considered an investment plum by many people. Sir Anthony was financing it largely. All the members of the expedition were contributing. It was rather in the nature of a strictly family party. No outsiders permitted. There could be no returns for some time."

"But a sum of three hundred pounds invested in it would be profitable in the long run, eh?"

Maitland seemed surprised.

"Three hundred pounds? You mean three thousand? Hundreds are of no use in such an enterprise."

The *juge* only nodded. Yes, he thought this rhymed fairly well with Mrs. Eastby's story. Mr. Maitland might think in thousands, but on an occasion, for an old friend, Sir Anthony had evidently condescended to include a small sum in the enterprise—doubtless a golden one.

The *juge* passed on to other questions, general ones, about Sir Anthony. His friendship with the Brownlows, for instance, Mr. Maitland said that the three had met long ago, but that, as far as he knew, Sir Anthony and the Brownlows had not seen anything of each other for many years.

"He wrote to Monsieur Brownlow a short time ago, we have been told." Maitland murmured that that was quite possible. The *juge* went on to detail the idea of Mrs. Brownlow that the husband was acting for Sir Anthony in some way.

Maitland listened very closely. He made no comment. Pressed for an opinion, he explained that he would know nothing of Sir Anthony's personal plans. Did he know whether Sir Anthony had come to Cluny at the Brownlows' suggestion or on his own initiative. Maitland was quite certain that the latter was the case. There was a letter, written by Sir Anthony— Maitland put his hand into his breast and drew out a letter-case, but after a glance at its contents, shook his head. He had not kept this particular letter to which he was referring, as it was not connected with business, he explained, but in it Anthony Cross had mentioned that he had suddenly decided to run down to Cluny for a couple of days. He had even asked him, Maitland, to join him there. If the *juge* had not just told him about the business link between the two dead men, Maitland went on to say that he would have suggested that possibly Sir Anthony had gone to Cluny for a quiet rest to think over the diamond thefts which were troubling him greatly—not because of their intrinsic value, though in view of the raised insurance rates, that was something, as because of the suspicion that it might be a member of their own firm out in Johannesburg who was, if not the actual thief, then in league with him.

The *juge*, remembering Mackay's assertion that Brownlow was connected with those thefts, questioned Mr. Maitland closely about them, or as closely as that gentleman would permit.

For Maitland explained that steps were even now being taken which any leakage would nullify, and he had had to promise their Mr. Oor to be silent concerning them.

The *juge* sat a moment thinking.

"Did Sir Anthony suspect Mr. Reginald Eastby of being connected with the thefts?" he asked suddenly.

"Yes," Maitland said, looking very grave; "yes, he did. Quite without foundation, in my belief, and in the belief of the other directors. Fortunately, Sir Anthony himself evidently found some reason to come over to our way of thinking, or he would not have written the letter pressing Reginald Eastby's claims in a—for him—singularly warm way to the new post in London. I understand that the head clerk, Mr. Heimbrot, brought you that letter?"

The *juge* said that they had seen it.

There was a pause. Then the magistrate wanted to know if Sir Anthony was interested in geology.

"Naturally," Maitland agreed with a smile. "His Mongolian expedition was to search for valuable minerals."

"A quarrel, or at least a discussion, was overheard not long before he was murdered, in which the word 'tufa' occurred in such a way as to suggest that it played an important part in the discussion. 'Not tufa!' were the exact words, said very sharply, and apparently angrily. Could you help us to understand this?"

Maitland had light blue eyes, of that clear color that is very pleasant to watch. Now they went black. The pupils had dilated suddenly. But otherwise he showed no sign.

" 'Not tufa!' " he repeated, stroking his chin thoughtfully; "that is not enough of a sentence to help much in guessing the conversation, beyond showing that the talk was geological in character."

"The word may have been misunderstood. Or the account of the interview may be unreliable," the *juge* murmured. He then questioned Mr. Maitland about the state of feeling between his dead friend and Mr. Reginald Eastby.

Mr. Maitland thought that Sir Anthony had not cared for Eastby personally, but that there was no use denying that the latter was a most suitable candidate for the London post. As to any friendship between the mother and the dead man, Maitland stiffened at the question. He grew as vague as Heimbrot. Sir Anthony and Colonel Eastby had been friends before the latter's accident cut him off from the outer world. Naturally he must have known Mrs. Eastby, perhaps quite well. Maitland really

could not say. He had never met Mrs. Eastby. His work
had lain in London. Even young Eastby he only knew
from his work and the correspondence which he had had
with him.

Mackay entered the room at that. He whispered a
word to Rondeau, who leaped from his seat and vanished
with him. A moment later Cambier rose. There was
something in the wind evidently. When his junior fled in
that hurried fashion it was as well to follow.

Rondeau was standing staring up at the pewter dish
at the end of the hall. "You are right. It does look like it.
But" —a second more and he had jerked the dish from its
holders, all but decapitating himself. On the floor, all
three bent over it—"this apparent second sun, *mon chef*,
Monsieur Mackay here thinks it—ah, it is!"

With these cryptic words Rondeau pried out a little
ball and held it in his hand. "Look, a revolver bullet!"

Cambier examined it carefully. "Flattened a bit, but
the mate to the one that killed Sir Anthony Cross. But
this is most extraordinary! I confess I have always taken
it for a mere repousse lump. Let this be a lesson to you,
Rondeau; you think I pay too much attention to trifles.
Here is an instance of not paying enough attention! This
is very strange—evidently that plaque hung in front of
the cedar room door. See the old marks of the hangers.
We will question the maids at once. Without saying why,
naturally. Carry this into the writing-room and lock the
door." Rondeau dragged it off. Cambier went into the
dining-room and held a review of the servants one by one.

The information he obtained was that the plaques had
hung in their right order the morning of the dance. Butler
as well as maids was positive of that. Also they had been
carefully cleaned that same morning. There had been a
suggestion of hanging them in a line in the ball-room
behind some clumps of pink geraniums, but Mrs.
Brownlow had finally preferred mirrors. As to the
possibility of any bullet having been at that time lodged
in the dish, the bullet had not been polished. But in the

dent behind it, a speck of sand had been driven into the metal. The plaques were scoured with sand and vinegar.

So two bullets had been fired from the pistol that killed Sir Anthony, or at least from a similar one. Was it at Brownlow that it had been fired, and had the murderer then remembered that he had provided himself with Anthony Cross's revolver to use on this man so as to suggest a duel? It was a very perplexed Cambier who finally re-entered the conference room where the *juge*, his questions done, was chatting amiably with Mr. Maitland and discussing the wines of the district. A glance at the commissaire and the *juge* begged Mr. Maitland not to let him detain him from resting after his journey.

Maitland seemed quite willing to leave.

When the door shut behind him, Cambier suggested a move into the writing-room. There the plaque was examined, the bullet was examined, and the butler was finally once more examined.

"It is a most enigmatical case!" murmured the *juge*.

"And, monsieur *le juge*" broke in Rondeau; "that geological talk, that word 'tufa'—I ask myself whether a science master, who was a geological expert—in other words, whether, after all, Monsieur Lascelles—"

"Do not be led away by what would be interesting!" counseled Cambier. "Monsieur Lascelles has an alibi that seems unshakable.

"Yet it is a thought!" mused the *juge*, dangling his glasses.

"It seems to me," put in Cambier, "that the finding of that bullet tends to exonerate all people not actually staying in the house. For it looks like some one who would have leisure to change the plaques. It suggests some one who was a friend—an inmate. Yes, to me it suggests Tibbitts."

"I will ask Monsieur Maitland, if he is still in the house, a few more questions," the *juge* said finally, as the result of his cogitations. He rang the bell. Mr. Maitland had not yet left. He was inquiring after Mrs. Brownlow, who still tossed and moaned and babbled on her bed overhead.

The *juge's* questions led to nothing fresh. He was just finishing the interview when a note was handed him. Mrs. Eastby wondered if she might speak to Mr. Maitland before he left. She wrote that she wanted to press for the return of the money handed by her to Sir Anthony for investment. Possibly the executor of the dead man would raise no objection to its being paid back at once, out of the estate. Sir Anthony's fortune had gone, as they had just been told, to a distant kinsman, the heir to the baronetcy, apart from charities bequests and a very handsome legacy to his executor, himself.

Mrs. Eastby was admitted at once. She and Mr. Maitland, who introduced himself, exchanged a few words of mutual regret on the sad occasion of the meeting, and Maitland went on to say a kind word about her son. Mrs. Eastby was very pale. She did not bring forward the reason which she had given in her note for wishing to meet the newly-arrived friend of the late Anthony Cross.

Instead she leaned forward to the *juge*.

"Might I have a few words with you when this gentleman has done?"

Maitland insisted on leaving at once. The others, intrigued by something in Mrs. Eastby's face, gathered around.

"That man—Mr. Maitland—that's the man I heard quarreling with Sir Anthony in the cedar room! That's the voice I heard. Oh, I could swear to it anywhere. And would."

The *juge* turned on her his cold scrutiny.

"Be very careful, madam. The point is important. Very."

"Of course. I know that. But it was his voice that I heard answering when Sir Anthony broke out into that angry cry of 'Not tufa!'"

She was questioned and cross-questioned. The men listened most intently, for, though she did not know this,

a man had told them only yesterday that he had seen a
stranger making his way across to the villa about
midnight dressed in a big loose coat and soft cap. The
man, a baker going on night work, had noticed him
because the evening was so warm, and he had wondered
at that coat. It did not conceal a fancy dress; he had
looked to see as much. The stranger was carrying a small
dispatch case. He claimed to have even seen him stop and
look at his watch once. The hour was about eleven.
Nothing had come of the efforts to trace this stranger,
and the police had decided that he was a certain traveling
salesman, who said that he had passed that way about
that time and had stopped at the lamp-post in question to
see the time. He had been wearing a top coat, but not
carrying a bag of any kind.

Now, however, the baker was questioned again. His
description, which had fitted the traveling salesman
badly, fitted Maitland very well indeed. A top coat meant
a car probably, since the man was wearing tweed
trousers. Around eleven—an express got into Macon in
time to bring a traveler, in a car, to Cluny around then.
Now, there are not many night garages in Macon. An
inquiry was put through at once. Meanwhile all the
attention of the French police was concentrated on the
new possibility—Maitland. Maitland, the dead man's
friend, the beneficiary by a large bequest, a party to that
new enterprise which Mrs. Eastby had been told by Sir
Anthony was so valuable.

There followed a few hours' intensive work, hours
which brought some interesting facts to light. Then Mr.
Maitland was asked to come to the *juge*'s room in the
Hotel de ville. The *juge* said that a man resembling him
had been seen the night of the dance making for the villa.
That a voice, definitely identified as his, had been heard
talking to Sir Anthony. Where had Mr. Maitland been the
night of the murders?

Mr. Maitland was not swift in his replies. He had a
way, from the first, of looking at his interlocutor before

speaking that gave him an air of caution. He now eyed the *juge* meditatively for a full second, then he said quietly:

"I motored over from Lyons the night of the dance to see Sir Anthony Cross."

"Indeed? This is the first we have heard of it—from you, monsieur." Maitland said nothing. He looked quite at his ease. But he was the kind of man to look at his ease with a boiler bursting beneath him.

"What hour was this interview, pray?"

Maitland seemed to ponder.

"I got out of the car around eleven. I was driving it myself, and left it in a field the other side of the river. I met Sir Anthony by chance in the garden. He had just posted that letter concerning Reginald Eastby, so he told me. We walked together through one of the open windows into a room, which I think must be the one you call the cedar room. Sir Anthony had been writing some letters there. We sat down and talked over a business matter, of which I regret that I am not at liberty to give you any particulars. Then I left by a little side door very close to the room, which Sir Anthony shut behind me. I motored back to Lyons and flew home to London. I think that is all."

"Indeed!" the *juge* permitted himself to be sarcastic. He opened a slip of paper that Rondeau had handed him. It was from Cambier, who was sitting in an adjoining room with Miss Young and the doctor's daughter. The latter identified the voice which had been thought to be Tibbitts's, the voice which she had heard during her stay in the garden talking in a very heated argument with Sir Anthony as that now speaking to the *juge.*

Vivian Young, on her part, was equally certain that it was not the voice of the young man in the long robe, the young man who had called her Jane, and who was now believed to be Eastby.

The *juge* destroyed the little note and turned again to Mr. Maitland.

He wanted to know if there had been any disagreement between Mr. Maitland and Sir Anthony. Maitland said that, unfortunately, there had been a distinct difference. About methods only.

"And are you still unable to explain the mention of the word 'tufa'?" the *juge* put in blandly, but at a venture. Maitland seemed to make an even longer pause than usual before replying:

"I fancy that must have referred to the possibility of some of the regions we intended to explore first of all being in a tufa belt. I was keen on not wasting our time, the time of the expedition, which was going to be an immensely costly affair, on baser metals. Tufa, as we rather loosely called it—I am no geologist nor yet a diamond expert—referred to those volcanic pipes in which diamonds are often found."

"And the question about 'money?' And the word 'thief'?" pressed the *juge*.

Maitland looked at him as though he considered him very dull wilted.

"Obviously the 'money' referred to the sums necessary to fit out the expedition. 'Thief,' on the other hand referred to the losses the combine was suffering."

The *juge* had copious notes taken throughout. He now asked Mr. Maitland if he himself were a friend of the Brownlows.

Maitland murmured that he could not claim that honor. Like Sir Anthony, he had met the couple many years ago in one of our colonies.

"But not since?"

"Not since," Maitland murmured positively.

The *juge* held out a lighter. It was a gunmetal and silver affair. On one corner were the initials "T.M." intertwined.

"Then how do you account for this?" he asked. "This is yours."

Cambier's note to the *juge* had finished with this suggestion. He now sat watching the scene like a cat licking its whiskers after creams. The idea was entirely his own. The lighter had been considered to belong to Tibbitts, and as such had not been given more than a passing glance, but the commissaire had noticed that if one read the monogram as T.M.— instead of M.T., as had been done—they were the same as those inside Mr. Maitland's hat now hanging on the hall-stand.

Mailtand went pale. At last a shot had got home. He turned the little case over in his hand. Would he deny it?

"It is mine," he said finally and carelessly; "I must have left it in the cedar room."

"It was not found in there."

"Probably some one picked it up, used it, and left it somewhere else," Maitland still spoke casually.

"The maid found it on the mantelshelf after Mrs. Brownlow and you had been talking in a small, little-used room off the billiard room," the *juge* said quietly.

The maid's story had been that during the dance Mrs. Brownlow had met her in the passage outside the room in question and asked her to give a message to Mr. Smith at once. The message had concerned some music that was to be played next. Mr. Smith was to talk it over with the conductor. The maid had carried out the instructions by passing the message on to a footman and had hurried back. It was the head housemaid who disliked Mrs. Brownlow. She had an impression, so she had told Cambier, that madam had only wanted to get her out of the way. She found no one in the passage or in the rooms opening out of it, but the little room next the billiard room smelled strongly of cigarette smoke. Not the kind that Mrs. Brownlow smoked, but a much stronger kind. And besides that, the maid was positive that some one had just burned some papers; the smell was unmistakable, so she claimed. On the mantelshelf she had found the case, which she had handed Cambier, and which had then been held to be marked with the initials of Mathew Tibbitts. Questioned afresh, the maid had said that the passage way smelt of the same cigarette smoke as she detected in the room. It ended in a door. And Maitland just now, in speaking of the door by which he had left the house, had referred to it.

"Just so," Maitland now said equably; "just what I suggested. Some one evidently picked it up after my talk with Cross and finally left it in some other room, where it was found later on."

"But this errand on which the maid was sent, monsieur, this message about the music to be played was before eleven, so the conductor can prove. And Sir Anthony Cross did not go to the cedar room to write, and eventually post, some letters until an hour later. In other words, monsieur, your lighter was found in the one room before it could, according to your story, have been left in the other room. The room in which two men were afterwards found murdered."

The *juge*'s voice was stern.

And then began one of those scenes of cleverly-put questions, and thundered denunciations, and subtle traps, of which the French *juges d'instruction* are pastmasters. It is a terrible thing to which to listen, when the mind of a man is driven from corner to corner, when its defences and barricades are pulled away one by one, when you can almost hear the blows rain down on it.

None of those listening but was moved, the Frenchmen, like bloodhounds on the trail, almost leaping from their seats with every point well driven home, the two men from Britain with set jaws.

But, as Mackay told himself, though it was the third degree of the United States, there was here no possibility of physical brutality added. And, horrible though it might be to hear, there was, therefore, no need for the innocent to dread it. No cross fire of questions, no cleverly-hidden traps can confuse the truth or the truth-teller.

But Maitland was confused. Though he maintained that there was a mistake, that he and Mrs. Brownlow had not met the night of the dance. In the end, he took his stand in silence, and with set lips refused to answer any more questions. Finally a paper was handed the *juge*. A wireless reply to a wireless inquiry.

"Tell me why," thundered the *juge*; "why did you resign from the English Law Society the morning after the murder of Sir Anthony and Mr. Brownlow? I have here an information that you, by your own letter of that date, no longer belong to that honored body of respected men."

This time Maitland spoke.

"Because of the enterprise on which Sir Anthony and I were about to embark—the Mongolian expedition, about some of whose preparations and itinerary we had quarreled, if one can call a somewhat acrimonious discussion a quarrel. I considered that the legality of certain of the steps contemplated were questionable and, therefore, as I did not wish to give up my association with the enterprise, I resigned from the Law Society."

"Because he threatened to denounce you if you did not!" the *juge* said harshly, and Mr. Maitland left the room for another on a floor above, with an agent beside him and two gendarmes bringing up the rear. Though not actually arrested, he was to be detained while further inquiries could be made. The *juge* made no secret of the fact that unless these brought some new facts to light— facts that should prove Maitland's innocence—he intended to send him up for trial, accused of the murder of both men. It was for Cambier to find out the motives.

Pointer did not think that the case against him would break down easily.

"His resignation from the Law Society will be made the most of. This mysterious expedition will be made the most of. He's in a tight place," Pointer said finally, as he and Mackay walked back to their hotel together. "Unlike Tibbitts there will be no escape for him. That sort of thing doesn't happen twice."

There was a silence.

"You don't think it was Maitland, do you?" Mackay

asked. "I don't. There's nae logic in sic a thought. He's in trouble, probably owing to some affair wi' Mrs. Brownlow, an auld admirer verra likely; the wumman seems to hae an extraordinary influence over men. That's the why I wadna meet her mair than I could help. But you don't think it was Maitland, do you?"

Pointer refused to give an opinion.

"It's not my case. I haven't worked it up. It's like judging a man from what you might read of the trial in a newspaper. Half the facts which would guide you to a decision are not given, and the other half are badly stated."

"But the clues so far?" Mackay wondered.

"There's no such thing as a clue. It all depends on who finds it. To use the jargon of the day, it's the detective's reactions to what he finds that turns things into clues."

"Aye, that's what Miss Young canna seem to get intae her head. It's no use asking me what I think o' this or that. This case doesna worrk oot according' to reason. I juist wait for the next think frae the bran pie to come to hand." He said as much to Vivian herself when she met him later on.

Vivian forebore to make any comment on his helplessness. At last she knew what it was to be helpless herself.

"They think the noo that it was Maitland wha helped Tibbitts to escape," Mackay said after a long pause. "That they twa are in collusion."

"My, Mr. Mackay, where will this tangle end!" she asked.

His expression was hopeless.

"I dinna ken. It seems to gang on for ever and a'."

"Here's this son of Mrs. Eastby, and now here's this friend of Sir Anthony's . . ." she mused.

"Yon professor at the villa was richt," Mackay said suddenly. "Aye. Ane violence brings anither. And it in its turn anither. And so on in rings."

"You've always maintained that Tibbitts was

innocent. How about this new-comer? Doesn't your second sight tell you about him?"

Mackay looked hurt.

"I micht ha'e known that you'd but laugh at me," he said reproachfully. "Na, Miss Young, the gift comes and gangs awa'. But my reasoning powers tell me that nae motive sufficient has been foond to account for Mr. Maitland, wealthy and respected, killing Sir Anthony. He had too much to lose. And not eno' to gain."

"And what about Mrs. Eastby?"

"Are you back again at her?" Mackay asked wearily.

"Why did she look so desperate that night before the dance?" Vivian said, in the tone of a woman who meant to know some day. "Nothing she's said explains her face outside the villa. Anthony's refusing to invest her money? Shucks! That's too silly to be mentioned—to me, who saw that look in her eyes."

"Hoo's Mrs. Brownlow?" he asked after a pause.

"She's still delirious. Say, Mr. Mackay, I'm coming down with brain fever next!"

There followed another silence full of thought. Vivian broke it.

"You know that umbrella of mine that got mixed?" she asked somewhat incoherently. Mackay said that he recollected the incident. "Well, this morning I was driven to have another look at the museum, and there sat this same man I spoke of, drawing a piece of cast-iron work, and drawing it real well too. But he pressed too hard on his pencil and broke the lead, then he sharpened it ta a needle's point, and then he dropped it and broke the point again and—my!"

"Ye shudna have stayed within earshot!" said Mackay virtuously.

"Oh, I was prepared for some swear words—I should have used a few myself! But it wasn't what he said, it was the voice, Mr. Mackay. It was Tibbitts's voice!"

Mackay's jaw actually dropped.

"But—but—why he's a Swedish art critic they told me

at the hotel!" "No, na, Miss Young. There's naething so misleading as a voice or even a likeness. Remember hoo you thocht that Mr. Lascelles—"

"Look here, my braw laddie," Vivian said tartly; "would a Swedish art critic say 'Now I've broken the bloody point again'?"

Mackay could not maintain that he would.

"You heard those actual words?" he asked.

"I shall never be the same again," she said, nodding her head.

Mackay stood as though rooted to the spot.

"Look here," he said swiftly, "you've often told me that my chance was in this case. Well, it's come!"

"It's been banging you on the head for days," she said huffily.

"Na, na; I mean the money. Mr. Davidson's thousand that I want to get back. Now, then, Miss Young, ye havna spoken o' this recognition, if one cud ca' it that?"

"You can. Even by the light of reason," she said shortly, then she softened at the worried, anxious look on his freckled face. "No, I haven't spoken of it to any one but you. You're the most trying young man I ever met, but if I have at last wound you up to go, thanks be!"

"Then not a worrd. I ha'e a plan. Ooch aye! But leave it tae me. And not a hint to any one mind, or it fails."

Mackay was really on the jump. Vivian promised absolute silence, and handed him over Tibbitts, the Swedish art critic, for his sole and only use. Though she had her doubts as to what the outcome would be.

CHAPTER THIRTEEN

Cambier dropped in for a chat with the chief inspector. Mackay happened to be out. When he returned, Pointer passed on to him the gist of the talk.

"He's hunting around for something to link the three men together, Sir Anthony, Brownlow, and Maitland. Tibbitts is considered to be merely Maitland's tool. Cambier, or rather the magistrate, thinks they will find the tie between the three men in some diamond-tufa proposition, that that was the business in which Brownlow was helping Sir Anthony, and the reason for which Maitland murdered both men. As to the key found in the garden, they think it's the key of a safe containing papers bearing on the proposition which Maitland took from Brownlow's dead body and then lost as he rushed away to his car. The safe is probably in London, they think. Maitland, according to what the police are going to try to prove, came back to the villa unseen, at dawn, to hunt for the key, and then had to give up. They think he has been in hiding nearby all along. As you know, they are certain that it was he who helped Tibbitts to escape— probably because the key was lost."

"Eh?" Mackay peered with knitted brows.

"The idea is that Tibbitts was to make him another as the price of rescue."

There was a short silence. Finally Mackay said:

"Of a' the preplaixing affairs. Ratiocination seems nae help at a'."

"The French may not be far out in the idea that there is a link between the three men," Pointer said after a pause, during which they sat smoking their pipes.

"You mean the diamond proposition?"

"I mean Touva." Pointer gave a short laugh. "I

shouldn't be surprised if that was the real word that Mrs. Eastby heard."

"Is that the way tufa should be pronounced?" Mackay asked a little shyly.

"Touva is not anything geological. It's the name of one of the new Soviet States lying between Siberia, I mean Soviet Russia, and Mongolia."

"Weel?"

"It's chief town is called Krasny," Pointer murmured, puffing away.

"What for no? I confess geography was the lesson I aye scamped at school. But we ken that Sir Anthony was interested in a Mongolian expedition—"

"Just so, and Mr. Brownlow is, or rather was, at the time of his death interested in Krasny, and it seems that young Jackson, the lad of whom Brownlow was supposed to have been jealous in Shanghai ten years ago, had been exploring the other side of the Gobi Desert. The new republic of Tannow Touva lies the other side of the desert too."

Mackay was all attention now.

"You've been making inquiries?" he asked.

"Strictly and only between ourselves," Pointer confessed, "though should they ask me, all I know is at the service of the men working on the case, of course—I have so far overstepped my official position as observer as to make a few inquiries about that murdered lad. For murdered I think he was. It seems as near proven as a thing not actually witnessed could be. Had any motive, other than jealousy, been found, nothing could have saved Brownlow from the gallows."

"But what's yon auld affair to do wi' Sir Anthony's murder?" Mackay spoke in the tone of a man who had no room for spare cargo.

"Cambier is hunting for a chain between the three men," the chief inspector explained. "I think its end is young Jackson. For Sir Anthony is the man who was briefed to defend Brownlow in the trial that never came off! He was attached to the British Supreme Court for China at Shanghai for a couple of years, as we learned in *Who's Who*."

"Losh!" muttered Mackay; "but surely they wadna, I mean Brownlow wadna, ha'e shot Anthony Cross because he had tried to get him off in an auld trial?" Mackay spoke in bewildered tones. "He *did* want to get him off, didn't he? If he was his counsel?"

"Oh, I think so. I'm told that Sir Anthony, like Abraham Lincoln, would never take on a case in which he didn't feel sure of his client's innocence. That really was one of the reasons why Brownlow was not absolutely done for, socially. A great many people argued that if Anthony Cross, who was as straight as he was brilliant, believed in him, Brownlow could only have acted hastily, not criminally."

"But the wife—" Mackay dropped his voice. "The widow, as she is the noo, talked to us as though she had nae doots—"

"Perhaps she hadn't," Pointer said a little dryly. "And also, just then, you were throwing so much doubt— justified doubt—on the idea of a duel having been fought over her, that she wanted to convince you of Brownlow's passionate nature."

"But hoo do you link up Mr. Maitland wi' a' this?" Mackay asked after another silence full of thought.

"Thomas Maitland was the consulate solicitor at that time. I shouldn't wonder if that was where he and Sir Anthony met. He seems to've been offered the post of solicitor to the Diamond Combine by the latter when he left to join the board of that big affair."

"Consulate solicitor—then he, too, wad ha'e been for the Brownlows—" murmured Mackay.

"Very much for them, I gathered, especially for Mrs. Brownlow."

"And a' this means?" pursued Mackay.

"That's to find out," Pointer said equably. He had a guess or two as to what would be found, but only guesses as yet. "Cambier and Rondeau are good hunting dogs. Once they strike the Touva—not tufa—trail, we shall have some quick developments; and Maitland will be past praying for. Cambier told me just now that they believed that Maitland aimed at Sir Anthony first as the latter entered the room, and then got him with the second bullet. He would know where Sir Anthony kept his revolver, and, so they think, had frightened Mrs. Brownlow into telling him where Brownlow kept his."

"And the revolver we did find by the body they think was put there by Mrs. Brownlow," Mackay went on, half to himself.

"Quite so," Pointer agreed; "according to him, the *juge*, too, thinks that Maitland terrorized Mrs. Brownlow. Either that, or that he was in some way an apparent friend to Sir Anthony, and, therefore, accepted by her as a friend of her husband's too. They're doubtful of the means he used, but they seem certain that it was under pressure exerted by Maitland during that preliminary interview with her that Mrs. Brownlow supported next morning the idea of a duel. Or, rather, helped to create it. They think, as I say, that she had been told to put that revolver down as soon as the room was opened. Their notion now is that Maitland wanted to be sure there were no fingerprints on the one found, and that it should only show one bullet fired.

"Rondeau has routed out a leather case of Brownlows, which shows that he had a brace of automatics, duplicates of each other, probably. They are too usual a make to be able to trace easily."

"And what do they think happened to the revolver that Brownlow used?" Mackay asked.

"They're going to look for it. It won't be difficult to find, probably."

"Think not?" Mackay wrinkled his forehead.

"I know where *I* should drop a revolver under those circumstances, supposing I wanted to drop it anywhere," Pointer said briskly.

"Ye mean—in the Grosne?" Mackay asked; and nodding at Pointer's assent, they went off to watch the work of salvage.

From the cornfields around came the yellow-hammer's notes, without which August would not know itself in the country. Down by the river the little sedge warblers were silent at last, their long season of song over. One missed their cheery chatter, heard on so many a summer's day, that it seems to belong by right to the murmur of every stream, like the splash of fish or the plop of voles.

In the trees around the ring-doves kept up their throaty notes of full content. The drone of insects sounded an undertone to the harvest noises. A peacock butterfly dipped and floated among the knap-weeds. It, too, belonged to that sound. Disturbed by the dozen from the nut-brown ears of wheat, its plainer cousins, the meadow browns, and whites, and blues, and coppers floated past, making the most of their short summers. That fair-weather sailor, the Red Admiral, was a splendid sight as, wings fluttering open and shut, he swung on a teasel.

Hardly lighter than they, thistledown was everywhere, and the tiny silk shuttlecocks of the rose bays. You could even catch the quick firing of the yellow gorse, as the pods cracked in the hot sun. Among the not yet cut oats, shimmering in silver-green as the air stirred them, danced gatekeeper butterflies, and tall as the oats themselves showed the blue-mauve heads of scabious in its prime. Black as their own shadows were most of the trees, except for the tufting green on the oaks ends, but the leaves of willows and poplars and ash, tossing over in the breeze, rippled among the dark green like wave crests at sea. Beauty was everywhere—the beauty of the country-side, in the full tide of summer. Only the warm, delicious scent of stocks from cottage gardens that spice the air of every English harvest scene was absent—as were the cottage gardens.

They found Rondeau directing his men in waders and armed with a net. The Grosne is swift, and its deepest pool well known. After half an hour's work a revolver was fished up, to the great surprise of a fat and stately old trout who lived there.

The weapon was the mate to that found beside Brownlow, but two shots had been fired from this, and it bore the mark of a silencer.

Rondeau hurried off well content. Mackay looked frowningly after him.

"We're juist dancing dervishes, that's what we a' are," he said disgustedly; "juist turning roond and roond oorseles wi' the murder in the cedar room in the center." He looked at his watch. Maitland was to be questioned anew within a few minutes, and the two men hurried away.

Rondeau had collected a good deal of fresh information in tiny bits. But like that wonderful Chinese enameling that is done on crushed egg shells, each little dot of information was added skilfully to another dot, until a pattern was formed. And the pattern, as composed by Cambier, showed that Maitland had certainly left the villa by the side door as he had said. But much earlier in the evening. The men thought that Mrs. Brownlow had let him out. After that he had not been seen until much later on; a dancer had noticed him step out of a cedar room window. Some one had shut the window after him and rolled down the steel shutter. Who, the dancer had not noticed, for inside the room the long curtains were drawn. Nor could he be sure of the time, except that it was past the wassail drinking. He thought some long time past, but as the *juge* extracted from him that he was waiting for a girl—his girl—to arrive with her people, it was highly probable that, like the poet, he had counted time "by heart-throbs not by figures on a dial." Of the fact, however, he was quite sure. He added details of the man's general appearance that confirmed those of other witnesses. He thought he saw the man in question toss something into the bushes as he passed out the gate. A cigarette stub he had fancied then. The police thought differently now. They thought the little key. Though why he had flung it away still eluded them.

Maitland refused to answer yea or nay, press him how they might. As for Mrs. Brownlow, she was still babbling of her husband, apparently back in some English home. Maitland was once returned to his rooms, and the French police worked on.

Vivian meanwhile had gone into Lyons. She seemed to be free from surveillance for the time being. Knowing that foreigners must show their passports to register at any hotel of repute overnight, and having given notice of the names of

the inmates of the villa at the frontier as "not to be allowed through," the French police were concentrating on Mr. Maitland's past and present. She was puzzling over the problem, which still was as impenetrable as ever to her eyes. And she could see as far into a brick wall as the next, she told herself. As to Mackay—well, the boy sure had bad luck to have this sort of a case drop on his head. But she was convinced that he would do his best, and perhaps win through after all with Davidson's commission.

She herself was trying to divert her mind by some necessary shopping. What Vivian thought of the average French shops had better be left unsaid.

A man joggled her arm, and half-spun her round with his heavy package, and standing so for a second, she found herself looking down a corner street, along which two people were passing just now. One was Mrs. Eastby, and the other— it was Mr. Murgatroyd. Vivian started. He sure was right about her being on the spot when things happened. She followed close on their heels. What they said she could not catch, but evidently it was not of a harmonious nature. Each of them, according to her scrutiny, was as mad as they could be. Finally Mrs. Eastby stopped so suddenly that Vivian only just had time to spin towards a shop window, but neither of the two were noticing her.

"I utterly refuse!" Mrs. Eastby was saying, firmly and yet with some suppressed emotion that made her voice tremble. "I utterly refuse."

Mr. Murgatroyd came closer and said something quietly and very low. It was not a short sentence. It looked like a threat. As it continued, Mrs. Eastby's defiance seemed to wither. She made some reply that Vivian could not catch, but which, judging by its tone, was grudgingly submissive, and again they walked on, this time only for a moment. Again they paused.

"I'd better not be seen," Vivian heard the man say, and then, murmuring some quick low words of farewell, he lifted his hat and turned away. She did not dare to follow Mrs. Eastby too closely now that the latter was alone, and in the end she lost her altogether.

Vivian herself went home by train deep in fruitless thought —thought of Mr. Murgatroyd, evidently able to meet Mrs. Eastby when he chose; thought of what little she had seen and heard of their meeting, and, most of all, thought of Tibbitts sharpening a pencil in the museum. What in the world had brought him back into such appalling danger? Who was the man with him? Mackay had refused to discuss his plans, but Vivian knew that he was hard at work. Would he succeed? He was not on hand on her return.

Late in the evening, and after some very dull games of patience that refused to come out, she went up to bed. But she could not sleep. Finally she got up again and decided that an hour's writing might quiet her mind. She was sending in an account of the Hotel de ville's most obvious treasures to a paper which always took any article of hers. After a few minutes' writing she stopped.

She was working with a brochure beside her to help her as to historical facts, and she had come on a word that she did not understand. She could not find it in her pocket dictionary. But downstairs was a big one. She slipped down to the library, wearing her soft bedroom slippers. The dictionary was not there. Then she remembered that it was now kept in the cedar room on the mantelshelf. She half-turned away. Then common sense came to her aid. After all, the daughter of a Texas ranger was not going to be frightened of entering a room because a tragedy, even a double tragedy, had happened there. She stepped quickly down the passage. As she came up to the door of the room at the end, she heard the sounds of some movement inside.

Who was in the library at this hour of night? By the clock she could see that it was close on twelve. She stood listening. Again she heard something stir inside, and this time made out a very light step and the soft sound of a chair or table shifted on a thick rug. She felt for the door-knob and turned it noiselessly. But the door was locked.

She could not get out through the front door without a noise. The same was true of hoisting one of the steel window shutters from any of the windows around. Yet whoever was inside must have got in from the outside, for, barring the servants, there was only herself and Mrs. Brownlow in the house. Suddenly she remembered that Smith's room had an outside balcony and staircase.

She crept up to his room, found the key in the lock, opened it, passed through the bedroom and let herself out by the door on to his balcony. To her surprise she found all the doors unlocked and the bolt on the balcony door unshot. So that some one in the library downstairs could have got in this way, supposing they knew of it. Tibbitts for one would know of it. So, of course, would any one probably who had stayed in the house. Should she wake the butler? He and the two footmen were stalwart fellows, and they slept on the floor above her own. But Vivian was an intrepid soul. She determined to find out for herself who was inside the villa to-night. She slipped down the outside stairs and turned towards the cedar room wing. All the windows were shuttered. She climbed the wooden stairs to Smith's room again. Entering, she locked the door behind her and put the key in her pocket . Then, for the first time, she looked about her in both bedroom and sitting-room. Here, too, the shutters were down, all the furniture was sheeted and covered, but on a chair lay a man's soft felt hat. Inside it was still warm to the touch. It was the kind of hat that nine men out of ten were wearing just now. Mr. Murgatroyd had been wearing one like it, she thought . She tucked it under her arm and laid it in a drawer in her room, locking the drawer. Vivian intended to disarrange as many of the plans of the person or persons in the house as possible.

In her room, too, she paused long enough to put on a black traveling coat, wind a scarf of thin silky stuff, also black, around her head and face, and finally draw on a pair of black gloves. That swiftly done, and with nothing light about her to catch the eye, she slipped down the stairs. Listening with her ear against the library hinges she heard the stealthy movements continue for some time longer. Then came the click of the lights turned out, and she flattened herself back into the shadow of a cabinet.

Cautiously the door opened, slowly the figure that had been in the room seemed to ooze out through it. It passed her and made for the stairs. It was a woman. Vivian crept up the stairs too. The figure turned down a passage leading in the direction of Mrs. Brownlow's room. Vivian slipped after her. She knew that Mrs. Brownlow had only one nurse now. And she, a sister from a convent nearby, slept in the sitting-room opening out of her patient's room, where she could be summoned at once or would hear any call or cry from the patient; but the latter's condition, though obstinate, was not getting worse, the doctor thought. It was simply a case of time and absolute quiet.

That meant, Vivian thought, that Mrs. Brownlow might be practically defenceless in her room. When she heard the door of her bedroom very cautiously opened and closed, she was close beside it, her ear against the panels. Faint stirrings reached her, fainter even than in the library. Then came, to her boundless surprise, the creak of a wooden bedstead and the rustle of sheets. Vivian was peering through the keyhole by this time. It showed her, by a faint night-light, the bed which was in a line with it. There was some one sitting up in bed, pulling the bedclothes straight. A second later Vivian caught sight of her face in the light. It was Mrs. Brownlow, but a Mrs. Brownlow with a most intelligent eye cocked in the direction of the sitting-room.

Evidently she too had caught a hint of stirring, but fancied it came from the sister there. A moment later she lay down noiselessly and Vivian could hear the deep sound of her breathing. A sound as of heavy sleep. Vivian stole away. So Mrs. Brownlow was not ill. Mrs. Brownlow was hunting for something in the library downstairs. For what? For what else, Vivian told herself, than for clues to her husband's murder. But why the deception by day? She had no time to waste in vain cogitation, however. Mrs. Brownlow might have been in the library, but she certainly had not entered by Mr. Smith's balcony, nor worn that felt hat now locked in Vivian's room. She slipped downstairs again, and stood by the newel post, listening intently. She thought she detected a creak here, a rustle there, that did not belong to the house. She herself made no sound. She hardly breathed as she put all her will power into increasing her sense of hearing. She did not close her eyes because, with Vivian, sight had often helped hearing. It did so now. For as she stood tense, something moved in the long corridor with its many shuttered windows on one side, its doors on the other, its tables and chests and chairs between, set flat against the wall.

Something or some one moved swiftly towards her. It was a man. She could not see his face, though that was a dim gray in the darkness. The electric battery of her torch had given out long ago, and could not be replaced in France, she had found. If she were to switch on the light, she would show herself. She waited, one hand on the post. She was afraid even to draw herself more compactly together for fear of a rustle. And then a hand was laid flat on hers. It was a very firm, warm hand. She was too startled to move now. She heard a low questioning, "Is that you Lascelles?" and a torch, just such a one as she would have liked to use, played over her. It struck her that she must look rather a ghastly figure in that house of death, with her black gown, and black gloves, and black veil twisted over her face so that it should not show as a face. Apparently she did, for she heard a stifled ejaculation, and some one passed her, taking the stairs three at a time in great, lithe bounds. Vivian slipped after him, but at a cautious distance. So cautious a one that she had to stand irresolute on the first landing, listening intently again. It was Smith. She was sure of that. Her blood was up—the blood of a first-class reporter, a getter of news unsurpassed in her own town. She stepped quickly, but without making a sound, to his room and gently felt for the door. It was standing open. At that she did draw back. That open door stopped her far more effectually than a barred one would have done. To what did it invite? It cost her an effort to enter. Listening again, if possible harder than ever, she felt sure that the room was empty. Then where had that figure gone? Mrs. Brownlow's rooms and a servant's staircase alone lay in the other direction. She turned now and all but ran towards them. As she ran, a low, suppressed cry rang out, so filled with almost unbearable fear that Vivian's very hair crisped. In a second she had leaped to Mrs. Brownlow's sitting-room and called out, "Sister! Is anything wrong?"

The door opened instantly. A very sleepy-eyed nun looked out, her finger to her lip.

"Sh-sh! It was only delirium. A bad dream. She is fast asleep."

Vivian came in. She saw in the farther room a white face on the pillow; a very, very white face, but the eyes were closed and she heard again that deep, softly hissing sound of breath drawn in and given out in profound slumber. The sound that she had heard a few minutes before while Mrs. Brownlow was sitting up in bed and eyeing the sitting-room attentively.

Vivian said something apologetic to the nun and left the room. Mrs. Brownlow's game—whatever it was—was not her business to-night. She wanted to search the villa.

She did. She found no one. But that proved nothing, as she told herself, with something of Mackay's baffled weariness in her thoughts. She did not know the cupboards nor the cellars of Villa Porte Bonheur. Smith and his friend, Lascelles, or his accomplice, Tibbitts, aye, or even Mr. Murgatroyd, might all be on the premises.

At long last she went to bed and fell fast asleep, thoroughly worn out, to find herself continuing in her dreams her article on the Hotel de ville's treasures. She was searching for the right words with which to describe Mrs. Brownlow's cry that was shut up in one of the glass cases along with her own umbrella, when sounds coming from down the corridor awoke her. The shrill tones of the head-housemaid, the butler's authoritative, but quiet voice. Then the steps of a man hurrying to her door, a tap, and the butler's voice asking:

"Is mademoiselle within? No, do not disturb yourself—I only wanted to be sure."

Vivian slipped into something and flung her door open.

Pointer was out fishing before breakfast, when he saw Mackay making towards him. It was then about half-past eight in the morning.

"Something's happened at the villa. The commissaire won't say what. But his car's on the road above. I told him we would both come along."

Pointer unjointed his rod with precision but with speed. He left his catch to look after themselves under a bush.

"I canna think what's happened the noo," muttered Mackay. "Can you?" he asked, wheeling suddenly.

"I can hazard a guess, but whether it's right or wrong—"

"A guess? What wad it be? I canna guess onything. But then I never could."

"That Mrs. Brownlow is missing," Pointer said quietly, as they hurried off. "I should expect that to be the next step."

Mackay stared at him. "Wow!" he muttered; "ye beat me! I canna see by what reasoning—"

"I wasn't talking of reasoning, but of guessing," was all that Pointer would say. He was right in his guess, whatever his grounds for it. Mrs. Brownlow was missing. The nun, on waking about eight, had found her patient's bedroom in wild disorder.

Cambier, fiery-eyed this time, was moving quickly about, darting here and there, rather like a tom-cat with whose preserves the mice have been taking liberties.

"*C'est trop!*" he muttered fiercely to Pointer. "Too much indeed. They mock us, these miscreants. But we shall see. And they shall see. . . ." His moustache bristled.

"What miscreants?" Pointer asked.

"Those who staged this scene. Bah, it belongs to the theater, not to the police. Rondeau is always asking himself questions, but I would like to tell him to look instead at one thing —one thing only!"

"And that is, *mon chef?*" Rondeau demanded eagerly.

Cambier pointed dramatically. "Tossed sheets, twisted mattress, bolster and pillow on the floor," he recapitulated, "chair overturned, window curtain half-torn off its hooks, creepers below the window half-torn down—bah! Look, Rondeau! No, do not think! Do not ask yourself anything at all! Just look! Merely look!"

Rondeau looked. But as always under such conditions did not see what he was expected to see.

"The stand lamp is overturned," he said slowly; "but the electric bulb itself is not—"

"I mean you to look at this!" hissed Cambier, waggling the flex leading from the lamp to the wall-plug. "See this wild confusion? Yet the wall-plug is still in the *prise*, and it comes out at a touch. Could this particular lamp have been overturned and it be still in the wall? It could not. The stage was set, Rondeau. Mrs. Brownlow left; she was not taken by force. It was a wet night. There are no footprints of any outsider in here. . . ."

"Overshoes, woolen socks . . ." murmured Rondeau doubtfully.

". . . Would leave marks on this rather stickily polished floor. Look at the tracks we ourselves have made, and we rubbed our feet well. There was no stranger in this room. There are no finger-prints but those of madam herself, or of the sister nursing her. Here is one of Mrs. Brownlow's far back in the room on this white wood which shows a faint mark of soil and green stain as well. From the creepers that she had just pulled loose. Oh, yes, my friends, this is all the doing of Madam Brownlow. That poor madam, who was too ill to be questioned. Who raved—bah, the doctor is one of her admirers —I should have remembered that. He would be easy to hood- wink—"

"But the nurses, the sister, *mon chef*—"

"The sisters? Rondeau do not exasperate me! The intelligence of a *religieuse*! I see by the chart here that madam's temperature was taken twice a day, mornings at eleven and afternoons around five. I learn from these notes at the side that she always has a cup of hot bouillon at eleven, and that the tea things are brought in before five. Well, it explains itself. A dip of the thermometer into bouillon or tea, and behold a high temperature. There are other ways of course. A hot-water bottle—there is even a way of rubbing it along a blanket —*enfin*, the thing was easy. And this poor invalid is laughing at us—at me!" He finished with a snap, "But have a care, madam!" He apostrophized the air in a way that made Pointer's face grow firmly wooden, while Mackay leaned far out of the window. It would not do to grin at the commissaire.

"We shall see who laughs in the end. Now, then,

Rondeau, I think we are all agreed on noticing that
Monsieur Tibbitts is at liberty. Oh, yes, we are fools
compared with madam, but that much we do notice. Also,
we know that at midnight last night a man was seen
walking away from the Villa Porte Bonheur in a most
secretive way, more suitable to a hunter after game than
to a man leaving a friend's house. The hour was just on
one in the morning. And the man was Monsieur Smith,
we are nearly sure, though he got away before my men
could close in on him. They gave him a good chase as it
was. Which was what he wanted. Which was what
madam wanted. It had been arranged between the three
of them, her and Smith and Tibbitts, that Smith was to
call my men off from the benevolent guard they were
keeping on the villa, while Tibbitts helped madam to get
out of her room by means of a ladder held for her to
descend comfortably, and then drove her off to some place
of safety. Oh, it was all quite simple and quite easy. But
we shall see; Monsieur Smith will see; Tibbitts will see;
Madame Brownlow will in good time see, too! This flight
of her's throws a most lurid light on the tragedy." And
with that, the commissaire transformed himself into a
whirlwind engine and zoomed off amid his men to meet
the *juge*, who had been hastily summoned to the Hotel de
ville.

The magistrate did not agree with the commissaire.

"You think there is nothing of Maitland in all this?"
he asked sceptically. "I do not agree. I think madam
escaped, fled if you like—"

"If I like!" snorted Cambier.

"In order to avoid having to give her evidence against
Maitland. Which can only mean that she knows it would
be damning. It is quite possible that she slipped away to
avoid the last, the inevitably terrible end of our inquiry—
the accusation, and in due time the trial and
condemnation of Maitland. In my opinion, Maitland made
her some proposal—to pass on to her husband. I think he
tried to blackmail him, or did blackmail him, through her,

in that interview before he killed the husband—and his other victim, Sir Anthony Cross."

Something like that was Cambier's idea. That in the wellborn and well-connected Mr. Maitland they had a secret blackmailer battening on the mistakes of the past.

He said as much now, but nothing would induce him to pardon that semblance of force which had been staged in the supposedly sick woman's room upstairs. He said that too.

The *juge* only pursed his lips and repeated:

"Madam was very timid. She is a woman who needs a man to look after her. A man of gentle manners, but iron principles." He shook off some thought and went on briskly, "As to how she escaped, I am on the whole inclined to think that Monsieur Smith actually helped her away, not merely assisted by serving as a decoy for our men. Oh, I do not pretend to have solved this difficult problem"—he eyed Cambier a little maliciously—"but that is how things look to me for the present. For the time being, I think we should suspend judgment on that sorely-tried woman, Madam Brownlow."

Cambier left him with a look, as though he could not trust himself to speak.

Mackay said that the *juge*, on the whole, was right. At least in thinking that Tibbitts had no share in the happenings.

"I was watching his hotel all last night," he confided to Vivian; "and he didna stir. I couldna tell the police that."

"Unless you put it down to second sight," she agreed. "In my belief, Mrs. Brownlow has gone off to rout out something. I think she's on some one's track. She was hunting for proofs in the library last night. I'm sure of that. But I can't get that suppressed scream of hers that I told you of out of my head. But for it, I shouldn't be worried. It was an awful little cry, Mr. Mackay. It haunts me. Suppose she had come on something and has been spirited away because of that? By some enemy? By whoever murdered her husband and Sir Anthony?"

"The French think she went off of her own free will," he reminded her doubtfully.

"Just like them!" was Vivian's compliment. "Say, Mr. Mackay, there's such a thing as going of your own free will, and yet absolutely against the grain. You can be terrified into doing something you would give a great deal not to do. If Mrs. Brownlow isn't gone for the sake of getting some evidence, then I sure do feel worried about her. It was Smith's voice that asked me 'Is that you, Lascelles?' in a queer, strange sort of tone. And look—" She held out a hat. "Do have some second sight for me, too, Mr. Mackay, and tell me who wore this and when?"

"I ha'e surprised people wi' the correctness o' ma descriptions before noo," he muttered, taking it from her and holding it tightly pressed against his breast, while he fixed his eyes straight ahead of him as he said slowly:

"It's nicht. A's dark. I see a big young man. Wi' a face that says creation did a fine piece of warrk the day it made him."

"Mr.   Smith?"   Vivian   was   half-laughing,   half-impressed.

"It's moonlight—na, na, it's raining, but I see him dimly slipping to this hoose and climbing the door to the balcony up yonder."

He handed her back the hat and rubbed his eyes.

"Am I richt?"

"I don't know." She told him where and how she had found the hat.

"It's Smith's," he assured her.

"You're certain?" she asked, a little doubtfully.

"Aye. I recognized it by a mark on the band when you handed it to me. He a' but burned a hole in it wi' his cigar when it was on a chair beside him the evening I watched him and Lascelles on the grass. The evening you met me."

He hurried off, leaving Vivian as before, half-angry, half-amused.

In about two hours she was called to the telephone.

She heard a man's steps pelting down the basement stairs as she went. Some policeman was racing for the extension below, she rightly guessed.

"Vivian—it's me," came the voice of Mrs. Brownlow. "I'm quite safe. I went away, just as I pretended to be so ill, because I couldn't face all the questions. I couldn't bear to be the one to get people into trouble, and quite the wrong people probably. I must stop at once; but I couldn't let you worry over me—" The voice ceased on that.

Below Vivian heard excited French voices. The agents did some swift work. They located the call within five minutes. It came from a *patisserie* in Lyons. But nothing was known of who had sent it. Vivian was relieved, and yet—she could not forget that strange, low cry that she had heard Mrs. Brownlow give just after Smith had gone on up the stairs. She went to her own room, trying to think things out "according to the light of reason," as Mackay would have said. She had just started a reply to a most incoherent, excited letter of condolence which she had received from Edith Montdore demanding, rather than asking, a full account from the inside of the extraordinary double murder at the villa, or supposing her dearest Vi could not bear to write of that, then at least an analysis of Mrs. Brownlow. Edith Montdore still called her "the vamp." Vivian had twice tried to begin a letter, and twice given it up. Her own thoughts were too vague, changing as cloud shapes change. What did she really think of Mrs. Brownlow?

She got up from the writing-table impatiently. Edith must wait for a clear summing-up of the widow's character. Wait, perhaps, for days, perhaps—as far as Vivian was concerned —for ever, and she again tore up the sheet of paper on which she had begun to write.

CHAPTER FOURTEEN

BY next day the French police were on the track of Maitland's connection with both Brownlow and Sir Anthony Cross in Shanghai. An association in a non-proven murder suspicion. The *juge* made the most of it. And Cambier promised to make more when fuller information was to hand.

Maitland did not break his silence. No taunt, no cajolery, got a word out of him.

"The typical blackmailer of the *haute monde,*" Cambier thought, and so thought the *juge.* That idea explained so much, fitted so many of the cogs and promised to fit all with a little patience.

At noon the chief inspector sat smoking his pipe in his sitting-room and thinking over the case, as far as it had gone, when the door opened and, without any announcement, Mrs. Eastby stepped in. She was staying at the same hotel, watched more or less carefully, chiefly less nowadays. For suspicion had shifted entirely away from her and her son.

She closed the door now very carefully behind her. Then she came up to the chief inspector. She was very pale. Even her lips were white. She had certainly gone through some ageing process here in Cluny.

"I've come to make a confession," she spoke almost in the voice of the confessional.

Pointer stopped her at once.

"I'd much rather you didn't." He spoke gravely but very kindly. "You're turning to me because I'm a man of your own country, and you're among strangers. But I can't let you forget that I'm a detective officer, though I am only acting as an observer in this case. Why not speak to Mr. Mackay?"

"Mr. Murgatroyd would only let me tell my story to you—or he intends to come forward and tell all that he knows to the *juge*. He's forcing me to speak." Her face worked. But she had herself in hand. "You are to make use of it if you must." Her pale face seemed to whiten still more. "Will you kindly let Mr. Murgatroyd know that I have really spoken to you, as I promised him yesterday."

"How can I communicate with him?" Pointer asked.

"He says that you worked on a case some months ago that took you to Paris, that you saved a young English diplomat there. Mr. Murgatroyd says that if you will wire to this young man 'Deposit received,' he will get it almost at once and un- derstand it as meaning that I have spoken. Oh, he didn't trust me!" She set her lips in a way that suggested that Mr. Murgatroyd was not entirely wrong in his doubts of her willingness to speak out unless she were given no alternative.

For a moment she and the Scotland Yard man sat in silence. He was looking at his shoes, she staring straight ahead of her.

"It had nothing to do with the murder of Anthony Cross," she began fiercely; "except, perhaps, that I had handed him that accursed money." Her voice faltered. "But Mr. Murgatroyd suspects my son—oh, he does! It's incredible, but he doesn't feel sure that somehow. . . . And because I had to say what I did against this Mr. Maitland, he is forcing me to—to tell you the whole story." The fire in her voice died down, smothered by some other feeling. She sat for some moments without speaking, and when she began again it was in a quiet, weary tone.

"As I think every one who knew us at the time guessed, Sir Anthony and I loved each other very dearly—long ago," she said finally. "Long, long ago. I was never in love with the man I married. Though I thought I was at the time. After he had an accident to his head, I fell ill myself. It was while I was getting well that I met Anthony Cross." There was a long pause. "I didn't run

away with him," she went on dreamily, "because of
Reggie. Even as a child he was so straight. But I very
nearly did. Very, very nearly. And I think Sir Anthony
never forgave me, and never forgave Reggie. You see, I
had let him make all his arrangements, and then at the
last moment, when I stepped into Reggie's room to say
good-bye to him asleep, I couldn't go—he was only ten—"
There followed a long pause.

"I'm telling you this because it alone explains why Sir
Anthony never did justice to Reggie's abilities or
character. He didn't want to give him a post really, but
I—well, I reminded him of what we had once felt for each
other. . . . Oh, this was years later, after Reggie had just
scraped through his pass. He gave him a post, and a good
one, but in some way he grudged him every little
success." Again there was a pause. "And now, chief
inspector," Mrs. Eastby went on in a very faint voice,
"comes the dreadful part. I—I—we were very hard up this
last year," came in a rush, as though to get the telling
over. "Harder up than usual. Living has gone up
frightfully in South Africa too. And I'm not a very good
manager. There were the heavy expenses for my
husband's removal from one nursing home and settling
him in another—and Reggie needed a holiday badly. And
one evening one of the men from the combine's counting-
house where Reggie worked talked to me a lot about how
little red-tape there was in their house. He said he often
wondered money wasn't taken by some of the smaller
employees, and pretended to think that it would never be
missed if it were taken. Or small stones either. Oh, he
chattered a lot about it all." She spoke wearily. "I believed
it, though I didn't know that I particularly listened. But
two days later I went to fetch Reggie for a tennis party to
which we were going together. I was shown into a
waiting-room in quite a different part of the building.
After a while, I got tired of waiting, and strolled off to
find his room. The names were put up on cards by the
doors. There was one room that had no name on it, and I

opened it, really to ask how Reggie's room could be reached. As I said, I was in a wing that I didn't know. The room was empty, but on the table were some packets of one-pound notes. There were three packets in all." Again she paused, then came a low, "I took them. Almost before I meant to do it it was done, and I was out of the room and down the corridor and out of the building. There were dozens of people coming and going. I felt sure that no one could ever know—ever guess even. Besides, what Mr. Barclay had said about how careless they were in checking-up came back to me. I thought I was quite safe." There came another pause but not so long. "Chief inspector, it was Reggie's own room! He had moved into a newer, larger room, and I think—*I* think—that the money was put there as a test. At any rate, he seemed to know nothing of it when he told me that night about his new quarters. I was horrified. And terrified. But next day came a note saying that he was to take his month's leave at once. Reggie was delighted. He thought it meant a promise of the post in London, of which he told me for the first time. I—I went with him, telling myself that all was all right—that no one would ever know. I spent some of the money on the trip.

"We went to Paris on our way to Switzerland. It was there that a letter came for him in Sir Anthony's writing. I was down at the breakfast table first. I wasn't sleeping well those day. ... It was only about four lines long, and was to say that Reginald was to bring the three hundred pounds that he had taken to Sir Anthony immediately at his hotel in Paris and send in his resignation. If he failed to do both at once, the combine would prosecute." Again there was one of those poignant pauses that marked her story.

"I went instead, and—Sir Anthony refused to believe my story. The true story. He thought I was shielding Reginald. He—oh, he had quite got over any feeling he once may have had for me." She pulled herself up. "No, that isn't fair. He did love me once, as I had loved him.

But that love, passionate and headstrong, had passed with our youth. He didn't love me now, and so I hadn't even that weapon. I had rather counted on it. I could do nothing with him. For if our love had gone, his jealousy— I think it really was a sort of unacknowledged jealousy— of Reggie had not gone. It seemed stronger than ever. Well"—Mrs. Eastby spread out her hands in a wide, weary gesture—"it's true, but very terrible, that you can do wrong in one moment of madness, and not put it right in weeks and weeks of agony and remorse. I followed him to Enghien, and again had an interview with him. I forced it on him. All I could do was to get him to put off the date when the money was to be paid back till the end of this month, when there was to be a big board meeting in London. He still absolutely refused to believe me. I—I think he didn't want to." Her voice shook. "I had been the romance of his youth. It was too horrible that it should end in—in the truth." Her voice was but a whisper now.

Pointer, his head resting on one hand, traced symbols on the blotting-pad with his pipe stem. He did not look up once, but his face was very kind.

"Fortunately my son had met a charming American girl, and he and she were quite content to stay at Enghien for the remainder of their lives. Or at least they thought so. The girl's father had a talk with me. He's rather a big man over in the United States. He wanted to see Sir Anthony about Reginald. I—I prevented that by saying that it would spoil Reggie's chances of getting that much-coveted post in London, to which he was sure to be appointed if nothing was done. He believed me, and let the affair between the two children continue on the understanding that if Reggie really got the post, he would have no objection to a marriage.

"I followed Sir Anthony down here. I made up my mind that if the worst came to the worst I would tell my story before Reggie too. I knew that in face of his horror and incredulity even Sir Anthony would have known that I was telling nothing but the truth. I tried over and over again to make him see it, but the night of the dance I was desperate. Time was all but out. All but! Sir Anthony would not extend it. He had told me so very sharply the night before when I spoke to him outside the house. So I got Reginald to come to the dance by saying that Jane would be there—as I've told already. And at the dance Sir Anthony refused me more curtly than ever. I practically was mad after that. I—I made up my mind to end everything. I wasn't going to tell Reggie. I couldn't lose all that was left me—his love. I couldn't live on after that. I felt that if I did make away with myself, Sir Anthony would know that I had not been shielding any one. I couldn't stand the dancing; I groped my way somehow to the upper first landing where I meant to wait until I saw Reggie come out and then tell him to take me away. I thought of throwing myself out of our hotel window—my room was on the fourth floor—but I ran into Mr. Murgatroyd, who was watching the dancers. He made some laughing remark to me.

"As I say I was mad. That people could dance when I was in such utter torment seemed to snap something inside my head. I don't know what I answered. I don't recollect clearly what happened. He must have taken me down into the writing-room. I must have told him the whole story. I had only a little over two hundred pounds out of the three hundred left." She flinched at the avowal anew. "And the bank wouldn't help me out. I don't know what I said to Mr. Murgatroyd. I only know that I was on my knees and crying as I've never cried in my life before. He was"—her face worked for a second, but she had great self-control; in a second she went on—"very wonderful. He told me not to despair, that he would make the sum up, and at once, to the three hundred, and that he would see Sir Anthony there and then and force him—*force* him to take my word for what had happened. I didn't believe him. I mean that he could do anything with Sir Anthony when I couldn't. And nothing else mattered. He hurried away and very nearly ran into Miss Young in the hall outside. Then, after she had gone on, and Mr. Murgatroyd had rushed off to his rooms, came my boy, still thinking that she was Jane. I only just got to the door of the cedar room in time to prevent him going in. He thought she had gone on in. I got him away by telling him, as I had told him before, that I had a big bet on the fact that no one should recognize him. You see, I had been terrified of his going up to Sir Anthony and of his learning everything from him. I think he thought it was some relation or friend of Jane's in the room. Luckily for me, oh, most luckily for me, he is where he won't look at newspapers for weeks. He really is in Bulgaria—or at least"—she shot a half-frightened glance towards the chief inspector—"at least very near there—in Serbia. And when I said Cyprus, I got it mixed with Sardinia."

Pointer made no comment on the geographical confusion that seemed to prevail in the lady's mind, and she hurried on with her story.

"Mr. Murgatroyd came back with the necessary money in notes to bring up the sum to the three hundred needed, then he went into the cedar room, and I heard voices, his very fierce at first. But, chief inspector, he succeeded! By some miracle, where I had failed, he succeeded! He rushed back for me and got a receipt made out. I didn't care about it then, but he thought it most important. He thought that if some accident happened to Sir Anthony, it might be all I should have to prove that I had given the money back, and that it had been taken back. Here is the receipt. I couldn't show it unless I was prepared to tell the story."

Pointer glanced through the paper she held out. It was in Sir Anthony Cross's writing. It said that Mrs. Eastby had by mistake taken three hundred pounds which she thought belonged to her son from the latter's room in the office of the combine in Johannesburg. That as soon as she had found out the mistake, she had at once endeavored to return it to Sir Anthony, and that the latter had now accepted it, together with her explanation, which completely satisfied him, and was restoring it to the combine on his return. That there was no question whatever of Mrs. Eastby's good faith in the matter, and the letter added that Reginald Eastby, neither at the time of the mistake nor of its return and acceptance by Sir Anthony, knew anything of the money.

This was the paper that Murgatroyd and Smith had signed.

"After everything was over, I sat on—alone—in the writing-room, getting myself in hand again. It seemed too good to be true. That was when I heard the voices in the next room arguing about tufa. And then I went back to the dancers, met my son, who had found out that Jane wasn't there, and was furious with me, and rushed off. He thought it was some kind of silly joke between Jane and me to find out whether he could mistake another girl for her or not. I had to tell him something. But I didn't care what he thought, as long as I now knew that it would never be the truth. Or at least, I thought so then. Though that Miss Young rather worried me. She's desperately sharp. However, I thought I was safely beyond the reach of harm that night at supper." She sighed. Her face lost its momentary look of vivacity. She held out her hand.

"I can't let even you keep that paper," she said a little tremulously; "but if need be, I can produce it. But I only lend you my story. Only if it must be told. Only if absolutely necessary," she repeated imploringly. She went on to say that when Sir Anthony was killed, and the money seemed to be lost, she was desperate again. Again Mr. Murgatroyd had come to her help, for before he left for Cluny in his hurried flight from questions whose answers he was afraid might drag in her story, he had sent her his address and told her that if there was any trouble, she was to let him know, as he would not be able to get hold of a newspaper easily.

At first she thought that she might have to appeal to him again, but she had seen Mr. Heimbrot and shown him the receipt—a wave of scarlet flooded her worn face.

Mr. Heimbrot pretended to believe it absolutely, and he had got the French authorities to hand him over the notes found on Tibbitts. He hadn't ventured to cash one before he was taken.

"Mr. Heimbrot cabled the money back to Jo'burg, and told me that he would guarantee that everything would be all right. He, of course, must have guessed," she whispered, torn by the anguish of a proud nature conscious of guilt. "But I think he was sorry for me."

Again came one of the pauses that marked the tragic story.

"But thanks to him I was able to tell Mr. Murgatroyd that his help had not been in vain. As I was back here in Cluny, so near to him, I wrote him, and we met in Lyons. Unfortunately, I told him how the inquiry was going on, and that I was sure Mr. Maitland was guilty. So is every one. But Mr. Murgatroyd actually fears lest in some way my son is implicated in a terrible way. Like so many good people, he evidently isn't at all clever."

Pointer reflected for a moment.

"I think I had better see Mr. Murgatroyd," he said finally, "and hear from him about his interview with Sir Anthony."

"He is staying with the Brothers of St. Peter Lateran outside Lyons. It's a sort of training school for Roman Catholic missionaries. He's great friends with the prior apparently. They never read the papers there, and besides, his name is quite a usual one." She got up and for a second stood in the shadow. "Thank you for listening so patiently," she said, with something very gentle and sweet in her face, something that gave a glimpse of the girl that once had captured Anthony Cross's by no means susceptible heart; "but I beg of you to remember that my confession is only for use in the last resort."

Pointer promised her. He did not think—now—that it would be needed. He expected a very quick wind-up to the Cluny problem.

As there seemed to him nothing of any interest going

on for the moment, he motored over to Lyons at once, changed into a tram, and then took a taxi to the big, bare building on the hill. Mr. Murgatroyd was in, and came down into the parlor at once.

He confirmed Mrs. Eastby's story as far as the night of the dance went. As to his part in it, he was as brief as he could well be.

"It was an awful thing to see her despair that night," he said gravely; "I've never seen anything so poignant. You see, she thought that she had ruined her son's career, and as well as broken to pieces his ideal of her. When she told me that Sir Anthony refused to let her speak to him any more on the subject, well"—he gave a faint smile—"I really think I saw red. That one fellow mortal should refuse to let another fellow mortal make restitution when restitution was possible." Murgatroyd smacked his open palm on the table between them, again stirred by the mere thought. His eyes flashed as they must have done the night that he talked to the distracted woman.

"I went into that cedar room as a man goes to a fight. But no sooner had I closed the door behind me than that feeling went. Have you ever felt confident before you did a thing that you could do it? I knew, as I stood there, that I should succeed. I did. And seeing what was to happen to him, I wonder now if both of us had an inner knowledge hidden from our conscious selves. My appeal was based simply on what would be his fate—my fate—the fate of any one of us—if our God were to deal with us at our death in steely justice. I think Mrs. Eastby's appeals to him were really working in him, though she thought that she had failed. Or else that wisdom of which I spoke—at any rate, he met me more than half-way. He admitted that he had been too harsh, that every man needs mercy shown him. He would show it to the boy. Let him make restitution and he should have another chance.

"That wouldn't do either. I told him her story as I had heard it—though only haltingly and not nearly so well or so pitifully. But his ears were opened. Not by me. By some power greater than either of us. He said that he had not understood, that he would like to speak to Mrs. Eastby again for a moment. He did, and then he drafted the receipt, read it over to me, and I got Smith to sign as my co-witness."

Pointer returned to Cluny and there had a brief talk with Heimbrot at the station, for that good man was leaving. The combine's business did not delay for such a trifle as the murder of a director.

"Easiest thing in the world to have happened," Heimbrot said earnestly as they walked up and down beside the train. "Of course, Mrs. Eastby thought it was her son's advance pay, seeing that she felt sure that he was as good as appointed to the post in London. We know what ladies are in money matters. I've told her that it's quite clear, and that her mistake can be put right in the office without any one knowing any thing about it. Between ourselves, chief inspector, it was Sir Anthony's idea of testing the honesty of the staff out there. He was a bit inclined to suspect Eastby—however, that's all over now. Mrs. Eastby thinks Sir Anthony's where he knows everything. Maybe. Pity he can't pass some information down to us. Such as who's helping themselves to those diamonds en route to Amsterdam—let alone who shot him and Brownlow, and why." With that the talk ended.

That night in Villa Porte Bonheur, a man with a cap pulled low over his eyes worked fast and well in the cedar room at a safe hidden in the wall. Another man was keeping watch outside the door. The shutters were down. No light showed. It was no wonder that the safe had not been discovered by the police, for the movable panel that concealed it was well made, sliding up into grooves in the fretted paneling which were in no wise different from other grooves around. The safe in Monsieur Pichegru's study had been searched by the police, but the man working at this was no policeman. It was Tibbitts. Across his face was a black mask, but his hands and long, powerful arms were unmistakable.

French safes cannot touch English or American ones, but even so, he was two hours at the job, and worked with the sweat standing in beads on his forehead. Oxyacetylene blowpipes are hot things. At last he laid down his tools and spat on his burning palms. "Done! And well done!" he muttered approvingly.

Nearly ten minutes ago, at his back, the outside steel shutter of one of the windows had been softly rising, an inch, then a foot. The window was open, to give the workman inside all possible ventilation. An *agent* had wormed his way through it into the room with infinite precautions. Getting to his feet now, he drew his baton and stepped on tiptoe towards the safe-breaker.

The club was actually lifting, when the door of the room was flung wide, and a man with a jet black face and hands sprang across the room in a lithe leap, and landed almost on the *agent's* back. There was a sense of distance and a sufficiency of movement in that leap that in itself would have told of a first-class boxer. If there had been any doubt, the punishing right hook as the policeman span around would have dispelled it. The club merely tapped Tibbitts and then dropped to the floor. The policeman's whistle went in a wide curve into a distant corner.

Now, as it happened, the *agent* was an admirer and imitator of Carpentier too. One of the best in the region. He avoided the well-meant punch and got in a long range thrust to the stomach that should have ended matters. But somehow it seemed to miss the desired effect. The black man got in a really brilliant left and right instead.

The policeman settled down to work. The man facing him was only about half his size. *Peste!* He went all out for a knock-down blow, but it was not to be had for the asking. Some of his efforts got home splendidly, yet in weight and substance he took more than he gave. And the funny thing was, that the blows which he received turned him black, just as those which he landed turned the black man fawn color or scarlet.

The *agent* was bursting with rage. His fury was almost comic. He was faster than the smaller man, but the other was as cool as a cucumber; his eyes, what could be seen of them, were steady and confident. At last he got in a blow that ended it as far as the agent was concerned.

It was only a few moments later that there came a shout from somewhere in the garden, and Chief Inspector Pointer was peering into the room. Two gendarmes ran to his call. The agent was attended to, the house was searched, but there was no sign of whoever it was that had so mauled the man on duty. The police stared at the safe door confronting them.

"A secret safe! And here! And Simon knocked about! This is a house of mysteries!"

The commissaire hurried in, followed by Rondeau. He, too, opened his eyes at the sight of the metal oblong in its wall of red-brown paneling.

But first of all he bent over the agent, who was now sitting up and groggily feeling his head.

"There were two men," he reported. "One opened the safe. I knocked him down when he got the door open. I waited till then. The other—he was a man painted black—"

"Painted black!" repeated Rondeau with great gusto. "*Saints!*"

"He and I fought—I don't know what has become of him or his mate. It was good boxing, though," the man muttered, "and fair hitting. The English school."

"Has that Smith been taking a hand again?" snorted Cambier.

"It was Tibbitts at the safe," the agent said; "he moved his mask to wipe his face once. Besides I knew him—"

"But naturally. The *portrait parle!*" Cambier nodded. "Pity he got away," Cambier repeated regretfully, "but it was lucky that you, monsieur, were on the spot, since Simon had had his whistle snatched from him."

"There is one spot in the road where you can see the

light from under the shutters reflected on the holly clump," the chief inspector reminded them. "I was just there—"

"It was very fortunate, and now—" Cambier swung the safe door open with the air of a man not expecting much except disappointment.

There came a gasp from his men, an exclamation from Rondeau, and a start from himself.

A heap of glittering stones lay on the floor of the little safe, sparkling and blinking. A pocket-book of dark green morocco lay to one side. On top of all lay an envelope with something written on it.

"Your arrival evidently prevented the thieves looting the safe," Cambier said joyfully to the chief inspector; "but this is most fortunate! And surely these are the jewels of Madam Brownlow so often described to us. Yes, these certainly look like them, including that necklace of black pearls she valued so highly. And here are her sapphires! And this " he opened the pocket-book and looked at its contents—"this is the pocket-book of Monsieur Davidson with the missing bearer bonds intact. All of them."

Only now did Cambier pick up—officially—the most interesting article in the safe. And that was the letter lying on top of all.

"A letter for Madam Brownlow—in Monsieur Brownlow's handwriting," he said solemnly.

There were no comments this time. Every eye had been fixed on that square of paper for the past minutes.

Cambier slowly opened it with great neatness. He read aloud the date. It was the date of the dance. In a still deeper hush if possible he read on:

"MY DEAR WIFE,—This will be a very long letter, and if it is incoherent in parts, put it down to hurry. For the game is up. I killed Peter Jackson in Shanghai, and not from jealousy, but because he had found a platinum field, and duly taken out his claim for some two hundred acres. He spoke to me of lumps of platinum the size of pigeons' eggs covering the ground, and an assayist in Shanghai gave a list of other valuable minerals, such as osmium and iridium, which were present in the ore samples. There was a huge fortune in the discovery. For one man. I drowned Jackson, and ran down the assayist who analysed his samples. But their deaths brought me no good. All the region where Jackson's find lies has been going through revolution after revolution, both at the time that he was there and ever since. I have not been able to get hold of any record of claims put in until just lately. The republic of Tanou Touva—Krasny is its chief town—has only now issued an edict, or whatever it should be called, stating that all land and mineral claims duly recorded since the fall of the monarchy, and paid for at the time, are to be considered as valid.

And now, when at last there is peace around Krasny, where Jackson's claim is entered, and I could get up a private expedition to work it, if a coup of mine which I'm planning in Lyons came off with Tibbitts's help—Anthony Cross has somehow got on to the truth. He intends to see me swing, he says.

I learned from him that Maitland was bringing him some papers dealing with that old Jackson affair, but that Maitland has just told him that, after a talk with you, he had burned the lot. Cross was furious. But I think Maitland could not bear to break your heart. He was in love with you years ago in Shanghai. I've often wondered if you were aware of that. You think Anthony Cross is, but there you're wrong, my dear. He intends to let you think it for a while. But it's me—not you—he's after. I made a bad break this evening in answering one of his questions. His suspicions had been entirely allayed, after his long talk with you yesterday evening, until I made that unfortunate slip. Well, he has rushed the truth out of me by putting this and that together and giving me no time to think over my answers. Having just been told by him that Maitland had destroyed all the papers, I shot

Cross, hoping that his death would settle the matter. Now I see by entries in his notebook that he's done me. He's posted some letters which will set wheels a-rolling that will crush me. I shall put my papers in order, and then, after arranging the room to look as though a duel— not a suicide—had taken place in it, I shall shoot myself. I have also seen to it that Tibbitts will not be able to blackmail you, should he want to. As I thought it safest to send in my claim at Krasny to Jackson's land in his, Tibbitts's name, it will be as well to have a hold over him. For he is a crook, picked up by me at Monte Carlo because of his skill in opening safes. Never mind how I knew of that skill. I had intended to arrange for some blunder on his part in the Lyons affair which would make him perfectly safe ever afterwards, but this will do as well for you. Which is why I am writing the whole truth here so badly."

"For you!" repeated Rondeau. "Ah, he little thought for whom he was writing these details."

"Madam shall see the letter," Cambier said promptly; "but certainly she shall!" He read on:

"And I have arranged matters so that Tibbitts thinks it was he who killed Anthony Cross. For which reason he is now putting as many miles as possible between here and himself I had intended to shoot Anthony Cross with his own revolver, so as to have his death look a suicide, as I have just written, but Tibbitts was too drunk to be able to open Cross's bag tonight. As things stand, it is just as well that I had to give up that intended artistic touch. As soon as Cross was dead I went upstairs to Tibbitts, woke him up, and told him that Cross had got on the track of our little exploit on the rapide the other week. For it was a put-up job. Incidentally, you will find the jewelery and the bonds of Davidson intact with this. I was waiting for another month or so before using either. For we are on the rocks, my dear, and have been so for some time past. I told Tibbitts, when I got him awake, that Cross was writing a letter which would mean prison for him. That he was to go into the cedar room, flourish a revolver, and demand the giving up of the letter, and get a promise from Cross that he would hold his tongue for to-night. I assured Tibbitts that Cross would give way if he acted exactly as I told him."Tibbitts is a gullible fool. I chose him chiefly for that when I picked him up at Monte. I intended using him for a plan of mine in Lyons, which would have meant wealth for all of us when I had brought it off. However, he did as I told him,took the revolver which I handed him and assured him was unloaded, and let me shove him ahead of me into the cedar room. He tripped on entering, and as I grabbed at him, his revolver went off. I saw to that. And also that it was fitted witha silencer before I used it the first time.

"Anthony Cross was sitting with his back to us at a writing-table. He was dead, of course, and of course I fired, not at him, but back over my shoulder when I touched Tibbitts. The shot went out through the still open door and buried itself in a leaden plate outside. I changed that plate afterwards to another position. And what Tibbitts tripped over was a line whichI had tied from Cross's arm to the cabinet by the door. Cross's body toppled over as the pistol went off. I rushed up to it, cutting the line, and called out 'My God, you've killed him! He's dead!' That finished Tibbitts. He babbled about it being an accident and so on, but I stuffed some notes that were in front of Cross into his pockets, and told him to beat it in my super-sports to Autun, where I would telephone him what to do. Should there be no telephone message waiting for him there, then he was to make for Paris and hide. It would mean that the police were after him in spite of all that I could do.

"He knows Paris all right. As I say, I don't think you'll ever see or hear from him again. He was so appalled that he forgot to ask about his share of the contents of the secret safe which I had discovered by chance one wet day while playing fives in the cedar room, and to which he finally fitted me akey. I shall leave the key and a slip of paper telling you to get this letter in your room in some secret place."

Here came a gap. Then the lines of the odd, precise, and yet irregular writing went on:

"I have just taken Cross's keys, had a dance with some oneso as not to be missed too long, gone upstairs, got his revolver from his bag, and fitted it with a silencer. I shall put his keys back in his pocket, and when everything is ready, lay beside me the revolver that I shot him with, and use his. On myself. No one will ever guess the truth. It will be taken for granted that his pistol skidded towards me in some jerk he made when dying."

On the line below came in a sudden, thickened scrawl the words:

"That fool Tibbitts has taken my revolver off with him."

Here came another gap. And then, irregularly below this:

"My head feels as though it were going. I've got blood all over my hands when I put Cross's keys back, and probably on my clothes as well. I've wiped them and burned the handkerchief, but even so, I daren't risk going up the stairs to our rooms again to get the mate to the automatic that fool has taken away with him. But there is that vanity-case of yours you told me to put somewhere for you a little while ago, as it didn't go with the blue of your dress as well as you thought. I told you that I had hung it on the same hook as your Burbery in the cloakroom. You will be pretty sure to get it before going upstairs, or to use it some time during the night. At least

I hope so. It's after all for your sake I'm taking all this trouble. I can reach the cloakroom unseen, with any luck. I'll chance it, and put in your case a slip with directions as to what you are to do directly the alarm is given. Be sure and do exactly as I say. Get my other revolver from my case, watch your chance and slip it beside me when you come into the room, and re- member that I had just learned that you were about to run away with Cross. I charge you on the slip that I shall write, and I charge you again, to carry out my wishes to the letter.

"Fortunately one cartridge was fired from the automatic that you will find in the case. And it, too, has a silencer. Should things go wrong you must show this. I am making it clear on purpose. I leave it in the safe, of which I have made certain that Pichegru has no idea, and shall drop the key with the slip in your bag. On the back will be a diagram showing you how to locate the safe. I am going to lock this up at once, then write a couple of business letters to London and post them—I can chance the darkness of the garden's outer paths, and then I shall put the slip in your bag, and come back and end it all."

There followed some words of leave-taking, but according to the letter, he had already said his real farewell to his wife on the slip of paper which he had placed where she would probably find it before learning of his death and Anthony Cross's murder.

There was a pause of complete stupefaction when the last word was read. Then came a babble of comment.

"It was he who lost the key then!" Rondeau finally said, "when he went out to post his letters after locking this safely up. But he must have been distracted! And I ask myself what madam thought when she read that there was a letter for her in a mysterious locked safe, and could not open it. He would be sure to say in the slip, which she evidently found when she went for her smelling-salts, how all important this document was. *Sapristi*, what a position for the poor woman!"

"Ah, yes, and Monsieur Smith told us how he had to insist that madam should not move her husband—she would be looking for the key, as well as placing the revolver," the sergeant thought.

"Mademoiselle Young asked herself," Rondeau agreed, "how it was that she did not see that revolver. So did the *juge*! We now know that it was not there when she first came into the room."

Again the talk became mixed. Piece by piece the story was tested and passed.

"So that is the truth of the Cluny problem!" Cambier said finally, scrutinizing the letter through a magnifying glass. "I think there is no doubt as to the genuineness of this letter. And—yes, I agree, it explains everything. Yes—everything. Well, well, I was afraid we were getting too much embroidery into it! A simple case after all. A sequel to an old scandal in China. Mixed up with other problems that do not concern us, but which were very perplexing. You agree with me, I know, *monsieur l'inspecteur en chef.* So the private investigator is right! Brownlow was the only criminal, though the reason for the crime will surprise Monsieur Mackay. And here is his client's money. Untouched. But we were on the track of Brownlow. But decidedly!"

"There is one thing," Rondeau was helping his *chef* put seals on the safe; "it was not Smith who boxed with Simon here. There is no reference to Smith throughout these papers."

"Nor who helped Tibbitts to escape," finished Cambier. "Some confederate of Tibbitts evidently. As to Tibbitts himself—well, it would have been a very difficult matter to bring any share in the crime home to him after Monsieur Maitland's arrival. So Maitland burned the papers, for Mrs. Brownlow's sake, that would have helped Sir Cross to convict her husband on that old affair in China! And refused to speak out—especially when he thought she was ill with inflammation of the brain. . . . He looks like a man of feeling. And to think that she knew all along that her husband was guilty. And did her best to deceive us."

"Did deceive us," Rondeau said with a youthful grin. "I do not think that the *juge*, for one, will find it in his heart to be hard on her."

Cambier's gesture recalled the younger man to official decorum. Pointer now took his leave for a short time, and the police dispersed. Rondeau and his chief stayed behind to make a few final notes for the magistrate.

"I ask myself if the *inspecteur en chef* will not have learned a great deal from our methods," Rondeau said, putting a sheet before the other to sign.

"It is that that distinguishes our work in France— method," Cambier agreed. He began to sign. "Finished! The Cluny problem," he murmured.

"Finished," Rondeau frowned down at the papers. "Though I still ask myself how it was that—"

"Ta-ta-ta!" Cambier had his pen between his teeth and was blotting furiously. "We must hurry or the *juge* will hear the story before he has our facts. Come, hurry, *mon cher!* No dreaming how complicated the story would have been had you written it! Let this case be an example to you. Even I was prepared to twist and tangle what we now know was quite a simple case. Truth is always simple!" And with that the two hurried off.

Mackay was busy in Lyons delving into some of Brownlow's and Tibbitts's activities—activities which now assumed a very sinister look. He refused to be called off until he had pretty well proven that the business could not be genuine, that there was no "backer," such as Brownlow had spoken of, behind him. But though he would not leave the town when he heard that the letter found in the safe was accepted as authentic, and that, therefore, the case was over, the problem was solved, and the money of Davidson was untouched, he asked Vivian Young to meet him on her way to Italy, where she was going next, and the two had a long talk. One that lasted, with intermissions, all the way to the American church in that dull but respectable old town.

"You won't mind the uncertainties ahead of us?" he asked finally, for he was selling his business, such as it was, and intended to start a new life elsewhere—with her.

"That's life. Uncertainty, and never knowing what's around the corners," she finished, with her eyes shining.

Mackay looked at her delightedly. This was a helpmate such as he wanted and needed.

CHAPTER FIFTEEN

POINTER flew from Lyons to London, where some really important matters were waiting for him. His leg was quite well now, and he was eager to be a worker again, not an observer merely. On his arrival, he had a long talk with the assistant commissioner, who, after the usual warm greetings, for he and Pointer were good friends, showed him a bulky pile of papers on a table near by.

"The digest of the Cluny problem. Fairly complete." The assistant commissioner moved over to them. "I know how impatient you are to be at work, and you can be as brief as you like in your replies. But there are just a few questions I want to put. I've jotted them down in what seems to me the order of their importance, and if we keep to that we shall soon be done. First of all"—he seated himself and pushed his tobacco jar across the table— "have you any idea how Anthony Cross got on the track that possibly young Jackson's valuable mineral claim might have been the real reason for his murder in Shanghai ten years ago? How could he learn of the existence of such a claim in the first place?"

"Very simply, I think, sir. Peter Jackson had a Chinese 'boy' called Cheng," Pointer was lighting up, "so they 'beamed' me from Shanghai. He was his employer's friend as well as servant. This Cheng had a relative Cheng, who had a remote connection Cheng—you know how these Tongs still run as one family—who regularly traded into the Soviet States of Central Asia."

"Of which this new republic of Touva is one." Major Pelham had looked up the place on a modern map.

"The 'boy' Cheng and Peter Jackson's younger brother between them tried to make out a case against Brownlow at the time, and, as we know, had to give it up. It was Sir Anthony Cross himself, by the way, who wrote to the Jackson family that they had nothing to go on. I fancy— or rather I feel sure —that the long-distance Cheng ran his eye over the list of claim-holders as soon as they became available, which was some four months ago now, at Krasny. He notified Jackson's Cheng, who was in touch, or got into touch with the dead man's younger brother, that he had found—"

"Of course! The name of Jackson on the list! And that younger brother to whom he wrote would find it quite easy to keep track of Sir Anthony Cross's whereabouts and career," Pelham finished—he was jotting down a line as he spoke. "I know there was a mother and a sister as well as this brother living at the time in Canada."

"The mother died of what was practically starvation the next winter," Pointer said slowly. "And the sister, who was consumptive at the time, followed her not long after. When Brownlow murdered Peter Jackson, he indirectly murdered the two women as well."

The assistant commissioner made a sound indicative of pity.

"So this brother writes to Cross," he went on, "and Sir Anthony goes down alone to Cluny, making his fiancé think that his visit had to do with the thefts of diamonds from his combine—"

"I think she jumped to that conclusion," Pointer struck in. "His words, as she told me them, might have equally applied to the Brownlow-Jackson affair. I think Sir Anthony only wanted to make sure that he would not have to introduce the Brownlows to her—in case they could not clear themselves."

"I see. Very likely indeed. At any rate, he went down to clear the matter up by a talk with the accused on the spot. Talk lasts a long time that first evening." The assistant commissioner had the tale at his fingers' ends. "Cross is not satisfied —that's how I read the lines, or between them—and wires for Maitland and the old papers. Maitland got there a little earlier than was expected, found all the doors open, walked in, met Mrs. Brownlow, who throws herself on his mercy. She gets him to burn the papers he has brought and to leave the villa without seeing Sir Anthony. Maitland yields to her begging, but once away his brain clears. He decided to return and tell Anthony Cross what he has done, and at once resign from the Law Society. He comes back. Has the stormy interview, bits of which were overheard. You think, too, don't you, that the 'thief and the 'money' and the 'tufa' all referred to Brownlow?"

Pointer did.

"Maitland leaves after that. When he is dragged into the affair, he cannot tell the truth because of Mrs. Brownlow. She probably told him that she was innocent, but her husband guilty, and that she cannot prove her own innocence. Eh?"

"Probably," Pointer thought.

"Now, why did Anthony Cross leave the hotel and put up at the villa for the remainder of the night of the dance?" Major Pelham wanted to know.

"To avoid Mrs. Eastby, I think," Pointer suggested. "I fancy that Mrs. Brownlow had very nearly satisfied him that there was no question of deliberate murder, of murder for gain, during her talk the early part of the night of the dance."

"And then Brownlow himself blundered in some reply, as he writes in that long letter of his, and Anthony Cross pounces on him. And the remainder of what happened—is it not written in the Third Book of Kings?" Major Pelham shot a not entirely appreciative glance at the mass of papers before him.

"Knowing how small a margin he had, Brownlow had laid quite a neat plan—for a 'suicide' of Anthony Cross should the worst come to the worst. How did he know that Cross had a revolver, by the way?" he asked next.

"The day before the dance, Mrs. Brownlow telephoned to him asking him to join them at the villa in a revolver-shooting contest; she added that some one could lend him a weapon if necessary—or a silencer if he had not one with him. Sir Anthony said that he would come if he had time, and added that he had an automatic fitted with a silencer with him and some cartridges. He didn't go to the villa, as a matter of fact."

"Mrs. Brownlow telephoned—" Major Pelham shot his under lip forward a moment, but he went on with the papers. "There's only one thing more, I think. What became of the whatever it was that Cross had in his second bag, the one he himself packed? Do you think they were business papers, which he posted himself late that night?"

"No, sir. I think Brownlow took them—after he had murdered Cross? And probably posted them to himself in town."

"I see." Major Pelham. rose from that particular table. "Thanks for clearing up all the vague points. By the way, the letter in the safe gave a fairly accurate idea of things, don't you think? As a rule, last letters are very one-sided, but the French police seem to think this was an accurate and careful account of what happened. Do you agree with them?"

"I think it was a careful account and fitted every point most neatly," Pointer said with a smile.

"And written by Brownlow, of course?" Pelham asked quickly.

"Written by the man who shot Brownlow," Pointer corrected quietly.

"Shot   Brownlow?"   the   assistant   commissioner wheeled on him. "What on earth do you mean, Pointer? Didn't Brownlow shoot himself? What on earth—"

"Mackay shot Brownlow, sir. Mackay Jackson, the younger brother of the murdered Peter Jackson."

"Mackay? You mean—you don't mean the man who was investigating Davidson's lost money at Cluny?"

"I do, sir."

"Then why the devil didn't you tell me so before?"

"But I was to answer your questions as you put them, sir, in the order of their importance," Pointer said politely.

Major Pelham burst out laughing. "Scored off me there. And you had this up your sleeve all the time? Come now, the story. The story that isn't written in, eh, the Third Book of Kings." And Pelham pushed the whole table away and wheeled up an arm-chair for himself.

"The tale runs like this, sir," Pointer began swiftly; "when his brother Peter was killed, Mackay Jackson had no money and no influence. He was just a poor little Canadian boy. But he never wavered in his certainty that his brother had been murdered by Brownlow and for something quite different from jealousy. He argued, rather shrewdly for a lad of sixteen, that his brother's murder would not remain Brownlow's only crime. He entered Pinkerton's and worked well. He was not considered brilliant, but absolutely fearless, and a quite remarkable shot. When he had sufficient experience, and had saved up some money, he got a chance to buy up a Scottish inquiry agency in Aberdeen. His only relative, his mother's sister, married a Mackay. Which accounts for his name probably, and the weird Scottish that he spoke—a bit of everything from Glasgow to Aberdeen. Yes, sir, Mackay shot Brownlow dead after the latter had killed Sir Anthony, and had fired full at him himself and missed. The shot that went into the pewter plate was meant for his head—and has had the deuce of a time saving suspects ever since," Pointer broke into a reminiscent chuckle. "It was all quite wrong, of course, and absolutely illegal, but it was funny too. Especially his Gift. His second sight!"

"He must have been put to it," murmured Pelham appreciatively. "I thought him an absolute fool when I came to that claim of his. Oh, yes, it's duly set down somewhere among those reams."

"He found it rather difficult, you see, to explain his absolute certainty that each person suggested as the criminal was not guilty. He couldn't very well say why he knew they were innocent!" The chief inspector had found Mackay's claim to occult knowledge very diverting.

Pelham laughed. "But go on," he urged; "what came after his purchase of the detective agency?"

"He promptly sent an account, and photographs, of the Brownlow couple, taken during the time in Shanghai, to one private detective agency in every large town of the world, offering a price for any information concerning the pair. The offer was renewed every anniversary of his brother's murder. And he has at last got his reward."

"So has Brownlow!" murmured Pelham.

"And when the last of the string of Chengs sent him word of the Jackson-Tibbitts sale of the claimed land in Touva, Mackay added the name of Tibbitts to the other two. This theft of Mrs. Brownlow's jewels and Davidson's money on the *rapide* came as a gift to Mackay. He was at once informed by several agencies that both the names that he was after had cropped up, the old and the new. Mackay Jackson came over to Paris at once, and offered his services to Davidson on the 'no success, no pay' understanding. By the way, sir, it was he who had himself offered his services as soon as he bought his business some years before to the diamond combine in which Sir Anthony Cross was a director, and he did some good work for them on the same understanding. As far as this my tale is vouched for by known facts, but from now on I'm only guessing—"

"Quite good enough for me," murmured Pelham; "guess on."

"I think that he immediately wrote to Sir Anthony, not as to the combine director this time, but as to the man who would have been counsel for the defence in that murder trial that never came off. He gave him—this is how I see it—the facts of his brother's claim having evidently been in existence at the time his brother was murdered, of the absolute absence of all papers relating to any such claim on the dead body, of the name of

Tibbitts as the present owner, who appears to be a friend of the man who killed his brother, whether in hot jealousy by a hasty shove, as was thought by those who were on his side, or in cold-blooded treachery. I imagine that Sir Anthony was better than Mackay Jackson hoped, and wrote to him to meet him in Cluny. Mackay does so, apparently while out fishing, the day after Cross's arrival. I take it that Mackay suggested a few bull's-eyes the other might score when questioning the Brownlows. The night of the murder, I believe that Mackay Jackson was listening outside the door of the cedar room and heard the fatal shot—heard Sir Anthony fall, and guesses what had happened. The shot would come without warning, we may be sure, from Brownlow. Mackay's one thought is to secure the papers which he thinks Maitland has brought Cross, and which he imagines will be in Sir Anthony's bag in his room, for they are too bulky to carry on him.

"He must get them before Brownlow does. For they will bring home the murder of Peter and of Anthony Cross—supposing that Cross is, as he guesses he is, badly hurt, if not dead. I think that thought was much more in his mind than even any idea of the claim at the moment. He ran up into the room allotted Sir Anthony Cross for the night and set to work. He would have to be very careful not to be caught with, possibly, a dead man downstairs. He finds nothing in the bag which he opens but a revolver of Cross's. He takes this and goes downstairs to the cedar room again, after nearly half an hour's work, for he had to pick the wardrobe door as well as the bag.

"Meanwhile, Brownlow has staged the little Tibbitts drama and sent him off. Mackay Jackson opens the door of the cedar room with his detective's nippers and finds Brownlow bending over Cross—"

"Judging from the distance that the bullet that entered the pewter plaque was probably fired?" asked Pelham briskly.

"Partly from that, and partly from the mix-up that followed over the revolvers. For the moment, however, Mackay shoots Brownlow, after getting a shot past his own head. Mackay doesn't miss. Brownlow dropped dead, and his revolver falls from his hand where he fell. Mackay, too, bends over Sir Anthony. He lays down the revolver with which he has just shot Brownlow—the revolver that is Sir Anthony's own —and tries to see if anything can be done. But Sir Anthony is dead. All this, as I say, sir, is purely guesswork, but I fancy it's fairly near what happened."

It was exactly what had happened.

"Then Mackay drags Brownlow over to the corner where there is a light—the opposite corner—searches him, and finds what looks like the key of another safe. He had heard from Miss Young about seeing Tibbitts in that very room with some black pearls, like the lost one of Mrs. Brownlow, in his hands. Can there be a safe in here? That would explain the missing papers. Mackay decided that he must hunt later on—during the inquiry. He picks up a revolver lying near Sir Anthony, remembering that he had laid the one down that he had fired, and hurries out when the coast is clear, locking the door from the outside, but with the key on the inside. The key showed double marks made by two uses of the ring nippers. As a matter of fact, the revolver with which Mackay had shot Brownlow had probably got shoved under Sir Anthony while Mackay raised him to see if he could do anything. That, at least, is where it was found. It was supposed that, twisting as he died, Sir Anthony had rolled over it a little. Mackay, of course, dropped the one that he had taken away in the Grosne, the river that runs beside the villa. And he also drops—most unintentionally, and in the garden—the key that looks like the key of a safe which he has taken from Brownlow's waistcoat pocket. For in order to look like a seedy debt collector at the dance—"

"A grim irony in his choice of that character," put in Major Pelham appreciatively.

"Mackay had ripped his coat lining and his pockets. So he loses the precious key on his way to the gate. Loses it, and looks for it desperately as soon as he can. He got to the villa gates just a little before the police next morning, I learned, and yet did not enter the villa except practically with them. He had another hunt for it, openly and officially this time, with the police, but he didn't find it. When it was discovered, he tried to get hold of it—'to send it to Davidson'—perhaps! But the police wouldn't let it out of their sight." The chief inspector was back in the hours at Cluny.

"When Mrs. Brownlow staged the idea of a duel by placing the mate to the revolver that killed Sir Anthony beside her husband, Mackay must have been staggered! It went against the grain with him for Brownlow to be considered merely the man of honor fighting for his wife. But he could prove nothing. He wanted the papers—that were burned. When Tibbitts was arrested he was in a bit of a hole. He tried his second sight, but it would only impress Miss Young. He did a very daring piece of work and got Tibbitts out."

"*He* got him out? Whew! But his French?"

"The mother of the Jacksons was a French-Canadian, sir, who couldn't speak more than a few words of broken English. Also, one of the jobs he had done for the combine was in Paris, and I found out that his French on that occasion had been perfect. So I wasn't surprised to find that he could pass himself off as Lenormand. I took care not to be at the hotel that night—just in case of what he might be planning."

"You knew who Mackay was all the time?"

"I guessed it. I'll tell you how, and why, afterwards, sir. And if so, it was Mackay's last chance for rescuing Tibbitts —before he should give himself away when the *juge* reconstructed the crime, as he intended to do. By the way, it was Mackay who had got Lenormand down to defend Tibbitts when he had no idea how desperate things were for that crook. And Mackay was a very poor man indeed. When he rescued Tibbitts, he evidently made his bargain with him. He felt sure that there was a hidden safe. So he got Tibbitts, in return for his safety, to stay around the villa well disguised, and burgle the safe at the first possible opportunity. Also, I take it, he arranged for the return to himself of any Jackson-Tibbitts claims in Touva. Mackay got a genuine Swedish antiquarian from Cook's in Paris to be sent to Dijon, a Swedish professor, moreover, who spoke English well, but not a word of French. Tibbitts was whisked to Dijon, made up en route, and well made up, and returned to Cluny with his Swedish friend as a Mr. Larsen. As far as strangers, and the French police go, a fellow Swede. Tibbitts would be sure to have some underground way of getting whatever papers he needed."

"What about the *portrait parle?*" asked Pelham in great amusement, "it seems to've been rather silent."

"Tibbitts as a Swedish savant with a passion for museums was evidently too much for it! Poor Mackay! He had his work all to do again when the suspicion shifted to Maitland."

"If he hadn't been a silly ass," Pelham put in, "he would have given Brownlow in charge when he entered the cedar room for the murder of Sir Anthony, his own attempted murder, and the murder, ten years ago, of his brother. Produced a copy of the claim located in Touva, and got off with the thanks of the congregation for putting such a dangerous criminal out of the way."

"Just so. That's where his impetuosity spoiled things. It used to amuse me—as it must have him—to hear Miss Young exhorting him to be a bit swifter. There was nothing slow about Mackay. Nor did he look it. Which rather puzzled the young lady, I think. She was a shrewd reader of faces, and Mackay's appealed to the daughter of a Texas ranger, however halting his words and slow his apparent actions might be. Well, when Maitland looked in a bad way, I decided that it would have to be a document that would save him. An escape couldn't succeed twice over. A posthumous confession seemed the best and most likely card, and when I found Mackay Jackson taking lessons from the commissaire in how to detect a forgery and exactly what points to look for— ostensibly, of course, over Sir Anthony's letter about young Eastby—why, the inference made itself. As to the whereabouts of the presently-to-be-found document, I remembered the key which the police had found. I wondered if there might not be a second, hidden safe. Tibbitts had certainly shown by his face that the key meant a great deal to him. And Mrs. Brownlow had a way of improving sufficiently at night, when the house was all quiet, to come down into the cedar room and tap the panels and work at them that suggested hunting for a safe."

"How do you know? Second sight too?"

"No, sir. I was asked to observe, so I observed."

"I wonder you didn't add 'by way of routine.'"

"It was by way of routine," the chief inspector said sturdily, "that I got into the habit of spending my nights tucked up under the cedar room couch. The lights were so placed that it was in the deep shadow."

"Tucked up!" scoffed the assistant commissioner.

"Well, I was asked to observe, wasn't I, sir?" Pointer repeated. "So I observed. The fight among other things. Very good show it was too. Gate money has been paid for worse. I knew Mackay could box, by the way he had jumped back to escape a car in the roads once or twice, jumped as a boxer does, keeping his weight forward. I crept out from under the couch as soon as he started in with the policeman. I also wanted to see what was inside that safe. So while the two were slogging away, I photographed all the most important looking papers I could find in it. To develop at my leisure afterwards. There were two packets. One was on top of the jewelry with blood marks on some of the papers. They were taken from Sir Anthony's dead, or not yet dead, body. Sir Anthony had evidently gone over his own notes of the

case when Mackay Jackson's letter reached him. I think
that was when Miss Young saw Mrs. Brownlow's
photograph—sent him by Mackay. It was still there. Then
there was one other packet in a drawer. Among these
were some papers which Brownlow must have taken
years ago from Peter Jackson, such as his original receipt
for the purchase of his claim, a document in Russian and
Turkish, stamped with a curious device which I am told is
the Wheel of Fate—Krasny's municipal stamp. Then
there was a forged Jackson-Tibbitts sale, dated just
before the murder, and witnessed by the dead analyst,
who was dead when Brownlow drew it up! There was also
the draft of a re-sale to Brownlow by Tibbitts, as yet
undated. There were other papers which I should have
liked to see, but I had to be quick, for Tibbitts was just
coming to as I worked. I slipped out of the door before the
agent was knocked out. I made for the garden through
the writing-room window, and watched, from under the
raised shutter of the cedar room, Mackay snatch all the
papers from the safe, toss in his own letter on top of the
jewels, grab Tibbitts, pull him to his feet, tell him to show
a leg for his life, and then the two made off towards a
little car which Mackay must have pulled under the
hedge of the orchard. As soon as they were safely off the
premises, I 'observed,' from the road where I was
standing, the light on the hollies behind the cedar room.
That told any one who saw it that the shutter was a least
partially up and a light in the room. I called for the police
and hurried to the window. And the rest of the doings of
that night is, as you say, sir, to be found in the Third
Book of Kings."

"Mackay went to Lyons, I suppose?" Pelham asked.

"I think so. Luckily Tibbitts can drive, for Mackay
himself had only one eye half-open, which couldn't have
looked around his cauliflower of a nose if it had tried. His
face would have needed some explaining. Rondeau would
certainly have asked himself a few questions if he had
caught sight of it. Which was why Mackay concentrated

on Brownlow's trail in Lyons, I fancy, and did that chiefly by telephoning, I'll wager. Though he arrived with his head nicely bandaged. He got that done at a convent hospital on the outskirts of the town as you drive in. Told the night sister that he had had an accident while motoring—a skid. She must have thought that he had skidded chiefly on his face, but she seems to have swallowed the story, and provided Mackay most obligingly with a head like a football. Also she let him telephone for a room to the hotel and again explain that he had had a slight accident and would arrive looking slightly the worse for wear. From the hotel he wrote and asked Miss Young to meet him there on her way to Italy."

"Do you think he told her the whole truth?" Pelham wondered. "I hope so."

"I'm sure so. Mackay would. And also, Miss Young would take it very quietly. The Texas ranger had accounted for some thirty bad men, she once told me. And certainly, by every standard, Brownlow was a bad 'un."

"And Tibbitts, what of him?"

" 'Mr. Larsen' and his fellow savant went on to Venice. There 'Mr. Larsen' terminated their connection. He went on alone, though still as Mr. Larsen, to Constantinople, and there joined Mr. and Mrs. Mackay Jackson. Mackay is giving him a new start in life. He needs a metal-worker to help him in Touva. I happened to overhear, or should I say 'observe,' a talk Mackay and Tibbitts had after Tibbitts had blundered in some way and Miss Young had recognized him. I think Mackay thought that Tibbitts had never had a decent chance in life. And I don't think Tibbitts ever had. He'll get it now. A fair and square deal."

There was a short pause.

"What took Smith to the villa that night Mrs. Brownlow left. If it was Smith?" the assistant commissioner wondered.

"A bogus message from Lascelles, so he told me. I dropped in for a chat on the way home. The message asked him to meet Lascelles without fail at midnight in the writing-room at Villa Porte Bonheur. If Lascelles was late, Smith was to wait for him for an hour, and then leave. He was told that it was most urgent. By the way, sir, Lascelles had been very keen on having a word with Sir Anthony. He would have given his eyes, so Smith says, to go with the Mongolian expedition, of which he had heard rumors through the Cambridge Association. In fact, he waited around while Sir Anthony and the Brownlows had their talk, and finally waylaid Sir Anthony on his walk back to his hotel. But he was told that the expedition was full up. Only tried men were to go on it. But now returning to Smith and the bogus message. He got the wind up after he'd been in the house only twenty minutes. Saw a black-robed figure —we know that it was Miss Young, but he didn't—by the cedar room door, and tried to slip out of the house by his balcony, the way he had entered. He found the balcony door bolted, and doubled down the corridor, past Mrs. Brownlow's room and down the servants' stairs, and so out by another side door. The police all but caught bim, but he managed to get back to Vichy unmolested. There, a tip of oriental magnificence made a night porter get a little mixed as to the hours, and tell the police that it was a good deal earlier when he saw Mr. Smith come in than it really was."

"I suppose that message was Mackay's doing again?"

Pointer nodded.

"I suppose so too, sir."

"Why? Red herring?"

"Partly, and partly to pay Smith out, I fancy. Mackay likes both to pay and collect his debts. I don't think Mackay had forgiven Smith his refusal to see him when he came down to Cluny. And I think he felt that he owed him a little discomfort on account of Smith's high and mighty airs to Miss Young. And also, in fairness, Smith was the only man available who would come on that sort of a message, and who wasn't suspected of being in the murder. Mackay did need a red herring to draw off the French police while he forced Mrs. Brownlow to leave Villa Porte Bonheur."

"Ah!" The assistant commissioner moved forward in his chair. "I was wondering how Mackay worked that. You think he distrusted her? I don't wonder!"

"Nor I either, sir! Though evidently Tibbitts told him nothing, could tell him nothing, that incriminated her— definitely. Still, once Vivian Young had recognized Tibbitts in one of the Swedish savants, I don't think Mackay had one easy moment. Everything—for him— turned on Tibbitts. And everything for both Tibbitts and himself turned on the latter not being taken again. Yet one incautious word of Miss Young's, especially if Mrs. Brownlow was in the original crime, would have meant the certain recapture of Tibbitts. So I think Mackay terrified Mrs. Brownlow by climbing into her window and telling her his real identity, at the same time ordering her to dress and follow him or be handed over to the police as her husband's accomplice. Like me, he must have watched her hunting that cedar room—for proofs of clues as to who killed her husband, Miss Young thought. Possibly that was the reason! At any rate, Mackay drove her off to Lyons, and there—well, she was a Frenchwoman born, you see, she wouldn't need to show her papers if she went under her maiden name or took another name. Probably she went to her own people in the south."

Pelham thought over what he had heard and nodded several times.

"And when did you suspect Mackay?"

"Pretty well from the first, sir. There were so many odd things about Mackay—apart from his remarkable Scottish accent. First of all, I heard that he had not yet been to see the body when the commissaire and I arrived, nor tried to see it. That struck me as extraordinary on the part of a private investigator, no matter whether he were on another crime or not. I felt sure that he had been in the room. That raised the question of when? Then, as a detective, he would be in possession of just such a pliers as would turn that key, and would have the requisite skill. Then, added to that, Miss Young told me that she saw him and Sir Anthony fishing in the same stream the day before the dance night. Now, I was at Macon then, and it was a wonderful day. Clear and sparkling. Not a day on which any fisherman would try to fish! In that light—Macon is only a few miles from Cluny, as you know, sir—a line of spiders' silk would have looked like a hawser, and not a trout of under six inches even could have been tempted to rise, not by any bait, nor any skill. Yet, I knew that Sir Anthony was a member of two very well-known anglers' clubs. So I talked fishing to Mackay over our first dinner, and he showed that he knew a good deal about it. Showed, too, that he knew of some flies that are only used in Canada, though he threw in references in the beginning to Scottish flies. You see, he really was a good fisherman, and got keen on the talk, and didn't quite notice how much he was giving away.

"Canadian flies! That gave me to think when I heard later on that young Jackson had been a Canadian, and had a younger brother who would be about Mackay's present age now. Then came the reply from Shanghai to a question of mine that the brother's name was Henry M. Jackson. The answer to another question told me that the M. stood for Mackay! Besides, too, I was certain that he had hunted that garden before any of us. There was the length of time before he reached the house after he left the hotel. And while I was with him, he let certain clumps quite alone, and only looked in certain others. Besides, his whole character—assumed character, I mean—was so at variance with his face! I felt sure that he was impersonating some Scot whom he had known, the original Uncle Mackay, very possibly. His talk of logic and going by 'the light of reason,' went quite comically with the most fearless, coldly daring face that I've ever seen—and a gait to match. Mackay's stride was that of a—well, I should fancy of a Texas ranger—according to Miss Young's glowing descriptions of them." Pointer gave a reminiscent chuckle.

"I wonder if he guessed, or guesses, that you know. . ." Major Pelliam said half to himself.

"I wonder, too, sir. He may. He risked that. Incidentally, I warned him that he had better hurry and get his final coup in before the French linked up with Touva—which might mean with him. Also I ventured on a wedding present of Copenhagen china. A couple of dogs."

"Dogs?"

"They were asleep," laughed the chief inspector as he rose.

"So you solved the Cluny problem in your own way. You would!"

Pointer shook his head.

"The real Cluny problem, sir, was and is Mrs. Brownlow. She's beyond me. Was she innocent? Was she guilty? And guilty all through? Who can say?"

"I wonder Mackay Jackson tried to shield her so completely in that final letter of his—the letter he signed as Brownlow," Pelham looked puzzled.

"I think he had promised her he would do as much when he made her leave the villa and go into hiding. And I think he wasn't sure—any more than I am—whether she were innocent or guilty, and knew that, as he never would be sure, he must give her the benefit of the doubt. And also, I shouldn't wonder if he didn't consider that her husband's death at his hand had settled the old score in full.

"She evidently knew what make of bullet killed Sir Anthony, since she was able to put the right weapon beside her husband—without that non-existent chit in her vanity-case to help her," the assistant commissioner said, after thinking things over.

"She did, sir. But there again ... we shall never know the truth . . . and the *juge,* though he will probably marry her, will never know. . . ."

"She didn't try to throw suspicion on any of the accused, or semi-accused persons," mused Major Pelham.

"But there again, sir, innocent or guilty? If she were in with her husband, she might well have been appalled at the idea of suspicion falling on Tibbitts, that husband's partner. Brownlow could doubtless have done a dozen things to suppress Tibbitts which she could not, without showing her hand, and that, always supposing she held one, she evidently was determined at all costs not to do. As for Mr. Maitland—well, she had to walk a very narrow ledge there, didn't she—innocent or guilty! I think the Scottish verdict of 'Not Proven,' the only one that fits that most enigmatic woman, for I ask myself, as Rondeau would put it, and I always shall, whether she were what she seemed or a most cunning accomplice."

And that was Chief Inspector Pointer's final utterance on the Cluny problem.

THE END

Other Resurrected Press Books in *The Chief Inspector Pointer Mystery* Series

The Eames-Erskine Case
The Footsteps that Stopped
The Clifford Affair
The Cluny Problem
The Craig Poisoning Mystery
The Tall House Mystery
Tragedy at Beechcroft
The Case of the Two Pearl Necklaces
Mystery at the Rectory
Scarecrow

MYSTERIES BY ANNE AUSTIN

Murder at Bridge

When an afternoon bridge party attended by some of Hamilton's leading citizens ends with the hostess being murdered in her boudoir, Special Investigator Dundee of the District Attorney's office is called in. But one of the attendees is guilty? There are plenty of suspects: the victim's former lover, her current suitor, the retired judge who is being blackmailed, the victim's maid who had been horribly disfigured accidentally by the murdered woman, or any of the women who's husbands had flirted with the victim. Or was she murdered by an outsider whose motive had nothing to do with the town of Hamilton. Find the answer in . . . **Murder at Bridge**

One Drop of Blood

When Dr. Koenig, head of Mayfield Sanitarium is murdered, the District Attorney's Special Investigator, "Bonnie" Dundee must go undercover to find the killer. Were any of the inmates of the asylum insane enough to have committed the crime? Or, was it one of the staff, motivated by jealousy? And what was is the secret in the murdered man's past. Find the answer in . . . **One Drop of Blood**

AVAILABLE FROM RESURRECTED PRESS!

THE EDWARDIAN DETECTIVES
LITERARY SLEUTHS OF THE EDWARDIAN ERA

The exploits of the great Victorian Detectives, Poe's C. Auguste Dupin, Gaboriau's Lecoq, and most famously, Arthur Conan Doyle's Sherlock Holmes, are well known. But what of those fictional detectives that came after, those of the Edwardian Age? The period between the death of Queen Victoria and the First World War had been called the Golden Age of the detective short story, but how familiar is the modern reader with the sleuths of this era? And such an extraordinary group they were, including in their numbers an unassuming English priest, a blind man, a master of disguises, a lecturer in medical jurisprudence, a noble woman working for Scotland Yard, and a savant so brilliant he was known as "The Thinking Machine."

To introduce readers to these detectives, Resurrected Press has assembled a collection of stories featuring these and other remarkable sleuths in The Edwardian Detectives.

- The Case of Laker, Absconded by Arthur Morrison
- The Fenchurch Street Mystery by Baroness Orczy
- The Crime of the French Café by Nick Carter
- The Man with Nailed Shoes by R Austin Freeman
- The Blue Cross by G. K. Chesterton
- The Case of the Pocket Diary Found in the Snow by Augusta Groner
- The Ninescore Mystery by Baroness Orczy
- The Riddle of the Ninth Finger by Thomas W. Hanshew
- The Knight's Cross Signal Problem by Ernest Bramah

- The Problem of Cell 13 by Jacques Futrelle
- The Conundrum of the Golf Links by Percy James Brebner
- The Silkworms of Florence by Clifford Ashdown
- The Gateway of the Monster by William Hope Hodgson
- The Affair at the Semiramis Hotel by A. E. W. Mason
- The Affair of the Avalanche Bicycle & Tyre Co., LTD by Arthur Morrison

RESURRECTED PRESS CLASSIC MYSTERY CATALOGUE

Journeys into Mystery
Travel and Mystery in a More Elegant Time

The Edwardian Detectives
Literary Sleuths of the Edwardian Era

Gems of Mystery
Lost Jewels from a More Elegant Age

E. C. Bentley
Trent's Last Case: The Woman in Black

Ernest Bramah
Max Carrados Resurrected:
The Detective Stories of Max Carrados

Agatha Christie
The Secret Adversary
The Mysterious Affair at Styles

Octavus Roy Cohen
Midnight

Freeman Wills Croft
The Ponson Case
The Pit Prop Syndicate

J. S. Fletcher
The Herapath Property
The Rayner-Slade Amalgamation
The Chestermarke Instinct
The Paradise Mystery
Dead Men's Money

The Middle of Things
Ravensdene Court
Scarhaven Keep
The Orange-Yellow Diamond
The Middle Temple Murder
The Tallyrand Maxim
The Borough Treasurer
In the Mayor's Parlour
The Saftey Pin

R. Austin Freeman
The Mystery of 31 New Inn from the Dr. Thorndyke Series
John Thorndyke's Cases from the Dr. Thorndyke Series
The Red Thumb Mark from The Dr. Thorndyke Series
The Eye of Osiris from The Dr. Thorndyke Series
A Silent Witness from the Dr. John Thorndyke Series
The Cat's Eye from the Dr. John Thorndyke Series
Helen Vardon's Confession: A Dr. John Thorndyke Story
As a Thief in the Night: A Dr. John Thorndyke Story
Mr. Pottermack's Oversight: A Dr. John Thorndyke Story
Dr. Thorndyke Intervenes: A Dr. John Thorndyke Story
The Singing Bone: The Adventures of Dr. Thorndyke
The Stoneware Monkey: A Dr. John Thorndyke Story
The Great Portrait Mystery, and Other Stories: A Collection of Dr. John Thorndyke and Other Stories
The Penrose Mystery: A Dr. John Thorndyke Story
The Uttermost Farthing: A Savant's Vendetta

Arthur Griffiths
The Passenger From Calais
The Rome Express

Fergus Hume
The Mystery of a Hansom Cab
The Green Mummy
The Silent House
The Secret Passage

Edgar Jepson
The Loudwater Mystery

A. E. W. Mason
At the Villa Rose

A. A. Milne
The Red House Mystery
Baroness Emma Orczy
The Old Man in the Corner

Edgar Allan Poe
The Detective Stories of Edgar Allan Poe

Arthur J. Rees
The Hampstead Mystery
The Shrieking Pit
The Hand In The Dark
The Moon Rock
The Mystery of the Downs

Mary Roberts Rinehart
Sight Unseen and The Confession

Dorothy L. Sayers
Whose Body?

Sir William Magnay
The Hunt Ball Mystery

Mabel and Paul Thorne
The Sheridan Road Mystery

Raoul Whitfield
Death in a Bowl

And much more!
Visit ResurrectedPress.com
for our complete catalogue

About Resurrected Press

A division of Intrepid Ink, LLC, Resurrected Press is dedicated to bringing high quality, vintage books back into publication. See our entire catalogue and find out more at www.ResurrectedPress.com.

About Intrepid Ink, LLC

Intrepid Ink, LLC provides full publishing services to authors of fiction and non-fiction books, eBooks and websites. From editing to formatting, from publishing to marketing, Intrepid Ink gets your creative works into the hands of the people who want to read them. Find out more at www.IntrepidInk.com.